Sir Thomas Malory
TALES OF
KING ARTHUR

*The crowning
of Arthur*

Sir Thomas Malory

TALES OF KING ARTHUR

edited and abridged
with an introduction by

MICHAEL SENIOR

Schocken Books · New York

First Schocken paperback edition 1982
First published by Schocken Books 1981
10 9 8 7 6 5 4 3 2   82 83 84

Published in the United Kingdom as *Sir Thomas Malory's
Tales of King Arthur*

© as to Introduction: Michael Senior 1980
© as to this abridged and edited version of
the text: Michael Senior 1980

Designed by Tim Higgins
Lettering by Gerald Mynott
Picture Research by Faith Perkins

Library of Congress Catalog Card No. 81—40412
Manufactured in the United States of America
ISBN 0—8052—3779—8 (hardback)
        0—8052—0719—8 (paperback)

*Frontispiece: Arthur in majesty, from
a fourteenth-century French tapestry*

Contents

Acknowledgments

The quotations from Professor Eugène Vinaver are taken from: *The Works of Sir Thomas Malory* edited by Eugène Vinaver. Clarendon Press, Oxford, 2nd edition 1967, reprinted with corrections and additions 1973.

The publishers would like to thank the following for their kind permission to use their illustrations:

KEY
BL: British Library
BM: British Museum
BN: Bibliothèque Nationale
Bod: Bodleian Library
BR: Bibliothèque Royale de Belgique
BS: Bayerische Staatsbibliothek
GR: Giraudon
PM: Pierpont Morgan Library

following page 22
Manchester City Art Gallery/Cooper Bridgeman Library. (top) Walker Art Gallery/Cooper Bridgeman Library; (bottom) Manchester City Art Gallery/Cooper Bridgeman Library.

following page 34
BL: MS Add., f.202v. Lambeth Palace Library. Bod: *Romance of Guiron le Courtois*, MS Douce 383, f.5v.

following page 66
BR: MS 9243, f.42v. Bod: *Romance of Guiron le Courtois* MS Douce 383, f.12v.

following page 98
Bod: *Romance of Guiron le Courtois* MS Douce 383, f.3. Bod: Ibid., f.17.

following page 130
Bod: *Romance of Guiron le Courtois* MS Douce 383, f.6. BN: MS Fr. 112, f.72. BM: MS Royal 20 Div/Cooper Bridgeman Library.

following page 162
Bod: *Roman de Lancelot du Lac* MS Douce 199, (top) f.221v; (bottom) f.299v. Bod: Ibid., (top) f.55; (bottom) f.98v. BN: MS Fr. 99, f.561. BN: MS Fr. 110, f.405.

following page 194
BN: MS Fr. 343, f.3. BN: Ibid., f.8v. BN: Ibid., f.4. (top) Bod: MS Douce 199 f.151v; (bottom) BN: MS Fr. 12577, f.18v.

following page 258
BN/GR: *Livre de Messire Lancelot du Lac* MS 3479. PM: MS 806, f.262 (both). Bod: (top) MS Douce, 199, f.44v; (bottom) MS Douce 199, f.252r.

following page 290
BR: MS 9243, f.45. BL: MS Harley 4379, f.43. BN: MS Fr.112, 3 vol., f.193v. BM: MS 10294, f.94.

Frontispiece: Picturepoint.
2 Bod: *Lestoire de Merlin* MS Douce 178, f.181v.
8 Hampshire County Council.
11 Janet and Colin Bord.
14–5 Ibid.
21 Fotomas Index.
26 BL: MS Roy 20 AII, f.3v.
28 Bod: *Lestoire de Merlin* MS Douce 178, f.378v.
29 Ibid., f.189v.
31 Ibid., (left) f.195v; (right) f.195.
35 BN: MS 4697, f.159v.
36 Bod: (top) *Lestoire de Merlin* MS Douce 178, f.189v;
(bottom) *Lancelot du Lac* MS Rawlinson Q.b.6., f.50.
37 Bod: *Lestoire de Merlin* MS Douce 178, (top) f.318v; (bottom) f.252.
38 Ibid., (top) f.385v; (bottom) f.389v.
39 Ibid., f.394v(b).
41 BL: MS Add. 38117, f.97v.
43 BM/BPC Picture Library.
44 GR: MS 403, f.7v.
45 Bod: *Lestoire de Merlin* MS Douce 178, f.384.
47 BL: MS Egerton 3028, f.30.
48 Bod: *Lestoire de Merlin* MS Douce 178, (top left) f.215v; (bottom left) f.296v; (top right) f.193; (bottom right) f.299.
49 Bod: Ibid., (top left) f.384v; (bottom left) f.411v; (top right) f.318(b); (bottom right) f.249.
56 Bod: *Lancelot du Lac* MS Rawlinson Q.b.6., f.293.
58 Bod: Ibid., f.371v.
59 Bod: Ibid., f.42.
60 BL: Wace Chronicle.
61 Bod: *Le Graal & Merlin* MS Douce 178, f.378.
62 Bod: *Lestoire de Merlin* MS Douce, 178, f.197b.
65 Bod: *Lestoire de Merlin* MS Douce 178, f.282(a).
67 Bod: *Le Graal & Merlin* MS Douce 178, f.397.
68 Bod: *Lestoire de Merlin* MS Douce 178, (top) f.262; (bottom) f.384.
71 Bod: Ibid., (left) f.202; (right) f.309.
72 GR: MS 3479, f.516.
75 Bod: (top) MS Douce 199, f.70v; (bottom) *Lestoire de Merlin* MS Douce 178, f.149v.
76 Bod: *Lancelot du Lac* MS Rawlinson Q.b.6., (left) f.154; (right) f.156.
77 Bod: Ibid., f.200.

80 Bod: Ibid., f.182.
85 Bod: *Le Mireur du Monde* MS Douce 336, f.56.
86 BS: MS Germ. 51, f.15v.
89 Ronald Sheridan.
106 BS: MS Germ. 51, f.90.
110 Bod: *Lancelot du Lac* MS Rawlinson Q.b.6., f.372v.
113 BS: MS Germ. 51, f.82.
114 Bod: *Lancelot du Lac* MS Rawlinson Q.b.6., f.33v.
117 Bod: *Lestoire de Merlin* MS Douce 178, f.387v.
122 GR: *Roman de Tristan* MS 646/316, f.239.
123 Bod: *Lancelot du Lac* MS Rawlinson Q.b.6., f.244.
124 Bod: *Le Mireur du Monde* MS Douce 336, f.78.
125 Bod: Ibid., f.58.
130 GR: *Roman de Tristan* MS 646/316, f.59.
139 Bod: *Lancelot du Lac* MS Rawlinson Q.b.6., f.246.
146 Bod: *Lancelot du Lac* MS Rawlinson Q.b.6., (left) f.211b; (right) f.312v.
149 Bod: Ibid., f.311v.
150 Bod: Ibid., f.158v.
152 Bod: Ibid., f.369.
156 GR: MS Fr. 112.
164 Bod: *Lancelot du Lac* MS Rawlinson Q.b.6, f.57.
165 Bod: *Lestoire de Merlin* MS Douce 178, f.275.

166 Bod: *Roman de Lancelot du Lac* MS Douce 199, f.151v.
168 Bod: *Lancelot du Lac* MS Rawlinson Q.b.6., (left) f.174; (right) f.267.
169 Bod: Ibid., f.324v.
175 Bod: *Lancelot du Lac* MS Rawlinson Q.b.6., (left) f.334v; (right) f.47v.
178 Bod: Ibid., f.236.
183 Bod: Ibid., (left) f.254v; (right) f.80.
191 Bod: *Romance of Lancelot du Lac* MS Douce 215, f.39.
192 Bod: *Lancelot du Lac* MS Rawlinson Q.b.6., f.352.
202 Bod: Ibid., f.56v.
203 Bod: Ibid., f.290b.
204 Bod: Ibid., f.365b.
206 Bod: Ibid., f.266.
207 Bod: *Romance de Lancelot du Lac* MS Douce 215, f.39v.
209 Bod: Ibid., f.301.
214 GR: MS Fr. 118, f.219v.
217 Bod: *Lancelot du Lac* MS Rawlinson Q.b.6., f.202.
225 Bod: *Romance of Guiron le Courtois* MS Douce 383, f.6.
226 GR: *Livre de Messire Lancelot du Lac* MS 3479, f.478.

228 Bod: *Lancelot du Lac* MS Rawlinson Q.b.6., f.372.
230 Bod: Ibid., f.69v.
231 Bod: Ibid., f.141.
244 BL/Robert Harding Associates.
250 Bod: *Lancelot du Lac* MS Rawlinson Q.b.6., (left) f.206v; (right) f.42v.
251 Bod: Ibid., f.190v.
252 PM: MS 806, f.158.
253 Bod: *Lancelot du Lac* MS Rawlinson Q.b.6., f.131.
263 Lambeth Palace Library: MS 6, f.43v.
272 Bod: *Lancelot du Lac* MS Rawlinson Q.b.6., f.398.
275 GR: *Livre de Messire Lancelot du Lac* MS 3479, f.539.
278 Bod: *Lancelot du Lac*, MS Rawlinson Q.b.6., f.389v.
279 Bod: Ibid., f.392v.
285 Bod: *Lancelot du Lac*, MS Rawlinson Q.b.6., f.137v.
294 GR: *Livre de Messire Lancelot du Lac* MS 3479, f.588.
298 Bod: *Lancelot du Lac* MS Rawlinson Q.b.6., f.397v.
303 Bod: *Lestoire de Merlin* MS Douce 178, f.1202.
305 BM/Cooper Bridgeman Library: MS Add. 10294.

Note on the text and illustrations

The text illustrations are taken from a variety of medieval manuscripts such as those which would have been available to Malory. These contain a great profusion of Arthurian stories, not all of which were incorporated in Malory's text, and in some cases we have chosen a scene which does not relate directly to episodes included in the text, but succeeds in conveying the mood and atmosphere of the tales. Details of the sources and manuscript numbers have been included in the acknowledgments above.

Cuts in the text have been marked with the following symbols:

 Shows that a lengthy section has been omitted.

 Shows that a paragraph or short section has been omitted.

. . .Shows that a sentence or a few words within a paragraph have been omitted.

Introduction

The work commonly known as *Le Morte d'Arthur* is now more than five hundred years old. It would be surprising if it had not undergone several changes of popularity over that period of cultural and social change. What is more significant is its durability. It has proved to contain elements which have a constant and infallible appeal.

The aim of this edition is to make available a version of these tales of Malory's which can be read by a contemporary reader purely for pleasure, without any sense of duty or effort. Malory was in many ways modern in outlook, to an extent which was only becoming possible in his own lifetime, and he wrote in a language which was approaching the form of our own. Hence it has been possible to do this version of Malory without any translating or rewriting of his text. The work has recently lost much of its popular audience, not because of any lack of appeal in its subject matter, but largely because it is burdened, in our estimation, by a massive load of matter extraneous to the main subjects which we no longer have the inclination to accept. We live in an impatient age. A need for relevance, for getting on with the business, impels even the most leisurely modern reader.

In pursuit of the above aim, I have used as one of the tests to decide what to include, what to omit, the question 'Is it enjoyable to read?' I hope that the result will retrieve the work from the remoteness of academic literary study, towards which it has seemed to be retreating, and to give it back to the readers for whom it was intended: that is, quite simply, all those who appreciate a good story well told.

For the same reason I do not intend to deal in any detail in this introduction with the sort of academic matters discussed and debated by the various Malory authorities. Scholars often give the impression that they are paid to disagree with one another, like barristers, and although such contests can sometimes be entertaining, it would obstruct our purpose here to investigate them at any length. Nevertheless there are some points about the work's background and the way it came into being which do add to an appreciation of it as an achievement.

First of all: who was Malory? The only clues he gives of himself, besides the inevitable revelation of taste and character presented by his writing, are that he was a knight, that he lived and wrote during the reign of Edward IV, and that for at least some of the time when he was composing his tales of Arthur he was in prison. Although there have been other candidates for the authorship, a Sir Thomas Malory of Newbold Revell, in Warwickshire, so comfortably fits the requirements that there is probably no need to seek further. If so, then the author of these stories was, in his private and not-so-private life, a remarkable man.

'The Tales of King Arthur' (as I propose to call them) were finished in the ninth year of the reign of Edward IV; somewhere, that is, between March 1469 and March 1470. The knight of Newbold Revell died in 1471. He had had an active military career during the campaigns of the Wars of the Roses, serving in the army of the Earl of Warwick, whose influence on the Yorkist side in support of Edward IV had earned him the nickname 'the King Maker'. It may well have been during Warwick's excursions in the north of England that Malory learnt his British geography, evident in his references, particularly towards the end of his works, to places such as Alnwick,

OPPOSITE *The Round Table in Winchester Great Hall*

9

Bamburgh, and Carlisle. Warwick's disposition towards king-making prompted him to change sides, exile Edward, and place on the throne the Lancastrian Henry VI. If Malory, as a loyal Warwickshire knight, changed sides along with his overlord, it might explain why Edward IV specifically excluded him from the pardons which he granted to the Lancastrians in 1468 and 1470.

There are several indications that this Sir Thomas fits the part of the 'knight prisoner' who wrote the Arthurian stories. Although we do not know that he was in prison during the years of the book's completion, we do know that when he died a year or so later he was buried at the church of the monastery of the Grey Friars, near Newgate prison. That monastery, we find from other sources, possessed a library, and if Malory served a long-term sentence at Newgate, this would help to explain how he acquired the sources from which he wrote.

There is, moreover, ample suggestion that this Sir Thomas Malory of Warwickshire might have spent an appreciable amount of time in one of Britain's major prisons. Admittedly, what evidence we have consists mostly of accusations, and there is no indication that he was guilty, or found guilty, of most of them. The charges might have been brought against him for other reasons; and indeed if he had done all that he was alleged to have done, he would not only have been busy but extremely foolish. But so much accusation tempts us to suppose at least a little guilt.

His alleged career really gets into its stride in the years 1450 and 1451. Early in 1450, we are told, he lay in ambush intending to assassinate no less a person than the Duke of Buckingham. One wonders how anyone, however reckless, could have expected to survive such an enterprise, if it had succeeded. At any rate the Duke survived, and the charge against Malory may have had a political motive. An accusation of rape follows immediately, combined with robbery, and then several cases of extortion. Cattle-rustling, malicious damage of property, the stealing of deer, are followed in the same year of 1451 by less rural pursuits. The indictment claims that he took to plundering monasteries. Finally he got himself arrested, in circumstances which suggest that a grain of truth may have existed in the later charges, and he proved his ability to indulge in lawlessness by escaping from

Coleshill jail by swimming the moat. The records assert that he at once went back to the habit of monastery-robbing, and consequently was arrested again.

For the rest of the 1450s we hear of him alternately in jail and being accused of various forms of banditry, mostly cattle-raiding. Several times he escaped, but ended up at Newgate in 1460. He was pardoned by King Edward in 1462, in time to begin the military phase of his career in Warwick's Northumbrian expedition that November.

Whether this remarkable biography (assuming it is our author's and not foisted on him by coincidence) has any relevance to the work of literature which he produced is at least debatable. All we can say is that such an active man could only have found the time for the vast amount of reading and scribing entailed if he was under forced constraint, such as that of prison. It is true also that writing about action is a sort of substitute for undertaking it, or compensation for being deprived of it; and in maturity or old age it would be natural for a man who had lived a violent life to want to record the essence of it. 'The Tales of King Arthur', however, are not all blood-and-thunder; they show a sensitivity and emotional depth which do not easily go with rape, cattle-stealing, and the robbing of monasteries. Yet one of the concerns of medieval man was to reconcile the conflict between emotion and action, sensitivity and violence, erudition and warfare. The idea of the whole man became explicit and important during the Renaissance, the man both of action and of learning, the cultured adventurer; it was an idea that developed out of the life-style of the preceding period, an attitude natural to many people up to, and during, as well as after Malory's time.

More than from any chronicles or law-court records we can learn about Malory from his choice of subject matter. The attitudes and dispositions he reveals in the process of selection itself are of such significance that we shall consider them further. But the themes were the traditional material of his native land, and in translating them into the English of his day he revealed a consciousness of his identity as an Englishman, in a sense which only became meaningful after the three streams of Celtic, Anglo-Saxon, and Norman peoples had become fully merged.

The earthworks of South Cadbury Castle

The matter which he chose was British and ancient, though (as we shall see) he drew it from Continental sources comparatively close to his own age. King Arthur himself, the prophet Merlin, Lancelot, Tristram, Guenever, Morgan le Fay, the themes of the Round Table and of the court at Camelot, the search for the Holy Grail, the treachery of Mordred, the fatal last battle and Arthur's disappearance to Avalon, along with the implied possibility of return: none of this was fictional literary material, none of it invented either by Malory or his sources or theirs, but rather it was part of the traditional lore of Britain. It will help us to understand what Malory was doing, and why the results are as they are, if we briefly trace the history of these elements.

King Arthur has two distinct streams to his make-up, one from early British history and one from folklore. This dual make-up is an important factor in his eternal appeal to the imagination of the British people. The question of whether Arthur ever existed, in the sense of someone of that name and answering that description, is not really relevant. The existence of Arthur lies in the stories and ideas associated with him, and there is no doubt that these became attached at a very early date to the character of a British military leader of the period of late Celtic independence and early Anglo-Saxon invasion. That such a leader did exist is historically probable. We can identify set-backs in the Saxon attack which indicate a spell of organized resistance. Archeologically we know that at such places as South Cadbury Castle (in local tradition identified as Camelot since the sixteenth century) sufficient national revival took place after the Roman occupation to give rise to a well-defended and wealthy court. There may have been one, or there may have been many, prototype Dark Age Arthurs. That we do not know. We do know that the idea of a British military leader of that period is a sound one, and bears crucial significance for our country's early identity.

We first hear of this figure in documents copied about the year 1100, but originally written very much earlier. One is a set of church annals, known as the *Annales Cambriae*, which end in the year 955. These, because they were composed year by year and collected periodically into groups, may originally date from the very year to which they refer. And there we hear of Arthur defeating his enemies at the Battle of Badon, and of his death in the year 539, along with 'Medraut', the prototype of Mordred, at the battle of Camlan.

These matters are somewhat expanded by our second early source. A fanciful and largely legendary *History of Britain* was composed or collected by a Welsh priest named Nennius in about AD 800. He tells us more or less explicitly that Arthur was fighting the Saxons, that he was the leader of the forces of resistance, and gives a list of twelve battles which Arthur fought, including the victory of Badon. The fact that Nennius does not say that Arthur was a king has led some to theorize that he was not. His role, in any case, is definitely that of leader.

This figure failed to become part of official British history for a curious reason. He is not mentioned at all by an earlier writer, Gildas, who would have been his younger contemporary if Arthur had been the Dark Age leader which the other sources imply. Whatever the explanation for Gildas's omission of the name of Arthur (though he mentions the battle of Badon to which that name later became attached), the result is that when Bede, writing about AD 730, drew from Gildas the first reliable documentation of British history, Arthur did not get included. Perhaps Gildas's omission was due to there having been no such person, and Bede was therefore, as so often, right. In any case we start our written history with Bede, and it does not feature Arthur.

That this is so has given a strength rather than a disadvantage to his effect on the national imagination. A pinned-down, historical Arthur could not have provided the vehicle for so many varied feelings and ideas. The flexibility and the power of the figure both owe something to that lack of documentation. But what finally established Arthur as a central figure in our national mythology was the merging of his two natures. The figure from our early history became effectively integrated with the character of the demigod, folk-hero, near-supernatural being, which had been growing at the same time.

This merging started early. In the same sources as those which tantalizingly hint at a real man, we find Arthur viewed as something much more than a man. His feats at the battle of Badon verge on the supernatural, and in a list of 'Marvels' attached to Nennius's *History* we find him with his wonderful hound hunting a magic boar. This is another sort of troop-leader, the terrible huntsman, the leader of a marvellous roving band, a character which ultimately has affinities with that universal folk-figure, the rider in the night sky, the conductor of the souls of the dead, and with other leaders of the Wild Hunt, such as our folk-figure Herne the Hunter, or the Norse god Odin.

This element in the make-up of Arthur is prominent in the early literature. And another of his most striking attributes there is his remarkable gravitational attraction. From a very early stage he shows the ability to trap into orbit around him tales and characters which previously were quite independent.

Merlin, for instance, as prophet and overseeing magician, had several forerunners in Celtic myth. They in turn merged with the folk-figure of the Wild Man of the woods, and the result became associated with a possibly historical sixth-century North British poet, Myrddin ap Morfryn. This compound was in turn put together with other tales, and the resulting synthesis given the name Merlin, by Geoffrey of Monmouth, in the mid-twelfth century. He, in fact, was largely responsible for formulating the collection of what would from then on be the Arthurian matter.

Strangely, Geoffrey neglected Tristram. Although the story seems certain to have been in existence in his time, since we find it along with other material in France shortly after, it bypassed Geoffrey and entered English literature in the metrical romances of the following centuries. But Tristram too, like Arthur and Merlin, was already extremely old. His name appears in the Welsh traditional material, the *Triads* and the stories known collectively as the *Mabinogion*. There is reason to think that his origins were Pictish, although surprisingly we find a stone commemorating someone with a Latinized version of the same name, Drustanus, standing above the Cornish village of Fowey. Since the story's later connections are with Cornwall rather than the north, we must suppose that it had moved south at a very early stage, and perhaps the Dark Age hero commemorated by the Drustan Stone was named after the originally Pictish hero of the tale.

Although not much is known of the pre-Arthurian career of Guenever, it is clear that in her original form, named in Welsh Gwenhwyfar, she was an independent figure of folk-tale (in some references named as the daughter of a giant), perhaps originally a minor goddess.

A clearer route to the same homeland can be traced for Morgan le Fay, who appears in Malory's stories as Arthur's sister, a sinister but seductive figure in the shadows around the civilized Arthurian court. As Morgan, or Morgain, she features in the early literature as a goddess of healing, the ruler of the mystic island of Avalon, evidently, to begin with, an afterworld containing a promise of rebirth. In Geoffrey of Monmouth's *Life of Merlin*, written about 1150, she is named as one of the enchantresses who took King Arthur to be healed after his last battle. Her connection with warfare originally wore a rather different aspect, since as the Morrigan she was originally an Irish battle-goddess, appearing to heroes such as CuChulainn in much the way that the deities became manifest on the battlefields of Troy. It was one of Malory's sources, the 'Vulgate Lancelot', which projected her as a fully-formed figure into the Arthurian legends.

The idea of Avalon, as an island to which one goes after death, again emerged early in Celtic literature. Indeed it had more importance for some of his predecessors than it did for Malory. With characteristic realism Malory himself plays it down. It seems that Geoffrey of Monmouth again drew the name into the story of Arthur, finding it in a French source. From the twelfth century onwards legend associated this mysterious island with the ancient religious centre of Glastonbury; in early times the central group of hills at Glastonbury was isolated by the inflow of the sea into that flat Somerset plain. Islands had always had an otherworld quality to the early British, and there is good reason to suppose that it was customary at one time to bury the dead across the insulating medium of a strip of water. During the monastic period the construction of sea-defences considerably reduced the flooding at Glastonbury, and it is perhaps as a result of this that Malory and his immediate source (the stanzaic poem of probably late-fourteenth-century date, 'Le Morte Arthur') describe Avalon as a 'vale', a term which fits Glastonbury well enough today.

Although the name Avalon, along with much of the material so far mentioned, stems from an ultimate Celtic source, this cannot be said with any confidence of Camelot. The name seems to have been an invention on the part of the late-twelfth-century French poet Chrétien de Troyes, writing at a distance about an England of an idealized past time. In our early native literature Arthur held his court not at some notional Camelot, but at the visible Roman town of Caerleon, in South Wales. When Malory re-imports the material he accepts the centrality of the new idea of an idealized court, yet locates Camelot firmly at Winchester. That ancient city was the seat of the kings of Wessex, and remained a royal headquarters even after the Norman invasion.

Is it coincidence that it was at Winchester, at Malory's Camelot, that the only so-far discovered manuscript copy of his work was found? Certainly it is not by chance that the Round Table has had a physical as well as traditional connection with the place since long before Malory's time. The board which still hangs in the Great Hall of Winchester castle reminds us that by the fourteenth century, when it was made, Winchester was firmly established as a centre of Arthurian tradition. It seems likely that this splendid large wooden disc, recently repaired and repainted, was made for Arthurian tournaments held by Edward III. The origins of the idea are unfortunately obscure; when the Round Table first enters literature it is assumed that we have already heard of it. The Norman poet Wace, writing in 1155, refers to it as famous. The point about it, as he makes clear, is that it prevents precedence. The knights could feel that they were all gathered equally about one board, none being 'able to boast that he was exalted above his fellow'. Like Wace, Chrétien de Troyes assumes that we are familiar with the idea. And it is firmly propelled into Arthurian literature by Robert de Boron, for whom it was a replica of the table on which stood the Holy Grail, itself modelled on that used at the Last Supper.

No emblem has received more investigation than that mystic vessel itself. The Grail has an ancientness and a power to convey wide and deep ideas which place it in the realm of religion rather than legend. Malory again subdues its mysticism, replacing the fervent spirituality of his sources with a human content, an emphasis on weakness, on vulnerability, on the failings of the flesh, which suits his own concerns and his portrayal of the participants better than the sermonizing of the French 'Queste del Saint Graal' from which he drew. But behind this late-medieval vessel for which his knights are rather vaguely searching lies a succession of vessels of plenty and vessels with testing powers, which stretch back far beyond Christianity into the worlds of British and Irish mythology and their archeological counterparts.

Of the remaining elements, Mordred, as we saw, was connected in our first sources with Arthur and with his death. Malory's favourite hero Lancelot, however, is quite a different matter. He came to Arthur's court at a late stage of its development, since he is not mentioned as part of the story in the Celtic material. No hero of mythology, however, comes to us without a past. And although the name Lancelot is again French, and again the contribution of Chrétien de Troyes, it can be traced back via various forms to its Celtic roots, and seems originally to have been derived from the Irish hero Lug and his Welsh counterpart Lleu, themselves the mythicized versions of the ancient European god known to the Romans as Lugus. After Chrétien, Lancelot became the central hero in the French 'Vulgate Cycle', the main part of which was called by his name.

The British material had been exported to France by various routes. After the Norman conquest barons who possessed territory in both Britain and France encouraged the movement of troubadours, and hence of their material. Because of the linguistic link through Brittany it became possible for matter to move from Wales to France, from the Welsh language to a Breton-speaking audience who would also understand it. At the culmination of this process Wace translated Geoffrey of Monmouth's great amalgamation (which was composed in Latin) into Norman French. Medieval French literature had for some time been occupied with two traditions: the 'Matter of Rome', which consisted mainly of extensions of the story of Troy, and the 'Matter of France', which centred on the semi-legendary exploits of the followers of Charlemagne. The

Glastonbury Tor rises above the flat Somerset plain

new complex of the stories loosely or closely connected with Arthur became, in the context of the new Anglo-French involvement, the 'Matter of Britain'. With the establishment of this idea, the immense popularity of the stories in Britain was shortly complemented by an equivalent fashion in France, and indeed it spread through Europe. We should not forget that while this expansion was taking place the material was also evolving in its homeland. Just as Wace conveyed Geoffrey's *History* to France, so Layamon, about the end of the twelfth century, made it available in vernacular to the English.

From these two directions Malory's immediate sources came into existence. In England he found the story of the expedition to Rome in an English alliterative poem of the fourteenth century known as 'Morte Arthure', itself based on the translations of Geoffrey. Towards the end of his work he used an English source again, though this time

in conjunction with the French cycle, perhaps basing some elements of the story of Lancelot and Guenever and certainly relying heavily in 'The Death of Arthur' on a stanzaic poem with a confusingly similar title, 'Le Morte Arthur'.

The birth, succession, and early career of Arthur, and the role and death of Merlin, Malory found in a thirteenth-century work known as 'La Suite de Merlin', a continuation of one of the later works of the 'Vulgate Cycle', the 'Merlin', itself a prose version of a poem by Robert de Boron. For the story of Tristram, and also for the affair of Lancelot and Elaine, he went to the 'Prose Tristan', a work of French prose again of about 1230, which drew on earlier Tristan poetry and on the 'Vulgate Lancelot', and which for the first time attached the Tristan story to the Arthurian collection. For the rest of his stories he relied on the vast and complex 'Vulgate Cycle' itself.

The last three works of this, in terms of narrative sequence, known collectively as 'The Prose Lancelot', form the main, and probably earliest, part of that great five-book cycle. Separately, they are the 'Lancelot', from which Malory took Lancelot's independent adventures, the 'Queste del Saint Graal', of which his Grail quest is an abbreviated translation, and the 'Mort Artu', which gave him much of the material of the romance of Lancelot and Guenever and the tragedy of its outcome.

'The Vulgate Cycle' (of which the remaining two works, the 'Estoire del Saint Graal' and the 'Merlin', do not immediately concern us) was composed by unknown writers between the years 1215 and 1230, and forms an expression of the convention of chivalry and courtliness in its later phase. Interesting as it is in itself, it is of more relevance here to consider what Malory made of it. The extent to which he reacted against its assumptions signals the ending of the outlook of the Middle Ages. His introduction of a fresh attitude and interest anticipates the mood of the Renaissance.

Malory's contribution of an approach which we recognize as modern consists of three main aspects: naturalism, in the sense of a tendency to describe events in convincing detail, set in a real geography; realism, consisting of a tendency to play down the magic and the supernatural and explain occurrences in terms of normal experience; and humanism, which follows from these and overlaps with them, by which the great sequences and crises are related less to political, religious or social ideals, or to literary conventions, and more to individual personalities.

We have already seen, for instance, how the French fantasy world of Camelot was placed by Malory very firmly in the real-world town of Winchester. Similarly, he specifies the geography of Astolat, where the fair maiden Elaine died for love of Lancelot: it was Guildford. When Guenever is abducted, the scene is again withdrawn from the vague and distant lands of Malory's sources, and said to be a short ride from Westminster, across the Thames. Malory shows an equivalent sense of the earthly necessities which surround even the most high-pitched emotional moments. In apologizing to Elaine of Astolat for his refusal to marry her, Lancelot, seeking a means of comforting her, offers her money: precisely, a settlement of a thousand pounds a year, 'to you and to your heirs'. This, one need hardly say, is not mentioned in the French work. Malory's eye for realistic detail is perhaps best brought out by Sir Ector's indignant explosion when, after a prolonged search instigated by Guenever, Lancelot is found, but refuses to come home: 'It hath cost my lady the queen twenty thousand pounds, the seeking of you.'

Malory's subduing of the supernatural and otherworldly in favour of explanations in terms of human experience shows itself most in his treatment of the magician Merlin and in his attitude towards the Holy Grail. Merlin's part in the story is quickly overshadowed by the rise of Arthur's political career. His death under the power of the damsel of the lake becomes a case of human infatuation, rather than of witchcraft and spell-binding. And when Malory turns to the task of translating the 'Quest of the Holy Grail', he makes a number of points which to his predecessor would have seemed grotesque, even sacrilegious. His prime hero Lancelot fails, as in the original, to achieve the Grail, being a sinner; yet in Malory this is made out to be no great disgrace, and Lancelot expresses satisfaction that he has come as near to the Grail as he has: 'for as I suppose no man in this world hath lived better than I have done to achieve that I have done.' And Malory's attitude is revealed in a striking way by Sir Bors, when he says that the purpose of the Grail Quest is a worldly, not a spiritual one: 'For he shall have much earthly worship that may bring it to an end.'

Of Malory's humanity we shall have more to say. It reveals itself in the details of characterization, in moments of irony or revelation of personal emotions. As the adultery between Lancelot and Guenever develops, we catch them almost winking at each other, Arthur innocently ignorant and trusting them both. 'What aileth you,' he asks Guenever, when Lancelot is absent in a moment of crisis, 'that ye cannot keep Sir Lancelot upon your side?' Explaining in front of Arthur why he could not love the maid of Astolat, Lancelot risks a statement about love: 'I love not to be constrained to love; for love must arise of the heart. . . .' We hear the delicate irony in his mistress's voice when she taunts him with not having been kinder to the dead maiden.

With typical consideration Malory allows his lesser characters too their moments of humanity. The maid of Astolat's brother, young Sir Lavaine, remarks that in dying rather than facing separation from Sir Lancelot, 'she doth as I do, for sithen I first saw my lord Sir Lancelot, I could never depart from him, nor nought I will and I may follow him.' And perhaps the fullest effect of his attention to human detail occurs in the exchanges between Guenever and the other Elaine, on whom Lancelot had sired Galahad, when they confront each other after Lancelot, spurned by Guenever, has gone mad. The two women, though bitter rivals, recognize that they have something in common: they have both lost Lancelot now.

These accumulated points of detail show the influence which Malory brought to bear on his material, and by which he transformed it from a beautiful, stylized medieval tableau into something of such relevance to our perennial experience that we respond to it with no difficulty today. On a more obvious and large-scale level he changed the material by imposing on it his own tastes in narrative style. He worked a complete re-shaping, using two means, that of severe abbreviation, and that of imposing a consecutive form of narration.

It should be explained at this point that the medieval cycles were not only extremely long, spun out with what seem to us to be irrelevant descriptions, but took the form of a continuous interweaving of a number of parallel themes. There was not one story going on, nor even a story and a sub-plot, but a whole collection of stories, each of which had equal status. These were told episodically, and instead of dealing with a substantial sequence of one, then turning to another, the cyclic story-teller would move constantly between them all. To Malory this seemed unsatisfactory; no doubt he was reflecting the new tastes of his time, which are, to an even greater extent, the tastes of ours. He therefore rearranged the matter, having considerably shortened it, always seeking a continuous narrative flow.

It is interesting to note that our age has taken these requirements further, and that much that Malory left in we now find inconveniently irrelevant. In this respect this edition is continuing the process which he started, since, in the words of Professor Vinaver, he reduced his mattter 'not by means of indiscriminate omission, but by a careful elimination of passages which seemed to him to delay the action'. Perhaps the structure and the bulk of the French romances obstructed this aim occasionally; much of the medieval style seems to us to have been retained. We find, in the full version of Malory's tales, rather too many instances of what Vinaver terms 'the typical "cyclic" method of interweaving a variety of different themes', a feature, as he put it, 'unpalatable to modern readers, and impossible to describe except by metaphors drawn from the language of tapestry'. Malory, however, had carried the re-shaping process a great distance. Fortunately it only requires a slight reduction to further clarify the narrative flow so that the story is palatable to the modern reader. In doing this I am, happily, pursuing Malory's own policy: that of discriminating adaptation to suit the tastes of a later age.

W e are fortunate that Malory undertook this task at the time when he did. The language in which he wrote was one which had, in effect, only comparatively recently come into being. French words had begun to enter the English language shortly before the Norman conquest, which of course turned that trickle into a flood, and by about the beginning of the fourteenth century the two languages had combined to form a definite language of literature. At the same time as new words were being introduced, a great many were becoming archaic and obsolete, so that by the end of the thirteenth century English had shed a large part of its exclusively Germanic make-up. Simplification of grammar had begun a considerable time before that, so that the language which grew out of the combination inherited a freedom from inflection and a tendency to neglect gender from its Middle English parent.

Malory's style is therefore based on an essential simplicity. The relatively young language had not yet begun to put on airs. In many respects his phrasing and syntax are more comprehensible than those of Shakespeare, writing about a hundred years later. This is partly due to the differences of intention and personality between the two great tale-tellers, since Malory is seldom, if ever, aiming at a poetic style. His prose is generally free from metaphor and imagery. He seems incapable of word-play, and one can hardly imagine him concocting the sort of multiple pun so loved by the later Renaissance. He is out to tell a story, and does so by the simplest means. All this helps to explain the almost complete comprehensibility of his prose. There are occasional unfamiliar forms (such as the use of 'and' to mean 'if'), but one adjusts to them remarkably quickly.

In view of the state of the language he used, it should not surprise us to find him experimenting and occasionally floundering. Along with the simplifications went a certain flexibility. As English has developed further it has become beset by rules and notions of correctness. For Malory it did not seem clumsy (for instance) to repeat a word several times within a sentence. And the double negative and double superlative were useful tools of emphasis, rather than errors.

But making all due allowances for differences of convention, it must still be said that Malory's prose is strikingly uneven in its quality. Particularly in the earlier books, he shows himself too easily influenced by the style of his source, often with unfortunate effects. Consequently we find occasional French constructions faithfully imitated, giving strange results in English. And when he is copying from the English sources, he tends to use alliterative phrases ('. . . King Arthur was so courageous that there might no manner of knights let him to land, and his knights fiercely followed him . . .') which seem artificially imposed on his generally unornamented prose. He is capable of an astounding clumsiness of sentence structure:

And then when it happened any of them to be of great worship by his noble deeds, then at the next feast of Pentecost, if there were any slain or dead, as there was none year that there failed but there were some dead, then was there chosen in his stead that was dead, the most men of worship that were called the Queen's Knights.

Yet the recognition of these deficiencies can only be a step towards acknowledgement of his final mastery of the cadences of English prose. Malory developed in confidence and ability as he progressed, and at the same time he became more deeply involved in the course of his story and more prone to original creation. In the last books his ear for the rhythm of the language is infallible. It comes into its own at moments of crisis, and specially in those long passages of monologue or dialogue, several of which find no parallel in his sources. Here the intensity of the emotion is matched by the simple pace of English diction in a perfect marriage of sense and form:

'Wherefore, madam, I pray you kiss me and never no more.'
'Nay,' said the queen, 'that shall I never do, but abstain you from such works.'
And they departed.

One feels that a more showy or self-conscious prose-writer would have failed to achieve the miraculous burden of passion and constraint which these passages bear. It is perhaps because he does not regard himself as a great stylist that in these moments of strong feeling he is able to use the short phrase, the steady sequence, and simple vocabulary, which he has used all along. When Lancelot expresses, at the end, his sense of the tragedy of all that has happened, and his own sense of remorse and regret, he resorts to no flowery images or allusions. Yet nothing could be more effective than the plain statement of his thoughts, in moderate, balanced English diction:

'Also when I remember how by my default, mine orgule and my pride, that they were both laid low, that were

peerless that ever was living of Christian people, wit you well,' said Sir Lancelot, 'this remembered, of their kindness and mine unkindness, sank so to mine heart, that I might not sustain myself.'

The dual roots of the English language, Germanic and Latin, to which it owes so much, mirrored the hybrid quality of the population of most of Britain; and it is not by chance that the originally Celtic material came to Malory from two different directions, the Middle English and the French, and that he combined them. The same process of amalgamation placed the Arthurian material at a cultural bridgehead in European history. In many ways the time again helps to explain why things happened as they did. If Britain had not been in the state in which it then was, Malory's work would not only not have been so important and successful, it might not have been undertaken at all.

When Malory finished composing his tales of Arthur, England had been in a state of civil war more or less continuously for fifteen years; the trouble had as long again to run, but the years in which he wrote formed a sort of watershed. Malory's probable overlord, the Earl of Warwick, who had secured the enthronement of Edward IV, at one point took the king prisoner and reintroduced, as an alternative king, the sporadically insane Henry VI. Even this apparent chaos was not extreme in that long and bitter struggle. No wonder that towards the end of his last book our author allowed himself a personal comment. Under the guise of describing the defection of the populace to the side of the usurping Mordred, he remarked:

Lo ye all Englishmen, see ye not what a mischief here was? For he that was the most king and noblest knight of the world, and most loved the fellowship of noble knights, and by him they were all upholden, now might not these Englishmen hold them content with him. Lo thus was the custom and usage of this land; and also men say that we of this land have not yet lost ne forgotten that custom and usage. Alas, this is a great default of us Englishmen, for there may nothing please us no term.

Arthur's role, from the beginning, had been to represent British national pride. First by fighting the Saxons, then restoring Britain's morale by defeating the Romans and becoming himself Emperor, he had symbolized the spirit of national resistance. In the high Middle Ages his immense popularity, following Geoffrey of Monmouth's revival of the national traditional material, owed not a little to the desire to see Britain as a country in its own right, as something older than and separate from the new Continental power blocks. Arthur's partial exile abroad had itself been symptomatic, mirroring Britain's own involvement with Europe during those centuries. In bringing him firmly home again Malory was serving a new national ideal, which was to reach its realization at the start of the Renaissance, with the ending of the struggle of the Wars of the Roses.

At the same time, while Arthur stood for strong government, security against outside influence, and national independence, he also contained in his background make-up the theme of internal division. The Mordred story was an original element, perhaps one of the first to become attached to his name; and it reflected a divisiveness in British politics which had been commented on by Tacitus and Gildas, and which, as Malory remarked, remains with us still. In Malory's telling, this political tendency is compounded by the more personal one of the final war against Lancelot, and the two combined destroy the security of Arthur's rule. This is a realistic outcome, no doubt influenced by the pessimism of a black time. 'Yet some men say in many parts of England that King Arthur is not dead, but had by the will of Our Lord Jesu into another place; and men say that he shall come again. . . . '

From time to time a nation feels the need to express to itself some large and important idea, and in times of that need our national hero has always been ready to come to our aid. It is widely recognized that one of the most important events in our history was the Battle of Hastings, which had the effect of making Britain, through its monarchy, a part of Europe. Rather less famous, but perhaps as important, was the event which ended the Wars of the Roses, the Battle of Bosworth. Not least among the significant effects of this was the change of dynasty which it brought about. Henry VII, of the Welsh family of Tudor, consciously and explicitly proclaimed himself to be of the original population of insular Britain. It is at least an indication of the mood of the time that the new king's first son, born in September 1486, was christened Arthur.

The Battle of Bosworth took place near Leicester, in the English Midlands, on 22 August, 1485. When William Caxton finished printing the work which he named *Le Morte d'Arthur*, at Westminster, he added the information that he did so on the last day of July of that same year. He could not have known that the event so soon to take place would render his work so appropriate. The 'Matter of Britain' was to be made available to a wide national readership at the very moment that Britain was to add a new dimension to its self-identity. The long-prophesied return was taking place in literature and politics at the same time.

W illiam Caxton was born in Kent in the early 1420s, but emigrated to the Low Countries and spent the first part of his career there and in Burgundy. The technique of printing was in use in Italy and Switzerland from the 1460s, and spread to France, the Netherlands, Belgium, Austria and Spain during the 1470s. Caxton probably saw it at first hand when on a visit to Cologne, and subsequently made use of it for reproducing his early translations. He returned to England as a printer in about 1476, at first producing his own translations of French works, and a number of pamphlets. The prologues and epilogues which he added to his works reveal a man of definite ideas and intentions. Of Malory's *Morte d'Arthur* he made some particularly pertinent comments:

After that I had accomplished and finished diverse histories, as well of contemplation as of other historical and worldly acts of great conquerors and princes, and also certain books of examples and doctrine, many noble and divers gentlemen of this realm of England camen and demanded me, many and ofttimes, wherefore that I have not do made and imprint the noble history of the Sangrailf and of the most renowned Christian king, first and chief, of the three best Christian and worthy, King Arthur, which ought most to be remembered among us English men tofore all other Christian kings. . . . To whom I answered, that divers men hold opinion that there was no such Arthur, and that all such books as be made of him be but feigned and fables, because that some chronicles make of him no mention nor remember him nothing, ne of his knights.

He goes on to list the items of evidence for Arthur's existence, many of which, such as the

Round Table at Winchester, hardly seem conclusive to us now. In deference to his patrons he accepted that 'I could not well deny but that there was such a noble king named Arthur', and proceeded, he tells us, 'after the simple cunning that God hath sent to me, . . . to imprint a book of the noble histories of the said King Arthur, and of certain of his knights, after a copy unto me delivered, which copy Sir Thomas Malory did take out of certain books of French, and reduced it into English'.

Caxton manifestly appreciated the work's good points. He referred to its 'joyous and pleasant histories, and noble and renowned acts of humanity, gentleness, and chivalries . . . And for to pass the time this book shall be pleasant to read in; but', he added in qualification, 'for to give faith and believe that all is true that is contained herein, ye be at your liberty.' He then went on to describe how he had divided the work into twenty-one books, and the books into chapters.

This he did somewhat arbitrarily. Several times, presumably for typographical reasons, a chapter begins in mid-sentence. It was early recognized that, as elsewhere, Caxton had probably exercised his editorial influence in the process of printing. Two copies of his edition of Malory survive, and a number of other early printings (two made by Caxton's apprentice, assistant, and eventual successor, Wynkyn de Worde) testify to the immediate success of the printed edition.

For a long time it was assumed that although Caxton had probably altered the text, this was as near to Malory as we would ever get. But early in the summer of 1934, a manuscript was found in the Fellows' Library of Winchester College, which had remained unidentified probably because it had lost some leaves from both ends. It turned out to be a fifteenth-century copy of Malory's works, made probably during the 1470s, a little after Malory's own writing and a little before Caxton's printing of it. It was not, it was at once established, the copy used by Caxton. In fact it was quite independent of it, containing both correct versions of Caxton's copy's mistakes and copyist's errors of which Caxton's original was free. By tracing back the history of scribal mistakes it can be established that neither the copy used by Caxton nor the Winchester manuscript was copied directly from Malory's own autograph. At least one other scribe had added his own mis-transcriptions in between.

It happened that at the time Professor Eugène Vinaver had been commissioned by the Clarendon Press of Oxford to produce, from the various printed editions extant, a critical edition of Malory's works. With the discovery of the manuscript his task changed, and instead he produced a critical edition of the manuscript text, with Caxton's variations given in footnotes.

Vinaver held that while the manuscript 'brings us nearer to what Malory really wrote', neither of the texts is to be regarded as having the prerogative of authenticity. The manuscript is 'at least as reliable as Caxton's text and quite independent of it. It supplies some of Caxton's obvious omissions . . . and often agrees with Malory's sources where Caxton is at variance with them. On the other hand, there are numerous readings in Caxton which, on the evidence of Malory's sources, appear to be more authentic than the corresponding readings in the Winchester MS. The two texts are, then,' he concludes, 'collateral versions of a common original, and each contains at least some elements of it which are not otherwise extant.'

Some of the differences are directly attributable to Caxton himself, so that in that respect at least the manuscript has the advanatge. In particular the book and chapter structure is an obvious imposition, as is the title, *Le Morte d'Arthur*, which, the manuscript makes clear, Malory only intended to refer to the last section. A heated debate (in which we shall not take part) has existed since Vinaver's first publication of the manuscript text, as to whether Malory was writing a single book or a series of loosely-related ones, which Caxton artificially united. Certainly Caxton omitted the first colophon, in which it appears that Malory had stopped, having run out of source material; and he added his own to Malory's at the very end, giving the whole work the title *Le Morte d'Arthur*, in spite of the fact that Malory said that the work he was ending was both 'The Death of Arthur' *and* 'the whole book of King Arthur, and of his noble knights of the Round Table,' of which the 'Death' was the last part.

Some of the slight word-changes appear to be Caxton's, and rather surprisingly he is occasionally a bit of a prude. He consistently altered the

The opening of Wynkyn de Worde's 1529 edition of Le Morte d'Arthur

¶Here begynneth the fyrst
boke of the moost noble and
worthy prince kyng Arthur
somtyme kyng of grete Bry
tayne/now called Englande
whiche treateth of his noble
actes and feates of armes ⁊
chyualrye/and of his noble
knyghtes of the table roūde
and this volume is deuyded
in to.xxi. bokes.

¶How Utherpendragon sente for the
duke of Cornewayle and Igrayne his
wyfe/and of theyr sodayn departynge
agayne.   Capm.j.

IT befell in the days
of y noble Utherpen
dragon whā he was
kynge of Englande
and so regned/there
was a myghty and
a noble duke in Cor
newayle that helde longe tyme warre
agaynst hym. And y duke was named
the duke of Tyntagyll/ ⁊ so by meanes
kynge Uther sente for this duke/char
gynge hym to brynge his wyfe w hym
for she was called a ryght fayre lady/⁊
a passynge wyse/⁊ Igrayne was her
name. So whan the duke ⁊ his wyfe
were comen to y kynge/by the meanes
of grete lordes they were bothe accor
ded/⁊ the kyng lyked ⁊ loued this lady
well/and made her grete chere out of

a

oath 'Pardie' (by God) to the feebler exclamation 'Forsooth'. And on one occasion, for which it is hard to forgive him, he renders as 'buttocks' the sound and ancient English monosyllable 'arse'.

Caxton's greatest change was the rewriting of a whole section, the story of the expedition to Rome. Why he did this we can only guess, but since this matter is taken directly from the Middle English alliterative poem 'Morte Arthure', and strongly shows the influence of that work's style, we must conclude that Caxton found the rather archaic English phraseology uncongenial. He had, after all, a largely Continental training. In contradiction to this we know that he enjoyed and respected Chaucer. The matter must remain something of a mystery, but his version of the Roman campaign is quite definitely Caxton rather than Malory.

I have therefore taken the text for that section from the manuscript rather than the printed version normally used. By contrast one has no choice but to present an unrevised Caxton text for the sections at the beginning and end which correspond to the manuscript's missing pages. In general I have often preferred the manuscript text elsewhere, favouring Caxton where he corrects an obvious mistake. Frequently one can decide which version is what Malory intended by referring back to the relevant passage of his French or English source. Since in other places we often cannot be sure what Malory wrote, and in some cases cannot even be sure whether a variation is due to a scribal error or to Caxton's editorial interference, there will inevitably be an element of collaboration about any composite text. Occasionally Caxton seems to have had a surer grasp of the sense than Malory. He remarks elsewhere that the English language was undergoing a great change during his lifetime, and that in his judgement 'the common terms that be daily used be lighter to be understood than the old and ancient English'. Accordingly he sometimes substitutes for a word he finds archaic one which to him, and to us, seems more comprehensible. I have allowed such revisions to stand. Either Caxton or the copyist who preceded him omitted, perhaps in the interests of speed, a great many titles such as 'Sir' and 'King'; and in such cases I felt that the effect of medieval formality was lost, and have replaced them.

More debatable are Caxton's attempts to tidy up Malory's sentence structure. Here, very occasionally, Caxton emerges as the better stylist. Since the cutting cannot be sensibly ascribed to copyists' errors, we owe to Caxton the magical restraint which makes Lancelot's climatic farewell to Guenever seem like a tightened spring: 'And if ye be hard bestad by any false tongues, lightly my lady send me word, and if any knight's hands may deliver you by battle, I shall deliver you.'

If the testimony of the Winchester manuscript is reliable here, Malory is more likely to have written the weaker, more loosely-structured sentence: 'And tell ye me, and if ye be hard bestad by any false tongues, but lightly, my good lady, send me word, and if any knight's hands under the heaven may deliver you by battle, I shall deliver you.'

Even the greatest writer can benefit from occasional discriminating editorial assistance, and one cannot apologize to Malory for perpetuating Caxton's rare improvements, since they are in accordance with his own best intentions. I repeat that such instances are rare. In general I have applied to the choice of text the two principles of readability and authenticity, and have usually not found them to conflict.

Throughout, I have modernized the spelling, carrying this process further than previous editors by (for instance) using our modern form 'damsel' for the archaic 'damosel', and using the forms of names (many of which Malory spells several different ways) which are most familiar to us now. For instance, I see no justification for perpetuating the spelling 'Launcelot', since the 'u' is only there to indicate a long 'a', as in 'laugh', a form evidently considered necessary when a French word was introduced into English, which has, incidentally, led us to adopt incorrect pronunciations of 'launch' (from French *'lancher'*) and 'haunch (from French *'hanche'*). 'Lyonesse'

Malory's idealized Arthurian world has proved a lasting inspiration, best exemplified by the widespread use of his themes by the Pre-Raphaelite artists during the nineteenth century
OPPOSITE
'The Lady of Shalott' by W. Holman Hunt
OVERLEAF
ABOVE *'Sir Galahad' by Arthur Hughes*
BELOW *'The Death of Arthur' by J. G. Archer*

(which Malory occasionally writes) seems more familiar and unambiguous than his more common 'Liones'.

As for punctuation, although the Winchester manuscript contains both stops and capitals, some are more appropriately rendered as commas than as the ends and starts of sentences. And neither the manuscript nor the Caxton print is set in paragraphs of the form we use today, but rather in long continuous sections; and neither contains inverted commas and the separation of direct speech. The punctuation of this text for modern readers is therefore a matter of decision, and I have adopted the form which seems most similar to that of contemporary literature.

So much for the actual text of this edition. As far as the selection of it is concerned, the principles of abridgement used are quite straightforward. The enormous length of the work was due to the inclusion of much material which has no appeal to a modern reader. It consists of detailed descriptions of tournaments and blow-by-blow accounts of battles, which presumably the contemporary audience demanded. There are also several passages of the adventures of minor characters which do not contribute in any way to the progress of the main narratives, but, by their intrusion, rather obstruct it. I have retained whatever promotes the telling of the stories, including occasional adventures, tournaments and minor incidents which contribute to the build-up of character or situation. I have omitted only what is extraneous and obstructive to the narrative flow.

There is so much material of that kind in Malory's original that this text is about one-third of the full version. In the process of editing, inevitably some likeable images and characters have been lost; to have allowed them to remain would have involved keeping large amounts of less appealing irrelevance. I particularly regret that Sir Palomides and his Questing Beast have suffered from this inevitable drawback; he remains, however, as a minor and supportive character in the Tristram episodes. The whole of the adventures of 'Beaumains', and the remarkably similar series of 'La Cote Mal Taile' have had to go, since they do not build up or press forward the main stories and themes. It is no use bewailing these losses. Let us instead consider what is left.

Whether or not Malory intended from the start to write a whole work, the stories grow out of a world of mystery and magic, and develop with his own confidence in his technique into solid and convincing elements of this real world. The conditions of the world of the magician Merlin still dominate the birth of Arthur and his accession to the throne. Old traditions permeate his marriage to Guenever and the scheming of his enchantress sister Morgan. But increasingly the world of political, social, and personal involvement takes over, together with that special heroic chivalry which Malory himself seems to have found sympathetic.

Malory's clear favourite, Lancelot, makes his appearance as a hero in his own right, and his knight-errant's adventures set the character which will be of such importance near the end. The independent story of Tristram parallels and prepares us for the later triangular love of Lancelot, Guenever, and Arthur. Lancelot's involvement with Elaine, the mother of Galahad, forms a sort of prelude to the Grail sequence, and that, in Malory, signals the start of the breaking up of the world of the Round Table. It clears the way for the final tragic love story, and leads us towards the emotional climax.

It is as we move surely towards that, that Malory comes into his own. Conforming to the medieval convention that a writer should copy rather than invent, he has tried in the early books to be faithful to his received material; hence the frequent references, which persist, to what the 'French book' says. But it is not his natural manner. He is by inclination something of a being of another time, the original creative artist. We can recognize now that his habit of mind, gradually asserting itself through the obstructing literary code of his time, is that of the modern novelist. His preoccupation is not with broad ideals, but with their practical human implications. He is not conveying episodes of pseudo-history, but rather investigating the minds and motivations of individual human beings. It becomes clear to us that his characters have become real to him, and that he cares about them deeply. They are no longer the puppets of an all-embracing code, the tools of literary or social convention; nor are they mainly the pawns of their fate. They are vulnerable and flawed, flesh-and-blood humanity, with real, unstylized aspirations and emotional conflicts.

One consequence of this concern of the author

is that as we near the end there are more original passages, together with a surer sense of direction which (in our present exercise) precludes the need for abridgement.

Much of Malory's original contribution consists of dialogue. He seems to have favoured direct expression as a way of conveying his characters' predicament. The sense of a personal involvement is strangely not diminished by the formality which he gives to their speeches. The high style of the diction reflects the high mode of their lives. They (we feel) are as aware as we are that they are not dealing with ordinary people or ordinary situations. A part of their emotional response seems to come from their recognition of the greatness and nobility in each other. Thus when Lancelot leaves Guenever he does so with an expression of her status and his knight's duty, but the phrases of respect in no way disguise the passion of a desperate parting after a night of making love:

'*Most noble Christian queen, I beseech you, as ye have been my special good lady, and I at all times your poor knight and true unto my power, and as I never failed you in right nor in wrong, sithen the first day King Arthur made me knight, that ye will pray for my soul if that I here be slain.*'

Some of Malory's additions in these later sections are slight, but their effect none the less telling. And they unfailingly rely on the sense that this great trio, King, Queen, and hero, are suffering as they are through a deeply human involvement. When at the end, on the eve of the last battle, Arthur has a dream in which he is warned by Gawain, recently dead, not to fight the following day, the dream occurs in both the sources, the French 'Mort Artu' and the English stanzaic poem 'Le Morte Arthur'. But Malory mentions two points his sources had not concerned themselves with. The dream comes when Arthur is falling asleep again after lying awake, but he is 'not sleeping nor thoroughly waking'. Then when he sees Sir Gawain he exclaims: 'I weened thou hadst been dead, and now I see thee alive, much am I beholding unto Almighty Jesu.'

They are small points of detail only, yet they are perceptions of experiences which everyone has had – the half-asleep, half-waking state in which vivid dreams come towards the end of a dreadful night; and the dream-revelation that someone whom one thought was dead is after all alive. As such they effectively make the point, on the eve of the last phase of the tragedy, that King Arthur is a fellow being as well as a king.

If I thank Malory for the details of his skill, it is because he will always be readily thanked for his broad conception. He has not only preserved for us in acceptable form the essence of our national tradition and ensured the immortality of its hero. He has given us the most poignant and perceptive rendering of the most penetrating of all human stories, that of the conflict of love with friendship and the destruction by love of bonds and loyalties and personal contentment.

MICHAEL SENIOR

Sir Thomas Malory

TALES OF KING ARTHUR

BOOK I

The Birth of Arthur

It befell in the days of Uther Pendragon, when he was king of all England, and so reigned, that there was a mighty duke in Cornwall that held war against him long time. And the duke was called the Duke of Tintagel. And so by means King Uther sent for this duke, charging him to bring his wife with him, for she was called a fair lady, and a passing wise, and her name was called Igraine.

So when the duke and his wife were comen unto the king, by the means of great lords they were accorded both. The king liked and loved this lady well, and he made them great cheer out of measure, and desired to have lain by her. But she was a passing good woman, and would not assent unto the king.

And then she told the duke her husband, and said, 'I suppose that we were sent for that I should be dishonoured. Wherefore, husband, I counsel you that we depart from hence suddenly, that we may ride all night unto our own castle.'

And in like wise as she said so they departed, that neither the king nor none of his council were ware of their departing.

All so soon as King Uther knew of their departing so sud-denly, he was wonderly wroth. Then he called to him his privy council, and told them of the sudden departing of the duke and his wife. Then they advised the king to send for the duke and his wife by a great charge:

'And if he will not come at your summons, then may ye do your best, then have ye cause to make mighty war upon him.'

So that was done, and the messengers had their answers, and that was this shortly, that neither he nor his wife would not come at him. Then was the king wonderly wroth. And then the king sent him plain word again, and bad him be ready and stuff him and garnish him, for within forty days he would fetch him out of the biggest castle that he hath.

When the duke had this warning, anon he went and furnished

OPPOSITE
Merlin reading a prophecy to King Uther with Igraine looking on from the battlements

The Birth of Arthur

and garnished two strong castles of his, of the which the one hight Tintagel, and the other castle hight Terrabil. So his wife Dame Igraine he put in the Castle of Tintagel, and himself he put in the Castle of Terrabil, the which had many issues and posterns out. Then in all haste came Uther with a great host, and laid a siege about the Castle of Terrabil, and there he pitched many pavilions, and there was great war made on both parties, and much people slain.

Then for pure anger and for great love of fair Igraine the King Uther fell sick. So came to the King Uther Sir Ulfius, a noble knight, and asked the king why he was sick.

'I shall tell thee,' said the king. 'I am sick for anger and for love of fair Igraine that I may not be whole.'

'Well, my lord,' said Sir Ulfius, 'I shall seek Merlin, and he shall do you remedy, that your heart shall be pleased.'

So Ulfius departed, and by adventure he met Merlin in a beggar's array, and there Merlin asked Ulfius whom he sought. And he said he had little ado to tell him.

'Well,' said Merlin, 'I know whom thou seekest, for thou seekest Merlin; therefore seek no farther, for I am he, and if King Uther will well reward me, and be sworn unto me to fulfil my desire, that shall be his honour and profit more than mine, for I shall cause him to have all his desire.'

'All this will I undertake,' said Ulfius, 'that there shall be nothing reasonable but thou shalt have thy desire.'

'Well,' said Merlin, 'he shall have his intent and desire. And therefore,' said Merlin, 'ride on your way, for I will not be long behind.'

Then Ulfius was glad, and rode on more than a pace till that he came to King Uther Pendragon, and told him he had met with Merlin.

'Where is he?' said the king.

'Sir,' said Ulfius, 'he will not dwell long.'

Therewithal Ulfius was ware where Merlin stood at the porch of the pavilion's door. And then Merlin was bound to come to the king. When King Uther saw him, he said he was welcome.

'Sir,' said Merlin, 'I know all your heart every deal. So ye will be sworn unto me as ye be a true king anointed, to fulfil my desire, ye shall have your desire.'

Then the king was sworn upon the four Evangelists.

'Sir,' said Merlin, 'this is my desire: the first night that ye shall lie by Igraine ye shall get a child on her; and when that is born, that it shall be delivered to me for to nourish thereas I will have it; for it shall be your worship, and the child's avail as mickle as the child is worth.'

*Merlin disguised
as a minstrel*

'I will well,' said the king, 'as thou wilt have it.'

'Now make you ready,' said Merlin, 'this night ye shall lie with Igraine in the Castle of Tintagel. And ye shall be like the duke her husband, Ulfius shall be like Sir Brastias, a knight of the duke's, and I will be like a knight that hight Sir Jordans, a knight of the duke's. But wait ye make not many questions with her nor her men, but say ye are diseased, and so hie you to bed, and rise not on the morn till I come to you, for the Castle of Tintagel is but ten miles hence.'

So this was done as they desired. But the Duke of Tintagel espied how the king rode from the siege of Terrabil, and therefore that night he issued out of the castle at a postern for to have distressed the king's host. And so, through his own issue, the duke himself was slain or-ever the king came at the Castle of Tintagel.

So after the death of the duke, King Uther lay with Igraine more than three hours after his death, and begat on her that night Arthur; and, or day came, Merlin came to the king, and bad him make him ready, and so he kissed the lady Igraine and departed in all haste. But when the lady heard tell of the duke her husband, and by all record he was dead or-ever King Uther came to her, then she marvelled who that might be that lay with her in likeness of her lord. So she mourned privily and held her peace.

Merlin on horseback leading two knights

Then all the barons by one assent prayed the king of accord betwixt the lady Igraine and him. The king gave them leave, for fain would he have been accorded with her. So the king put all the trust in Ulfius to entreat between them. So by the entreaty at the last the king and she met together.

'Now will we do well,' said Ulfius. 'Our king is a lusty knight and wifeless, and my lady Igraine is a passing fair lady; it were great joy unto us all, and it might please the king to make her his queen.'

Unto that they all well accorded and moved it to the king. And anon, like a lusty knight, he assented thereto with good will, and so in all haste they were married in a morning with great mirth and joy.

And King Lot of Lothian and of Orkney then wedded Margawse that was Gawain's mother, and King Nentres of the land of Garlot wedded Elaine. All this was done at the request of King Uther. And the third sister Morgan le Fay was put to school in a nunnery, and there she learned so much that she was a great clerk of necromancy. And after she was wedded to King Uriens of the land of Gore, that was Sir Uwain's le Blanchemains father.

Then Queen Igraine waxed daily greater and greater. So it befell after within half a year, as King Uther lay by his queen, he asked her, by the faith she ought to him, whose was the child within her body; then [was] she sore abashed to give answer.

'Dismay you not,' said the king, 'but tell me the truth, and I shall love you the better, by the faith of my body.'

'Sir,' said she, 'I shall tell you the truth. The same night that my lord was dead, the hour of his death, as his knights record, there came into my castle of Tintagel a man like my lord in speech and in countenance, and two knights with him in likeness of his two knights Brastias and Jordans, and so I went unto bed with him as I ought to do with my lord, and the same night, as I shall answer unto God, this child was begotten upon me.'

'That is truth,' said the king, 'as ye say; for it was I myself that came in the likeness. And therefore dismay you not, for I am father to the child; and there he told her all the cause, how it was by Merlin's counsel. Then the queen made great joy when she knew who was the father of her child.

Soon came Merlin unto the king, and said, 'Sir, ye must purvey you for the nourishing of your child.'

'As thou wilt,' said the king, 'be it.'

'Well,' said Merlin, 'I know a lord of yours in this land, that is a passing true man and a faithful, and he shall have the nourishing of your child; and his name is Sir Ector, and he is a lord of fair livelihood in many parts in England and Wales. And this lord, Sir Ector, let him be sent for, for to come and speak with you, and desire him yourself, as he loveth you, that he will put his own child to nourishing to another woman, and that his wife nourish yours. And when the child is born let it be delivered to me at yonder privy postern unchristened.'

So like as Merlin devised it was done. And when Sir Ector was come he made fiance to the king for to nourish the child like as the king desired; and there the king granted Sir Ector great rewards. Then when the lady was delivered, the king commanded two knights and two ladies to take the child, bound in a cloth of gold, 'and that ye deliver him to what poor man ye meet at the postern gate of the castle.' So the child was delivered unto Merlin, and so he bare it forth unto Sir Ector, and made an holy man to christen him, and named him Arthur. And so Sir Ector's wife nourished him with her own pap.

Then within two years King Uther fell sick of a great malady. And in the meanwhile his enemies usurped upon him, and did a great battle upon his men, and slew many of his people.

'Sir,' said Merlin, 'ye may not lie so as ye do, for ye must to the field though ye ride on an horse-litter; for ye shall never have the better of your enemies but if your person be there, and then shall ye have the victory.'

So it was done as Merlin had devised, and they carried the king

FAR LEFT *Merlin leading an army*

LEFT *Merlin directing a battle*

forth in an horse-litter with a great host toward his enemies. And at St Albans there met with the king a great host of the north. And that day Sir Ulfius and Sir Brastias did great deeds of arms, and King Uther's men overcame the northern battle and slew many people, and put the remnant to flight. And then the king returned unto London, and made great joy of his victory.

And then he fell passing sore sick, so that three days and three nights he was speechless; wherefore all the barons made great sorrow, and asked Merlin what counsel were best.

'There is none other remedy,' said Merlin, 'but God will have his will. But look ye all, barons, be before King Uther to-morn, and God and I shall make him to speak.'

So on the morn all the barons with Merlin came tofore the king; then Merlin said aloud unto King Uther,

'Sire, shall your son Arthur be king, after your days, of this realm with all the appurtenance?'

Then Uther Pendragon turned him, and said in hearing of them all,

'I give him God's blessing and mine, and bid him pray for my soul, and righteously and worshipfully that he claim the crown upon forfeiture of my blessing.' And therewith he yielded up the ghost. And then was he interred as longed to a king, wherefore the queen, fair Igraine, made great sorrow, and all the barons.

BOOK 2

Arthur becomes King

hen stood the realm in great jeopardy long while, for every lord that was mighty of men had made him strong, and many weened to have been king. Then Merlin went to the Archbishop of Canterbury, and counselled him for to send for all the lords of the realm, and all the gentlemen of arms, that they should to London come by Christmas, upon pain of cursing; and for this cause: that Jesus, that was born on that night, that He would of his great mercy show some miracle, as He was come to be king of mankind, for to show some miracle who should be rightwise king of this realm. So the Archbishop, by the advice of Merlin, sent for all the lords and gentlemen of arms that they should come by Christmas even unto London. And many of them made them clean of their life, that their prayer might be the more acceptable unto God.

So in the greatest church of London (whether it were Paul's or not the French book maketh no mention) all the estates were long or day in the church for to pray. And when matins and the first mass was done, there was seen in the churchyard, against the high altar, a great stone four square, like unto a marble stone, and in midst thereof was like an anvil of steel a foot on high, and therein stuck a fair sword naked by the point, and letters there were written in gold about the sword that saiden thus: WHOSO PULLETH OUT THIS SWORD OF THIS STONE AND ANVIL, IS RIGHTWISE KING BORN OF ALL ENGLAND. Then the people marvelled, and told it to the Archbishop.

'I command,' said the Archbishop, 'that ye keep you within your church, and pray unto God still; that no man touch the sword till the high mass be all done.'

So when all the masses were done all the lords went to behold the stone and the sword. And when they saw the scripture, some assayed, such as would have been king. But none might stir the sword nor move it.

'He is not here,' said the Archbishop, 'that shall achieve the sword, but doubt not God will make him known. But this is my counsel,' said the Archbishop, 'that we let purvey ten knights, men of good fame, and they to keep this sword.'

So it was ordained, and then there was made a cry, that every man should assay that would, for to win the sword. And upon New Year's Day the barons let make a jousts and a tournament, that all knights that would joust or tourney there might play. And all this was ordained for to keep the lords together and the com-mons, for the Archbishop trusted that God would make him known that should win the sword.

So upon New Year's Day, when the service was done, the barons rode unto the field, some to joust and some to tourney, and so it happed that Sir Ector, that had great livelihood about London, rode unto the jousts, and with him rode Sir Kay his son, and young Arthur that was his nourished brother; and Sir Kay was made knight at All Hallowmass afore. So as they rode to the jousts-ward, Sir Kay had lost his sword, for he had left it at his father's lodging, and so he prayed young Arthur for to ride for his sword.

'I will well,' said Arthur, and rode fast after the sword.

And when he came home the lady and all were out to see the jousting.

Then was Arthur wroth, and said to himself, 'I will ride to the churchyard, and take the sword with me that sticketh in the stone, for my brother Sir Kay shall not be without a sword this day.' So when he came to the churchyard, Sir Arthur alit and tied his horse to the stile, and so he went to the tent, and found no knights there, for they were at jousting; and so he handled the sword by the handles, and lightly and fiercely pulled it out of the stone, and took his horse and rode his way until he came to his brother Sir Kay, and delivered him the sword.

And as soon as Sir Kay saw the sword, he wist well it was the sword of the stone, and so he rode to his father Sir Ector, and said,

'Sir, lo here is the sword of the stone, wherefore I must be king of this land.'

When Sir Ector beheld the sword, he returned again and came to the church, and there they alit all three, and went into the church. And anon he made Sir Kay swear upon a book how he came to that sword.

'Sir,' said Sir Kay, 'by my brother Arthur, for he brought it to me.'

'How gat ye this sword?' said Sir Ector to Arthur.

'Sir, I will tell you. When I came home for my brother's sword, I found nobody at home to deliver me his sword, and so I thought my brother Sir Kay should not be swordless, and so I came hither eagerly and pulled it out of the stone without any pain.'

'Found ye any knights about this sword?' said Sir Ector.

'Nay,' said Arthur.

'Now,' said Sir Ector to Arthur, 'I understand ye must be king of this land.'

'Wherefore I?' said Arthur, 'and for what cause?'

'Sir,' said Ector, 'for God will have it so, for there should never man have drawn out this sword, but he that shall be rightwise king of this land. Now let me see whether ye can put the sword there as it was, and pull it out again.'

'That is no mastery,' said Arthur, and so he put it in the stone; therewithal Sir Ector assayed to pull out the sword and failed.

'Now assay,' said Sir Ector unto Sir Kay.

And anon he pulled at the sword with all his might, but it would not be.

'Now shall ye assay,' said Sir Ector to Arthur.

'I will well,' said Arthur, and pulled it out easily.

And therewithal Sir Ector knelt down to the earth, and Sir Kay.

'Alas,' said Arthur, 'my own dear father and brother, why kneel ye to me?'

'Nay, nay, my lord Arthur, it is not so. I was never your father nor of your blood, but I wot well ye are of an higher blood than I weened ye were.'

And then Sir Ector told him all, how he was betaken him for to nourish him, and by whose commandment, and by Merlin's deliverance. Then Arthur made great dole when he understood that Sir Ector was not his father.

'Sir,' said Ector unto Arthur, 'will ye be my good and gracious lord when ye are king?'

'Else were I to blame,' said Arthur, 'for ye are the man in the world that I am most beholding to, and my good lady and mother your wife, that as well as her own hath fostered me and kept. And if ever it be God's will that I be king as ye say, ye shall desire of me what I may do, and I shall not fail you, God forbid I should fail you.'

'Sir,' said Sir Ector, 'I will ask no more of you, but that ye will make my son, your foster brother, Sir Kay, seneschal of all your lands.'

'That shall be done,' said Arthur, 'and more, by the faith of my body, that never man shall have that office but he, while he and I live.'

Therewithal they went unto the Archbishop, and told him how the sword was achieved, and by whom. And on Twelfth-day all the barons came thither, and to assay to take the sword, who that

OPPOSITE
*Arthur with his
tutor Merlin*

OVERLEAF
*The coronation
of Arthur*

FACING PAGE 35
*Knights in combat at a
joust; a recurrent theme
throughout the medieval
Arthurian material*

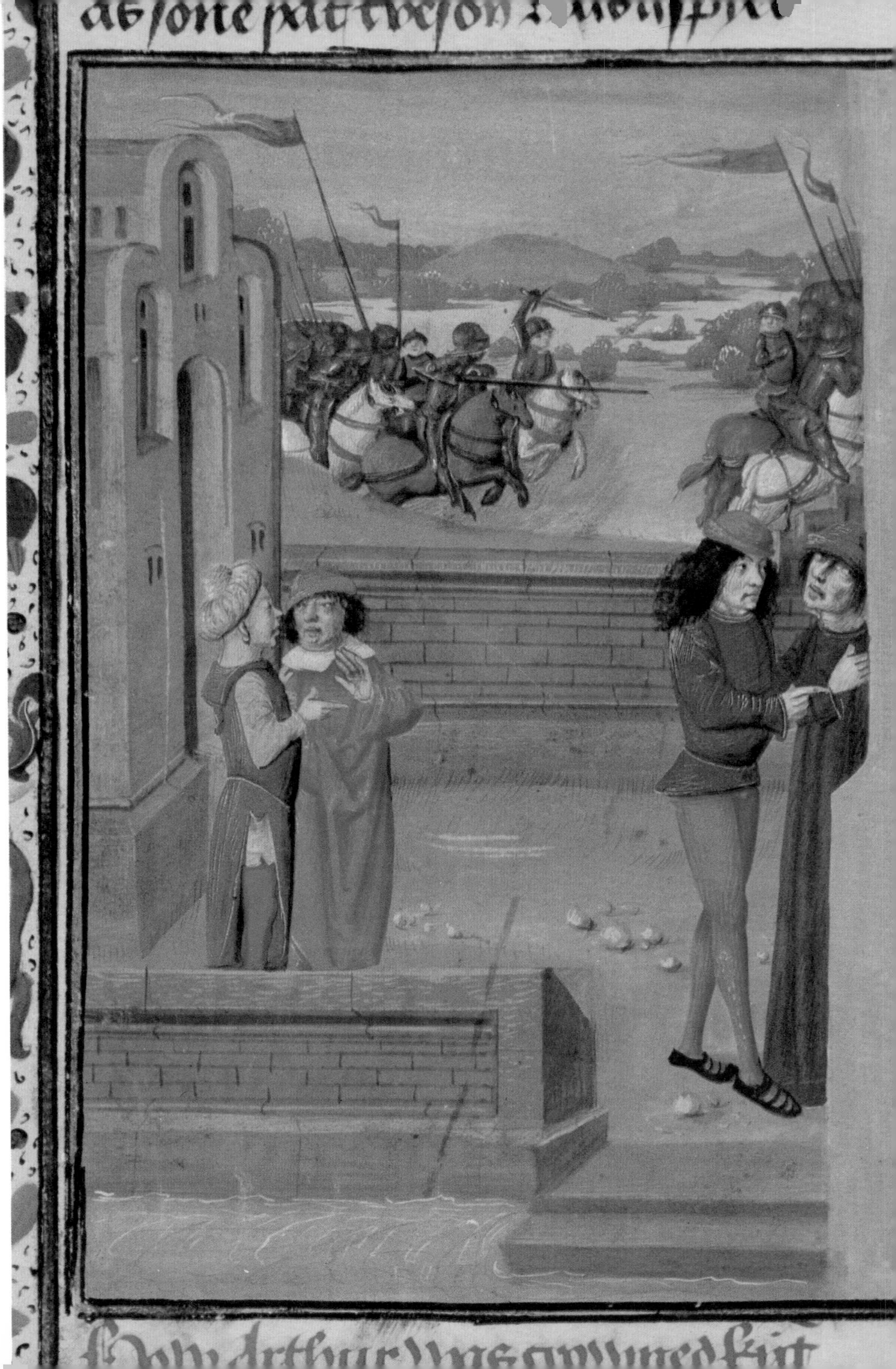

Coment lucanoz le grant ou

et lors aporta lespee toute nue en
tre ses mains si le menerent alau
tel et si le mit sus·

T quant il l'ot mise si le sacre
rent et enonissent et enfiser
toutes iceles coses que ondoit

*Merlin riding
with Arthur and
his knights*

would assay. But there afore them all, there might none take it out
but Arthur; wherefore there were many lords wroth, and said it
was great shame unto them all and the realm, to be over-governed
with a boy of no high blood born, and so they fell out at that time,
that it was put off till Candlemas, and then all the barons should
meet there again; but alway the ten knights were ordained to watch
the sword day and night, and so they set a pavilion over the stone
and the sword, and five always watched.

So at Candlemas many more great lords came thither for to have
won the sword, but there might none prevail. And right as
Arthur did at Christmas, he did at Candlemas, and pulled out the
sword easily, whereof the barons were sore aggrieved and put it off
in delay till the high feast of Easter. And as Arthur sped before, so
did he at Easter, yet there were some of the great lords had indigna-
tion that Arthur should be king, and put it off in a delay till the
feast of Pentecost. Then the Archbishop of Canterbury by Merlin's providence let purvey then of the best knights that they might
get, and such knights as Uther Pendragon loved best and most
trusted in his days. And such knights were put about Arthur as
Sir Baudwin of Britain, Sir Kay, Sir Ulfius, Sir Brastias. All these
with many other were always about Arthur, day and night, till
the feast of Pentecost.

And at the feast of Pentecost all manner of men assayed to pull at
the sword that would assay, but none might prevail but Arthur,
and he pulled it out afore all the lords and commons that were
there, wherefore all the commons cried at once,

'We will have Arthur unto our king; we will put him no more
in delay, for we all see that it is God's will that he shall be our king,
and who that holdeth against it, we will slay him.'

And therewith they all kneeled at once, both rich and poor,
and cried Arthur mercy because they had delayed him so long.
And Arthur forgave them, and took the sword between both his
hands, and offered it upon the altar where the Archbishop was,
and so was he made knight of the best man that was there.

And so anon was the coronation made. And there was he sworn
unto his lords and the commons for to be a true king, to stand with
true justice from thenceforth the days of this life. Also then he
made all lords that held of the crown to come in, and to do service
as they ought to do. And many complaints were made unto Sir
Arthur of great wrongs that were done since the death of King
Uther, of many lands that were bereaved lords, knights, ladies, and
gentlemen. Wherefore King Arthur made the lands to be given
again unto them that ought them.

When this was done, that the king had stablished all the countries about London, then he let make Sir Kay Seneschal of

*Arthur enthroned
being acclaimed
by the lords
and commons*

PAGE 35
*Arthur draws the sword
from the stone and is
acclaimed king*

England; and Sir Baudwin of Britain was made constable; and Sir Ulfius was made chamberlain; and Sir Brastias was made warden to wait upon the north from Trent forwards, for it was that time the most part the king's enemies. But within few years after, Arthur won all the north, Scotland, and all that were under their obeissance. Also Wales, a part of it, held against Arthur, but he overcame them all, as he did the remnant, through the noble prowess of himself and his knights of the Round Table.

Then the king removed into Wales, and let cry a great feast that it should be holden at Pentecost after the incoronation of him at the city of Caerleon.

And thither came to him King Lot's wife, of Orkney, in manner of a message, but she was sent thither to espy the court of King Arthur; and she came richly beseen, with her four sons Gawain, Gaheris, Agravain, and Gareth, with many other knights and ladies. For she was a passing fair lady, wherefore the king cast great love unto her, and desired to lie by her. And so they were agreed, and he begat upon her Mordred. And she was sister, on the mother's side, Igraine, unto Arthur. So there she rested her a month, and at the last she departed.

Arthur in combat with King Lot of Orkney

Then the king dreamed a marvellous dream whereof he was sore adread. But all this time King Arthur knew not that King Lot's wife was his sister. Thus was the dream of Arthur:

Him thought there was come into this land griffins and serpents, and him thought they burnt and slew all the people in the land, and then him thought he fought with them, and they did him passing great harm, and wounded him full sore, but at the last he slew them.

When the king awaked, he was passing heavy of his dream, and so to put it out of thoughts, he made him ready with many knights to ride on hunting. And as soon as he was in the forest the king saw a great hart before him.

'This hart will I chase,' said King Arthur.

And so he spurred his horse, and rode after long, and so by fine force often he was like to have smitten the hart. Wherefore as the king had chased the hart so long, that his horse had lost his breath, and fell down dead; then a yeoman fetched the king another horse.

Merlin disguised as a small boy

Then the king sat in a study, and bad his men fetch his horse as fast as ever they might. Right so came by him Merlin like a child of fourteen year of age, and saluted the king, and asked him why he was so pensive.

'I may well be pensive,' said the king, 'for I have seen the marvellest sight that ever I saw.'

'That know I well,' said Merlin, 'as well as thyself, and of all

37

ABOVE *Merlin as an old man explaining a dream*

BELOW *Merlin warning Arthur to prepare for war*

thy thoughts, but thou art but a fool to take thought, for it will not amend thee. Also I know what thou art, and who was thy father, and of whom thou were begotten; for King Uther Pendragon was thy father, and begat thee on Igraine.'

'That is false' said King Arthur, 'How shouldest thou know it, for thou art not so old of years to know my father?'

'Yes,' said Merlin, 'I know it better than ye or any man living.'

'I will not believe thee,' said Arthur, and was wroth with the child.

So departed Merlin, and came again in the likeness of an old man of fourscore year of age, whereof the king was passing glad, for he seemed to be right wise.

Then said the old man, 'Why are ye so sad?'

'I may well be sad,' said Arthur, 'for many things. For right now there was a child here, and told me many things that me-seemeth he should not know, for he was not of age to know my father.'

'Yes,' said the old man, 'the child told you truth, and more would he have told you and ye would have suffered him. But ye have done a thing late that God is displeased with you, for ye have lain by your sister, and on her ye have gotten a child that shall de-troy you and all the knights of your realm.'

'What are ye,' said Arthur, 'that tell me these tidings?'

'Sir, I am Merlin, and I was he in the child's likeness.'

'Ah,' said King Arthur, 'ye are a marvellous man, but I marvel much of thy words that I must die in battle.'

'Marvel not,' said Merlin, 'for it is God's will your body should be punished for your foul deeds. But I may well be sorry,' said Merlin, 'for I shall die a shameful death to be put in the earth quick, and ye shall die a worshipful death.'

And as they talked thus, came one with the king's horse, and so the king mounted on his horse, and Merlin on another, and so rode unto Caerleon.

And anon the king asked Ector and Ulfius how he was be-gotten, and they told him Uther Pendragon was his father and Queen Igraine his mother.

Then he said to Merlin, 'I will that my mother be sent for, that I may speak with her; and if she say so herself, then will I believe it.'

So in all haste, the queen was sent for, and she came and brought with her Morgan le Fay, her daughter, that was as fair a lady as any might be. And the king welcomed Igraine in the best manner.

Right so came Ulfius, and said openly that the king and all might hear that were feasted that day,

'Ye are the falsest lady in the world, and the most traitress unto the king's person.'

'Beware,' said Arthur, 'what thou sayest; thou speakest a great word.'

'Sir, I am well ware,' said Ulfius, 'what I speak, and here is my glove to prove it upon any man that will say the contrary, that this Queen Igraine is causer of your great damage, and of your great war. For, and she would have uttered it in the life of King Uther Pendragon, of the birth of you, and how ye were begotten, ye had never had the mortal wars that ye have had. For the most part of your barons of your realm knew never whose son ye were, nor of whom ye were begotten; and she that bare you of her body should have made it known openly in excusing of her worship and yours, and in likewise to all the realm. Wherefore I prove her false to God and to you and to all your realm, and who will say the contrary I will prove it on his body.'

Then spake Igraine and said, 'I am a woman and I may not fight, but rather than I should be dishonoured, there would some good man take my quarrel. More,' she said, 'Merlin knoweth well, and ye Sir Ulfius, how King Uther came to me in the Castle of Tintagel in the likeness of my lord, that was dead three hours tofore, and thereby gat a child that night upon me. And after the thir-teenth day King Uther wedded me, and by his commandment when the child was born it was delivered unto Merlin and fostered by him. And so I saw the child never after, nor wot not what is his name, for I knew him never yet.'

And there Ulfius said to the queen, 'Merlin is more to blame than ye.'

'Well I wot,' said the queen, 'I bare a child by my lord King Uther, but I wot not where he is become.'

Then Merlin took the king by the hand, saying, 'This is your mother.' And therewith Sir Ector bare witness how he nourished him by Uther's commandment. And therewith King Arthur took his mother, Queen Igraine, in his arms and kissed her, and either wept upon other. And then the king let make a feast that lasted eight days.

*   *   *

*Merlin advising
Arthur*

BOOK 3

Excalibur

[Then the king and Merlin departed]

nd as they rode, King Arthur said, 'I have no sword.'

'No force,' said Merlin, 'hereby is a sword that shall be yours, and I may.'

So they rode till they came to a lake, the which was a fair water, and broad. And in the midst of the lake Arthur was ware of an arm clothed in white samite, that held a fair sword in that hand.

samite: *rich silk*

'Lo!' said Merlin, 'yonder is that sword that I spake of.'

With that they saw a damsel going upon the lake.

'What damsel is that?' said Arthur.

'That is the Lady of the Lake,' said Merlin; 'and within that lake is a rock, and therein is as fair a place as any on earth, and richly beseen; and this damsel will come to you anon, and then speak ye fair to her that she may give you that sword.'

So anon came the damsel unto Arthur, and saluted him, and he her again.

'Damsel,' said Arthur, 'what sword is that yonder, that the arm holdeth above the water? I would it were mine, for I have no sword.'

'Sir Arthur, king,' said the damsel, 'that sword is mine, and if ye will give me a gift when I ask it you, ye shall have it.'

'By my faith,' said Arthur, 'I will give you what gift ye will ask.'

'Well!' said the damsel, 'Go ye into yonder barge, and row yourself to the sword, and take it and the scabbard with you. And I will ask my gift when I see my time.'

So King Arthur and Merlin alit and tied their horses to two trees, and so they went into the barge, and when they came to the sword that the hand held, then King Arthur took it up by the handles, and took it with him, and the arm and the hand went under the water.

Then King Arthur looked on the sword, and liked it passing well.

40

*Arthur sending
the children to sea
in an attempt to
destroy Mordred*

'Whether like you better,' said Merlin, 'the sword or the scabbard?'

'I like better the sword,' said Arthur.

'Ye are the more unwise,' said Merlin, 'for the scabbard is worth
ten of the swords, for whiles ye have the scabbard upon you, ye
shall lose no blood be ye never so sore wounded. Therefore keep
well the scabbard always with you.'

So they came unto Caerleon, whereof his knights were passing
glad. And when they heard of his adventures, they marvelled
that he would jeopard his person so, alone. But all men of worship said it was merry to be under such a chieftain, that would put
his person in adventure as other poor knights did.

Then King Arthur let send for all the children born on Mayday, begotten of lords and born of ladies; for Merlin told King
Arthur that he that should destroy him should be born on Mayday. Wherefore he sent for them all, upon pain of death; and so
there were found many lords' sons, and many knights' sons, and
all were sent unto the king. And so was Mordred sent by King
Lot's wife. And all were put in a ship to the sea, and some were
four weeks old, and some less.

And so by fortune the ship drove unto a castle, and was all toriven, and destroyed the most part save that Mordred was cast up,
and a good man found him, and fostered him till he was fourteen
year old, and then he brought him to the court, as it rehearseth
afterward, toward the end of 'The Death of Arthur'.

So many lords and barons of this realm were displeased, for
their children were so lost, and many put the wite on Merlin
more than on Arthur; so what for dread and for love, they held
their peace.

41

BOOK 4

Guenever

In the beginning of Arthur, after he was chosen king by adventure and by grace, for the most part of the barons knew not that he was Uther Pendragon's son, but as Merlin made it openly known, but yet many kings and lords held great war against him for that cause, but well Arthur overcame them all, for the most part the days of his life he was ruled much by the counsel of Merlin.

So it fell on a time King Arthur said unto Merlin, 'My barons will let me have no rest, but needs I must take a wife, and I will none take but by thy counsel and by thine advice.'

'It is well done,' said Merlin, 'that ye take a wife, for a man of your bounty and noblesse should not be without a wife. Now is there any that ye love more than another?'

'Yea,' said King Arthur, 'I love Guenever the King's daughter Leodegrance, of the land of Camelerd, the which holdeth in his house the Table Round that ye told he had of my father Uther. And this damsel is the most valiant and fairest lady that I know living, or yet that ever I could find.'

'Sir,' said Merlin, 'as of her beauty and fairness she is one of the fairest alive. But and ye loved her not so well as ye do, I should find you a damsel of beauty and of goodness that should like you and please you, and your heart were not set. But there as a man's heart is set, he will be loth to return.'

'That is truth,' said King Arthur.

But Merlin warned the king covertly that Guenever was not wholesome for him to take to wife, for he warned him that Lancelot should love her, and she him again; and so he turned his tale to the adventures of Sangrail.

Then Merlin desired of the king for to have men with him that should enquire of Guenever, and so the king granted him, and Merlin went forth unto King Leodegrance of Camelerd, and told him of the desire of the king that he would have unto his wife Guenever his daughter.

OPPOSITE
*Arthur enthroned with
his queen, Guenever*

42

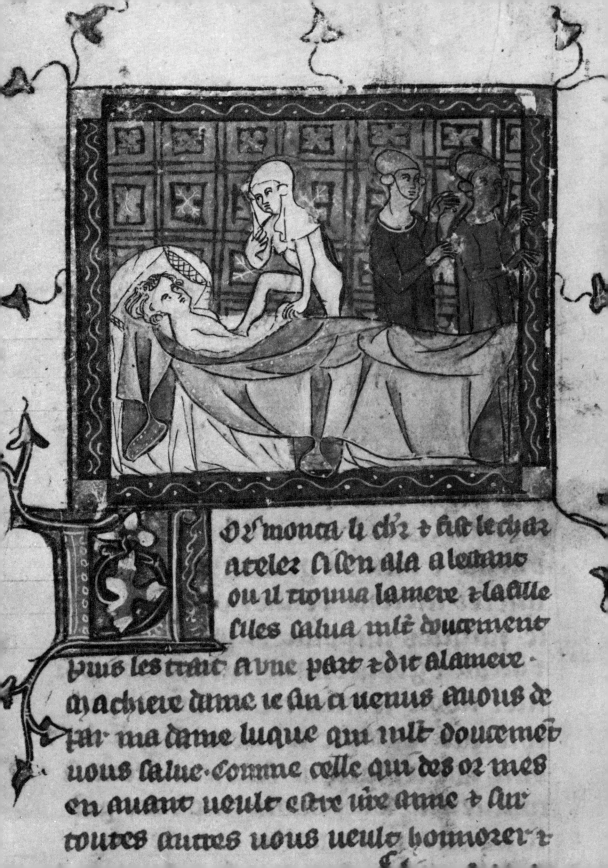

Or monta li chr̄ z fist le char
ateler si sen ala a lettant
ou il trouua lamere z lafille
siles salua mlt douement
puis les traist a une part z dit alamere.
ha achiere dame ie su ci uenus enuois de
fir ma dame luque qui mlt douteme
uous salue. comme celle qui des or mes
en auant ueult estre ure amie z sur
toutes autres uous ueult honnorer z

'That is to me,' said King Leodegrance, 'the best tidings that ever I heard, that so worthy a king of prowess and noblesse will wed my daughter. And as for my lands, I will give him, wist I it might please him, but he hath lands enow, him needeth none. But I shall send him a gift shall please him much more, for I shall give him the Table Round, the which Uther, his father, gave me, and when it is full complete, there is an hundred knights and fifty. And as for an hundred good knights I have myself, but I want fifty, for so many have been slain in my days.'

And so King Leodegrance delivered his daughter Guenever unto Merlin, and the Table Round with the hundred knights, and so they rode freshly, with great royalty, what by water and by land, till that they came nigh unto London.

When King Arthur heard of the coming of Guenever and the hundred knights with the Table Round, then King Arthur made great joy for her coming, and that rich present, and said openly,

'This fair lady is passing welcome unto me, for I have loved her long, and therefore there is nothing so lief to me. And these knights with the Round Table please me more than right great riches.'

lief: dear

And in all haste the king let ordain for the marriage and the coronation in the most honourable wise that could be devised.

'Now, Merlin,' said King Arthur, 'go thou and espy me in all this land fifty knights which be of most prowess and worship.'

So within short time Merlin had found such knights that should fulfil twenty and eight knights, but no more he could find. Then the Bishop of Canterbury was fetched, and he blessed the sieges with great royalty and devotion, and there set the eight and twenty knights in their sieges.

sieges: seats

And when this was done Merlin said, 'Fair sirs, you must all arise and come to King Arthur for to do him homage; he will have the better will to maintain you.'

And so they arose and did their homage, and when they were gone Merlin found in every siege letters of gold that told the knights' names that had sitten therein. But two sieges were void.

And so anon came young Gawain and asked the king a gift.

'Ask,' said the king, 'and I shall grant it you.'

'Sir, I ask that ye will make me knight that same day ye shall wed fair Guenever.'

'I will do it with a good will,' said King Arthur, 'and do unto you all the worship that I may, for I must by reason ye are mine nephew, my sister's son.'

Then was the high feast made ready, and the king was wedded at Camelot unto Dame Guenever in the Church of Saint Stephen's, with great solemnity.

ABOVE *Arthur shows his knights their places at the Round Table*

OPPOSITE *Guenever steps into Arthur's bed on their wedding night*

BOOK 5

The Death of Merlin

So after these quests . . .
it fell so that Merlin fell in a dotage on the damsel
that King Pellinor brought to court and she was
one of the damsels of the Lady of the Lake, that
hight Nimue. But Merlin would let have her no
rest, but always he would be with her. And ever
she made Merlin good cheer till she had learned of him all manner
that she desired; and he was assotted upon her, that he might not
be from her.

So on a time he told King Arthur that he should not dure long,
but for all his crafts he should be put in the earth quick. And so he
told the king many things that should befall, but always he warned
the king to keep well his sword and the scabbard, for he told him
how the sword and the scabbard should be stolen by a woman
from him, that he most trusted. Also he told King Arthur that he
should miss him,

'Yet had ye lever than all your lands to have me again.'

'Ah,' said the king, 'since ye know of your adventure, purvey for
it, and put away by your crafts that misadventure.'

'Nay,' said Merlin, 'it will not be.' So he departed from the
king.

And within a while the Damsel of the Lake departed, and
Merlin went with her evermore wheresomever she went. And
oftentimes Merlin would have had her privily away by his subtle
crafts; then she made him to swear that he should never do none
enchantment upon her if he would have his will. And so he
sware. Then she and Merlin went over the sea unto the land of
Benwick, thereas King Ban was king that had great war against
King Claudas. And there Merlin spake with King Ban's wife,
a fair lady and a good, and her name was Elaine, and there
he saw young Lancelot. There the queen made great sorrow for
the mortal war that King Claudas made on her lord and on her
lands.

OPPOSITE
*One of the many
legends of Merlin
told how he erected
Stonehenge*

46

Cil sunt as pieds ankes
er̓es devour et de tr̓auers
Iou ont eu poyng̃ et bn̓ boter
et bien retrait et bn̓ crole
ue par fd̓rce a la meniom̓
e purrent fair̓ pridre un tour̃

Trahez uous dit ger̓lin en sus
a par fd̓rce ne feres plus
r̓e tirez engine et dmou
ēt ce verru de corps uall̃
mic alaid auaint si festuet̃
ntour par dak le leue nuit

Various scenes from the legends of Merlin

TOP LEFT *Merlin leading two kings*

BOTTOM LEFT *Merlin explaining a dream to a king*

TOP RIGHT *Merlin in attendance on two kings*

BOTTOM RIGHT *Merlin disguised as a stag*

'Take none heaviness,' said Merlin, 'for this same child young Lancelot within this twenty year shall revenge you on King Claudas, that all Christendom shall speak of it; and this same child shall be the most man of worship of the world. And his first name is Galahad, that know I well,' said Merlin, 'and since ye have confirmed him Lancelot.'

'That is truth,' said the queen, 'his first name was Galahad. O Merlin,' said the queen, 'shall I live to see my son such a man of prowess?'

'Yea, lady, on my peril ye shall see it, and live many winters after.'

Then so soon after the lady and Merlin departed, and by the way Merlin showed her many wonders, and so came into Cornwall. And always Merlin lay about the lady to have her maidenhood, and she was ever passing weary of him, and fain would have been delivered of him, for she was afeared of him because he was a devil's son, and she could not be skift of him by no mean.

skift: *rid*

And so on a time it happened that Merlin showed to her in a rock whereas was a great wonder, and wrought by enchantment, that went under a great stone. So by her subtle working she made Merlin to go under that stone to let her wit of the marvels there, but she wrought so there for him that he came never out for all the craft he could do. And so she departed and left Merlin.

TOP LEFT AND
RIGHT *Merlin
bids farewell to
Arthur and leaves him*

BOTTOM LEFT
Merlin imprisoned

BOTTOM RIGHT
*Merlin teaching
magic to Nimue*

So, as [a knight named] Sir Bagdemagus rode to see many adventures, it happed him to come to the rock thereas the Lady of the Lake had put Merlin under the stone, and there he heard him make great dole; whereof Sir Bagdemagus would have holpen him, and went unto the great stone, and it was so heavy that an hundred men might not lift it up. When Merlin wist that he was there, he bad leave his labour, for all was in vain; for he might never be holpen but by her that put him there. . . .

BOOK 6

Morgan le Fay

hen it befell that Arthur and many of his knights rode on hunting into a great forest, and it happed King Arthur, King Uriens, and Sir Accolon of Gaul, followed a great hart, for they three were well horsed, and so they chased so fast that within a while they three were then ten mile from their fellowship. And at the last they chased so sore that they slew their horses underneath them. Then were they all three on foot, and ever they saw the hart afore them passing weary and ambushed.

bestad: beset

'What will we do?' said King Arthur, 'We are hard bestad.'

'Let us go on foot,' said King Uriens, 'till we may meet with some lodging.'

brachet: female hound
dight: prepared

Then were they ware of the hart that lay on a great water bank, and a brachet biting on his throat, and more other hounds came after. Then King Arthur blew the prize and dight the hart.

Then the king looked about the world, and saw before him in a great water a little ship, all apparelled with silk down to the water; and the ship came right unto them and landed on the sands. Then Arthur went to the bank and looked in, and saw none earthly creature therein.

'Sirs,' said the king, 'come thence, and let us see what is in this ship.'

So they went in all three, and found it richly behanged with cloth of silk. By then it was dark night, and there suddenly were about them an hundred torches set upon all the sides of the ship boards, and it gave great light; and therewithal there came twelve fair damsels and saluted King Arthur on their knees, and called him by his name, and said he was right welcome, and such cheer as they had he should have of the best. The king thanked them fair. Therewithal they led the king and his two fellows into a fair chamber, and there was a cloth laid richly beseen of all that longed to a table, and there were they served of all wines and meats that they could think of. But of that the king had great marvel, for he fared never better in his life as for one supper.

And so when they had supped at their leisure, King Arthur was led into a chamber, a richer beseen chamber saw he never none; and so was King Uriens served, and led into such another chamber; and Sir Accolon was led into the third chamber passing richly and well beseen. And so they were laid in their beds easily. And anon they fell asleep, and slept marvellously sore all the night.

And on the morrow King Uriens was in Camelot abed in his wife's arms, Morgan le Fay. And when he awoke he had great marvel, how he came there, for on the even afore he was two days' journey from Camelot. And when King Arthur awoke he found himself in a dark prison, hearing about him many complaints of woeful knights.

Anon, therewithal there came a damsel unto Arthur, and asked him, 'What cheer?'

'I cannot say,' said he.

'Sir,' she said, 'and ye will fight for my lord, ye shall be delivered out of prison, and else ye escape never the life.'

'Now,' said Arthur, 'that is hard, yet had I lever to fight with a knight than to die in prison; with this,' said Arthur, 'I may be delivered and all these prisoners, I will do the battle.'

'Yes,' said the damsel.

'Then I am ready,' said Arthur, 'and I had horse and armour.'

'Ye shall lack none,' said the damsel.

'Meseemeth, damsel, I should have seen you in the court of Arthur.'

'Nay,' said the damsel, 'I came never there. I am the lord's daughter of this castle.'

Yet was she false, for she was one of the damsels of Morgan le Fay.

Now turn we unto Accolon of Gaul, that when he awoke he found himself by a deep well-side, within half a foot, in great peril of death. And there came out of that fountain a pipe of silver, and out of that pipe ran water all on high in a stone of marble. When Sir Accolon saw this, he blessed him and said,

'Jesu, save my lord King Arthur, and King Uriens, for these damsels in this ship have betrayed us. They were devils and no women; and if I may escape this misadventure, I shall destroy them, all that I may find of these false damsels that usen enchantments.'

Right with that there came a dwarf with a great mouth and a flat nose, and saluted Sir Accolon, and told him how he came from Queen Morgan le Fay,

'And she greeteth you well, and biddeth you be of strong heart, for ye shall fight to-morn with a knight at the hour of prime, and therefore she hath sent you here Excalibur, Arthur's sword, and the scabbard, and she biddeth you as ye love her, that ye do the battle to the uttermost, without any mercy, like as ye had promised her when ye spake last together in private. And what damsel that bringeth her the knight's head, which ye shall fight withal, she will make her a queen.'

'Now I understand you well,' said Accolon, 'I shall hold that I have promised her now I have the sword. When saw ye my lady Queen Morgan le Fay?'

'Right late,' said the dwarf.

Then Accolon took him in his arms and said, 'Recommend me unto my lady queen, and tell her all shall be done that I have promised her, and else I will die for it. Now I suppose,' said Accolon, 'she hath made all these crafts and enchantments for this battle.'

'Sir, ye may well believe it,' said the dwarf.

Right so there came a knight and a lady with six squires, and saluted Accolon, and prayed him for to arise, and come and rest him at his manor. And so Accolon mounted upon a void horse, and went with the knight unto a fair manor by a priory, and there he had passing good cheer.

Then Sir Arthur mounted upon horseback, and there were all the knights and commons of that country; and so by all their advices there were chosen twelve good men of the country for to wait upon the two knights.

And right as Arthur was on horseback there came a damsel from Morgan le Fay, and brought unto Sir Arthur a sword like unto Excalibur, and the scabbard, and said unto Arthur, 'Morgan le Fay sendeth here your sword for great love.'

And he thanked her, and weened it had been so, but she was false, for the sword and the scabbard was counterfeit, and brittle, and false.

And then they dressed them on both parts of the field, and let their horses run so fast that either smote other in the midst of the shield with their spear's head, that both horse and man went to the earth; and then they start up both, and pulled out their swords.

The meanwhile that they were thus at the battle, came the damsel of the lake into the field, that put Merlin under the stone; and she came thither for love of King Arthur, for she knew how Morgan le Fay had so ordained that King Arthur should have been slain that day, and therefore she came to save his life.

And so they went eagerly to the battle, and gave many great strokes. But always Arthur's sword bit not like Accolon's sword; but for the most part, every stroke that Accolon gave he wounded sore Arthur, that it was marvel he stood, and always his blood fell from him fast. When Arthur beheld the ground so sore be-bled he was dismayed; and then he deemed treason that his sword was changed, for his sword bit not steel as it was wont to do. Therefore he dread him sore to be dead, for ever him seemed that the sword in Accolon's hand was Excalibur, for at every stroke that Accolon struck he drew blood on Arthur.

'Now, knight,' said Accolon unto Arthur, 'keep thee well from me.'

But Arthur answered not again, and gave him such a buffet on the helm that he made him to stoop, nigh falling down to the earth. Then Sir Accolon withdrew him a little and came on with Excalibur on high, and smote Sir Arthur such a buffet that he fell nigh to the earth. Then were they wroth both, and gave each other many sore strokes. But always Sir Arthur lost so much blood that it was marvel he stood on his feet, but he was so full of knighthood that knightly he endured the pain. And Sir Accolon lost not a deal of blood, therefore he waxed passing light; and Sir Arthur was passing feeble, and weened verily to have died; but for all that he made countenance as though he might endure, and held Accolon as short as he might. But Accolon was so bold because of Excalibur that he waxed passing hardy. But all men that beheld him said they saw never knight fight so well as Arthur did considering the blood that he bled.

So was all the people sorry for him . . .; then always they fought together as fierce knights, and Sir Arthur withdrew him a little for to rest him, and Sir Accolon called him to battle and said, 'It is no time for me to suffer thee to rest.' And therewith he came fiercely upon Arthur, and Sir Arthur was wroth for the blood that he had lost, and smote Accolon on high upon the helm, so mightily, that he made him nigh to fall to the earth; and therewith Arthur's sword brast at the cross, and fell in the grass among the blood, and the pommel and the sure handles he held in his hands. When Sir Arthur saw that, he was in great fear to die, but always he held up his shield and lost no ground, nor bated no cheer.

Then Sir Accolon began with words of treason, and said, 'Knight, thou art overcome, and mayst not endure, and also thou art weaponless, and thou has lost much of thy blood, and I am full loth to slay thee. Therefore yield thee to me as recreant.'

'Nay,' said Sir Arthur, 'I may not so, for I have promised by the faith of my body to do this battle to the uttermost, while my life lasteth, and therefore I had lever to die with honour than to live with shame. And if it were possible for me to die an hundred times, I had lever to die so oft than yield me to thee; for though I lack weapon, I shall lack no worship, and if thou slay me weaponless that shall be thy shame.'

'Well,' said Accolon, 'as for the shame I will not spare, now keep thee from me, for thou art but a dead man.'

And therewith Accolon gave him such a stroke that he fell nigh to the earth, and would have had Arthur to have cried him mercy. But Sir Arthur pressed unto Accolon with his shield, and gave him with the pommel in his hand such a buffet that he reeled three strides aback.

When the damsel of the lake beheld Arthur, how full of prowess his body was, and the false treason that was wrought for him to have had him slain, she had great pity that so good a knight and such a man of prowess should so be destroyed. And at the next stroke Sir Accolon struck at him such a stroke that by the damsel's enchantment the sword Excalibur fell out of Accolon's hand to the earth.

And therewithal Sir Arthur lightly leapt to it, and gat it in his hand, and forthwithal he knew that it was his sword Excalibur.

'Ah,' said Arthur, 'thou hast been from me all too long, and much damage hast thou done me.'

And therewith he espied the scabbard hanging by his side, and suddenly he start to him and pulled the scabbard from him, and threw it from him as far as he might throw it.

'Ah, sir knight,' said Arthur, 'this day hast thou done me great damage with this sword. Now are ye come unto your death, for I shall not warrant you but ye shall be as well rewarded with this sword or ever we depart as ye have rewarded me, for much pain have ye made me to endure, and much blood have I lost.'

And therewith Sir Arthur rushed on him with all his might and pulled him to the earth, and then rushed off his helm, and gave him such a buffet on the head that the blood came out at his ears, his nose, and his mouth.

'Now will I slay thee,' said Arthur.

'Slay me ye may well,' said Accolon, 'and it please you, for ye are the best knight that ever I found, and I see well that God is with you. But for I promised,' said Accolon, 'to do this battle to the uttermost, and never to be recreant while I lived, therefore shall I never yield me with my mouth, but God do with my body what He will.'

Then Sir Arthur remembered him, and thought he should have seen this knight.

'Now tell me,' said Arthur, 'or I will slay thee, of what country art thou, and of what court?'

'Sir knight,' said Sir Accolon, 'I am of the royal court of King Arthur, and my name is Accolon of Gaul.'

Then was Arthur more dismayed than he was beforehand; for then he remembered him of his sister Morgan le Fay, and of the enchantment of the ship.

'O sir knight,' said he, 'I pray you tell me who gave you this sword, and by whom ye had it.'

Then Sir Accolon bethought him, and said, 'Woe worth this sword, for by it I have gotten my death.'

'It may well be,' said the king.

'Now, sir,' said Accolon, 'I will tell you: this sword hath been in my keeping the most part of this twelvemonth; and Morgan le Fay, King Urien's wife, sent it me yesterday by a dwarf, to this intent, that I should slay King Arthur, her brother. For ye shall understand King Arthur is the man in the world that she hateth most, because he is most of worship and of prowess of any of her blood. Also she loveth me out of measure as paramour, and I her again. And if she might bring about to slay Arthur by her crafts, she would slay her husband King Uriens lightly. And then had she me devised to have me king in this land, and so to reign, and she to be my queen; but that is now done,' said Accolon, 'for I am sure of my death.'

'Well,' said Sir Arthur, 'I feel by you ye would have been king in this land. Yet it had been great damage to have destroyed your lord,' said Arthur.

'It is truth,' said Accolon, 'but now I have told you the truth, wherefore I pray you tell me of whence ye are, and of what court?'

'O Accolon,' said King Arthur, 'now I let thee wit that I am King Arthur, to whom thou hast done great damage.'

When Accolon heard that he cried aloud, 'Fair, sweet lord, have mercy on me, for I knew not you.'

'O Sir Accolon,' said King Arthur, 'mercy shalt thou have, because I feel by thy words at this time thou knowest me not; but I understand well by thy words that thou hast agreed to the death of my person, and therefore thou art a traitor; but I wit thee the less, for my sister Morgan le Fay by her false crafts made thee to agree and consent to her false lusts, but I shall be sore avenged upon her and I live, that all Christendom shall speak of it. God knoweth I have honoured her and worshipped her more than all my kin, and more have I trusted her than mine own wife and all my kin after.'

Then Sir Arthur called the keepers of the field, and said, 'Sirs, cometh hither, for here are we two knights that have foughten unto a great damage unto us both, and likely each one of us to have slain other, if it had happed so; and had any of us known other, here had been no battle, nor stroke stricken.'

Then all aloud cried Accolon unto all the knights and men that were then there gathered together, and said to them in this manner.

'O lords, this noble knight that I have foughten withal, the which me sore repenteth, is the most man of prowess, of manhood,

alther: *of all*

and of worship in the world, for it is himself King Arthur, our alther liege lord, and with mishap and with misadventure have I done this battle with the king and lord that I am holden withal.'

Then all the people fell down on their knees and cried King Arthur mercy.

'Mercy shall ye have,' said Arthur. 'Here may ye see what sudden adventures befallen often of errant knights, how that I have foughten with a knight of mine own unto my great damage and his both.

So the king took his leave of all the people, and mounted upon horseback, and Sir Accolon with him. And when they were come to the abbey, he let fetch leeches and searched his wounds and Accolon's both; but Sir Accolon died within four days, for he had bled so much blood that he might not live, but King Arthur was well recovered.

So when Accolon was dead he let send him on an horse-bier with six knights unto Camelot, and said,

'Bear him to my sister Morgan le Fay, and say that I send her him to a present. And tell her I have my sword Excalibur and the scabbard.'

So they departed with the body.

The meanwhile Morgan le Fay had weened King Arthur had been dead. So on a day she espied King Uriens lay in his bed sleeping. Then she called unto her a maiden of her counsel, and said,

'Go fetch me my lord's sword, for I saw never better time to slay him than now.'

'O madam,' said the damsel, 'and ye slay my lord ye can never escape.'

'Care thee not,' said Morgan le Fay, 'for now I see my time it is best to do it, and therefore hie thee fast and fetch me the sword.'

Then the damsel departed, and found Sir Uwain sleeping upon a bed in another chamber, so she went unto Sir Uwain, and waked him, and bad him,

'Arise, and wait on my lady your mother, for she will slay the king your father sleeping in his bed, for I go to fetch his sword.'

'Well,' said Sir Uwain, 'go on your way, and let me deal.'

Anon the damsel brought Morgan the sword with quaking hands. And lightly she took the sword, and pulled it out, and went boldly unto the bed's side, and awaited how and where she might slay him best.

And as she lifted up the sword to smite, Sir Uwain leapt unto his mother, and caught her by the hand, and said,

'Ah, fiend, what wilt thou do? And thou wert not my mother, with this sword I should smite off thy head. Ah,' said Sir Uwain, 'men saith that Merlin was begotten of a devil, but I may say an earthly devil bare me.'

A damsel carries a message to the Lady of the Lake

'O fair son, Uwain, have mercy upon me, I was tempted with a devil, wherefore I cry thee mercy; I will never more do so; and save my worship and discover me not.'

'On this covenant,' said Sir Uwain, 'I will forgive it you, so ye will never be about to do such deeds.'

'Nay, son,' said she, 'and that I make you assurance.'

Then came tidings unto Morgan le Fay that Accolon was dead, and his body brought unto the church, and how King Arthur had his sword again. But when Queen Morgan wist that Accolon was dead, she was so sorrowful that near her heart to-brast. But because she would not it were known, outward she kept her countenance, and made no semblant of sorrow. But well she wist and she abode till her brother Arthur came thither, there should no gold go for her life. Then she went unto Queen Guenever, and asked her leave to ride into the country.

'Ye may abide,' said Queen Guenever, 'till your brother the king come home.'

'I may not, Madam,' said Morgan le Fay, 'for I have such hasty tidings, that I may not tarry.'

'Well,' said Guenever, 'ye may depart when ye will.'

So early on the morn, or it was day, she took her horse and rode all that day and most part of the night, and on the morn by noon she came to the same abbey of nuns whereas lay King Arthur; and she knowing he was there, she asked where he was. And they answered how he had laid him in his bed to sleep, for he had had but little rest these three nights.

'Well,' said she, 'I charge you that none of you awake him till I do.'

And then she alit off her horse, and thought for to steal away Excalibur his sword.

And so she went straight unto his chamber, and no man durst disobey her commandment, and there she found Arthur asleep in his bed, and Excalibur in his right hand naked. When she saw that, she was passing heavy that she might not come by the sword without she had awaked him, and then she wist well she had been dead. Then she took the scabbard and went her way on horseback.

When the king awoke and missed his scabbard, he was wroth, and he asked who had been there, and they said his sister, Queen Morgan had been there, and had put the scabbard under her mantle and was gone.

'Alas,' said Arthur, 'falsely ye have watched me.'

'Sir,' said they all, 'we durst not disobey your sister's commandment.'

'Ah,' said the king, 'let fetch the best horse may be found, and bid Sir Ontzlake arm him in all haste, and take another good horse and ride with me.'

So anon the king and Ontzlake were well armed, and rode after this lady, and so they came by a cross and found a cowherd, and they asked the poor man if there came any lady late riding that way.

'Sir,' said this poor man, 'right late came a lady riding with a forty horses, and to yonder forest she rode.'

Then they spurred their horses, and followed fast, and within a while Arthur had a sight of Morgan le Fay. Then he chased as fast as he might. When she espied him following her, she rode a greater pace through the forest till she came to a plain, and when she saw she might not escape, she rode unto a lake thereby, and said,

'Whatsoever come of me, my brother shall not have this scab⸗ bard.'

And then she let throw the scabbard in the deepest of the water. So it sank, for it was heavy of gold and precious stones. Then she rode into a valley where many great stones were, and when she saw she must be overtake, she shaped herself, horse and man, by en⸗ chantment unto a great marble stone.

Anon withal came Sir Arthur and Sir Ontzlake whereas the king might know his sister and her men, and one knight from another.

'Ah,' said the king, 'here may ye see the vengeance of God, and now am I sorry that this misadventure is befall.'

And then he looked for the scabbard, but it would not be found, so he returned to the abbey where he came from.

So when Arthur was gone she turned all into the likeness as she and they were before, and said, 'Sirs, now may we go where we will.'

Then said Morgan, 'Saw ye Arthur, my brother?'

'Yea,' said her knights, 'right well, and that ye should have found and we might have stirred from one stead, for by his army⸗ vestal countenance he would have caused us to have fled.'

'I believe you,' said Morgan.

When the king had well rested him at the abbey, he rode unto Camelot, and found his queen and his barons right glad of his coming. And when they heard of his strange adventures as is afore rehearsed, then all had marvel of the falsehood of Morgan le Fay; many knights wished her burnt.

'Well,' said the king, 'she is a kind sister; I shall so be avenged on her and I live, that all Christendom shall speak of it.'

So on the morn there came a damsel from Morgan to the king, and she brought with her the richest mantle that ever was seen in that court, for it was set as full of precious stones as one might stand by another, and there were the richest stones that ever the king saw. And the damsel said, 'Your sister sendeth you this mantle, and desireth that ye should take this gift of her; and in what thing she

Arthur and his knights leaving Morgan le Fay

armyvestal: *Caxton's variant of manuscript reading 'amyvestal', but neither word exists elsewhere. Perhaps intended to mean 'warlike'*

hath offended you, she will amend it at your own pleasure.'

When the king beheld this mantle it pleased him much, but he said but little.

With that came the Damsel of the Lake unto the king, and said, 'Sir, I must speak with you in private.'

'Say on,' said the king, 'what ye will.'

'Sir,' said the damsel, 'put not on you this mantle till ye have seen more, and in no wise let it not come on you nor on no knight of yours till ye command the bringer thereof to put it upon her.'

'Well,' said King Arthur, 'it shall be done as ye counsel me.'

And then he said unto the damsel that came from his sister, 'Damsel, this mantle that ye have brought me, I will see it upon you.'

Arthur in consultation with a damsel

'Sir,' she said, 'It will not beseem me to wear a king's garment.'

'By my head,' said Arthur, 'ye shall wear it or it come on my back, or on any man's that here is.'

And so the king made it to be put upon her. And forthwithal she fell down dead, and never more spake word after, and burnt to coals.

Then was the king wonderly wroth, more than he was tofore, hand, and said unto King Uriens,

'My sister, your wife, is alway about to betray me, and well I wot either ye, or my nephew, your son, is of counsel with her to have me destroyed; but as for you,' said the king to King Uriens, 'I deem not greatly that ye be of her counsel, for Accolon confessed to me by his own mouth, that she would have destroyed you as well as me, therefore I hold you excused; but as for your son, Sir Uwain, I hold him suspect. Therefore I charge you put him out of my court.'

So Sir Uwain was discharged. And when Sir Gawain wist that, he made him ready to go with him, and said, 'Whoso banish, eth my cousin germain shall banish me.'

So they two departed, and rode into a great forest, and so they came to an abbey of monks, and there were well lodged. But when the king wist that Sir Gawain was departed from the court, there was made great sorrow among all the estates.

'Now,' said Gaheris, Gawain's brother, 'we have lost two good knights for the love of one.'

Here endeth this tale, as the French book saith, from the marriage of King Uther unto King Arthur that reigned after him and did many battles . . . who that will make any more, let him seek other books of King Arthur, or of Sir Lancelot or Sir Tristram. For this was drawn by a knight prisoner, Sir Thomas Malory, that God send him recover. Amen. EXPLICIT.

Q ue sont estour merueillouse
V ne ne uie plus pillouse
B ien furent bednet 7 sir kes
P leur gels barons en airt le kes
k es seneschals gels loielers
Q uit seruet bien des bridnes dasters
Ⓜ ais bednet sest solemet alle
L i kens boes lad enotre
B ednet ferist par mi le cors
E t fist passer le fer de tors
B ednet chiet le chor li pait
L aime sen uit ihu la gard
k es ad troue bednet mort
C uidelent ad qi len port

BOOK 7

The Expedition to Rome

t befell, when King Arthur had wedded Queen Guenever and fulfilled the Round Table, and so after his marvellous knights and he had vanquished the most part of his enemies, then soon after came Sir Lancelot du Lake unto the court, and Sir Tristram came that time also; and then King Arthur held a royal feast and Table Round.

So it befell that the Emperor Lucius, Procuror of the Public Weal of Rome, sent unto Arthur messengers commanding him for to pay his truage, that his ancestors had paid before him. When King Arthur wist what they meant, he looked up with his gray eyes, and angered at the messengers passing sore. Then were these messengers afeared, and kneeled still and durst not arise, they were so afeared of his grim countenance. Then one of the knights messengers spake aloud, and said,

truage: *tribute*

'Crowned king, misdo no messengers; for we be come at his commandment, as servants should.'

Then spake the Conqueror: 'Thou recreant and coward knight, why fearest thou my countenance? There be in this hall, and they were sore aggrieved, thou durst not for a dukedom of lands look in their faces.'

'Sir,' said one of the senators, 'so Christ me help, I was so afeared when I looked in thy face that mine heart would not serve for to say my message. But sithen it is my will for to say my errand, thee greets well Lucius, the Emperor of Rome, and commands thee, upon pain that will follow, to send him the truage of this realm that thy father Uther Pendragon paid; or else he will bereave thee all thy realms that thou wieldest – and thou as rebel, not knowing him as thy sovereign, withholdest and retainest, contrary to the statutes and decrees made by the noble and worthy Julius Caesar, conqueror of this realm.'

'Thou sayest well,' said Arthur, 'but for all thy brim words I will not be over-hasty. And therefore thou and thy fellows shall

OPPOSITE
*Arthur in combat
with Lucius, the
Emperor of Rome*

ABOVE *A messenger
arrives at Camelot*

brim: *fierce*

abide here seven days; and shall call unto me my counsel of my most trusty knights and dukes, and regent kings, and earls and barons, and of my most wise doctors; and when we have taken our *avisement* ye shall have your answer plainly, such as I shall abide by.'

avisement: advice

Then some of the young knights, hearing this their message, would have run on them to have slain them, saying it was a rebuke to all the knights there being present to suffer them to say so to the king. And anon the king commanded that none of them upon pain of death to *missay* them, nor do them any harm.

missay: insult

Then the noble king commanded Sir Clegis to look that these men be settled and served with the best, that there be no dainties spared upon them, that neither *child* nor horse fault nothing.

child: youth

'For they are full royal people. And though they have grieved me and my court, yet we must remember on our worship.'

So they were led into chambers and served as richly of dainties that might be gotten. So the Romans had thereof great marvel.

Then the king unto counsel called his noble lords and knights, and within a tower there they assembled, the most part of the knights of the Round Table. Then the king commanded them of their best counsel.

'Sir,' said Sir Cador of Cornwall, 'as for me I am not heavy of this message, for we have by many days rested now. The letters of Lucius the Emperor likes me well, for now shall we have war and worship.'

lieve: believe
spiteous:
contemptuous

'By Christ, I lieve well,' said the king, 'Sir Cador, this message likes thee. But yet they may not be so answered, for their spiteous speech grieveth so my heart. That truage to Rome will I never pay. Therefore counsel me, my knights, for Christ's love, of Heaven. For this much have I found in the chronicles of this land, that Sir Belin and Sir Brine, of my blood elders, that born were in Britain, and they hath occupied the Empireship eight score winters; and after, Constantine our kinsmand conquered it; and Dame Elen's son, of England, was Emperor of Rome; and he recovered the cross that Christ died upon. And thus was the Empire kept by my kind elders, and thus have we evidence enough to the Empire of Holy Rome.'

Arthur giving instructions to his knights

Then the King of Little Britain said unto King Arthur, 'Sir, answer these aliens and give them their answer, and I shall summon my people, and thirty thousand men shall ye have, at my costs and wages.'

'Ye say well,' said the King Arthur.

Then leap in young Sir Lancelot du Lake with a light heart, and said unto King Arthur,

'Though my lands march nigh thine enemies, yet shall I make

mine avow after my power, that of good men of arms after my blood thus many I shall bring with me: twenty thousand helms and hauberks attired, that shall never fail you while our lives lasteth.'

'Now I thank you,' said the king, 'with all my true heart. I suppose by the end be done and dealt, the Romans had been better to have left their proud message.'

So when the seven-night was at an end, the senators besought the king to have an answer.

'It is well,' said the king. 'Now say ye to your Emperor that I shall in all haste me ready make with my keen knights, and by the river of Rome hold my Round Table. And I will bring with me the best people of fifteen realms, and with them ride on the mountains in the mainlands, and mine down the walls of Milan the proud, and sith ride unto Rome with my royalest knights. Now ye have your answer, hie you that ye were hence, and from this place to the port there ye shall pass over. And I shall give you seven days to pass unto Sandwich. Now speed you, I counsel you, and spare not your horses. And look ye go by Watling Street and no way else. And where night falls on you, look ye there abide, be it fell or town, I take no keep. For it longeth not to none aliens for to ride on   *keep: care* nights. And may any be found a spear-length out of the way, and that ye be in the water by the seven-night's end, there shall no gold under God pay for your ransom.'

'Sir,' said these senators, 'this is an hard conduct. We beseech you that we may pass safely.'

'Care ye not,' said the king. 'Your conduct is able.'

Thus they passed from Carlisle unto Sandwich-ward, that had but seven days for to pass through the land; and so Sir Cador brought them on their ways. But the senators spared for no horse, but hired them hackneys from town to town, and by the sun was set at the seven days' end they came unto Sandwich. So blithe were they never.

And so the same night they took the water and passed into Flanders, Almain, and after that over the great mountain that   *Almain: Germany* hight Godard, and so after through Lombardy and through Tuscany, and soon after they came to the Emperor Lucius. And there they showed him the letters of King Arthur, and how he was the gastfullest man that ever they on looked. When the Emperor   *gastful: fearful* Lucius had read the letters and understood them well of their credence, he fared as a man were rased out of his wit.   *rased: torn*

'I weened that Arthur would have obeyed you and served you himself unto your hand, for so he beseemed, or any king christened, for to obey any senator that is sent from my person.'

'Sir,' said the senators, 'let be such words; for that we have

saws: *speech*
list: *wish*

escaped on live we may thank God for ever; for we would not pass again to do that message for all your broad lands. And therefore, sir, trust to our saws, ye shall find him your utter enemy. And seek ye him and ye list, for into this land will he come, and that shall ye find within this half-year, for he thinks to be Emperor himself. For he saith ye have occupied the Empire with great wrong, for all his true ancestors save his father Uther were Emperors of Rome.

'And of all the sovereigns that we saw ever, he is the royalest king that liveth on earth, for we saw on New Year's Day at his Round Table nine kings, and the fairest fellowship of knights are with him that dures on live, and thereto of wisdom and of fair speech and all royalty and riches they fail of none. Therefore, sir, by my counsel, rear up your liege people and send kings and dukes to look unto your marches, and that the mountains of Almain be mightily kept.'

'By Easter,' said the Emperor, 'I cast me for to pass Almain and so forth into France, and there bereave him his lands. I shall bring with me many giants of Genoa, that one of them shall be worth an hundred of knights, and perilous passage shall be surely kept with my good knights.'

Then the Emperor sent forth his messengers of wise old knights unto . . . Alexandria, to India, to Armenia that the river of Euphrates runs by, and to Asia, Africa, and Europe the Large, and to Irritayne and Elamet, to the Outer Isles, to Arabia, to Egypt, to Damascus, and to Damietta, and to noble dukes and earls . . . . Thus all these kings and dukes and admirals noble assembled with sixteen kings at once. And so they came unto Rome with great multitude of people.

When the Emperor understood their coming, he made ready all his noble Romans and all men of war betwixt him and Flanders. Also he had gotten with him fifty giants that were engendered with fiends, and all those he let ordain for to await on his person, and for to break the battle of the front of Arthur's knights; but they were so much of their bodies that horses might not bear them. And thus the Emperor with all his horrible people drew to pass Almain to destroy Arthur's land, that he won through war of his noble knights.

Now leave we Sir Lucius and speak we of King Arthur, that commanded all that were under his obeisance, after the utas of St Hilary, that all should be assembled for to hold a Parliament at York, within the walls. And there they concluded shortly to arrest all the ships of this land, and within fifteen days to be ready at Sandwich.

utas: *eighth day*

'Now sirs,' said Arthur, 'I purpose me to pass many perilous ways, and to occupy the Empire that mine elders afore have claimed. Therefore I pray you, counsel me that may be best and most worship.'

The kings and knights gathered them unto counsel, and were condescended for to make two chieftains, that was Sir Baudwin of Britain, an ancient and an honourable knight, for to counsel and comfort; Sir Cador's son of Cornwall, that was at the time called Sir Constantine, that after was king after Arthur's days. And there in the presence of all the lords the king resigned all the rule unto these two lords, and Queen Guenever.

And Sir Tristram at that time beleft with King Mark of Cornwall, for the love of La Beale Isoud, wherefore Sir Lancelot was passing wroth.

Then Queen Guenever made great sorrow that the king and all the lords should so be departed, and there she fell down in a swoon, and her ladies bear her to her chamber. Then the king commended them to God, and beleft the queen in Sir Constantine's and Sir Baudwin's hands, and all England wholly to rule as themselves deemed best. And when the king was on horseback, he said in hearing of all the lords:

'If that I die in this journey, here I make thee, Sir Constantine, my true heir; for thou art next of my kin save Sir Cador, thy father; and therefore, if that I die, I will that ye be crowned king.'

Right so he sought, and his knights, towards Sandwich, where he found before him many galyard knights, for there were the most part of all the Round Table, ready on those banks for to sail when the king liked. Then in all haste that might be they shipped their horses and harness and all manner of ordnance that falleth for the war, and tents and pavilions many were trussed, and so they shot from the banks many great carracks and many ships of forestage, with cogs and galleys and pinnaces full noble, with galleys and galleots, rowing with many oars. And thus they stroke forth into the streams, many sad hundreds.

Gawain arranging the mustering of ships

galyard: *valiant*

carrack: *large ship*
forestage: *forecastle*
cog: *broad ship*
galleot: *small boat*

Here followeth the Dream of King Arthur

As the king was in his cog and lay in his cabin, he fell in a slumbering, and dreamed how a dreadful dragon did drench much of his people, and came flying on wing out of the west parts. And his head, him seemed, was enamelled with azure, and his shoulders shone as the gold, and his womb was like mails of a marvellous hue, and his tail was full of tatters, and his feet were flourished as it were fine sable. And his claws were like clean gold, and an hideous flame of fire there flowed out of his mouth, like as the land and the water had flamed all on fire.

Then him seemed there came out of the Orient a grimly bear,

all black, in a cloud, and his paws were as big as a post .... He roamed and roared so rudely that marvel it were to tell.

Then the dreadful dragon dressed him against him, and come in the wind like a falcon, and freshly strikes the bear. ... And so he renteth the bear and burns him up clean, that all fell on powder, both the flesh and the bones, and so it fluttered abroad on the sea.

Anon the king waked, and was sore abashed of his dream; and in all haste he sent for a philosopher, and charged him to tell what signified his dream.

'Sir,' said the philospher, 'the dragon thou dreamest of betokens thine own person, that thus here sails with these siker knights; and the colour of his wings is thy kingdoms that thou hast with thy knights won. And his tail that was all to-tattered signified your noble knights of the Round Table. And the bear that the dragon slew above in the clouds betokens some tyrant that torments thy people, or thou art like to fight with some giant boldly in battle by thyself alone. Therefore of this dreadful dream dread thee but a little, and care not now, Sir Conqueror, but comfort thyself.'

Then within a while they had a sight of the banks of Normandy, and at the same tide the king arrived at Barfleur, and found there ready many of his great lords, as he had commanded at Christmas before himself.

On the morn from Barfleur removeth the king with all his great battle proudly arrayed, and so they shook over the streams into a fair champaign, and thereby down in a valley they pitched up their tents.

And even at the meat-while came two messengers, that one was the Marshal of France, that said to the king how the Emperor was entered into France,

'And hath destroyed much of our marches, and is come into Burgundy, and many boroughs hath destroyed, and hath made great slaughter of your noble people. And where that he rideth, all he destroys. And now he is come into Douce France, and there he burns all clean. Now all the douze-peers, both dukes and other, and the peers of Paris town, are fled down into the Low Country towards Roon, and but if thou help them the sooner they must yield them all at once, both the bodies and the towns. They can none other succour, but the needs they must yield them in haste.'

Then the king bids Sir Bors:

'Now, busk thee blithe, and Sir Lionel and Sir Bedevere, look that ye fare, with Sir Gawain, my nephew, with you, and take as many good knights, and look that ye ride straight unto Sir Lucius and say I bid him in haste to remove out of my lands. And if he will not, so bid him dress his battle, and let us redress our rights

siker: *trusty*

champaign: *meadowland*

meat-while: *mealtime*

Roon: *Probably Rhone, but geography might support Rouen. Vinaver suggests Rhine*

OPPOSITE
Arthur in combat with a Roman tribune

Tantost quilz furent entrez ou
camp sans plente dattente ilz
auallerent les lances lun côtre
laultre z ferment cheuaulx des
esperons qui les emporterent de
telle raideur quil sambloit que
ce fuist fouldze tellement fai
soient ilz la terre resonner. si fe
rirent en ce venir lun laultre ens
es pis si durement qil comunt
le dit flolon verser a terre tout
plat estendu z le roy passa oult

qui prestement retourna z auoit
ia sacquiet son espee pour ferir
le dit flolon le quel flolon es
toit ia releuez côme tous côfus
z honteux. et en tresptant desir
de venuier sa honte auoit ahers
sa lance qui ly estoit volee par
et sen vint de grant ire embrasez
deuers le roy et assist sa lance
ens es ars du cheual artus tel
lement que il le tua mort par
terre z quey le cheual z le roy

with our hands. And that is more worship than thus to override masterless men.'

Then anon in all haste they dressed them to horseback, those noble knights, and when they came to the green wood they saw before them many proud pavilions of silk of diverse colours, that were set in a meadow beside a river, and the Emperor's pavilion was in the midst with an eagle displayed on loft. Then through the wood our knights rode till that they came unto the Emperor's tent. But behind them they left stuff of men of arms in a bushment; and there they left in the bushment Sir Lionel and Sir Bedevere. Sir Gawain and Sir Bors went with the message.

bushment: ambush

So they rode worthily into the Emperor's tent, and spoke both at once with haughty words:

'Now give thee sorrow, Sir Emperor, and all thy soldiers thee about. For why occupiest thou with wrong the Empireship of Rome? That is King Arthur's heritage, by kind of his noble elders; there lacked none but Uther, his father. Therefore, the king commandeth thee to ride out of his lands, or else to fight for all and knightly it win.'

'Ye say well,' said the Emperor, 'as your lord hath you commanded. But say to your lord I send him greeting, but I have no joy of your ranks thus to rebuke me and my lords. But say your lord I will ride down by Seine and win all that thereto longs, and after ride unto Rhone and win it up clean.'

The Emperor of Rome receiving news of Arthur's advance

Rhone: see note above
elf: creature

'It beseems thee ill,' said Sir Gawain, 'that any such an elf should brag such words, for I had lever than all France to fight against thee.'

'Other I,' said Sir Bors, 'than to wield all Britain or Burgundy the noble.'

Then a knight that hight Sir Gayus, that was cousin unto the Emperor, he said these words:

'Lo, how these English Britons be braggers of kind, for ye may see how they boast and brag as they durst beat all the world.'

Then grieved Sir Gawain at his great words, and with his burly brand that bright seemed he stroke off the head of Sir Gayus the knight.

And so they turned their horses and rode over waters and woods, into they come nigh the bushment there Sir Lionel and Sir Bedevere were hoving still. Then the Romans followed fast on horseback and on foot over a fair champaign unto a fair wood. But yet or they went and depart, our bushment brake on both sides of the Romans, and there the bold Bedevere and Sir Lionel bare down the Romans on every side. There our noble knights of merry England bear them through the helms and bright shields and slew them down, and there the whole rout returned unto the

OPPOSITE
Arthur with his knights approaches a fortified city

Emperor, and told him at one word his men were destroyed, ten thousand, by battle of tired knights:

'For they are the brimmest men that ever we saw in field.'

But always Sir Bors and Sir Gawain freshly followed on the Romans even unto the Emperor's tents.

Then King Arthur dispersed all his host in divers parties, that they should not escape, but to fight them behoves.

When the Emperor was entered into the Vale of Soissons, he might see where King Arthur hoved in battle with banners displayed. On every side was he beset, that he might not escape, but either to fight either to yield him, there was none other boot.

'Now I see well,' said Sir Lucius, 'yonder traitor hath betrayed me.'

Then he redresses his knights on diverse parts, and set up a dragon with eagles many one enhued with sable, and then he let blow up with trumpets and with tabours, that all the vale dindled. And then he let cry on loud, that all men might hear:

'Sirs, ye know well that the honour and worship hath ever followed the Romans. And this day let it never be lost for the default of heart, for I see well by yonder ordnance this day shall die much people. And therefore do doughtily this day, and the field is ours.'

Then Sir Lancelot leap forth with his steed even straight unto Sir Lucius, and in his way he smote through a king that stood alther-next him, and his name was Jacound, a Saracen full noble. And then he rushed forth unto Sir Lucius and smote him on the helm with his sword, that he fell to the earth. And sith he rode thrice over him on a row, and so took the banner of Rome and rode with it away unto Arthur himself. And all said that it saw, there was never knight did more worship in his days.

By then the bowmen of England and of Britain began to shoot, and these other, Romans and Saracens, shot with darts and with cross-bows. There began a strong battle on every side and much slaughter on the Romans' party, and the Dutchmen with quarrels did much harm, for they were with the Romans with their bows of horn. And the great giants of Genoa killed down many knights, with clubs of steel crushed out their brains. Also they squat out the brains of many coursers.

When Arthur had espied the giants' works he cried on loud that knights might hear, and said:

'Fair lords, look your name be not lost! Lose not your worship for yonder bare-legged knaves, and ye shall see what I shall do as for my true part.'

He took there out Excalibur, and girds towards Galapas that grieved him most. He cut him off by the knees cleanly there in sunder:

boot: *remedy*

dindled: *trembled*

ABOVE *Arthur in the thick of a battle*

BELOW *Arthur strikes off the head of an opponent*

'Now art thou of a size,' said the king, 'like unto our feeries.' *feeries: companions*
And then he strake off his head swiftly.

So forth they went with the king, those knights of the Round
Table. Was never king neither knights did better since God
made the world. They laid on with long swords and swapped
through brains. Shields neither sheen arms might them not with- *sheen: bright*
stand, till they laid on the earth ten thousand at once. Then the
Romans reeled a little, for they were somewhat rebuked, but King
Arthur with his prize knights pressed sore after.

Anon as King Arthur had a sight of the Emperor Lucius, for
king neither for captain he tarried no longer. And either with
their swords swapped at other. So Sir Lucius with his sword hit
Arthur overthwart the nose and gave him a wound nigh unto the
tongue. Sir Arthur was wroth, and gave him another with all the
might that in his arm was left, that from the crest of his helm unto
the bare paps it went adown; and so ended the Emperor.

And then relieved the king, with his noble knights, and ran- *relieved: rallied*
sacked all the fields for his bold barons. And those that were
dead were buried as their blood asked, and they that might be
saved, there was no salve spared neither no dainties too dear that
might be gotten for gold or silver. And thus he let save many
knights that weaned never to recover, but for Sir Kay's recovery
and of Sir Bedevere the rich was never man under God so glad as
himself was.

Then the king rode straight thereas the Emperor lay, and gart *gart: commanded*
lift him up lordly with barons full bold, and the Sultan of Syria,
and of Ethiopia the king, and of Egypt and of India two knights
full noble, with seventeen other kings, were taken up also, and also
sixty senators of Rome that were honoured full noble men, and all
the elders. The king let balm all these with many good gums, and
. . . let close them in chests full cleanly arrayed, and their banners
above on their bodies, and their shields turned upward, that every
man might know of what country they were.

So on the morn they found in the heath three senators of Rome.
When they were brought to the king he said these words:

'Now, to save your lives I take no force great, with that ye will
move on my message unto great Rome, and present these corpses
unto the proud Potestate, and after show him my letters and my
whole intent. And tell them in haste they shall see me, and I trow
they will beware how they bourd with me and my knights.' *bourd: jest*

Then the Emperor himself was dressed in a chariot, and every
two knights in a chariot sued after, and the senators come after by *sue: follow*
couples in a cord.

'Now say ye to the Potestate and all the lords after, that I send
them tribute that I owe to Rome, for this is the true tribute that I

and mine elders have lost this ten score winters. And say them as meseems I have sent them the whole sum, and if they think it not enough, I shall amend it when that I come. And furthermore I charge you to say to them never to demand tribute nor tax of me nor of my lands, for such treasure must they take as happens us here.'

So on the morn these senators raked unto Rome, and within eighteen days they come to the Potestate and told him how they had brought the tax and the truage of ten score winters, both of England, Ireland, and of all the East Lands.

❡ Now turn we to Arthur with his noble knights, that entereth straight into Luxemburg and so through Flanders, and then to Lorraine. He laught up the lordships, and sithen he drew him into Almain and unto Lombardy the rich, and set laws in that land that dured long after.

❡ Then into Tuscany he turned, when he time seemed, and there he wins towers and towns full high . . . . Then he speeds toward Spoleto, with his speedful knights, and so unto Viterbo he victualed his knights, and to the Vale of Vycecounte he devised there to lie, in that virtuous vale among vines full. And there he sojourns, that sovereign, with solace at his heart, for to wit whether the senators would him of succour beseech.

But soon after, on a Saturday, sought unto King Arthur all the senators that were on live, and of the cunningest cardinals that dwelt in the court, and prayed him of peace and proffered him full large; and besought him as a sovereign, most governor under God, for to give them licence for six weeks large, that they might be assembled all, and then in the city of . . . Rome to crown him there kindly, with chrismed hands, with sceptre, forsooth, as an Emperor should.

'I assent me,' said the king, 'as ye have devised, and comely by Christmas to be crowned, hereafter to reign in my estate, and to keep my Round Table, with the rents of Rome to rule as me likes. And then, as I am advised, to get me over the salt sea with good men of arms to deem for His death that for us all on the rood died.'

When the senators had this answer, unto Rome they turned and made ready for his crownment in the most noble wise. And at the day assigned, as the romance me tells, he was crowned Emperor by the Pope's hands, with all the royalty in the world to wield for ever. There they sojourned that season till after the time, and stablished all the lands from Rome unto France, and gave lands and rents unto knights that had them well deserved. There was none that plained on his part, rich neither poor. Then he commanded Sir Lancelot and Sir Bors to take keep unto their fathers' lands, that King Ban and King Bors wielded, and their fathers.

laught: seized

FAR LEFT
*The victorious Arthur
rides with his army*

LEFT *Arthur
and his companions
returning to England*

Sir Lancelot and Sir Bors de Ganis thanked the king fair, and said their hearts and service should ever be his own.

Thus the king gave many lands. There was none that would ask that might plain of his part, for of riches and wealth they had all their will. Then the knights and lords that to the king longs called a counsel upon a fair morn, and said:

'Sir King, we beseech thee for to hear us all. We are under your lordship well stuffed, blessed be God, of many things. And also we have wives wedded. We will beseech your good grace to release us to sport us with our wives, for, worship be Christ, this journey is well overcome.'

'Ye say well,' said the king, 'for enough is as good as a feast. For to attempt God overmuch I hold it not wisdom. And therefore make you all ready and turn we into England.'

Then there was trussing of harness with carriage full noble. And the king took his leave of the Holy Father the Pope, and patriarchs and cardinals and senators full rich, and left good governance in that noble city and all the countries of Rome for to ward and to keep on pain of death, that in no wise his commandment be broken. Thus he passeth through the countries of all parts.

And so King Arthur passed over the sea unto Sandwich haven. When Queen Guenever heard of his coming, she met with him at London, and so did all the other queens and noble ladies. For there was never a solemner meeting in one city together, for all manner of riches they brought with them at the full.

Here endeth the tale of the noble King Arthur, that was Emperor himself through dignity of his hands.

And here followeth after many noble tales of Sir Lancelot du Lake.

est auſſi gentil; home come bous eſtes · Ma̅
Eſtor ne l'entendi mie · En nom dieu fait l'eſtue
il dort que ia dieux ne li aiſt · et dit que ſe ſes ſu
ne fuſt malade qu'il le meiſt ſus de ſon cheual ·

Ores hauſa le troncon de la
lance qu'il tenoit · ſi feru le ch
Eſtor enn le biés ſi qu'il le fiſt
uoler en pieces · et puis le pr
par le ſram ſi le ſacha a li m
du venient ſi que par vn p
qu'il ne cheï a terre et le fiſt
gemir ſur les deux piez derrieres · Et eſtor laiſt
ſon penſe ſi bit l'eſtuier qui bien ſambloit felon
Et li dit que ſe il l'eſbit li qu'il n'auoit le col buſſe &
pourquoy beau ſire fait Eſtor pourquoy ſu
fait il ſi comenca a iuuer trop du vient le dif
ſcable fait il bous auoient endormi que par b
pour que bous n'auez a eſtache · J · cha · naure
a tant ſ'en ala · Et la dame qu'il le tenoit dit li ſi
ſcable bous ſont chautier vne cha ay

BOOK 8

Lancelot

oon after that King Arthur was come from Rome into England, then all the knights of the Table Round resorted unto the king, and made many jousts and tournaments. And some there were that were but knights, which increased so in arms and worship that they passed all their fellows in prowess and noble deeds, and that was well proved on many.

But in especial it was proved on Sir Lancelot du Lake, for in all tournaments and jousts and deeds of arms, both for life and death, he passed all other knights, and at no time was he overcome but if it were by treason or enchantment. So this Sir Lancelot increased so marvellously in worship, and in honour, therefore is he the first knight that the French book maketh mention of after King Arthur came from Rome. Wherefore Queen Guenever had him in great favour above all other knights, and in certain he loved the queen again above all other ladies days of his life, and for her he did many deeds of arms, and saved her from the fire through his noble chivalry.

Thus Sir Lancelot rested him long with play and game. And then he thought himself to prove himself in strange adventures, and bad his nephew, Sir Lionel, for to make him ready, 'for we two will seek adventures.'

So they mounted on their horses, armed at all rights, and rode into a deep forest and so into a plain. And then the weather was hot about noon, and Sir Lancelot had great lust to sleep. Then Sir Lionel espied a great apple tree that stood by an hedge, and said,

'Brother, yonder is a fair shadow, there may we rest us on our horses.'

'It is well said, fair brother,' said Sir Lancelot, 'for this seven year I was not so sleepy as I am now.'

And so they there alighted and tied their horses unto sundry trees, and Sir Lancelot laid him down under this apple tree, and his helm he laid under his head. And Sir Lionel waked while he slept. So Sir Lancelot slept passing fast.

And in the meanwhile there came three knights riding, as fast fleeing as ever they might ride. And there followed them three but one knight. And when Sir Lionel saw him, he thought he saw never so great a knight, nor so well faring a man, neither so well apparelled unto all rights.

So within a while this strong knight had overtaken one of the three knights, and there he smote him to the cold earth that he lay still. And then he rode unto the second knight, and smote him so that man and horse fell down. And then straight to the third knight he rode, and smote him behind his horse's arse a spear length. And then he alit down and reined his horse on the bridle and bound all three knights fast with the reins of their own bridles.

When Sir Lionel had seen him do thus, he thought to assay him, and made him ready, and stilly and privily he took his horse, and thought not for to awake Sir Lancelot. And when he was mounted upon his horse, he overtook this strong knight, and bad him turn, and the other smote Sir Lionel so hard that horse and man he bare to earth, and so he alit down and bound him fast, and threw him overthwart his own horse, and so he served them all four, and rode with them away to his own castle.

And when he came there he unarmed them, and beat them with thorns all naked, and after put them in a deep prison where were many more knights that made great dolour.

Now leave we these knights prisoners, and speak we of Sir Lancelot du Lake that lieth under the apple tree, sleeping. About the noon there come by him four queens of great estate; and, for the heat should not nigh them, there rode four knights about them, and bare a cloth of green silk on four spears, betwixt them and the sun. And the queens rode on four white mules.

Thus as they rode they heard by them a great horse beside them grimly neigh. Then they looked and were ware of a sleeping knight, that lay all armed under an apple tree; and anon as these queens looked on his face, they knew well it was Sir Lancelot. Then they began to strive for that knight, and every one of them said they would have him to her love.

'We shall not strive,' said Morgan le Fay, that was King Arthur's sister, 'I shall put an enchantment upon him that he shall not awake in six hours, and then I will lead him away unto my castle. And when he is surely within my hold, I shall take the enchantment from him, and then let him choose which of us he will have unto paramour.'

So this enchantment was cast upon Sir Lancelot, and then they laid him upon his shield, and bare him so on horseback betwixt

two knights, and brought him unto the castle Chariot, and there they laid him in a chamber cold, and at night they sent unto him a fair damsel with his supper ready dight. By that the enchantment was past. And when she came she saluted him, and asked him what cheer.

Morgan le Fay and the queens find Lancelot asleep

'I cannot say, fair damsel,' said Sir Lancelot, 'for I wot not how I came into this castle but it be by an enchantment.'

'Sir,' said she, 'ye must make good cheer, and if ye be such a knight as it is said ye be, I shall tell you more to-morn by prime of the day.'

'Gramercy, fair damsel,' said Sir Lancelot, 'of your good will I require you.'

And so she departed. And there he lay all that night without any comfort. And on the morn early came these four queens, pas-singly well beseen, and all they bidding him good morn, and he them again.

'Sir knight,' the four queens said, 'thou must understand thou art our prisoner, and we know thee well that thou art Sir Lancelot du Lake, King Ban's son. And because we understand your worthi-ness, that thou art the noblest knight living, and as we know well there can no lady have thy love but one, and that is Queen Guenever, and now thou shalt lose her love for ever, and she thine. For it behoveth thee now to choose one of us four.'

'I am the Queen Morgan le Fay, queen of the land of Gore, and

Morgan le Fay imprisons Lancelot

75

maugre: *in spite of*

here is the Queen of Northgales, and the Queen of Eastland, and the Queen of the Out Isles; now choose one of us which thou wilt have to thy paramour, for thou mayest not choose or else in this prison to die.'

'This is an hard case,' said Sir Lancelot, 'that either I must die or else choose one of you. Yet had I lever to die in this prison with worship, than to have one of you to my paramour maugre my head. And therefore ye be answered: I will none of you, for ye be false enchantresses. And as for my lady, Dame Guenever, were I at my liberty as I was, I would prove it on you or on yours, that she is the truest lady unto her lord living.'

'Well,' said the queens, 'is this your answer, that ye will refuse us?'

'Yea, on my life,' said Sir Lancelot, 'refused ye be of me.'

So they departed and left him there alone that made great sorrow.

Right so at the noon came the damsel unto him with his dinner and asked him what cheer.

'Truly, fair damsel,' said Sir Lancelot, 'in my life days never so ill.'

'Sir,' she said, 'that me repentest, but and ye will be ruled by me, I shall help you out of this distress, and ye shall have no shame nor villainy, so that ye hold me a promise.'

'Fair damsel, I will grant you; but sore I am of these queens' crafts afeared, for they have destroyed many a good knight.'

'Sir,' said she, 'that is sooth, and for the renown and bounty that they hear of you they would have your love. And, sir, they say your name is Sir Lancelot du Lake, the flower of knights, and they be passing wroth with you that ye have refused them. But sir, and ye would promise me to help my father on Tuesday next coming, that hath made a tournament betwixt him and the King of Northgales, for the last Tuesday past my father lost the field through three knights of Arthur's court – and if ye will be there on Tuesday next coming, and help my father, to-morn by prime by the grace of God I shall deliver you clean.'

'Fair maiden,' said Sir Lancelot, 'tell me what is your father's name, and then I shall give you an answer.'

'Sir knight,' she said, 'my father is King Bagdemagus, that was foul rebuked at the last tournament.'

'I know your father well,' said Sir Lancelot, 'for a noble king and a good knight, and by the faith of my body, ye shall have my body ready to do your father and you service at that day.'

'Sir,' she said, 'gramercy, and to-morn look ye be ready betimes, and I shall deliver you, and take you your armour and your horse, shield and spear. And hereby, within this ten mile, is an abbey of white monks, and there I pray you to abide me, and thither shall I bring my father unto you.'

'All this shall be done,' said Sir Lancelot, 'as I am true knight.'

And so she departed, and came on the morn early, and found him ready. Then she brought him out of twelve locks, and brought him his armour and his own horse; and lightly he saddled him and took a great spear in his hand, and so rode forth, and said,

'Fair damsel, I shall not fail you, by the grace of God.'

Now leave we there and speak of Sir Lancelot that rode a great while in a deep forest. And as he rode he saw a black brachet, seeking in manner as it had been in the feute of an hurt deer. And therewith he rode after the brachet, and he saw lie on the ground a large feute of blood. And then Sir Lancelot rode faster, and ever the brachet looked behind her, and so she went through a great marsh, and ever Sir Lancelot followed.

feute: track

And then was he ware of an old manor, and hither ran the brachet, and so over a bridge. So Sir Lancelot rode over that bridge that was old and feeble; and when he came in midst of a great hall, there he saw lie a dead knight that was a seemly man, and that brachet licked his wounds.

And therewithal came out a lady weeping and wringing her hands, and said,

'O knight, too much sorrow hast thou brought me.'

'Why say ye so?' said Sir Lancelot, 'I did never this knight no harm, for hither by feute of blood this brachet brought me; and therefore, fair lady, be not displeased with me, for I am full sore aggrieved for your grievance.'

'Truly, sir,' she said, 'I trow it be not ye that hath slain my husband, for he that did that deed is sore wounded, and he is never likely to recover, that I shall ensure him.'

'What was your husband's name?' said Sir Lancelot.

Lancelot meets a weeping lady

'Sir,' said she, 'his name was called Sir Gilbert the Bastard, one of the best knights of the world, and he that hath slain him I know not his name.'

'Now God send you better comfort,' said Sir Lancelot.

And so he departed and went into the forest again, and there he met with a damsel, the which knew him well, and she said aloud,

'Well be ye found, my lord; and now I require thee, on thy knighthood, help my brother that is sore wounded, and never stinteth bleeding; for this day he fought with Sir Gilbert the Bastard and slew him in plain battle, and there was my brother sore wounded. And there is a lady, a sorceress, that dwelleth in a castle here beside, and this day she told me my brother's wound should never be whole till I could find a knight that would go into the Chapel Perilous, and there he should find a sword and a bloody cloth that the wounded knight was lapped in, and a piece of that cloth and sword should heal my brother's wounds, with that his wounds were searched with the sword and the cloth.'

'This is a marvellous thing,' said Sir Lancelot, 'but what is your brother's name?'

'Sir,' she said, 'his name was Sir Meliot de Logris.'

'That me repenteth,' said Sir Lancelot, 'for he is a fellow of the Table Round, and to his help I will do my power.'

'Then, sir,' said she, 'follow even this highway, and it will bring you unto the Chapel Perilous; and there I shall abide till God send you here again. And, if you speed not, I know no knight living that may achieve that adventure.'

Right so Sir Lancelot departed, and when he came to the Chapel Perilous he alit down, and tied his horse unto a little gate. And as soon as he was within the churchyard he saw on the front of the chapel many fair rich shields turned up-so-down, and many of the shields Sir Lancelot had seen knights bear beforehand. With that he saw by him there stand a thirty great knights, more by a yard than any man that ever he had seen, and all those grinned and gnashed at Sir Lancelot.

And when he saw their countenance he dread him sore, and so put his shield afore him, and took his sword ready in his hand ready unto battle. And they were all armed in black harness, ready with their shields and their swords drawn. And when Sir Lancelot would have gone through them, they scattered on every side of him, and gave him the way, and therewith he waxed all bold, and entered into the chapel. And then he saw no light but a dim lamp burning, and then was he ware of a corpse hilled with a cloth of silk.

Then Sir Lancelot stooped down, and cut a piece away of that cloth, and then it fared under him as the earth had quaked a little; therewithal he feared. And then he saw a fair sword lie by the dead knight, and that he gat in his hand and hied him out of the chapel. Anon as ever he was in the chapel yard all the knights spake to him with grimly voices, and said,

'Knight Sir Lancelot, lay that sword from thee or else thou shalt die.'

hilled: *covered*

'Whether that I live or die,' said Sir Lancelot, 'with no great words get ye it again, therefore fight for it and ye list.'

Then right so he passed throughout them. And beyond the chapel yard there met him a fair damsel, and said,

'Sir Lancelot, leave that sword behind thee, or thou will die for it.'

'I leave it not,' said Sir Lancelot, 'for no threating.'

'No,' said she, 'and thou didst leave that sword, Queen Guenever should thou never see.'

'Then were I a fool and I would leave this sword,' said Lancelot.

'Now, gentle knight,' said the damsel, 'I require thee to kiss me but once.'

'Nay,' said Sir Lancelot, 'that God me forbid.'

'Well, sir,' said she, 'and thou hadst kissed me thy life days had been done, and now, alas,' she said, 'I have lost all my labour, for I ordained this chapel for thy sake, and for Sir Gawain. And once I had Sir Gawain within me, and at that time he fought with that knight that lieth there dead in yonder chapel, Sir Gilbert the Bastard; and at that time he smote the left hand off of Sir Gilbert the Bastard. And, Sir Lancelot, now I tell thee: I have loved thee this seven year, but there may no woman have thy love but Queen Guenever. And sithen I may not rejoice thee to have thy body alive, I had kept no more joy in this world but to have thy body dead. Then would I have balmed it and sered it, and so have kept it my life days, and daily I should have clipped thee, and kissed thee, despite of Queen Gunever.'

sered: waxed

'Ye say well,' said Sir Lancelot. 'Jesu preserve me from your subtle crafts.'

And therewithal he took his horse and so departed from her. And as the book saith, when Sir Lancelot was departed she took such sorrow that she died within a fortnight, and her name was Hellawes the sorceress, Lady of the Castle Nigramous.

Anon Sir Lancelot met with the damsel, Sir Meliot's sister. And when she saw him she clapped her hands, and wept for joy. And then they rode unto a castle thereby where lay Sir Meliot. And anon as Sir Lancelot saw him he knew him, but he was passing pale as the earth for bleeding.

When Sir Meliot saw Sir Lancelot he kneeled upon his knees and cried on high, 'O lord Sir Lancelot, help me!'

Anon Sir Lancelot leapt unto him and touched his wounds with Sir Gilbert's sword. And then he wiped his wounds with a part of the bloody cloth that Sir Gilbert was wrapped in, and anon an wholer man in his life was he never.

And then there was great joy between them, and they made Sir Lancelot all the cheer that they might. And so on the morn

Lancelot

Sir Lancelot took his leave, and bad Sir Meliot hie him 'to the court of my lord Arthur, for it draweth nigh to the feast of Pentecost, and there by the grace of God ye shall find me.' And therewith they departed.

And so Sir Lancelot rode through many strange countries, over moors and valleys, till by fortune he came to a fair castle. And as he passed beyond the castle him thought he heard bells ring.

And then was he ware of a falcon came over his head flying towards an high elm, and long lunes about her feet, and she flew unto the elm to take her perch. The lunes overcast about a bough, and when she would have taken her flight she hung by the legs fast; and Sir Lancelot saw how she hung, and beheld the fair falcon perigot, and he was sorry for her.

lunes: *leashes*

The meanwhile came a lady out of the castle and cried on high, 'O Lancelot, Lancelot, as thou art flower of all knights, help me to get my hawk; for and my hawk may be lost my lord will destroy me, for I kept the hawk and she slipped from me. And if my lord my husband wit it he is so hasty that he will slay me.

'What is your lord's name?' said Sir Lancelot.

'Sir,' she said, 'his name is Sir Phelot, a knight that longeth unto the King of Northgales.'

'Well, fair lady, since that ye know my name, and require me of knighthood to help you, I will do what I may to get your hawk, and yet God knoweth I am an ill climber, and the tree is passing high, and few boughs to help me withal.'

A detail from one of the many legends of Lancelot showing him being taken prisoner on a bridge

And therewith Sir Lancelot alit, and tied his horse to the same tree, and prayed the lady to unarm him. And so when he was unarmed, he put off all his clothes unto his shirt and his breech, and with might and great force he clomb up to the falcon and tied the lunes to a great rotten bush, and threw the hawk down with the bush.

Anon the lady gat the hawk in her hand; and therewithal came out Sir Phelot out of the groves suddenly, that was her husband, all armed and with his naked sword in his hand, and said:

'O knight Lancelot, now have I found thee as I would,' he standing at the bole of the tree to slay him.

'Ah, lady,' said Sir Lancelot, 'why have ye betrayed me?'

'She hath done,' said Sir Phelot, 'but as I commanded her, and therefore there nis none other boot but thine hour is come that thou must die.'

'That were shame unto thee,' said Sir Lancelot, 'thou an armed knight to slay a naked man by treason.'

'Thou gettest none other grace,' said Sir Phelot, 'and therefore help thyself and thou can.'

'Truly,' said Sir Lancelot, 'that shall be thy shame, but since thou wilt do none other, take mine harness with thee, and hang my sword upon a bough that I may get it, and then do thy best to slay me and thou canst.'

'Nay, nay,' said Sir Phelot, 'for I know thee better than thou weenest. Therefore thou gettest no weapon and I may keep thee therefrom.'

'Alas,' said Sir Lancelot, 'that ever a knight should die weapon-less.'

And therewith he waited above him and under him, and over his head he saw a rough spike, a big bough leafless, and therewith he brake it off by the body. And then he came lower and awaited how his own horse stood, and suddenly he leapt on the further side of the horse, froward the knight.

And then Sir Phelot lashed at him eagerly, to have slain him. But Sir Lancelot put away the stroke with the rough spike, and therewith he smote him on the one side of the head, that he fell down in a swoon to the ground. So then Sir Lancelot took his sword out of his hand, and struck his neck from the body.

Then cried the lady, 'Alas! why hast thou slain my husband?'

'I am not causer,' said Sir Lancelot, 'for with falsehood ye would have slain me with treason, and now it is fallen on you both.'

And then she swooned as though she would die. And therewith Sir Lancelot gat all his armour as well as he might, and put it upon him for dread of more resort, for he dread that the knight's castle was so nigh. And as soon as he might he took his horse and departed, and thanked God that he had escaped that adventure.

So Sir Lancelot rode many wild ways, throughout marsh and many wild ways.

*   *   *

BOOK 9

Tristram

here was a king that hight Meliodas, and he was lord and king of the country of Lionesse. And this Meliodas was a likely knight as any was that time living. And by fortune he wedded King Mark's sister of Cornwall, and she was called Elizabeth that was called both good and fair.

And at that time King Arthur reigned, and he was whole king of England, Wales, and Scotland, and of many other realms: howbeit there were many kings that were lords of many countries, but all they held their lands of King Arthur; for in Wales were two kings, and in the north were many kings; and in Cornwall and in the west were two kings; also in Ireland were two or three kings, and all were under the obeissance of King Arthur. So was the King of France, and the King of Brittany, and all the lordships unto Rome.

So when this King Meliodas had been with his wife, within a while she waxed great with child. And she was a full meek lady, and well she loved her lord, and he her again, so there was great joy betwixt them.

So there was a lady in that country that had loved King Meliodas long, and by no mean she never could get his love; therefore she let ordain upon a day, as King Meliodas rode an-hunting, for he was a great chaser of deer, and there by enchantment she made him chase an hart by himself alone till that he came to an old castle, and there anon he was taken prisoner by the lady that him loved.

When Elizabeth, King Meliodas' wife, missed her lord, and she was nigh out of her wit, and also, as great with child as she was, she took a gentlewoman with her, and ran into the forest suddenly to seek her lord. And when she was far in the forest she might no farther, for she began to travail fast of her child. And she had many grimly throes; but her gentlewoman halp her all that she might. And so by miracle of Our Lady of Heaven she was delivered with great pains. But she had taken such cold for the default of help that deep draughts of death took her, that needs she must die and depart out of this world, there was none other boot.

When this Queen Elizabeth saw that there was none other boot, then she made great dole, and said unto her gentlewoman,

'When ye see my lord, King Meliodas, recommend me unto him, and tell him what pains I endure here for his love and how I must die here for his sake for default of good help; and let him wit that I am full sorry to depart out of this world from him, therefore pray him to be friend to my soul. Now let me see my little child, for whom I have had all this sorrow.'

And when she saw him she said thus: 'Ah, my little son, thou hast murdered thy mother, and therefore I suppose, thou art a murderer so young, thou art full likely to be a manly man in thine age. And because I shall die of the birth of thee, I charge thee, gentlewoman, that thou pray my lord, King Meliodas, that when he is christened let call him Tristram, that is as much to say as a sorrowful birth.'

And therewith this queen gave up the ghost and died. Then the gentlewoman laid her under an umbre of a great tree, and then she lapped the child as well as she might for cold.

Right so there came the barons of King Meliodas, following after the queen, and when they saw that she was dead, and understood none other but the king was destroyed, then certain of them would have slain the child, because they would have been lords of the country of Lionesse. But then through the fair speech of the gentlewoman, and by the means that she made, the most part of the barons would not assent thereto. And then they let carry home the dead queen, and much sorrow was made for her.

Then this meanwhile Merlin delivered King Meliodas out of prison on the morn after his queen was dead. And so when the king was come home the most part of the barons made great joy. But the sorrow that the king made for his queen that might no tongue tell. So then the king let inter her richly, and after he let christen his child as his wife had commanded before her death. And then he let call him Tristram, 'the sorrowful born child.'

Then the King Meliodas endured after that seven years without a wife, and all this time Tristram was fostered well. Then it befell that King Meliodas wedded King Howel of Brittany's daughter, and anon she had children by King Meliodas. Then was she heavy and wroth that her children should not rejoice the country of Lionesse, wherefore this queen ordained for to poison young Tristram.

So she let poison be put in a piece of silver in the chamber where Tristram and her children were together, unto that intent that when Tristram were thirsty he should drink that drink. And so it fell upon a day, the queen's son, as he was in that chamber, espied the piece with poison, and he weened it had been good drink, and because the child was thirsty he took the piece with poison and drank freely; and therewithal the child suddenly brast and was dead.

When the queen [of] Meliodas wist of the death of her son, wit ye well that she was heavy. But yet the king understood nothing of her treason. Notwithstanding the queen would not leave this, but eft she let ordain more poison, and put it in a piece.

And by fortune King Meliodas, her husband, found the piece with wine wherein was the poison, and he that was much thirsty took the piece to drink thereout. And as he would have drunken thereof the queen espied him, and ran unto him, and pulled the piece from him suddenly. The king marvelled why she did so, and remembered him suddenly how her son was slain with poison. And then he took her by the hand, and said,

'Thou false traitress, thou shalt tell me what manner of drink this is, or else I shall slay thee.'

And therewith he pulled out his sword, and sware a great oath that he should slay her but if she told him truth.

'Ah! mercy, my lord,' said she, 'and I shall tell you all.'

And then she told him why she would have slain Tristram, because her children should rejoice this land.

'Well,' said King Meliodas, 'and therefore shall ye have the law.'

And so she was damned by the assent of the barons to be burnt; and then was there made a great fire, and right as she was at the fire to take her execution, this same young Tristram kneeled afore King Meliodas, and besought him to give him a boon.

'I will well,' said the king again.

Then said young Tristram, 'Give me the life of thy queen, my stepmother.'

'That is unrightfully asked,' said King Meliodas, 'for thou ought of right to hate her, for she would have slain thee with that poison and she might have had her will; and for thy sake most is my cause that she should die.'

'Sir,' said Tristram, 'as for that, I beseech you of your mercy that ye will forgive her. And as for my part, God forgive it her, and I do; and so much it liked your highness to grant me my boon, for God's love I require you hold your promise.'

'Sithen it is so,' said the king, 'I will that ye have her life. Then,' said the king, 'I give her to you, and go ye to the fire and take her, and do with her what ye will.'

So Sir Tristram went to the fire, and by the commandment of the king delivered her from the death. But after that King Meliodas would never have ado with her as at bed and at board. But by the good means of young Tristram he made the king and her accorded. But then the king would not suffer young Tristram to abide no longer in his court.

And then he let ordain a gentleman that was well learned and taught, his name was Gouvernail; and then he sent young Tristram with Gouvernail into France to learn the language, and nurture, and deeds of arms. And there was Tristram more than seven years. And then when he well could speak the language, and had learned all that he might learn in that countries, then he came home to his father, King Meliodas, again.

And so Tristram learned to be an harper passing all other, that there was none such called in no country, and so in harping and on instruments of music he applied him in his youth for to learn. And after, as he growed in might and strength, he laboured ever in hunting and in hawking – never gentleman more, that ever we heard read of. And as the book saith, he began good measures of blowing of beasts of venery, and beasts of chase, and all manner of vermins, and all these terms we have yet of hawking and hunting. And therefore the book of venery, of hawking, and hunting, is called the book of Sir Tristram.

Wherefore, as meseemeth, all gentlemen that bearen old arms ought of right to honour Sir Tristram for the goodly terms that gentlemen have and use, and shall do to the day of doom, that thereby in a manner all men of worship may dissever a gentleman from a yeoman, and from a yeoman a villain. For he that gentle is

A manuscript detail of a deer hunt

will draw him unto gentle tatches, and to follow the customs of noble gentlemen.

tatches: qualities

Thus Tristram endured in Cornwall until he was big and strong, of the age of eighteen years. And then the King Meliodas had great joy of young Tristram, and so had the queen, his wife. For ever after in her life, because Sir Tristram saved her from the fire, she did never hate him more after, but ever loved him after, and gave Tristram many great gifts; for every estate loved him, where that he went.

Then it befell that King Anguish of Ireland sent unto King Mark of Cornwall for his truage, that Cornwall had paid many winters. And all that time King Mark was behind of the truage for seven years.

And King Mark and his barons gave unto the messenger of Ireland these words and answer, that they would none pay; and bad the messenger go unto his king Anguish,

'And tell him we will pay him no truage, but tell your lord, and he will always have truage of us of Cornwall, bid him send a trusty knight of his land, that will fight for his right, and we shall find another to defend our right.'

With this answer the messengers departed into Ireland. And when King Anguish understood the answer of the messengers he was wonderly wroth. And then he called unto him Sir Marhaus, the good knight, that was nobly proved, and a knight of the Round Table. And this Marhaus was brother unto the Queen of Ireland. Then the king said thus:

'Fair brother, Sir Marhaus, I pray you go into Cornwall for my sake, to do battle for our truage that of right we ought to have; and whatsoever ye spend ye shall have sufficiently more than ye shall need.'

'Sir,' said Marhaus, 'wit ye well that I shall not be loth to do battle in the right of you and your land with the best knight of the Table Round; for I know them, for the most part, what be their deeds; and for to advance my deeds and to increase my worship I will right gladly go unto this journey for our right.'

So in all haste there was made purveyance for Sir Marhaus, and he had all thing that him needed; and so he departed out of Ireland, and arrived up in Cornwall even fast by the Castle of Tintagel. And when King Mark understood that he was there arrived to fight for Ireland, then made King Mark great sorrow when he understood that the good and noble knight Sir Marhaus was come. For they knew no knight that durst have ado with him. For at that time Sir Marhaus was called one of the famousest and renowned knights of the world.

And thus Sir Marhaus abode in the sea, and every day he sent

OPPOSITE
Scenes from Tristram's boyhood. At the top he is baptized; in the centre he learns the skills of a courtly knight; at the bottom he travels by sea to Cornwall

unto King Mark for to pay the truage that was behind of seven year, other else to find a knight to fight with him for the truage. This manner of message Sir Marhaus sent daily unto King Mark.

Then they of Cornwall let make cries in every place, that what knight would fight for to save the truage of Cornwall, he should be rewarded so that he should fare the better the term of his life.

Then some of the barons said to King Mark, and counselled him to send to the court of King Arthur for to seek Sir Lancelot du Lake, that was that time named for the marvellous knight of all the world. Then there were some other barons that counselled the king not to do so, and said that it was labour in vain, because Sir Marhaus was a knight of the Round Table, 'therefore any of them will be loth to have ado with other, but if it were any knight at his own request would fight disguised and unknown.' So the king and all his barons assented that it was no boot to seek any knight of the Round Table.

This meanwhile came the language and the noise unto King Meliodas, how that Sir Marhaus abode fast by Tintagel, and how King Mark could find no manner knight to fight for him. When young Tristram heard of this he was wroth, and sore ashamed that there durst no knight in Cornwall have ado with Marhaus of Ireland.

Therewithal Tristram went unto his father, King Meliodas, and asked him counsel what was best to do for to recover Cornwall from truage.

'For, as meseemeth,' said Tristram, 'it were shame that Sir Marhaus, the Queen's brother of Ireland, should go away unless that he were foughten withal.'

'As for that,' said King Meliodas, 'wit you well, son Tristram, that Sir Marhaus is called one of the best knights of the world, and knight of the Table Round; and therefore I know no knight in this country that is able to match with him.'

'Alas,' said Tristram, 'that I am not made knight. And if Sir Marhaus should thus depart into Ireland, God let me never have worship; and I were made knight I should match him. And sir,' said Tristram, 'I pray you give me leave to ride to King Mark; and so ye be not displeased, of King Mark will I be made knight.'

'I will well,' said King Meliodas, 'that ye be ruled as your courage will rule you.'

Then Tristram thanked his father much. And then he made him ready to ride into Cornwall.

In the meanwhile there came a messenger with letters of love from King Faramon of France's daughter unto Tristram, that were full piteous letters, and in them were written many complaints of love; but Tristram had no joy of her letters not regard unto her. Also she

A tile from Chertsey Abbey showing an unidentified scene from the story of Tristram

sent him a little brachet that was passing fair. But when the king's daughter understood that Tristram would not love her, as the book saith, she died for sorrow. And then the same squire that brought the letter and the brachet came again unto Tristram, as after ye shall hear in the tale following.

So after this young Tristram rode unto his eme King Mark of Cornwall. And when he came there he heard say that there would no knight fight with Sir Marhaus.

eme: uncle

Then yede Tristram unto his eme and said, 'Sir, if ye will give me the order of knighthood, I will do battle with Sir Marhaus.'

'What are ye,' said the king, 'and from whence be ye come?'

'Sir,' said Tristram, 'I come from King Meliodas that wedded your sister, and a gentleman wit ye well I am.'

King Mark beheld Tristram and saw that he was but a young man of age, but he was passingly well made and big.

'Fair sir,' said the king, 'what is your name, and where were ye born?'

'Sir,' said he again, 'my name is Tristram, and in the country of Lionesse was I born.'

'Ye say well,' said the king; 'and if ye will do this battle I shall make you knight.'

'Therefore I come to you,' said Tristram, 'and for none other cause.'

But then King Mark made him knight. And therewithal, anon as he had made him knight, he sent a messenger unto Sir Marhaus with letters that said that he had found a young knight ready for to take the battle to the uttermost.

'It may well be so,' said Sir Marhaus; 'but tell King Mark I will not fight with no knight but he be of blood royal, that is to say, other king's son, other queen's son, born of a prince or princess.'

When King Mark understood that, he sent for Sir Tristram de Lionesse and told him what was the answer of Sir Marhaus.

Then said Sir Tristram, 'Sithen that he sayeth so, let him wit that I am comen of father side and mother side of as noble blood as he is: for, sir, now shall ye know that I am King Meliodas' son, born of your own sister, Dame Elizabeth, that died in the forest in the birth of me.'

'O Jesu,' said King Mark, 'ye are welcome fair nephew to me.'

Then in all the haste the king horsed Sir Tristram, and armed him in the best manner that might be had or gotten for gold or silver. And then King Mark sent unto Sir Marhaus, and did him to wit that a better born man than he was himself should fight with him, 'and his name is Sir Tristram de Lionesse, begotten of King Meliodas, and born of King Mark's sister.' Then was Sir Marhaus glad and blithe that he should fight with such a gentleman.

And so by the assent of King Mark and of Sir Marhaus they let ordain that they should fight within an island nigh Sir Marhaus' ships; and so was Sir Tristram put into a vessel both his horse and he, and all that to him longed both for his body and for his horse, that he lacked nothing. And when King Mark and his barons of Cornwall beheld how young Sir Tristram departed with such a carriage to fight for the right of Cornwall, there was neither man ne woman of worship but they wept to see and understand so young a knight to jeopard himself for their right.

So to shorten this tale, when Sir Tristram was arrived within the island he looked to the farther side, and there he saw at an anchor six other ships nigh to the land; and under the shadow of the ships, upon the land, there hoved the noble knight, Sir Marhaus of Ireland. Then Sir Tristram commanded his servant Gouvernail to bring his horse to the land, and dress his harness at all manner of rights.

And then Sir Marhaus advised Sir Tristram, and said thus: 'Young knight, Sir Tristram, what dost thou here? Me sore repenteth of thy courage, for wit thou well I have been assayed with many noble knights, and the best knights of this land have been assayed of my hands, and also I have matched with the best knights of the world. And therefore by my counsel return again unto thy vessel.'

'Ah, fair knight, and well-proved knight,' said Sir Tristram, 'thou shalt well wit I may not forsake thee in this quarrel, for I am for thy sake made knight. And thou shalt well wit that I am a king's son, born and gotten upon a queen; and such promise I have made at my nephew's request and mine own seeking, that I shall fight with thee unto the uttermost, and deliver Cornwall from the old truage. And also wit thou well, Sir Marhaus, that this is the greatest cause that thou couragest me to have ado with thee, for thou art called one of the most renowned knights of the world. And because of that noise and fame that thou hast thou givest me courage to have ado with thee, for never yet was I proved with good knight; and sithen I took the order of knighthood this day, I am right well pleased that I may have ado with so good a knight as thou art. And now wit thou well, Sir Marhaus, that I cast me to get worship on thy body; and if that I be not proved, I trust to God that I shall be worshipfully proved upon thy body, and to deliver the country of Cornwall for ever from all manner of truage from Ireland for ever.'

When Sir Marhaus had heard him say what he would, he said thus again:

'Fair knight, sithen it is so that thou castest to win worship of me, I let thee wit worship may thou none lose by me if thou mayest stand me three strokes; for I let thee wit for my noble deeds, proved and seen, King Arthur made me knight of the Table Round.'

Then they began to fewter their spears, and they met so fiercely together that they smote either other down, both horse and man. But Sir Marhaus smote Sir Tristram a great wound in the side with his spear. And then they avoided their horses, and pulled out their swords, and threw their shields afore them. And then they lashed together as men that were wild and courageous. And when they had stricken together long that their arms failed, then they left their strokes, and foined at their breasts and visors; and when they saw that that might not prevail them, then they hurtled together like rams to bear either other down.

fewter: fix in rest

foined: thrust

Thus they fought still together more than half a day, and either of them were wounded passing sore, that the blood ran down freshly from them upon the ground. By then Sir Tristram waxed more fresher than Sir Marhaus, and better winded and bigger; and with a mighty stroke he smote Sir Marhaus upon the helm such a buffet that it went through his helm, and through the coif of steel, and through the brain-pan, and the sword stuck so fast in the helm and in his brain-pan that Sir Tristram pulled three times at his sword or ever he might pull it out from his head. And there Sir Marhaus

coif: cap

fell down on his knees, the edge of Sir Tristram's sword left in his brain-pan. And suddenly Sir Marhaus rose grovelling, and threw his sword and his shield from him, and so he ran to his ships and fled his way. And Sir Tristram had ever his shield and his sword.

And when Sir Tristram saw Sir Marhaus withdraw him, he said, 'Ah! sir knight of the Round Table, why withdrawest thou thee? Thou dost thyself and thy kin great shame, for I am but a young knight, or now I was never proved, and rather than I should withdraw me from thee, I had rather be hew in piece-meal.'

Sir Marhaus answered no word but yede his way sore groaning.

'Well, sir knight,' said Sir Tristram, 'I promise thee thy sword and thy shield shall be mine; and thy shield shall I wear in all places where I ride on mine adventures, and in the sight of King Arthur and all the Round Table.'

So Sir Marhaus and his fellowship departed into Ireland. And as soon as he came to the king, his brother, they searched his wounds. And when his head was searched a piece of Sir Tristram's sword was founden therein and might never be had out of his head for no surgeons. And so he died of Sir Tristram's sword; and that piece of the sword the queen, his sister, kept it for ever with her, for she thought to be revenged and she might.

Now turn we again unto Sir Tristram, that was sore wounded, and full sore bled that he might not within a little while stand, when he had taken cold, unnethe stir him of his limbs. And then he set him down softly upon a little hill, and bled fast. Then anon came Gouvernail, his man, with his vessel; and the king and his barons came with procession against Sir Tristram.

And when he was come unto the land, King Mark took him in his arms, and the king and Sir Dinas, the Seneschal, led Sir Tristram into the Castle of Tintagel. And then he was searched in the best manner, and laid in his bed. And when King Mark saw his wounds he wept heartily and so did all his lords.

'So God me help,' said King Mark, 'I would not for all my lands that my nephew died.'

So Sir Tristram lay there a month and more, and ever he was like to die of that stroke that Sir Marhaus smote him first with the spear. For, as the French book saith, the spear's head was envenomed, that Sir Tristram might not be whole. Then was King Mark and all his barons passing heavy, for they deemed none other but that Sir Tristram should not recover. Then the king let send after all manner of leeches and surgeons, both unto men and women, and there was none that would behote him the life.

Then came there a lady that was a right wise lady, and she said plainly unto King Mark, and to Sir Tristram, and to all his barons, that he should never be whole but if Sir Tristram went into the same country that the venom came from, and in that country should he be holpen or else never. Thus said the lady unto the king. When King Mark understood that, he let purvey for Sir Tristram a fair vessel, well victualled, and therein was put Sir Tristram, and Gouvernail with him, and Sir Tristram took his harp with him. And so he was put into the sea to sail into Ireland.

And so by good fortune he arrived up in Ireland, even fast by a castle where the king and the queen was; and at his arrival he sat and harped in his bed a merry lay, such one heard they never none in Ireland before that time. And when it was told the king and the queen of such a knight that was such an harper, anon the king sent for him, and let search his wounds, and then asked him his name.

Then he answered, 'I am of the country of Lionesse, and my name is Tramtrist, that thus was wounded in a battle as I fought for a lady's right.'

'So God me help,' said King Anguish, 'ye shall have all the help in this land that ye may have here. But I let you wit, in Cornwall I had a great loss as ever had king, for there I lost the best knight of the world; his name was Marhaus, a full noble knight, and knight of the Table Round;' and there he told Sir Tristram wherefore Sir Marhaus was slain. Sir Tristram made semblant as he had been sorry, and better knew he how it was than the king.

Then the king for great favour made Tramtrist to be put in his daughter's ward and keeping, because she was a noble surgeon. And when she had searched him she found in the bottom of his wound that therein was poison, and so she healed him in a while; and therefore Tramtrist cast great love to La Beale Isoud, for she was at that time the fairest maid and lady of the world. And there Tramtrist learned her to harp, and she began to have a great fantasy unto him.

Thus was Sir Tramtrist long there well cherished with the king and with the queen, and namely with La Beale Isoud.

So upon a day the queen and La Beale Isoud made a bain for Sir Tramtrist. And when he was in his bain the queen and Isoud, her daughter, roamed up and down in the chamber, the whiles Gouvernail and Hebes attended upon Tramtrist. And the queen beheld his sword there as it lay upon his bed. And then by unhap the queen drew out his sword and beheld it a long while, and both they thought it a passing fair sword; but within a foot and an half of the point there was a great piece thereof out broken of the edge. And when the queen espied that gap in the sword, she remembered her of a piece of a sword that was found in the brain-pan of Sir Marhaus, the good knight that was her brother.

'Alas then,' said she unto her daughter, La Beale Isoud, 'this is the same traitor knight that slew my brother, thine eme.'

bain: bath

When Isoud heard her say so she was passing sore abashed, for passing well she loved Tramtrist, and full well she knew the cruelness of her mother the queen.

Anon therewithal the queen went unto her own chamber, and sought her coffer, and there she took out the piece of the sword that was pulled out of Sir Marhaus' head after that he was dead. And then she ran with that piece of iron to the sword that lay upon the bed. And when she put that piece of steel and iron unto the sword, it was as meet as it might be when it was new broken.

And then the queen gripped that sword in her hand fiercely, and with all her might she ran straight upon Tramtrist where he sat in his bain. And there she had rived him through had not Sir Hebes gotten her in his arms, and pulled the sword from her, and else she had thrust him through.

Then when she was letted of her evil will she ran to the King Anguish, her husband, and said on her knees, 'O my lord, here have ye in your house that traitor knight that slew my brother and your servant, that noble knight, Sir Marhaus.'

'Who is that,' said the king, 'and where is he?'

'Sir,' she said, 'it is Sir Tramtrist, the same knight that my daughter healed.'

'Alas,' said the king, 'therefore I am right heavy, for he is a full noble knight as ever I saw in field. But I charge you,' said the king to the queen, 'that ye have not ado with that knight, but let me deal with him.'

Then the king went into the chamber unto Sir Tramtrist, and then was he gone unto his chamber, and the king found him all ready armed to mount upon his horse. When the king saw him all ready armed to go unto horseback, the king said,

'Nay, Tramtrist, it will not avail to compare thee against me; but thus much I shall do for my worship and for thy love; in so much as thou art within my court it were no worship for me to slay thee; therefore upon this condition I will give thee leave for to depart from this court in safety, so thou wilt tell me who was thy father, and what is thy name, and if thou slew Sir Marhaus, my brother.'

'Sir,' said Tristram, 'now I shall tell you all the truth: my father's name is Sir Meliodas, King of Lionesse, and my mother hight Elizabeth, that was sister unto King Mark of Cornwall; and my mother died of me in the forest, and because thereof she commanded or she died that when I were christened they should christen me Tristram; and because I would not be known in this country I turned my name and let call me Tramtrist; and for the truage of Cornwall I fought for my eme's sake, and for the right of Cornwall that ye had posseded many years. And wit you well,' said Sir Tristram unto the king, 'I did the battle for the love of mine uncle, King Mark, and for the love of the country of Cornwall, and for to increase mine honour; for that same day that I fought with Sir Marhaus I was made knight, and never or then did I do battle with no knight, and from me he went alive, and left his shield and his sword behind.'

'So God me help,' said the king, 'I may not say but ye did as a knight should do, and it was your part to do for your quarrel, and to increase your worship as a knight should do; howbeit I may not maintain you in this country with my worship, unless that I should displease many of my barons, and my wife and her kin.'

'Sir,' said Sir Tristram, 'I thank you of your good lordship that I have had with you here, and the great goodness of my lady, your daughter, hath showed me. And therefore,' said Sir Tristram, 'it may so be that ye shall win more by my life than by my death, for in the parts of England it may happen I may do you service at some season, that ye shall be glad that ever ye showed me your good lordship. With more I promise you as I am true knight, that in all places I shall be my lady, your daughter's, servant, and knight in all right and in wrong, and I shall never fail her to do as much as a knight may do. Also I beseech your good grace that I may take my leave at my lady, your daughter, and at all the barons and knights.'

'I will well,' said the king.

Then Sir Tristram went unto La Beale Isoud and took his leave of her. And then he told her all, what he was, and how he had changed his name because he would not be known, and how a lady told him that he should never be whole till he came into this country where the poison was made, 'wherethrough I was near my death had not your ladyship been.'

'O gentle knight,' said La Beale Isoud, 'full woe am I of thy departing, for I saw never man that I ought so good will to' And therewithal she wept heartily.

'Madam,' said Sir Tristram, 'ye shall understand that my name is Sir Tristram de Lionesse, gotten of King Meliodas, and born of his queen. And I promise you faithfully that I shall be all the days of my life your knight.'

'Gramercy,' said La Beale Isoud, 'and I promise you there/against that I shall not be married this seven years but by your as/sent; and to whom that ye will I shall be married to, him will I have, and he will have me if ye will consent.'

And then Sir Tristram gave her a ring, and she gave him another; and therewith he departed from her, leaving her making great dole and lamentation.

And he straight went unto the court among all the barons, and there he took his leave at most and least, and openly he said among them all,

Tristram

'Fair lords, now it is so that I must depart. If there be any man here that I have offended unto, or that any man be with me grieved, let complain him here afore me or that ever I depart, and I shall amend it unto my power. And if there be any that will proffer me wrong, or say of me wrong or shame behind my back, say it now or never, and here is my body to make it good, body against body.'

And all they stood still, there was not one that would say one word; yet were there some knights that were of the queen's blood, and of Sir Marhaus' blood, but they would not meddle with him.

So Sir Tristram departed, and took the sea, and with good wind he arrived up at Tintagel in Cornwall. And when King Mark was whole in his prosperity there came tidings that Sir Tristram was arrived, and whole of his wounds: thereof was King Mark passing glad, and so were all the barons. And when he saw his time he rode unto his father, King Meliodas, and there he had all the cheer that the king and the queen could make him. And then largely King Meliodas and his queen departed of their lands and goods to Sir Tristram.

Then by the licence of King Meliodas, his father, he returned again unto the court of King Mark, and there he lived in great joy long time, until at the last there befell a jealousy and an unkindness betwixt King Mark and Sir Tristram, for they loved both one lady. And she was an earl's wife that hight Sir Segwarides. And this lady loved Sir Tristram passingly well. And he loved her again, for she was a passing fair lady, and that espied Sir Tristram well. Then King Mark understood that and was jealous, for King Mark loved her passingly well.

So it fell upon a day this lady sent a dwarf unto Sir Tristram, and bad him, as he loved her, that he would be with her the night next following.

'Also she charged you that ye come not to her but if ye be well armed, for her lord was called a good knight.'

Sir Tristram answered to the dwarf, 'Recommend me unto my lady, and tell her I will not fail but I shall be with her the term that she hath set me.'

And with this answer the dwarf departed. And King Mark espied that the dwarf was with Sir Tristram upon message from Segwarides' wife; then King Mark sent for the dwarf, and when he was comen he made the dwarf by force to tell him all, why and wherefore that he came on message from Sir Tristram. And then he told him.

'Now,' said King Mark, 'go where thou wilt, and upon pain of death that thou say no word that thou spakest with me.'

So the dwarf departed from the king. And that same night that the steven was set betwixt Segwarides' wife and Sir Tristram, King

steven: *appointment*

96

Mark armed him, and made him ready, and took two knights of his council with him; and so he rode afore for to abide by the way, for to await upon Sir Tristram.

And as Sir Tristram came riding upon his way with his spear in his hand, King Mark came hurtling upon him with his two knights suddenly. And all three smote him with their spears, and King Mark hurt Sir Tristram on the breast right sore. And then Sir Tristram fewtered his spear, and smote his uncle, King Mark, so sore, that he rashed him to the earth, and bruised him that he lay still in a swoon, and long it was or ever he might wield himself. And then he ran to the one knight, and eft to the other, and smote them to the cold earth, that they lay still.

And therewithal Sir Tristram rode forth sore wounded to the lady, and found her abiding him at a postern. And there she welcomed him fair, and either halsed other in arms.

halsed: embraced

And so she let put up his horse in the best wise, and then she unarmed him. And so they supped lightly, and went to bed with great joy and pleasance; and so in his raging he took no keep of his green wound that King Mark had given him. And so Sir Tristram bled both the over sheet and the nether sheet, and the pillows, and the head sheet.

And within a while there came one afore, that warned her that her lord was near hand within a bow draught. So she made Sir Tristram to arise, and so he armed him, and took his horse, and so departed. By then was come Sir Segwarides, her lord, and when he found her bed troubled and broken, and went near and beheld it by candle light, then he saw that there had lain a wounded knight.

'Ah, false traitress,' then he said, 'why hast thou betrayed me?' And therewithal he swung out a sword, and said, 'But if thou tell me who hath been here, here thou shalt die.'

'Ah, my lord, mercy,' said the lady, and held up her hands, saying, 'Slay me not, and I shall tell you all who hath been here.'

'Tell anon' said Segwarides, 'to me all the truth.'

Anon for dread she said, 'Here was Sir Tristram with me, and by the way as he came to meward, he was sore wounded.'

'Ah, false traitress,' said Segwarides, 'where is he become?'

'Sir,' she said, 'he is armed, and departed on horseback, not yet hence half a mile.'

'Ye say well,' said Segwarides.

Then he armed him lightly, and gat his horse, and rode after Sir Tristram the straight way unto Tintagel. And within a while he overtook Sir Tristram. And then he bad him, 'Turn, false traitor knight.'

And Sir Tristram anon turned him against him. And therewithal Segwarides smote Sir Tristram with a spear that it all

Tristram

to-brast; and then he swung out his sword and smote fast at Sir Tristram.

'Sir knight,' said Sir Tristram, 'I counsel you that ye smite no more. Howbeit for the wrongs that I have done you I will forbear you as long as I may.'

'Nay,' said Segwarides, 'that shall not be, for either thou shalt die or I.'

Then Sir Tristram drew out his sword, and hurtled his horse unto him fiercely, and through the waist of the body he smote Sir Segwarides that he fell to the earth in a swoon.

And so Sir Tristram departed and left him there. And so he rode unto Tintagel and took his lodging secretly, for he would not be known that he was hurt. Also Sir Segwarides' men rode after their master, whom they found lying in the field sore wounded, and brought him home on his shield, and there he lay long or that he were whole, but at the last he recovered.

Also King Mark would not be aknown of that Sir Tristram and he had met that night. And as for Sir Tristram, he knew not that King Mark had met with him. And so the king came askance to Sir Tristram, to comfort him as he lay sick in his bed. But as long as King Mark lived he loved never Sir Tristram after that; though there was fair speech, love was there none.

And thus it passed many weeks and days, and all was forgiven and forgotten; for Sir Segwarides durst not have ado with Sir Tristram, because of his noble prowess, and also because he was nephew unto King Mark; therefore he let it overslip: for he that hath a privy hurt is loth to have a shame outward.

Then when this was done King Mark cast all the ways that he might to destroy Sir Tristram. And then he imagined in himself to send Sir Tristram into Ireland for La Beale Isoud. For Sir Tristram had so praised her for her beauty and her goodness that King Mark said that he would wed her, whereupon he prayed Sir Tristram to take his way into Ireland for him on message. And all this was done to the intent to slay Sir Tristram. Notwithstanding, Sir Tristram would not refuse the message for no danger nor peril that might fall, for the pleasure of his uncle. So to go he made him ready in the most goodliest wise that might be devised. For Sir Tristram took with him the most goodliest knights that he might find in the court; and they were arrayed, after the guise that was then used, in the goodliest manner. So Sir Tristram departed and took the sea with all his fellowship.

And anon, as he was in the broad sea a tempest took him and his fellowship, and drove them back into the coast of England; and there they arrived fast by Camelot, and full fain they were to take the land. And when they were landed Sir Tristram set up his

OPPOSITE
Tristram arrives in the anteroom of a castle

Ores dist lhistoire
que quant trist
tan se fut party
de la damoiselle
si comme ie vo9
ay compte il cheuaulcha tant quil
vint au chastel dessus la mer ou

la royne dillande demouroit et
yseut et brangam Et il y vint de
nuit tout a escient Car il ne vou
loit pas que lon le cong neust si
descendy deuant vnij praxel et
osta ses armes et les mist delez
vne fontaine et atacha son cheal

Icy commence le quart volume de Guiron le courtois / Et dist comment
vne damoiselle vint a la court du roy artus / et de son message.

u temps que
le roy artus ren
gnoit en sa plus
grant prosperite
honneur et haul
tesse et quil estoit aime de ses subgies
et voisins Craint et doubte de ses

ennemis Et que par sa grant
largesse et bonte de chevalerie
tout le monde pres et lonng par
loit de sa bonte qui estoit tele que
a son pouoir exaulchoit lordre
de chevalerie et pour ce & tous
chevaliers estoit aime et servi.

pavilion upon the land of Camelot, and there he let hang his shield upon the pavilion.

Then it fell that Sir Bleoberis and Sir Blamor de Ganis, that were brethren, they had assummoned the King Anguish of Ireland for to come to Arthur's court upon pain of forfeiture of King Arthur's good grace. And if the King of Ireland came not in at the day assigned and set, the king should lose his lands.

So by it happened that at the day assigned, King Arthur neither Sir Lancelot might not be there for to give the judgement, for King Arthur was with Sir Lancelot at the Castle Joyous Gard. And so King Arthur assigned King Carados and the King of Scots to be there that day as judges.

So when the kings were at Camelot King Anguish of Ireland was come to know his accusers. Then was there Blamor de Ganis, and appeled the King of Ireland of treason, that he had slain a cousin of his in his court in Ireland by treason.

The king was sore abashed of his accusation, for why he was come at the summons of King Arthur, and or that he came at Camelot he wist not wherefore he was sent for. And when the king heard Sir Blamor say his will, he understood well there was none other remedy but to answer him knightly, for the custom was such in those days, that and any man were appeled of any treason or murder he should fight body for body, or else to find another knight for him. And all manner of murders in those days were called treason.

So when King Anguish understood his accusing he was passing heavy, for he knew Sir Blamor de Ganis that he was a noble knight, and of noble knights comen. Then the King of Ireland was but simply purveyed of his answer; therefore the judges gave him respite by the third day to give his answer. So the king departed unto his lodging.

Then when Sir Tristram was in his pavilion, Gouvernail, his man, came and told him how that King Anguish of Ireland was come thither, and he was in great distress; and there Gouvernail told Sir Tristram how King Anguish was summoned and appeled of murder.

'So God me help,' said Sir Tristram, 'these be the best tidings that ever came to me this seven year, for now shall the King of Ireland have need of my help; for I dare say there is no knight in this country that is not of Arthur's court that dare do battle with Sir Blamor de Ganis; and for to win the love of the King of Ireland I will take the battle upon me; and therefore Gouvernail bring me, I charge thee, to the king.'

Then Gouvernail went unto King Anguish of Ireland, and saluted him fair. The king welcomed him and asked him what he would.

OPPOSITE
A damsel arrives at the court of King Arthur

'Sir,' said Gouvernail, 'here is a knight near hand that desireth to speak with you: he bad me say he would do you service.'

'What knight is he?' said the king.

'Sir,' said he, 'it is Sir Tristram de Lionesse, that for the good grace that ye showed him in your lands will reward you in these countries.'

'Come on, fellow,' said the king, 'with me anon and bring me unto Sir Tristram.'

So the king took a little hackney and but few fellowship with him, until he came unto Sir Tristram's pavilion. And when Sir Tristram saw the king he ran unto him and would have holden his stirrup. But the king leapt from his horse lightly, and either halsed other in arms.

'My gracious lord,' said Sir Tristram, 'gramercy of your great goodness showed unto me in your marches and lands: and at that time I promised you to do my service and ever it lay in my power.'

'And, gentle knight,' said the king unto Sir Tristram, 'now have I great need of you, never had I so great need of no knight's help.'

'How so, my good lord?' said Sir Tristram.

'I shall tell you,' said the king: 'I am assummoned and appeled from my country for the death of a knight that was kin unto the good knight Sir Lancelot; wherefore Sir Blamor de Ganis, brother to Sir Bleoberis, hath appeled me to fight with him, other to find a knight in my stead. And well I wot,' said the king, 'these that are come of King Ban's blood, as Sir Lancelot, and these other, are passing good knights, and hard men for to win in battle as any that I know now living.'

'Sir,' said Sir Tristram, 'for the good lordship ye showed unto me in Ireland, and for my lady your daughter's sake, La Beale Isoud, I will take the battle for you upon this condition that ye shall grant me two things: one is that ye shall swear to me that ye are in the right, that ye were never consenting to the knight's death. Sir, then,' said Sir Tristram, 'when that I have done this battle, if God give me grace that I speed, that ye shall give me a reward, what thing reasonable that I will ask of you.'

'So God me help,' said the king, 'ye shall have whatsomever ye will ask.'

'It is well said,' said Sir Tristram. 'Now make your answer that your champion is ready, for I shall die in your quarrel rather than to be recreant.'

'I have no doubt of you,' said the king, 'that and ye should have ado with Sir Lancelot du Lake.'

'Sir,' said Sir Tristram, 'as for Sir Lancelot, he is called the noblest knight of the world, and wit ye well that the knights of his blood are noble men, and dread shame; and as for Bleoberis, brother to Sir Blamor, I have done battle with him. Therefore upon my head it is no shame to call him a good knight.'

'Sir, it is noised,' said the king, 'that Sir Blamor is the hardier knight.'

'As for that, let him be. He shall never be refused, and he were the best knight that now beareth shield or spear.'

So King Anguish departed unto King Carados and the kings that were that time as judges, and told them that he had found his champion ready. Then by the commandments of the kings Sir Blamor de Ganis and Sir Tristram were sent for to hear the charge. . . . So when they had taken their charge they withdrew them to make ready to do battle.

Then said Sir Bleoberis unto his brother, Sir Blamor, 'Fair dear brother,' said he, 'remember of what kin we be come of, and what a man is Sir Lancelot du Lake, neither farther nor nearer but brother's children, and there was never none of our kin that ever was shamed in battle; but rather suffer death, brother, than to be shamed.'

'Brother,' said Sir Blamor, 'have ye no doubt of me, for I shall never shame none of my blood; howbeit I am sure that yonder knight is called a passing good knight as of his time any in the world, yet shall I never yield me, nor say the loth word. Well may he happen to smite me down with his great might of chivalry, but rather shall he slay me than I shall yield me as recreant.'

'God speed you well,' said Sir Bleoberis, 'for ye shall find him the mightiest knight that ever ye had ado withal, for I know him, for I have had ado with him.'

'God me speed,' said Sir Blamor de Ganis. And therewith he took his horse at the one end of the lists, and Sir Tristram at the other end of the lists, and so they fewtered their spears and came together as it had been thunder; and there Sir Tristram through great might smote down Sir Blamor and his horse to the earth.

Then anon Sir Blamor avoided his horse and pulled out his sword and threw his shield before him, and bad Sir Tristram alight, 'For though an horse hath failed me, I trust to God the earth will not fail me.'

And then Sir Tristram alit, and dressed him unto battle; and there they lashed together strongly, rasing, foining and dashing, many sad strokes, that the kings and knights had great wonder that they might stand; for ever they fought like wood men, so that there were never knights seen fight more fiercely than they did; for Sir Blamor was so hasty he would have no rest, that all men wondered that they had breath to stand on their feet; and all the place was bloody that they fought in. And at the last, Sir Tristram smote Sir

Blamor such a buffet upon the helm that he there fell down upon his side, and Sir Tristram stood still and beheld him.

Then when Sir Blamor might speak, he said thus:

'Sir Tristram de Lionesse, I require thee, as thou art a noble knight, and the best knight that ever I found, that thou wilt slay me out, for I would not live to be made lord of all the earth, for I have lever die with worship than live with shame; and needs, Sir Tristram, thou must slay me, or else thou shalt never win the field, for I will never say the loth word. And therefore if thou dare slay me, slay me, I require thee.'

When Sir Tristram heard him say so knightly, he wist not what to do with him, he remembering him of both parts, of what blood he was comen, and for Sir Lancelot's sake he would be loth to slay him; and in the other part in no wise he might not choose, but that he must make him to say the loth word, or else to slay him.

Then Sir Tristram start aback, and went to the kings that were judges, and there he kneeled down tofore them, and besought them of their worships, and for King Arthur's and Sir Lancelot's sake, that they would take this matter in their hands.

'For, my fair lords,' said Sir Tristram, 'it were shame and pity that this noble knight that yonder lieth should be slain; for ye hear well, shamed will he not be, and I pray to God that he never be slain nor shamed for me. And as for the king for whom I fight for, I shall require him, as I am his true champion and true knight in this field, that he will have mercy upon this knight.'

'So God me help,' said King Anguish, 'I will for your sake, Sir Tristram, be ruled as ye will have me, for I know you for my true knight; and therefore I will heartily pray the kings that be here as judges to take it in their hands.'

Then the kings that were judges called Sir Bleoberis to them, and asked him his advice.

'My lords,' said Sir Bleoberis, 'though my brother be beaten, and have the worse through might of arms, I dare say, though Sir Tristram hath beaten his body he hath not beaten his heart, and I thank God he is not shamed this day; and rather than he should be shamed I require you,' said Sir Bleoberis, 'let Sir Tristram slay him out.'

'It shall not be so,' said the kings, 'for his party adversary, both the king and the champion, have pity of Sir Blamor's knighthood.'

'My lords,' said Bleoberis, 'I will right well as ye will.'

Then the kings called the King of Ireland, and found him goodly and treatable. And then, by all their advices, Sir Tristram and Sir Bleoberis took up Sir Blamor, and the two brethren were accorded with King Anguish, and kissed and made friends for ever. And then Sir Blamor and Sir Tristram kissed together, and there they made their oaths that they would never none of them two brethren fight with Sir Tristram, and Sir Tristram made them the same oath. And for that gentle battle all the blood of Sir Lancelot loved Sir Tristram for ever.

Then King Anguish and Sir Tristram took their leave, and sailed into Ireland with great noblesse and joy. So when they were in Ireland the king let make it known throughout all the land how and in what manner Sir Tristram had done for him. Then the queen and all that there were made the most of him that they might. But the joy that La Beale Isoud made of Sir Tristram there might no tongue tell, for of all men earthly she loved him most.

Then upon a day King Anguish asked Sir Tristram why he asked not his boon, for whatsomever he had promised him he should have it without fail.

'Sir,' said Sir Tristram, 'now is it time, Sir, this is all that I will desire, that ye will give me La Beale Isoud, your daughter, not for myself, but for mine uncle, King Mark, that shall have her to wife, for so I have promised him.'

'Alas,' said the king, 'I had lever than all the land that I have ye would have wedded her yourself.'

'Sir, and I did so, I were ashamed for ever in this world, and false of my promise. Therefore,' said Sir Tristram, 'I require you hold your promise that ye promised me; for this is my desire, that ye shall give me La Beale Isoud to go with me unto Cornwall for to be wedded to King Mark, mine uncle.'

'As for that,' said King Anguish, 'ye shall have her with you to do with her what it please you; that is for to say if that ye list to wed her yourself, that is me levest, and if ye will give her unto King Mark, your uncle, that is in your choice.'

So to make short conclusion, La Beale Isoud was made ready to go with Sir Tristram. And Dame Bragwaine went with her for her chief gentlewoman, with many other.

Then the queen, Isoud's mother, gave to Dame Bragwaine, her daughter's gentlewoman, and unto Gouvernail, a drink, and charged them that what day King Mark should wed, that same day they should give him that drink, so that King Mark should drink to La Beale Isoud, 'and then,' said the queen, 'I undertake either shall love the other the days of their life.' So this drink was given unto Dame Bragwaine, and unto Gouvernail.

So Sir Tristram took the sea, and La Beale Isoud; and when they were in their cabin, it happed so that they were thirsty, and they saw a little flacket of gold stand by them, and it seemed by the colour and the taste that it was noble wine.

flacket: *flask*

Then Sir Tristram took the flacket in his hand, and said, 'Madam Isoud, here is the best drink that ever ye drank, that

Dame Bragwaine, your maiden, and Gouvernail, my servant, have kept for themself.'

Then they laughed and made good cheer, and either drank to other freely, and they thought never drink that ever they drank was so sweet nor so good. But by that drink was in their bodies, they loved either other so well that never their love departed for weal neither for woe. And thus it happed first the love betwixt Sir Tristram and La Beale Isoud, the which love never departed the days of their life.

And anon they [Mark and Isoud] were richly wedded with great nobley. But ever, as the French book saith, Sir Tristram and La Beale Isoud loved ever together. Then was there great jousts and great tourneying, and many lords and ladies were at that feast, and Sir Tristram was most praised of all other. . . . Thus they lived with joy and play a long while. But ever Sir Andred, that was nigh cousin to Sir Tristram, lay in a watch to wait betwixt Sir Tristram and La Beale Isoud, for to take them and slander them.

So upon a day Sir Tristram talked with La Beale Isoud in a window, and that espied Sir Andred, and told it to the king. Then King Mark took a sword in his hand and came to Sir Tristram, and called him false traitor, and would have stricken him. But Sir Tristram was nigh him, and ran under his sword, and took it out of his hand.

And then the king cried, 'Where are my knights and my men? I charge you slay this traitor.'

But at that time there was not one would move for his words.

When Sir Tristram saw that there was not one would be against him, he shook the sword to the king, and made countenance, as though he would have stricken him. And then King Mark fled, and Sir Tristram followed him, and smote upon him five or six strokes flatling on the neck, that he made him fall on the nose.

And then Sir Tristram yede his way and armed him, and took his horse and his men, and so he rode into that forest. And there upon a day Sir Tristram met with two brethren that were knights with King Mark, and there he struck off the head of the one, and wounded the other to the death; and he made him to bear his brother's head in his helm unto the king, and thirty more there he wounded. And when that knight came before the king to say his message, he died there before the king and the queen. Then King Mark called his council unto him, and asked advice of his barons what was best to do with Sir Tristram.

'Sir,' said the barons, in especial Sir Dinas, the Seneschal, 'Sir, we will give you counsel for to send for Sir Tristram, for we will that ye wit many men will hold with Sir Tristram and he were hard bestad.'

'And sir,' said Sir Dinas, 'ye shall understand that Sir Tristram is called peerless and makeless of any Christian knight, and of his might and hardiness we knew none so good a knight, but if it be Sir Lancelot du Lake. And if he depart from your court and go to King Arthur's court, wit ye well he will get him such friends there that he will not set by your malice. And therefore, sir, I counsel you to take him to your grace.'

'I will well,' said the king, 'that he be sent for, that we may be friends.'

Then the barons sent for Sir Tristram under a safe conduct. And so when Sir Tristram came to the king he was welcome, and no rehearsal was made, and there was game and play. And then the king and queen went an-hunting, and Sir Tristram.

Then Sir Tristram used daily and nightly to go to Queen Isoud when he might, and ever Sir Andred his cousin watched him night by night for to take him with La Beale Isoud.

And so upon a night Sir Andred espied the hour and the time when Sir Tristram went to his lady. Then Sir Andred gat unto him twelve knights, and at midnight he set upon Sir Tristram secretly and suddenly. And there Sir Tristram was taken naked abed with La Beale Isoud, and then was he bound hand and foot, and so was he kept until day.

And then by the assent of King Mark, and of Sir Andred, and of some of the barons, Sir Tristram was led unto a chapel that stood upon the sea rocks, there for to take his judgement: and so he was led bounden with forty knights. And when Sir Tristram saw that there was none other boot but needs that he must die, then said he,

'Fair lords, remember what I have done for the country of Cornwall, and in what jeopardy I have been in for the weal of you all; for when I fought for the truage of Cornwall with Sir Marhaus, the good knight, I was promised to be better rewarded, when ye all refused to take the battle; therefore, as ye be good gentle knights, see me not thus shamefully to die, for it is shame to all knighthood thus to see me die. For I daresay,' siad Sir Tristram, 'that I never met with no knight but I was as good as he, or better.'

'Fie upon thee,' said Sir Andred, 'false traitor that thou art, with thine avaunting; for all thy boast thou shalt die this day.'

'O Andred, Andred,' said Sir Tristram, 'thou shouldst be my kinsman, and now thou art to me full unfriendly. But and there were no more but thou and I, thou wouldst not put me to death.'

'No?' said Sir Andred, and therewith he drew his sword, and would have slain him.

When Sir Tristram saw him make such countenance he looked upon both his hands that were fast bounden unto two knights, and

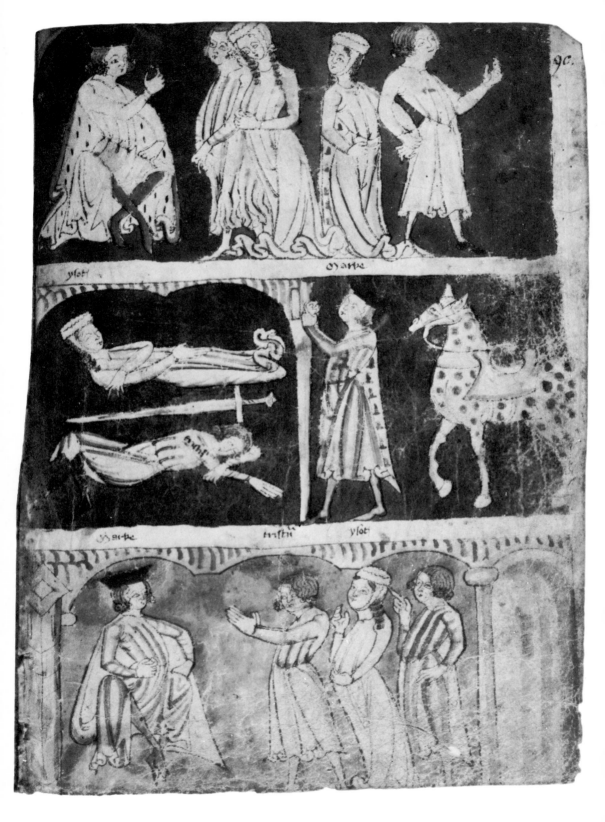

suddenly he pulled them both to him, and unwrast his hands, and leapt unto his cousin, Sir Andred, and wrothe his sword out of his hands; then he smote Sir Andred that he fell to the earth, and so Sir Tristram fought till that he had killed ten knights. So then Sir Tristram gat the chapel and kept it mightily.

wrothe: twisted

Then the cry was great, and the people drew fast unto Sir Andred, more than an hundred. When Sir Tristram saw the people draw unto him, he remembered he was naked, and sparred fast the chapel door, and brake the bars of a window, and so he leapt out and fell upon the crags in the sea. And so at that time Sir Andred nor none of his fellows might get to him.

But when they were departed, Gouvernail, and Sir Lambegus, and Sir Sentraille de Lushon, that were Sir Tristram's men, sought their master. When they heard he was escaped then they were passing glad; and on the rocks they found him, and with towels they pulled him up. And then Sir Tristram asked them where was La Beale Isoud, for he weened she had been had away of Andred's people.

'Sir,' said Gouvernail, 'she is put in a lazar-cote.'

lazar-cote: leper hut

'Alas,' said Sir Tristram, 'that is a full ungoodly place for such a fair lady, and if I may she shall not be long there.'

And so he took his men and went thereas was La Beale Isoud, and fetched her away, and brought her into a forest to a fair manor, and Sir Tristram there abode with her.

So now this good knight bad his men depart, for at that time he might not help them. So they departed all save Gouvernail.

And so upon a day Sir Tristram yede into the forest for to disport him, and then it happened that there he fell asleep; and there came a man that Sir Tristram aforehand had slain his brother, and when this man had found him he shot him through the shoulder with an arrow, and Sir Tristram leapt up and killed that man.

And in the meantime it was told King Mark how Sir Tristram and La Beale Isoud were in that same manor, and as soon as ever he might thither he came with many knights to slay Sir Tristram. And when he came there he found him gone; and anon he took La Beale Isoud home with him, and kept her strait that by no mean never she might write nor send unto Tristram, nor he unto her.

OPPOSITE
Various scenes from a German version of the story of Tristram. At the top, King Mark sends Tristram and Isoud into exile; in the centre he finds the lovers asleep with a sword between them; at the bottom he allows them to return to court

And then when Sir Tristram came toward the old manor he found the track of many horses, and looked about in the place and knew that his lady was gone. And then Sir Tristram took great sorrow, and endured with great pain long time, for the arrow that he was hurt withal was envenomed.

Then by the mean of La Beale Isoud she told a lady that was cousin unto Dame Bragwaine, and she came to Sir Tristram, and told him that he might not be whole by no means: 'For thy lady, La Beale Isoud, may not help thee, therefore she biddeth you haste into Brittany to King Howel, and there ye shall find his daughter, Isoud la Blanche Mains, and she shall help you.'

Then Sir Tristram and Gouvernail gat them shipping, and so sailed into Brittany. And when King Howel wist that it was Sir Tristram he was full glad of him.

'Sir,' he said, 'I am comen into this country to have help of your daughter, for it is told me that there is none other may heal me but she.'

And so within a while she healed him.

Then by the great means of the king and his son, by great prof'fers, there grew great love betwixt Isoud and Sir Tristram for that lady was both good and fair, and a woman of noble blood and fame. And for because Sir Tristram had such cheer and riches, and all other pleasance that he had almost forsaken La Beale Isoud.

And so upon a time Sir Tristram agreed to wed this Isoud la Blanche Mains. And so at last they were wedded, and solemly held their marriage.

And so when they were abed both, Sir Tristram remembered him of his old lady, La Beale Isoud. And then he took such a thought suddenly that he was all dismayed, and other cheer made he none but with clipping and kissing; as for other fleshly lusts Sir Tristram had never ado with her: such mention maketh the French book. Also it maketh mention that the lady weened there had been no pleasure but kissing and clipping.

clipping: *embracing*

And in the meantime there was a knight in Brittany, his name was Sir Suppinabiles, and he came over the sea into England, and then he came into the court of King Arthur, and there he met with Sir Lancelot du Lake, and told him of the marriage of Sir Tristram.

Then said Sir Lancelot, 'Fie upon him, untrue knight to his lady that so noble a knight as Sir Tristram is should be found to his first lady and love untrue, that is, La Beale Isoud, the Queen of Cornwall. But say ye him this,' said Sir Lancelot, 'that of all knights in the world I have loved him most, and had most joy of him, and all was for his noble deeds. And let him wit that the love between him and me is done for ever, and that I give him warning from this day forth I will be his mortal enemy.'

So departed Sir Suppinabiles unto Brittany again, and there he found Sir Tristram and told him that he had been in King Arthur's court.

Then said Sir Tristram, 'Heard ye anything of me?'

'So God me help,' said Sir Suppinabiles, 'there I heard Sir

Lancelot speak of you great shame, and that ye are a false knight to your lady. And he bad me do you to wit that he will be your mortal enemy in every place where he may meet you.'

'That me repenteth,' said Tristram, 'for of all knights I loved most to be in his fellowship.'

Then Sir Tristram was ashamed and made great moan that any noble knight should defame him for the sake of his lady.

And so in this meanwhile La Beale Isoud made a letter unto Queen Guenever, complaining her of the untruth of Sir Tristram, how he had wedded the king's daughter of Brittany.

So Queen Guenever sent her another letter, and bad her be of good comfort, for she should have joy after sorrow, for Sir Tristram was so noble a knight called, that by crafts of sorcery ladies would make such noble men to wed them.

'But in the end,' Queen Guenever said, 'it should be thus, that he shall hate her, and love you better than ever he did.'

Now . . . turn we unto Sir Tristram de Lionesse that was in Brittany. When La Beale Isoud understood that he was wedded she sent to him by her maid, Dame Bragwaine, as piteous letters as could be thought and made, and her conclusion was thus, that if it pleased Sir Tristram, that he would come to her court, and bring with him Isoud la Blanche Mains; and they should be kept as well as she herself.

Then Sir Tristram called unto him Sir Kehydius, and asked him whether he would go with him into Cornwall secretly. He answered him that he was ready at all times. And then he let ordain privily a little vessel, and therein they sailed, Sir Tristram, Sir Kehydius, and Dame Bragwaine and Gouvernail, Sir Tristram's squire . . . and so they sailed into Cornwall all wholly together.

And by assent and information of Dame Bragwaine when they were landed they rode unto Sir Dinas, the Seneschal, a trusty friend of Sir Tristram's. And so Sir Dinas and Dame Bragwaine rode to the court of King Mark, and told the queen, La Beale Isoud, that Sir Tristram was nigh her in that country.

Then for very pure joy La Beale Isoud swooned; and when she might speak she said,

'Gentle knight, seneschal, help that I might speak with him, other my heart will brast.'

Then Sir Dinas and Dame Bragwaine brought Sir Tristram and Sir Kehydius privily into the court, unto her chamber whereas La Beale Isoud assigned it; and to tell the joys that were betwixt La Beale Isoud and Sir Tristram there is no maker can make it, nor no heart can think it, nor no pen can write it, nor no mouth can speak it.

Tristram

peron: *stone*

❧Then departed Sir Tristram and rode straight to Camelot, to the peron that Merlin had made to fore, where Sir Lanceor, that was the King's son of Ireland, was slain by the hands of Sir Balin. . . . And at that time Merlin prophesied that in that same place should fight two the best knights that ever were in King Arthur's days, and the best lovers. . . . Then was he ware of a seemly knight came riding against him all in white, with a covered shield. When he came nigh Sir Tristram he said on high,

'Ye be welcome, sir knight, and well and truly have ye hold your promise.'

And then they dressed their shields and spears, and came together with all their mights of their horses; and they met so fiercely that both their horses and knights fell to the earth, and, as fast as they might, avoided their horses, and put their shields afore them; and they struck together with bright swords, as men that were of might, and either wounded other wonderly sore, that the blood ran out upon the grass. And thus they fought the space of four hours, that never one would speak to other one word, and of their harness they had hewn off many pieces.

A tournament at Camelot

❧Then at the last spake Sir Lancelot and said, 'Knight, thou fightest wonderly well as ever I saw knight, therefore, and it please you, tell me your name.'

'Sir,' said Sir Tristram, 'that is me loth to tell any man my name.'

'Truly' said Sir Lancelot, 'and I were required, I was never loth to tell my name.'

'It is well said,' said Sir Tristram. 'Then I require you to tell me your name.'

'Fair knight,' he said, 'my name is Sir Lancelot du Lake.'

'Alas,' said Sir Tristram, 'what have I done? For ye are the man in the world that I love best.'

'Now, fair knight,' said Sir Lancelot, 'tell me your name.'

'Truly, Sir,' said he, 'my name is Sir Tristram de Lionesse.'

'O Jesu,' said Sir Lancelot, 'what adventure is befall me!'

And therewith Sir Lancelot kneeled down and yielded him up his sword. And therewith Sir Tristram kneeled adown, and yielded him up his sword. And so either gave other the degree. And then they both forthwithal went to the stone, and set them down upon it, and took off their helms to cool them, and either kissed other an hundred times.

And then anon after they took their horses and rode to Camelot. And there they met with Sir Gawain and with Sir Gaheris that had made promise to Arthur never to come again to the court till they had brought Sir Tristram with them.

'Return again,' said Sir Lancelot, 'for your quest is done, for I have met with Sir Tristram: lo, here is his own person!'

Then was Sir Gawain glad, and said to Sir Tristram,

'Ye are welcome, for now have ye eased me greatly of my labour. For what cause,' said Sir Gawain, 'came ye into this country?'

'Fair sir,' said Sir Tristram, 'I came into this country because of Sir Palomides; for he and I had assigned at this day to have done battle together at the peron, and I marvel I hear not of him. And thus by adventure my lord Sir Lancelot and I met together.'

With this came King Arthur, and when he wist that Sir Tristram was there, then he ran unto him and took him by the hand and said,

'Sir Tristram, ye are as welcome as any knight that ever came to this court.'

And when the king had heard how Sir Lancelot and he had foughten, and either had wounded other wonderly sore, then the king made great dole.

Then King Arthur took Sir Tristram by the hand and went to the Table Round. Then came Queen Guenever and many ladies with her, and all those ladies saiden at one voice,

'Welcome, Sir Tristram!'

'Welcome,' said the damsels.

'Welcome,' said knights.

'Welcome,' said King Arthur, 'for one of the best knights, and the gentlest of the world, and the man of most worship; for of all manner of hunting thou bearest the prize, and of all measures of blowing thou art the beginning and of all the terms of hunting and hawking ye are the beginner, of all instruments of music ye are the best; therefore, gentle knight,' said King Arthur, 'ye are welcome to this court. And also, I pray you,' said King Arthur, 'grant me a boon.'

'Sir, it shall be at your commandment,' said Sir Tristram.

'Well,' said King Arthur, 'I will desire of you that ye will abide in my court.'

'Sir,' said Sir Tristram, 'thereto is me loth, for I have to do in many countries.'

'Not so,' said Arthur, 'ye have promised it me, ye may not say nay.'

'Sir,' said Sir Tristram, 'I will as ye will.'

Then went King Arthur unto the sieges about the Round Table, and looked in every siege which were void that lacked knights. And then the king saw in the siege of Marhaus letters that said: THIS IS THE SIEGE OF THE NOBLE KNIGHT, SIR TRISTRAM. And then Arthur made Sir Tristram a knight of the Round Table, with great nobley and great feast as might be thought.

For Sir Marhaus was slain afore by the hands of Sir Tristram in an island; and that was well known at that time in the court of King Arthur. For this Sir Marhaus was a worthy knight. And for evil deeds that he did to the country of Cornwall Sir Tristram and he fought. And they fought so long, tracing and traversing, till they fell bleeding to the earth; for they were so sore wounded that they might not stand for bleeding. And Sir Tristram by fortune recovered, and Sir Marhaus died through the stroke he had in the head.

So leave we of Sir Tristram and turn unto King Mark.

Then King Mark had great despite of the renown of Sir Tristram, and then he chased him out of Cornwall. Yet was he nephew unto King Mark, but he had great suspicion unto Sir Tristram because of his queen, La Beale Isoud; for him seemed that there was too much love between them both. So when Sir Tristram departed out of Cornwall into England King Mark heard of the great prowess that Sir Tristram did there, the which grieved him sore.

So he sent on his part men to espy what deeds he did. And the queen sent privily on her part spies to know what deeds he had done, for great love was between them twain. So when the messengers were come home they told the truth as they had heard, that he passed all other knights but if it were Sir Lancelot. Then King Mark was right heavy of these tidings, and as glad was La Beale Isoud.

Then in great despite he took with him two good knights and two squires, and disguised himself, and took his way into England, to the intent for to slay Sir Tristram. And one of these two knights hight Sir Bersules, and the other knight was called Amant. So as they rode King Mark asked a knight that he met, where he might find King Arthur.

'Sir' he said, 'at Camelot.'

Also he asked the knight after Sir Tristram, whether he heard of him in the court of King Arthur.

'Wit you well,' said the knight, 'ye shall find Sir Tristram there for a man of as great worship as is now living . . . . And the last battle that ever he did he fought with Sir Lancelot; and that was a marvellous battle. And not by force Sir Lancelot brought Sir Tristram to the court. And of him King Arthur made passing great joy, and so made him knight of the Table Round; and his seat was where Sir Marhaus the good knight's seat was.'

Then was King Mark passing sorry when he heard of the honour of Sir Tristram; and so they departed. Then said King Mark unto his two knights.

'Now will I tell you my counsel, for ye are the men that I most trust on live. And I will that ye wit my coming hither is to this

intent, for to destroy Sir Tristram by some wiles or by treason; and it shall be hard if ever he escapes our hands.'

'Alas,' said Sir Bersules, 'my lord, what mean you? For and ye be set in such a way ye are disposed shamefully; for Sir Tristram is the knight of most worship that we know living. And therefore I warn you plainly I will never consent to the death of him; and therefore I will yield him my service, and forsake you.'

When King Mark heard him say so, suddenly he drew his sword and said, 'Ah, traitor!' and smote Sir Bersules on the head, that the sword went to his teeth.

'When Sir Amant, his fellow, saw him do that villainous deed, and his squires, they said it was foul done, and mischievously; 'Wherefore we will do thee no more service. And wit ye well, we will appeach you of treason afore King Arthur.'

Then was King Mark wonderly wroth and would have slain Amant; but he and the two squires held them together, and set nought by his malice. So when King Mark saw he might not be revenged on them, he said thus unto the knight, Amant,

'Wit thou well, and thou appeach me of treason I shall thereof defend me afore King Arthur; but I require thee that thou tell not my name, that I am King Mark, whatsomever come of me.'

'As for that,' said Sir Amant, 'I will not discover your name.'

And so they departed. And Sir Amant and his fellows took the body of Bersules and buried it.

Then King Mark rode till he came to a fountain, and there he rested him, and stood in a doubt whether he would ride to King Arthur's court or none, or return again to his country.

And so he rode as fast as he might unto Camelot; and the same day he found there Sir Amant, the knight, ready, that afore King Arthur had appelled him of treason; and so, lightly the king commanded them to do battle. And by misadventure King Mark smote Sir Amant through the body. And yet was Amant in the righteous quarrel . . . . But when Sir Tristram knew all the matter he made great dole and sorrow out of measure, and wept for sorrow for the loss of the noble knights, Sir Bersules and of Sir Amant.

When Sir Lancelot espied Sir Tristram weep he went hastily to King Arthur, and said,

'Sir, I pray you give me leave to return again to yonder false king and knight.'

'I pray you,' said King Arthur, 'fetch him again, but I would not that ye slew him, for my worship.

Then Sir Lancelot armed him in all haste, and mounted upon a great horse, and took a spear in his hand and rode after King Mark. And from thence a three mile English Sir Lancelot overtook him and bad him: 'Turn recreant king and knight, for whether thou

Lancelot armed and mounted

wilt or not thou shalt go with me to King Arthur's court.'

Then King Mark returned and looked upon Sir Lancelot, and said,

'Fair sir, what is your name?'

'Wit thou well,' said he, 'my name is Sir Lancelot, and therefore defend thee.'

And when King Mark knew that it was Sir Lancelot, and came so fast upon him with a spear, he cried then aloud, and said,

'I yield me to thee, Sir Lancelot, honourable knight.'

But Sir Lancelot would not hear him, but came fast upon him. King Mark saw that, and made no defence, but tumbled adown out of his saddle to the earth as a sack, and there he lay still, and cried Sir Lancelot mercy.

'Arise, recreant knight and king!'

'Sir, I will not fight,' said King Mark, 'but whither that ye will I will go with you.'

'Alas, alas,' said Sir Lancelot, 'that I may not give thee one buffet for the love of Sir Tristram and of La Beale Isoud, and for the two knights that thou hast slain traitorly.'

And so he mounted upon his horse and brought him to King Arthur; and there King Mark alit in that same place, and threw his helm from him upon the earth, and his sword, and fell flat to the earth of King Arthur's feet, and put him in his grace and mercy.

'So God me help,' said King Arthur, 'ye are welcome in a manner, and in a manner ye are not welcome. In this manner ye are welcome, that ye come hither maugre your head, as I suppose.'

'That is truth,' said King Mark, 'and else I had not been here, for my lord, Sir Lancelot, brought me hither through his fine force, and to him am I yielden to as recreant.'

'Well,' said King Arthur, 'ye understand ye ought to do me service, homage, and fealty. And never would ye do me none, but ever ye have been against me, and a destroyer of my knights; now how will ye acquit you?'

'Sir,' said King Mark, 'right as your lordship will require me, unto my power, I will make a large amends.' For he was a fair speaker, and false thereunder.

Then for great pleasure of Sir Tristram, to make them two accorded, the king withheld King Mark as at that time and made a broken love day between them.

Now pass we our matter, . . . and speak of King Arthur, that on a day said unto King Mark,

'Sir, I pray you give me a gift that I shall ask you.'

'Sir,' said King Mark, 'I will give you what gift I may give you.'

Tristram

'Sir, gramercy,' said King Arthur. 'This will I ask you, that ye will be good lord unto Sir Tristram, for he is a man of great honour; and that ye will take him with you into Cornwall, and let him see his friends, and there cherish him for my sake.'

'Sir,' said King Mark, 'I promise you by my faith, and by the faith that I owe to God and to you, I shall worship him for your sake all that I can or may.'

'Sir,' said King Arthur, 'and I will forgive you all the evil will that ever I ought you, and you swear that upon a book afore me.'

'With a good will,' said King Mark. And so he there sware upon a book afore him and all his knights, and therewith King Mark and Sir Tristram took either other by the hands hard knit together. But for all this King Mark thought falsely, as it proved after, for he put Sir Tristram in prison, and cowardly would have slain him.

Then soon after King Mark took his leave to ride into Cornwall, and Sir Tristram made him ready to ride with him, whereof the most part of the Round Table were wroth and heavy, and in especial Sir Lancelot, and Sir Lamorak, and Sir Dinadan, were wroth out of measure. For well they wist King Mark would slay or destroy Sir Tristram.

'Alas,' said Dinadan, 'that my lord, Sir Tristram, shall depart.'

And Sir Tristram took such sorrow that he was amazed like a fool.

'Alas,' said Sir Lancelot unto King Arthur, 'what have ye done, for we shall lose the most man of worship that ever came into your court.'

'Sir, it was his own desire,' said King Arthur, 'and therefore I might not do withal, for I have done all that I can and made them at accord.'

'Accord?' said Sir Lancelot. 'Now fie on that accord. For ye shall hear that he shall slay Sir Tristram, or put him in prison, for he is the most coward and the villainest king and knight that is now living.'

And therewith Sir Lancelot departed, and came to King Mark and said to him thus:

'Sir king, wit thou well the good knight Sir Tristram shall go with thee. Beware, I rede thee, of treason, for and thou mischief that knight by any manner of falsehood or treason, by the faith I owe to God and to the order of knighthood, I shall slay thee mine own hands.'

'Sir Lancelot,' said the king, 'overmuch have ye said to me, and I have sworn and said over largely afore King Arthur in hearing of all his knights, that I shall not slay nor betray him. It were to me overmuch shame to break my promise.'

'Ye say well,' said Sir Lancelot, 'but ye are called so false and full of treason that no man may believe you. Pardie, it is known well for what cause ye came into this country, and for none other cause but to slay Sir Tristram.'

So with great dole King Mark and Sir Tristram rode together. For it was by Sir Tristram's will and his means to go with King Mark, and all was for the intent to see La Beale Isoud, for without the sight of her Sir Tristram might not endure.

Now ... turn we again unto King Arthur. There came a knight out of Cornwall, his name was Sir Fergus, a fellow of the Round Table. And there he told the king and Sir Lancelot good tidings of Sir Tristram, and there were brought goodly letters, and how he left him in the Castle of Tintagel.

Then came a damsel that brought goodly letters unto King Arthur and unto Sir Lancelot, and there she had passing good cheer of the king, and of the queen, and of Sir Lancelot. Then so they wrote goodly letters again. But Sir Lancelot bad ever Sir Tristram beware of King Mark, for ever he called him in his letters King Fox, as who saith, he fareth all with wiles and treason. Whereof Sir Tristram in his heart thanked Sir Lancelot.

Then the damsel went unto La Beale Isoud, and bare her letters from the king and from Sir Lancelot, whereof she was in great joy.

'Fair damsel,' said La Beale Isoud, 'how fareth my lord Arthur, and Queen Guenever, and the noble knight, Sir Lancelot?'

She answered, and to make short tale, 'Much the better that ye and Sir Tristram be in joy.'

'God reward them,' said La Beale Isoud, 'for Sir Tristram suffereth great pain for me, and I for him.'

So the damsel departed, and brought the letters to King Mark. And when he had read them, and understood them, he was wroth with Sir Tristram, for he deemed that he had sent the damsel unto King Arthur. For King Arthur and Sir Lancelot in a manner threatened King Mark in these letters. And as King Mark read these letters he deemed treason by Sir Tristram.

'Damsel,' said King Mark, 'will ye ride again and bear letters from me unto King Arthur?'

'Sir,' she said, 'I will be at your commandment to ride when ye will.'

'Ye say well,' said the king; 'come again to-morn, and fetch your letters.'

Then she departed and came to La Beale Isoud and to Sir Tristram and told them how she should ride again with letters to King Arthur.

'Then we pray you,' said they, 'that when ye have received your letters, that ye would come by us that we may see the privity of your letters.'

A lady arriving at King Arthur's court accompanied by a dwarf

'All that I may do, madam, ye wot well I must do for Sir Tristram, for I have been long his own maiden.'

So on the morn the damsel went to King Mark to have received his letters and to depart.

'Damsel, I am not advised,' said King Mark, 'as at this time to send my letters.'

But so privily and secretly he sent letters unto King Arthur, and unto Queen Guenever, and unto Sir Lancelot. So the varlet departed, and found the king and the queen in Wales, at Caerleon. And as the king and the queen were at mass the varlet came with the letters. And when mass was done the king and the queen opened the letters privily by themself. And to begin, the king's letters spake wonderly short unto King Arthur, and bad him intermit with himself and with his wife, and of his knights, for he was able enough to rule and keep his wife.

When King Arthur understood the letter, he mused of many things, and thought on his sister's words, Queen Morgan le Fay, that she had said betwixt Queen Guenever and Sir Lancelot. And in this thought he studied a great while. Then he bethought him again how his own sister was his enemy, and that she hated the queen and Sir Lancelot to the death, and so he put all that out of his thought. Then King Arthur read the letter again, and the latter clause said that King Mark took Sir Tristram for his mortal enemy; wherefore he put King Arthur out of doubt he would be revenged of Sir Tristram. Then was King Arthur wroth with King Mark.

And when Queen Guenever read her letter and understood it, she was wroth out of measure, for the letter spake shame by her and by Sir Lancelot. And so privily she sent the letter unto Sir Lancelot.

And when he wist the intent of the letter he was so wroth that he laid him down on his bed to sleep, whereof Sir Dinadan was ware, for it was his manner to be privy with all good knights. And as Sir Lancelot slept he stole the letter out of his hand, and read it word by word. And then he made great sorrow for anger. And so Sir Lancelot wakened, and went to a window, and read the letter again, which made him angry.

'Sir,' said Dinadan, 'wherefore be ye angry? I pray you discover you heart to me; for pardie ye wot well I owe you good will, howbeit I am a poor knight and a servitor unto you and to all good knights. For though I be not of worship myself I love all those that be of worship.'

'It is truth,' said Sir Lancelot, 'ye are a trusty knight, and for great trust I will show you my counsel.'

And when Dinadan understood all, he said,

'Sir, this is my counsel: set you right nought by these threats, for King Mark is so villainous, that by fair speech shall never man get ought of him. But ye shall see what I shall do: I will make a lay for him, and when it is made I shall make an harper to sing it afore him.'

And so anon he went and made it, and taught it an harper that hight Eliot. And when he could it he taught it to many harpers. And so by the will of Sir Lancelot, and of King Arthur, the harpers went straight into Wales, and into Cornwall, to sing the lay that Sir Dinadan made by King Mark, which was the worst lay that ever harper sang with harp or with any other instruments.

Now ... speak we of the harpers that Sir Lancelot and Sir Dinadan had sent into Cornwall. And at the great feast that King Mark made . . ., then came Eliot the harper with the lay that Dinadan had made, and secretly brought it unto Sir Tristram, and told him the lay that Dinadan had made by King Mark.

And when Sir Tristram heard it, he said, 'O Lord Jesu, that Dinadan can make wonderly well and ill, there he should make evil!'

'Sir,' said Eliot, 'dare I sing this song afore King Mark?'

'Yea, on my peril,' said Sir Tristram, 'for I shall be thy warrant.'

So at the meat came in Eliot the harper, and because he was a curious harper men heard him sing the same lay that Dinadan had made, which spake the most villainy by King Mark of his treason that ever man heard. When the harper had sung his song to the end King Mark was wonderly wroth, and said,

'Thou harper, how durst thou be so bold, on thy head, to sing this song afore me.'

'Sir,' said Eliot, 'wit you well I am a minstrel, and I must do as I am commanded of these lords that I bear the arms of. And sir, wit ye well that Sir Dinadan, a knight of the Table Round, made this song, and made me to sing it afore you.'

'Thou sayest well,' said King Mark, 'and because thou art a minstrel thou shalt go quit. But I charge thee hie thee fast out of my sight.'

So the harper departed and went to Sir Tristram, and told him how he had sped. Then Sir Tristram let make letters as goodly as he could to Lancelot and to Sir Dinadan. And so he let conduct the harper out of the country.

But to say that King Mark was wonderly wroth, he was, for he deemed that the lay that was sung afore him was made by Sir Tristram's counsel, wherefore he thought to slay him and all his well-willers in that country.

Now turn we from this matter, and speak of Sir Tristram, of whom this book is principal of. And leave we the king and the queen, Sir Lancelot, ... and here beginneth the treason of King Mark, that he ordained against Sir Tristram.

There was cried by the coasts of Cornwall a great tournament and jousts, and all was done by Sir Galahaut the Haut Prince and King Bagdemagus, to the intent to slay Sir Lancelot, or else utterly to destroy him and shame him, because Sir Lancelot had always the higher degree; therefore this prince and this king made this jousts against Sir Lancelot. And thus their counsel was discovered unto King Mark, whereof he was glad. Then King Mark bethought him that he would have Sir Tristram unto that tournament disguised that no man should know him, to that intent that the Haut Prince should ween that Sir Tristram were Sir Lancelot.

And so at these jousts came in Sir Tristram. And at that time Sir Lancelot was not there, but when they saw a knight disguised do such deeds of arms, they weened it had been Sir Lancelot. And in especial King Mark said it was Sir Lancelot plainly.

Then they set upon him, both King Bagdemagus, and the Haut Prince, and their knights, that it was wonder that ever Sir Tristram might endure that pain. Notwithstanding for all the pain that he had, Sir Tristram won the degree at that tournament, and there he hurt many knights and bruised them, and they hurt him and bruised him wonderly sore.

So when the jousts were all done they knew well that it was Sir Tristram de Lionesse; and all that were on King Mark's party were glad that Sir Tristram was hurt, and all the remnant was sorry for his hurt; for Sir Tristram was not so behated as was Sir Lancelot, not within the realm of England.

Then came King Mark unto Sir Tristram and said, 'Fair nephew, I am sorry of your hurts.'

'Gramercy my lord,' said Sir Tristram.

Then King Mark made Sir Tristram to be put in an horse bier in great sign of love, and said,

'Fair cousin, I shall be your leech myself.'

And so he rode forth with Sir Tristram, and brought him to a castle by daylight. And then King Mark made Sir Tristram to eat. And after that he gave him a drink, the which as soon as he had drunk he fell asleep. And when it was night he made him to be carried to another castle, and there he put him in a strong prison, and there he ordained a man and a woman to give him his meat and his drink. So there he was a great while.

Then was Sir Tristram missed, and no creature wist where he was become.

And in the meanwhile there came into the country Sir Percival de Gales to seek Sir Tristram. And when he heard that Sir Tristram was in prison, Sir Percival made clearly the deliverance of Tristram by his knightly means. And when he was so delivered he made great joy of Sir Percival, and so did each one of other. Then Sir Tristram said unto Sir Percival,

'And ye will abide in these marches I will ride with you.'

'Nay,' said Sir Percival, 'in this country I may not tarry, for I must needs into Wales.'

So Sir Percival departed from Sir Tristram, and rode straight unto King Mark, and told him how he had delivered Sir Tristram; and also he told the king that he had done himself great shame for to put Sir Tristram in prison, 'for he is now the knight of most renown in this world living. And wit thou well that the noblest knights of the world love Sir Tristram, and if he will make war upon you ye may not abide it.'

'That is truth,' said King Mark, 'but I may not love Sir Tristram because he loveth my queen and my wife, La Beale Isoud.'

'Ah, fie for shame,' said Sir Percival, 'say ye never so more. Are ye not uncle unto Sir Tristram, and he your nephew? Ye should never think that so noble a knight as Sir Tristram is, that he would do himself so great a villainy to hold his uncle's wife; howbeit,' said Sir Percival, 'he may love your queen sinless, because she is called one of the fairest ladies of the world.'

Then Sir Percival departed from King Mark. So when he was departed King Mark bethought him of more treason: notwithstanding he granted unto Sir Percival never by no manner of means to hurt Sir Tristram.

Then Sir Tristram sent a letter unto La Beale Isoud, and prayed her to be his good lady; and said, if it pleased her to make a vessel ready for her and him, he would go with her unto the realm of Logris, that is this land.

When La Beale Isoud understood Sir Tristram's letters and his intent she sent him another, and bad him be of good comfort, for she would do make the vessel ready, and all manner of thing to purpose. Then La Beale Isoud sent unto Sir Dinas, and to Sadok, and prayed them in anywise to take King Mark, and put him in prison, unto the time that she and Sir Tristram were departed unto the realm of Logris.

When Sir Dinas the Seneschal understood the treason of King Mark he promised her to do her commandment, and sent her word again that King Mark should be put in prison. And as they devised it so it was done. And then Sir Tristram was delivered out of prison; and anon in all the haste Queen Isoud and Sir Tristram went and took their counsel, and so they took with them what they list best. And so they departed.

Then La Beale Isoud and Sir Tristram took their vessel, and came by water into this land. And so they were not four days in this land but there came a cry of a jousts and tournament that King Arthur let make. When Sir Tristram heard tell of that tournament he disguised himself, and La Beale Isoud, and rode unto that tournament. And when he came there he saw many knights joust

Ldit secompte q̃

cellui chastel est

moult bel et m̃

riche et si estoit

and tourney; and so Sir Tristram dressed him to the range, and to make short conclusion he overthrew fourteen knights of the Round Table.

When Sir Lancelot saw these knights of the Round Table thus overthrown, he dressed him to Sir Tristram. And that saw La Beale Isoud how Sir Lancelot was come into the field. Then La Beale Isoud sent unto Sir Lancelot a ring, and bad him wit that it was Sir Tristram de Lionesse. When Sir Lancelot understood that there was Sir Tristram he was full glad, and would not joust. And then Sir Lancelot espied whither Sir Tristram yede, and after him he rode; and then either made great joy of other.

And so Sir Lancelot brought Sir Tristram and Isoud unto Joyous Gard, that was his own castle, that he had won with his own hands. And there Sir Lancelot put them in, to wield it for their own. And wit ye well that castle was garnished and fur-nished for a king and a queen royal there to have sojourned. And Sir Lancelot charged all his people to honour them and love them as they would do himself.

So Sir Lancelot departed unto King Arthur; and then he told Queen Guenever how he that jousted so well at the last tourna-ment was Sir Tristram. And there he told her how he had with him La Beale Isoud maugre King Mark. And so Queen Guenever told all this to King Arthur. And when King Arthur wist that Sir Tristram was escaped and comen from King Mark, and had brought La Beale Isoud with him, then was he passing glad. So because of Sir Tristram King Arthur let make a cry, that on May Day should be a jousts before the Castle of Lonazep; and that castle was fast by Joyous Gard.

And thus Arthur devised, that all the knights of this land, and of Cornwall, and of North Wales, should joust against all these countries: Ireland and Scotland, and the remnant of Wales, and the country of Gore, and Surluse, and of Listinoise, and they of Northumberland, and all they that held lands of King Arthur on this half the sea. So when this cry was made many knights were glad and many were sad.

'Sir,' said Sir Lancelot unto King Arthur, 'by this cry that ye have made ye will put us that be about you in great jeopardy, for there be many knights that have great envy of us; therefore when we shall meet at the day of jousts there will be hard skift for us.'

'As for that,' said Arthur, 'I care not; there shall we prove who shall be best of his hands.'

So when Sir Lancelot understood wherefore King Arthur made this jousting, then he made such purveyance that La Beale Isoud should behold the jousts in a secret place that was honest for her estate.

Lancelot rides in company with a knight and his lady

OPPOSITE
Tristram and Isoud take ship for England

Tristram

Now turn we unto Sir Tristram and to La Beale Isoud, how they made great joy together daily with all manner of mirths that they could devise. And every day Sir Tristram would go ride an-hunting, for Sir Tristram was called that time the best chaser of the world, and the noblest blower of an horn of all manner of measures. For as books report, of Sir Tristram came all the good terms of venery and of hunting, and all the sizes and measures of all blowing with an horn; and of him we had first all the terms of hawking, and which were beasts of chase and beasts of venery, and which were vermins; and all the blasts that longed to all manner of game. First to the uncoupling, to the seeking, to the finding, to the rechase, to the flight, to the death, and to strake, and many other blasts and terms, that all manner of gentlemen have cause to the world's end to praise Sir Tristram, and to pray for his soul.

strake: signal in hunting

So on a day La Beale Isoud said unto Sir Tristram,

'I marvel me much,' said she, 'that ye remember not yourself, how ye be here in a strange country, and here be many perilous knights; and well ye wot that King Mark is full of treason; and that ye will ride thus to chase and to hunt unarmed ye might be soon destroyed.'

'My fair lady and my love, I cry you mercy, I will no more do so.'

So then Sir Tristram rode daily an-hunting armed, and his men bearing his shield and his spear.

Now turn we unto Sir Tristram, that as he rode an-hunting he met with Sir Dinadan, that was comen into that country to seek Sir Tristram. Then Sir Dinadan told Sir Tristram his name, but Sir Tristram would not tell him his name, wherefore Sir Dinadan was wroth.

Hounds are unleashed at the climax of a boar hunt

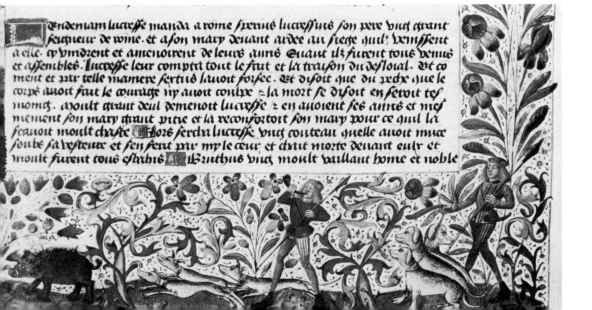

'For such a foolish knight as ye are,' said Sir Dinadan, 'I saw but late this day lying by a well, and he fared as he slept; and there he lay like a fool grinning, and would not speak, and his shield lay by him, and his horse also stood by him; and well I wot he was a lover.'

'Ah, fair sir,' said Sir Tristram, 'are ye not a lover?'

'Marry, fie on that craft!' said Sir Dinadan.

'Sir, that is evil said,' said Sir Tristram, 'for a knight may never be of prowess, but if he be a lover.'

'It is well said,' said Sir Dinadan; 'now tell me your name, sith ye be such a lover, or else I shall do battle with you.'

'As for that,' said Sir Tristram, 'it is no reason to fight with me but I tell you my name; and as for that my name shall ye not wit as at this time.'

'Fie for shame,' said Dinadan, 'art thou a knight and darst not tell thy name to me? Therefore, sir, I will fight with you.'

'As for that,' said Sir Tristram, 'I will be advised, for I will not do battle but if me list. And if I do battle with you,' said Sir Tristram, 'ye are not able to withstand me.'

'Fie on thee, coward,' said Sir Dinadan.

And thus as they hoved still, they saw a knight come riding against them.

'Lo,' said Sir Tristram, 'see where cometh a knight riding, which will joust with you.'

Anon, as Sir Dinadan beheld him he said,

'That same is the doted knight that I saw lie by the well, neither sleeping ne waking.'

'Well,' said Sir Tristram, 'I know that knight well with the covered shield of azure, he is the King's son of Northumberland,

A hunter plunges into a lake to kill a stag brought to bay

Tristram

his name is Sir Epinogrus; and he is as great a lover as I know, and he loveth the King's daughter of Wales, a full fair lady. And now I suppose,' said Sir Tristram, 'and ye require him he will joust with you, and then shall ye prove whether a lover be a better knight, or ye that will not love no lady.'

'Well,' said Sir Dinadan, 'now shalt thou see what I shall do.'

And therewithal Sir Dinadan spake on high and said,

'Sir knight, make thee ready to joust with me, for it is the custom of knights errant one to joust with other.'

'Sir,' said Sir Epinogrus, 'is that the rule of you knights errant for to make a knight to joust will he or nill he?'

'As for that,' said Sir Dinadan, 'make thee ready, for here is for me.'

And therewithal they spurred their horses and met together so hard that Sir Epinogrus smote down Sir Dinadan.

Then Sir Tristram rode to Sir Dinadan and said, 'How now? Meseemeth the lover hath well sped.'

'Fie on thee, coward,' said Sir Dinadan, 'and if thou be a good knight revenge me.'

'Nay,' said Sir Tristram, 'I will not joust as at this time, but take your horse and let us go hence.'

'God defend me,' said Sir Dinadan, 'from thy fellowship, for I never sped well since I met with thee.' And so they departed.

'Well,' said Sir Tristram, 'peradventure I could tell you tidings of Sir Tristram.'

'God save me,' said Sir Dinadan, 'from thy fellowship. For Sir Tristram were mickle the worse and he were in thy company.' And then they departed.

'Sir,' said Sir Tristram, 'yet it may happen that I shall meet with you in other places.'

So rode Sir Tristram unto Joyous Gard.

So Sir Tristram told La Beale Isoud of all this adventure, as ye have heard tofore. And when she heard him tell of Sir Dinadan,

'Sir,' she said, 'is not that he that made the song by King Mark?'

bourder: *jester*

'That same is he,' said Sir Tristram, 'for he is the best bourder and japer that I know, and a noble knight of his hands, and the best fellow that I know, and all good knights love his fellowship.'

'Alas, sir,' said she, 'why brought ye not him with you hither?'

'Have ye no care,' said Sir Tristram, 'for he rideth to seek me in this country; and therefore he will not away till he have met with me.'

And there Sir Tristram told La Beale Isoud how Sir Dinadan held against all lovers.

Right so there came in a varlet and told Sir Tristram how there was come an errant knight into the town, with such colour upon his shield.

'By my faith, that is Sir Dinadan,' said Sir Tristram. 'Therefore, madam, wit ye what ye shall do: send ye for him, my lady Isoud, and I will not be seen, and ye shall hear the merriest knight that ever ye spake withal, and the maddest talker; and I pray you heartily that ye make him good cheer.'

So anon La Beale Isoud sent into the town, and prayed Sir Dinadan that he would come into the castle and repose him there with a lady.

'With a good will,' said Sir Dinadan.

And so he mounted upon his horse and rode into the castle; and there he alit, and was unarmed, and brought into the hall.

And anon La Beale Isoud came unto him, and either saluted other; then she asked him of whence that he was.

'Madam,' said Sir Dinadan, 'I am of the court of King Arthur, and knight of the Table Round, and my name is Sir Dinadan.'

'What do ye in this country?' said La Beale Isoud.

'Forsooth, madam,' said he, 'I seek Sir Tristram the good knight, for it was told me that he was in this country.'

'It may well be,' said La Beale Isoud, 'but I am not ware of him.'

'Madam,' said Dinadan, 'I marvel at Sir Tristram and more other such lovers, what aileth them to be so mad and so sotted upon women.'

'Why,' said La Beale Isoud, 'are ye a knight and are no lover? It is great shame to you: wherefore ye may not be called a good knight but if ye make a quarrel for a lady.'

'God defend me,' said Sir Dinadan, 'for the joy of love is too short, and the sorrow thereof, and what cometh thereof, is duras over long.'　　　*duras: pain*

'Ah,' said La Beale Isoud, 'say ye never more so, for here fast by was the good knight Sir Bleoberis, that fought with three knights at once for a damsel, and he won her afore the King of Northumberland. And that was worshipfully done,' said La Beale Isoud.

'Forsooth, it was so,' said Sir Dinadan, 'for I know him well for a good knight and a noble, and comen he is of noble blood; and all be noble knights of the blood of Sir Lancelot du Lake.'

'Now I pray you, for my love,' said La Beale Isoud, 'will ye fight for me with three knights that do me great wrong? And insomuch as ye be a knight of King Arthur's I require you to do battle for me.'

'Then,' Sir Dinadan said, 'I shall say you be as fair a lady as ever I saw any, and much fairer than is my lady Queen Guenever, but wit ye well at one word, I will not fight for you with three knights, Jesu defend me.'

Then Isoud laughed, and had good game at him. So he had all the cheer that she might make him, and there he lay all that night.

And on the morn early Sir Tristram armed him, and La Beale Isoud gave him a good helm; and then he promised her that he would meet with Sir Dinadan. And so they two would ride together unto Lonazep, where the tournament should be.

'And there shall I make ready for you where ye shall see all the fight.'

So departed Sir Tristram with two squires that bare his shield and his spears that were great and long.

And on the morn they were apparelled to ride toward Lonazep. So Sir Tristram had three squires, and La Beale Isoud had three gentlewomen, and both the queen and they were richly apparelled; and other people had they none with them, but varlets to bear their shields and their spears. And thus they rode forth.

'Now upon what party,' said Sir Tristram, 'is it best we be withal as to-morn?'

'Sir,' said Sir Palomides, 'ye shall have mine advice to be against King Arthur as to-morn, for on his party will be Sir Lancelot and many good knights of his blood with him. And the more men of worship that they be, the more worship we shall win.'

'That is full knightly spoken,' said Sir Tristram; 'and right so as ye counsel me, so will I do.'

'In the name of God,' said they all.

So that night they were lodged with the best. And on the morn when it was day they were arrayed all in green trappers, shields and spears, and La Beale Isoud in the same colour, and her three damsels. And right so these four knights came into the field endlong and through. And so they led La Beale Isoud thither as she should stand and behold all the jousts in a bay window; but always she was wimpled, that no man might see her visage. And then these knights rode straight unto the party of the King of Scots.

When King Arthur had seen him do all this he asked Sir Lancelot what were these knights and that queen.

'Sir,' said Sir Lancelot, 'I cannot say you in certain, but if Sir Tristram be in this country, or Sir Palomides, wit ye well it be they in certain, and La Beale Isoud.'

Then Arthur called to him Sir Kay and said,

'Go lightly and wit how many knights there be here lacking of the Table Round, for by the sieges ye may know.'

So went Sir Kay and saw by the writing in the sieges that there lacked ten knights, 'and these be their names that be not here: Sir Tristram, Sir Palomides, Sir Percival, Sir Gareth, Sir Gaheris, Sir Epinogrus, Sir Mordred, Sir Dinadan, Sir La Cote Male Taile, and Sir Pelleas the noble knight.'

'Well,' said Arthur, 'some of these I dare undertake are here this day against us.'

This meanwhile as they stood thus talking there came into the place Sir Tristram upon a black horse. And or ever he stint he smote down with one spear four good knights of Orkney that were of the kin of Sir Gawain; and here Sir Gareth and Sir Dinadan every each of them smote down a good knight.

'Jesu!' said Arthur, 'yonder knight upon the black horse doth mightily and marvellously well.'

'Abide you,' said Sir Gawain. 'That knight on the black horse began not yet.' .... And then Sir Tristram drew his sword and rode into the thickest of the press against them of Orkney; and there he smote down knights, and rashed off helms, and pulled away their shields, and hurtled down many knights. And so he fared so that Sir Arthur and all knights had great marvel to see any one knight do so great deeds of arms. And ... ever Sir Tristram did so much deeds of arms that they of Orkney waxed weary of him, and so withdrew them unto Lonazep.

Then was the cry of heralds and all manner of common people: 'The green knight hath done marvellously, and beaten all them of Orkney.' And there the heralds numbered that Sir Tristram that sat upon the black horse had smitten down with spears and swords thirty knights; and Sir Palomides had smitten down twenty knights, and the most part of these fifty knight were of the house of King Arthur and proved knights.

'So God me help,' said King Arthur unto Sir Lancelot, 'this is a great shame to us to see four knights beat so many knights of mine. And therefore make you ready, for we will have ado with them.'

'Sir,' said Sir Lancelot, 'wit ye well that there are two passing good knights, and great worship were it not to us now to have ado with them, for they have this day sore travailed.'

'As for that,' said King Arthur, 'I will be avenged; and therefore take with you Sir Bleoberis and Sir Ector, and I will be the fourth,' said King Arthur.

'Well, sir,' said Sir Lancelot, 'ye shall find me ready, and my brother Sir Ector, and my cousin Sir Bleoberis.'

And so when they were ready and on horseback, 'Now choose,' said King Arthur unto Sir Lancelot, 'with whom that ye will encounter withal.'

'Sir,' said Sir Lancelot, 'I will meet with the green knight upon the black horse;' (that was Sir Tristram) 'and my cousin Sir Bleoberis shall match the green knight upon the white horse; (that was Sir Palomides) 'and my brother Sir Ector shall match with the green knight upon the white horse,' (that was Sir Gareth).

OVERLEAF
Tristram in combat
with Palomides

129

Triſtan

N ceſte partie dit li
compte que apes ce
que ſir ſe fu parti
de ſes compaignoe

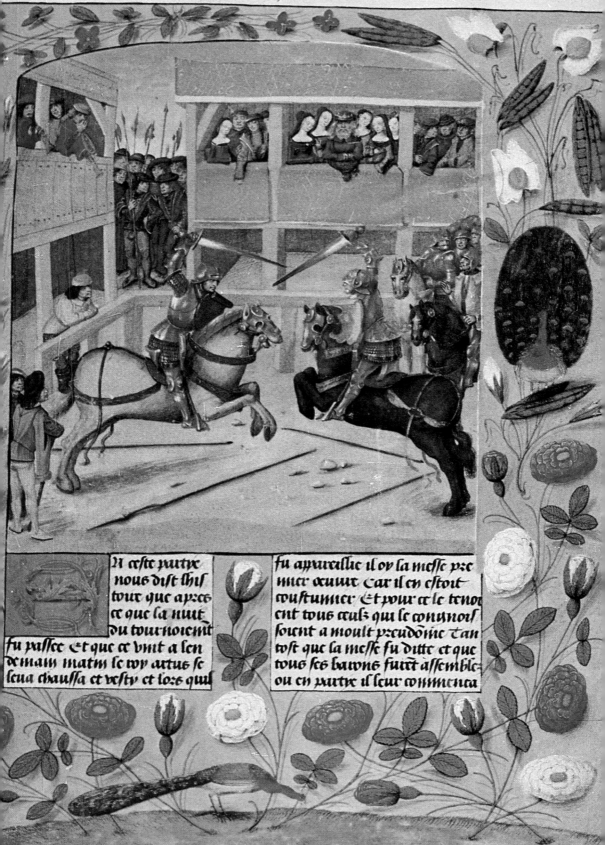

En ceste partie
nous dist lhis
toire que apres
ce que la nuit
du tournoiement
fu passee et que ce vint a len
demain matin le roy artus se
leua chaussa et vesty et lors quil

fu appareille il oy la messe pre
mier ceuure Car il en estoit
coustumier Et pour ce le tenoi
ent tous ceulx qui le congnoi
ssoient a moult preudomme tan
tost que la messe fu ditte et que
tous ses barons furet assemble
ou en partie il leur commenca

la ueille de la pentecou
ste q̃nt tout li compaig
non de la table ronde fu
rent uenu a camaelot ⁊ il orent
oi le seruice / il fisent mettre les ta

'Then must I,' said King Arthur, 'have ado with the green knight upon the grizzled horse,' (and that was Sir Dinadan).

'Now every man take heed to his fellow,' said Sir Lancelot. And so they trotted on together, and there encountered Sir Lancelot against Sir Tristram. So Sir Lancelot smote Sir Tristram sore upon the shield that he bare horse and man to the earth; but Sir Lancelot weened that it had been Sir Palomides, and so he passed forth. . . . And then the noble King Arthur encountered with Sir Dinadan, and he smote him quite from his saddle. And then the noise turned awhile how the green knights were slain down.

And therewith Sir Tristram mounted upon his horse, and there he met with King Arthur, and he gave him such a buffet upon the helm with his sword that King Arthur had no power to keep his saddle. . . . Then was there great press about King Arthur for to horse him again; but Sir Palomides would not suffer King Arthur to be horsed again, but ever Sir Palomides smote on the right hand and on the left hand and raced off helms mightily as a noble knight.

And this meanwhile Sir Tristram rode through the thickest of the press, and smote down knights on the right hand and on the left hand, and raced off helms, and so passed forth unto his pavilions, and left Sir Palomides on foot; and Sir Tristram changed his horse and disguised himself all in red, horse and harness.

And when Queen Isoud saw Sir Tristram unhorsed, and she wist not where he was, then she wept greatly. But Sir Tristram when he was ready came dashing lightly into the field, and then La Beale Isoud espied him. And so he did great deeds of arms; with one spear that was great Sir Tristram smote down five knights or ever he stint.

So when La Beale Isoud espied Sir Tristram again upon his horseback she was passing glad, and then she laughed and made good cheer. And as it happened, Sir Palomides looked up toward her where she was in the window, and he espied how she laughed. And therewith he took such a rejoicing that he smote down, what with his spear and with his sword, all that ever he met; for through the sight of her he was so enamoured in her love that he seemed at that time, that and both Sir Tristram and Sir Lancelot had been both against him they should have won no worship of him. And in his heart, as the book saith, Sir Palomides wished that with his worship he might have ado with Sir Tristram before all men, because of La Beale Isoud.

Then Sir Palomides began to double his strength, and he did so marvellously that all men had wonder of him, and ever he cast up his eye unto La Beale Isoud. And when he saw her make

FACING PAGE 130
*Arthur and his court
watch single combat at
a tournament*

OVERLEAF
*Lancelot jousting
before the King and
Queen*

OPPOSITE
*Arthur and his
knights at a feast*

such cheer he fared like a lion, that there might no man withstand him.

And then Sir Tristram beheld him, how that Sir Palomides bestirred him; and then he said unto Sir Dinadan,

'So God me help, Sir Palomides is a passing good knight and a well enduring, but such deeds saw I him never do, nor never heard I tell that ever he did so much in one day.'

'It is his day,' said Sir Dinadan; and he would say no more unto Sir Tristram; but to himself he said, 'And if ye knew for whose love he doth all those deeds of arms, soon would Sir Tristram abate his courage.'

And then King Arthur sent out many knights of the Table Round; and Sir Palomides was ever in the foremost front, and Sir Tristram did so strongly well that the king and all other had marvel.

And then the king let blow to lodging; and because Sir Palomides began first, and never he went nor rode out of the field to repose, but ever he was doing marvellously well other on foot or on horseback, and longest during, King Arthur and all the kings gave Sir Palomides the honour and the gree as for that day.

gree: *prize*

Then Sir Tristram commanded Sir Dinadan to fetch the queen, La Beale Isoud, and bring her to his two pavilions that stood by the well. And so Sir Dinadan did as he was commanded. But when Sir Palomides understood and knew that Sir Tristram was in the red armour, and on the red horse, wit ye well that he was glad, and so was Sir Gareth and Sir Dinadan, for they all weened that Sir Tristram had been taken prisoner.

And then every knight drew to his inn.

So on the morn Sir Lancelot departed, and Sir Tristram was ready, and La Beale Isoud with Sir Palomides and Sir Gareth. And so they rode all in green full freshly beseen unto the forest. And Sir Tristram left Sir Dinadan sleeping in his bed. And so as they rode it happed the king and Lancelot stood in a window, and saw Sir Tristram ride and Isoud.

'Sir,' said Lancelot, 'yonder rideth the fairest lady of the world except your queen, Dame Guenever.'

'Who is that?' said King Arthur.

'Sir,' said he, 'it is Queen Isoud that, out-take my lady your queen, she is makeless.'

'Take your horse,' said King Arthur, 'and array you at all rights as I will do, and I promise you,' said the king, 'I will see her.'

Then anon they were armed and horsed, and either took a spear and rode unto the forest.

'Sir,' said Sir Lancelot, 'it is not good that ye go too nigh them, for wit ye well there are two as good knights as any now are living, and therefore, sir, I pray you be not too hasty. For peradventure there will be some knights that will be displeased and we come suddenly upon them.'

'As for that,' said King Arthur, 'I will see her, for I take no force whom I grieve.'

'Sir,' said Sir Lancelot, 'ye put yourself in great jeopardy.'

'As for that,' said the king, 'we will take the adventure.'

Right so anon the king rode even to her, and saluted her, and said, 'God you save.'

'Sir,' said she, 'ye are welcome.'

Then the king beheld her, and liked her wonderly well. So with that came Sir Palomides unto King Arthur, and said, 'Thou uncourteous knight, what seekest thou here? For thou art uncourteous to come upon a lady thus suddenly. Therefore withdraw thee.'

But King Arthur took none heed of Sir Palomides' words, but ever he looked still upon Queen Isoud. Then was Sir Palomides wroth, and therewith he took a spear, and came hurtling upon King Arthur, and smote him down with a spear, a great fall.

When Sir Lancelot saw that despite of Sir Palomides, he said to himself,

'I am loth to have ado with yonder knight, and not for his own sake but for Sir Tristram's. And one thing I am sure of: if I smite down Sir Palomides I must have ado with Sir Tristram, and that were too much to match them both for me alone, for they are two noble knights. Notwithstanding whether I live or I die needs must I revenge my lord Arthur, and so I will whatsomever befall me.'

And therewith Sir Lancelot cried to Sir Palomides, 'Keep thee from me.'

And then Sir Lancelot and Sir Palomides rashed together with two spears strongly; but Sir Lancelot smote Sir Palomides so hard that he went quite out of his saddle, and had a great fall.

When Sir Tristram saw Sir Palomides have that fall, he said to Sir Lancelot,

'Sir knight, keep thee, for I must joust with thee.'

'As for to joust with me,' said Sir Lancelot, 'I will not fail you, for no dread I have of you; but I am loth to have ado with you and I might choose, for I will that ye wit that I must revenge my special lord and my most bedread friend, that was unhorsed unwarly and unknightly. And therefore, sir, though I revenge that fall, take ye no displeasure, for he is to me such a friend that I may not see him shamed.'

Anon Sir Tristram understood by his person and by his knightly words that it was Sir Lancelot du Lake, and truly Sir Tristram deemed that it was King Arthur that Sir Palomides had smitten down. And then Sir Tristram put his spear from him, and got Sir Palomides again on horseback, and Sir Lancelot got King Arthur again on horseback and so departed.

'So God me help,' said Sir Tristram unto Palomides, 'ye did not worshipfully when ye smote down that knight so suddenly as ye did. And wit ye well ye did yourself great shame, for the knights came hither of their gentleness to see a fair lady; and that is every good knight's part, to behold a fair lady; and ye had not ado to play such masteries afore my lady. Wit thou well it will turn to anger, for he that ye smote down was King Arthur, and that other was the good knight Sir Lancelot. But I shall not forget,' said Sir Tristram, 'the words of Sir Lancelot when that he called him a man of great worship, thereby I wist that it was King Arthur. And as for Sir Lancelot, and there had been an hundred knights in the meadow, he would not have refused them, and yet he said he would refuse me. And by that again I knew that it was Sir Lancelot, for ever he forbeareth me in every place, and showeth me great kind-ness; and of all knights, I out-take none, say what men will say, he beareth the flower of all chivalry, assay him whosomever will. And he be well angered, and that him list to do his utterance without any favour, I know him not alive but Sir Lancelot is over hard for him, be it on horseback or on foot.'

'Sir, I may never believe,' said Sir Palomides, 'that King Arthur will ride so privily as a poor errant knight.'

'Ah,' said Sir Tristram, 'ye know not my lord King Arthur, for all knights may learn to be a knight of him. And therefore ye may be sorry,' said Sir Tristram, 'of your unknightly deeds to so noble a king.'

'And a thing that is done, sir, it can not be undone,' said Sir Palomides.

Then they blew unto lodging, and Queen Isoud was led unto her pavilions.

And therewithal two knights armed came unto the pavilion, and there they alit both, and came in armed at all pieces.

'Fair knights,' said Sir Tristram, 'ye are to blame to come thus armed at all pieces upon me while we are at our meat; and if ye would anything with us when we were in the field, there might ye have eased your hearts.'

'Not so sir,' said one of those knights, 'we come not for that in-tent, but wit ye well, Sir Tristram, we be come hither as your friends. And I am come here for to see you, and this knight is come for to see your queen.'

Then said Sir Tristram, 'I require you do off your helms that I may see you.'

'That will we do at your desire,' said the knights.

And when their helms were off, Sir Tristram thought that he should know them.

Then said Sir Dinadan privily unto Sir Tristram, 'Sir, that is Sir Lancelot du Lake that spake unto you first, and the other is my lord King Arthur.'

Then said Sir Tristram unto La Beale Isoud, 'Madam arise, for here is my lord, King Arthur.'

Then the king and queen kissed, and Sir Lancelot and Sir Tristram braced either other in arms, and then there was joy without measure; and at the request of La Beale Isoud, King Arthur and Sir Lancelot were unarmed, and then there was merry talking.

'Madam,' said King Arthur, 'it is many a day ago sithen I desired first to see you, for ye have been praised so fair a lady. And now I dare say ye are the fairest that ever I saw, and Sir Tristram is as fair and as good a knight as any that I know. And therefore me seemeth ye are well beset together.'

'Sir, God thank you,' said the noble knight, Sir Tristram, and Isoud; 'of your great goodness and largess ye are peerless.'

And thus they talked of many things and of all the whole jousts.

'But for what cause,' said King Arthur, 'were ye, Sir Tristram, against us? Ye are a knight of the Table Round; of right ye should have been with us.'

'Sir,' said Sir Tristram, 'here is Sir Dinadan, and Sir Gareth your own nephew, caused me to be against you.'

'My lord Arthur,' said Sir Gareth, 'I may well bear the blame, for my back is broad enough. But it were Sir Tristram's own deeds.'

'By God, that I may repent,' said Sir Dinadan, 'for this unhappy Sir Tristram brought us to this tournament, and many great buffets he hath caused us to have.'

Then the king and Lancelot laughed that they might not sit.

And then they of Lionesse sent letters unto Sir Tristram of recommendation, and many great gifts to maintain Sir Tristram's estate; and ever between Sir Tristram resorted unto Joyous Gard whereas La Beale Isoud was that loved him as her life.

BOOK 10

Lancelot and Elaine

ow . . . speak we of Sir Lancelot du Lake, and of Sir Galahad, Sir Lancelot's son, how he was gotten, and in what manner.

As the book of French maketh mention, afore the time that Sir Galahad was begotten or born, there came in an hermit unto King Arthur upon Whitsunday, as the knights sat at the Table Round. And when the hermit saw the Siege Perilous, he asked the king and all the knights why that siege was void.

Then King Arthur for all the knights answered and said,

'There shall never none sit in that siege but one, but if he be destroyed.'

Then said the hermit, 'Sirs, wot ye what is he?'

'Nay,' said King Arthur and all the knights, 'we know not who is he that shall sit there.'

'Then wot I,' said the hermit, 'for he that shall sit there is unborn and unbegotten, and this same year he shall be begotten that shall sit in that Siege Perilous, and he shall win the Sangrail.'

When this hermit had made this mention he departed from the court of King Arthur.

And then after this feast Sir Lancelot rode on his adventure, till on a time by adventure he passed over the Pounte of Corbin; and there he saw the fairest tower that ever he saw, and thereunder was a fair little town full of people. And all the people, men and women, cried at once,

'Welcome, Sir Lancelot du Lake, the flower of all knighthood, for by thee all we shall be holpen out of danger.'

'What mean ye,' said Sir Lancelot, 'that ye cry so upon me?'

'Ah, fair knight,' said they all, 'here is within this tower a dolorous lady that hath been there in pains many winters and days, for ever she boileth in scalding water; and but late,' said all the people, 'Sir Gawain was here and he might not help her, and so he left her in pain still.'

'So may I,' said Sir Lancelot, 'leave her in pain as well as Sir Gawain did.'

'Nay,' said the people, 'we know well that it is Sir Lancelot that shall deliver her.'

'Well,' said Lancelot, 'then tell me what I shall do.'

And so anon they brought Sir Lancelot into the tower; and when he came to the chamber thereas this lady was, the doors of iron unlocked and unbolted. And so Sir Lancelot went into the chamber that was as hot as any stew. And there Sir Lancelot took the fairest lady by the hand that ever he saw, and she was naked as a needle. And by enchantment Queen Morgan le Fay and the Queen of Northgales had put her there in that pains, because she was called the fairest lady of that country; and there she had been five years, and never might she be delivered out of her great pains unto the time the best knight of the world had taken her by the hand.

Then the people brought her clothes. And when she was arrayed, Sir Lancelot thought she was the fairest lady that ever he saw, but if it were Queen Guenever.

Then this lady said to Sir Lancelot, 'Sir, if it please you will ye go with me hereby into a chapel that we may give loving and thanking unto God?'

'Madam,' said Sir Lancelot, 'cometh on with me, and I will go with you.'

So when they came there and gave thankings to God all the people, both learned and lewd, gave thankings unto God and him, and said,

'Sir knight, since ye have delivered this lady, ye shall deliver us from a serpent that is here in a tomb.'

Then Sir Lancelot took his shield and said,

'Sirs, bring me thither, and what I may do unto the pleasure of God and of you I shall do.'

So when Sir Lancelot came thither he saw written upon the tomb letters of gold that said thus: HERE SHALL COME A LEOPARD OF KINGS' BLOOD, AND HE SHALL SLAY THIS SERPENT, AND THIS LEOPARD SHALL ENGENDER A LION IN THIS FOREIGN COUNTRY, THE WHICH LION SHALL PASS ALL OTHER KNIGHTS.

So then Sir Lancelot lift up the tomb, and there came out an horrible and a fiendly dragon, spitting fire out of his mouth. Then Sir Lancelot drew his sword and fought with that dragon long, and at the last with great pain Sir Lancelot slew that dragon.

And therewithal came King Pelles, the good and noble knight, and saluted Sir Lancelot, and he him again.

'Fair knight,' said the king, 'what is your name? I require you of your knighthood tell me!'

'Sir,' said Sir Lancelot, 'wit you well my name is Sir Lancelot du Lake.'

'And my name is King Pelles, king of the foreign country, and cousin nigh unto Joseph of Arimathea.'

And then either of them made much of other, and so they went into the castle to take their repast. And anon there came in a dove at a window, and in her mouth there seemed a little censer of gold. And therewithal there was such a savour as all the spicery of the world had been there. And forthwithal there was upon the table all manner of meats and drinks that they could think upon.

So there came in a damsel passing fair and young, and she bare a vessel of gold betwixt her hands; and thereto the king kneeled devoutly, and said his prayers, and so did all that were there.

'O Jesu!' said Sir Lancelot, 'What may this mean?'

'Sir,' said the king, 'this is the richest thing that any man hath living. And when this thing goeth about, the Round Table shall be broken; and wit thou well,' said the king, 'this is the holy Sangrail that ye have here seen.'

So the king and Sir Lancelot led their life the most part of that day together. And fain would King Pelles have found the mean that Sir Lancelot should have lain by his daughter, fair Elaine. And for this intent: the king knew well that Sir Lancelot should get a child upon his daughter, which should be named Sir Galahad, the good knight, by whom all the foreign country should be brought out of danger, and by him the Holy Grail should be achieved.

Then came forth a lady that hight Dame Brisen, and she said unto the king,

'Sir, wit ye well Sir Lancelot loveth no lady in the world but all only Queen Guenever; and therefore work ye by counsel, and I shall make him lie with your daughter, and he shall not wit but that he lieth by Queen Guenever.'

'O fair lady, Dame Brisen,' said the king, 'hope ye that ye may bring this matter about?'

'Sir,' said she, 'upon pain of my life let me deal.' For this Dame Brisen was one of the greatest enchantresses that was at that time in the world living.

And so anon by Dame Brisen's wit she made one to come to Sir Lancelot that he knew well. And this man brought him a ring from Queen Guenever like as it had come from her, and such one as she was wont for the most part to wear; and when Sir Lancelot saw that token wit ye well he was never so fain.

'Where is my lady,' said Sir Lancelot.

'In the Castle of Case,' said the messenger, 'but five mile thence.'

Then Sir Lancelot thought to be there the same night. And then this Dame Brisen by the commandment of King Pelles let send Elaine to this castle with twenty-five knights unto the Castle of Case.

Then Sir Lancelot against night rode unto that castle, and there anon he was received worshipfully with such people, to his seeming, as were about Queen Guenever secret. So when Sir Lancelot was alit, he asked where the queen was. So Dame Brisen said she was in her bed; and then the people were avoided, and Sir Lancelot was led unto her chamber.

And then Dame Brisen brought Sir Lancelot a cupful of wine; and anon as he had drunken that wine he was so assotted and mad that he might make no delay, but withouten any let he went to bed. And so he weened that maiden Elaine had been Queen Guenever. And wit you well that Sir Lancelot was glad, and so was that lady Elaine that she had gotten Sir Lancelot in her arms. For well she knew that that same night should be begotten upon her Sir Galahad, that should prove the best knight of the world.

And so they lay together until undern of the morn; and all the windows and holes of that chamber were stopped that no manner of day might be seen.

undern: 9 o'clock in the morning

And then Sir Lancelot remembered him, and he arose up and went to the window. And anon as he had unshut the window the enchantment was gone; then he knew himself that he had done amiss.

'Alas,' he said, 'that I have lived so long; now I am shamed.'

So then he gat his sword in his hand and said, 'Thou traitoress, what art thou that I have lain by all this night? Thou shalt die right here of my hands.'

Then this fair lady Elaine skipped out of her bed all naked, and kneeled down afore Sir Lancelot, and said,

'Fair courteous knight, Sir Lancelot, ye are comen of kings' blood, and therefore I require you have mercy upon me. And as thou art renowned the most noble knight of the world, slay me not, for I have in my womb begotten of thee that shall be the most noblest knight of the world.'

'Ah, false traitoress,' said Sir Lancelot, 'why hast thou betrayed me? Anon tell me what thou art.'

Lancelot threatening to kill Elaine

'Sir,' she said, 'I am Elaine, the daughter of King Pelles.'

'Well,' said Sir Lancelot, 'I will forgive you this deed.' And therewith he took her up in his arms, and kissed her, for she was as fair a lady, and thereto lusty and young, and as wise, as any was that time living.

'So God me help,' said Sir Lancelot, 'I may not wit this to you; but her that made this enchantment upon me and between you and me, and I may find her, that same Dame Brisen shall lose her head

for witchcrafts, for there was never knight deceived so as I am this night.'

And then she said, 'My lord Sir Lancelot, I beseech you see me as soon as ye may, for I have obeyed me unto the prophecy that my father told me. And by his commandment to fulfil this pro-phecy I have given thee the greatest riches and the fairest flower that ever I had, and that is my maidenhood that I shall never have again. And therefore, gentle knight, owe me your goodwill.'

And so Sir Lancelot arrayed him and armed him, and took his leave mildly at that young lady Elaine. And so he departed, and rode till he came to the Castle of Corbin, where her father was.

And as fast as her time came she was delivered of a fair child, and they christened him Galahad. And wit ye well that child was well kept and well nourished, and he was so named Galahad be-cause Sir Lancelot was so named at the fountain stone; and after that, the Lady of the Lake confirmed him Sir Lancelot du Lake.

Then after the lady was delivered and churched, there came a knight unto her, his name was Sir Bromel la Pleche, the which was a great lord; and he had loved that lady Elaine long, and he ever-more desired to wed her; and so by no mean she could put him off, till on a day she said to Sir Bromel,

'Wit thou well, sir knight, I will not love you, for my love is set upon the best knight of the world.'

'Who is that?' said Sir Bromel.

'Sir,' she said, 'it is Sir Lancelot du Lake that I love and none other, and therefore woo me no longer.'

'Ye say well,' said Sir Bromel, 'and sithen ye have told me so much, ye shall have but little joy of Sir Lancelot, for I shall slay him wheresomever I meet him.'

'Sir,' said the Lady Elaine, 'do to him no treason, and God for-bid that ye spare him.'

'Wit ye well, my lady,' said Bromel, 'and I promise you this twelvemonth I shall keep the Pounte of Corbin for Sir Lancelot's sake, that he shall neither come ne go unto you, but I shall meet with him.'

Then as it fell by fortune and adventure, Sir Bors de Ganis, that was nephew unto Sir Lancelot, came over that bridge and there Sir Bromel and Sir Bors jousted, and Sir Bors smote Sir Bromel such a buffet that he bare him over his horse's croup.

And then Sir Bromel, as an hardy man, pulled out his sword, and dressed his shield to do battle with Sir Bors. And anon Sir Bors alit and avoided his horse, and there they dashed together many sad strokes; and long thus they fought, till at the last Sir Bromel was laid to the earth, and there Sir Bors began to unlace his helm to slay him. Then Sir Bromel cried Sir Bors mercy, and yielded him.

'Upon this covenant thou shalt have thy life,' said Sir Bors, 'so thou go unto Sir Lancelot upon Whitsunday that next cometh, and yield thee unto him as knight recreant.'

'Sir, I will do it,' said Sir Bromel. And so he sware upon the cross of the sword.

And so he let him depart, and Sir Bors rode unto King Pelles, that was within Corbin. And when the king and Elaine his daughter knew that Sir Bors was nephew unto Sir Lancelot, they made him great cheer.

Then said Dame Elaine, 'We marvel where Sir Lancelot is, for he came never here but once, that ever I saw.'

'Madam, marvel ye not,' said Sir Bors, 'for this half year he hath been in prison with Queen Morgan le Fay, King Arthur's sister.'

'Alas,' said Dame Elaine, 'that me sore repenteth.'

And ever Sir Bors beheld that child in her arms, and ever him seemed it was passing like Sir Lancelot.

'Truly,' said Elaine, 'wit you well this child he begat upon me.'

Then Sir Bors wept for joy, and he prayed to God it might prove as good a knight as his father was.

And so came in a white dove, and she bare a little censer of gold in her mouth, and there was all manner of meats and drinks; and a maiden bare that Sangrail, and she said there openly,

'Wit you well, Sir Bors, that this child is Galahad, that shall sit in the Siege Perilous, and achieve the Sangrail, and he shall be much better than ever was Sir Lancelot du Lake, that is his own father.'

And then they kneeled down and made their devotions, and there was such a savour as all the spicery in the world had been there. And as the dove had taken her flight, the maiden vanished with the Sangrail as she came.

'Sir,' said Sir Bors then unto King Pelles, 'this castle may be named the Castle Adventurous, for here be many strange adventures.'

'That is sooth,' said the king, 'for well may this place be called the adventurous place. For there come but few knights here that go away with any worship; be he never so strong, here he may be proved. And but late ago Sir Gawain, the good knight, gat but little worship here. For I let you wit,' said King Pelles, 'here shall no knight win worship but if he be of worship himself and of good living, and that loveth God and dreadeth God. And else he getteth no worship here, be he never so hardy a man.'

'That is a wonderful thing,' said Sir Bors. 'What ye mean in this country I wot not, for ye have many strange adventures. And therefore I will lie in this castle this night.'

'Sir, ye shall not do so,' said King Pelles, 'by my counsel, for it is hard and ye escape without a shame.'

'I shall take the adventure that will befall me,' said Sir Bors.

'Then I counsel you,' said the king, 'to be clean confessed.'

'As for that,' said Sir Bors, 'I will be shriven with a good will.'

So Sir Bors was confessed. And for all women Sir Bors was a virgin, save for one, that was the daughter of King Brandegoris, and on her he gat a child that hight Elaine. And save for her Sir Bors was a clean maiden.

And so Sir Bors was led unto bed in a fair large chamber, and many doors were shut about the chamber. When Sir Bors espied all those doors, he avoided all the people, for he might have nobody with him; but in no wise Sir Bors would unarm him, but so he laid him down upon the bed.

And right so he saw a light come that he might well see a spear great and long that came straight upon him pointling, and to Sir Bors seemed that the head of the spear burnt like a taper. And anon, or Sir Bors wist, the spear head smote him into the shoulder an handbreath in deepness, and that wound grieved Sir Bors passing sore.

And then he laid him down again for pain. . . . And then he heard and felt much noise in that chamber, and then Sir Bors espied that there came in, he wist not whether at doors or at windows, shot of arrows and of quarrels so thick that he marvelled, and many fell upon him and hurt him in the bare places.

quarrels: *short arrows*

And then Sir Bors was ware where came in an hideous lion. So Sir Bors dressed him unto the lion, and anon the lion bereft him his shield, and with his sword Sir Bors smote off the lion's head.

Right so Sir Bors forthwithal saw a dragon in the court passing perilous and horrible, and there seemed to him that there were letters of gold written in his forehead; and Sir Bors thought that the letters made a signification of 'King Arthur'.

Right so there came an horrible leopard and an old, and there they fought long, and did great battle together. And at the last the dragon spit out of his mouth as it had been an hundred dragons; and lightly all the small dragons slew the old dragon and tare him all to pieces.

Anon withal there came an old man into the hall, and he sat him down in a fair chair, and there seemed to be two adders about his neck. And then the old man had an harp, and there he sang an old song how Joseph of Arimathea came into this land. And when he had sungen, this old man bad Sir Bors to go from thence.

'For here shall ye have no more adventures; yet full worshipfully have ye achieved this, and better shall ye do hereafter.'

And then Sir Bors seemed that there came the whitest dove that ever he saw, with a little golden censer in her mouth. And anon therewithal the tempest ceased and passed away, that afore was marvellous to hear. So was all that court full of good savours.

Then Sir Bors saw four children bearing four fair tapers, and an old man in the midst of these children with a censer in his one hand, and a spear in his other hand, and that spear was called the spear of vengeance.

'Now,' said that old man to Sir Bors, 'go ye to your cousin, Sir Lancelot, and tell him of this adventure the which had been most convenient for him of all earthly knights; but sin is so foul in him he may not achieve such holy deeds, for had not been his sin he had passed all the knights that ever were in his days. And tell thou Sir Lancelot, of all worldly adventures he passeth in manhood and prowess all other, but in these spiritual matters he shall have many his better.'

And then Sir Bors saw four gentlewomen come by him, poorly beseen; and he saw where that they entered into a chamber where was great light as it were a summer light; and the women kneeled down before an altar of silver with four pillars, and as it had been a bishop kneeled down afore that table of silver. And as Sir Bors looked over his head he saw a sword like silver, naked, hoving over his head, and the clearness thereof smote so in his eyen that as at that time Sir Bors was blind. And there he heard a voice which said,

'Go hence, thou Sir Bors, for as yet thou art not worthy for to be in this place.'

And then he yede backward to his bed till on the morn.

And on the morn King Pelles made great joy of Sir Bors; and then he departed and rode to Camelot, and there he found Sir Lancelot du Lake, and told him of the adventures that he had seen with King Pelles at Corbin.

And so the noise sprang in Arthur's court that Lancelot had gotten a child upon Elaine, the daughter of King Pelles, wherefore Queen Guenever was wroth, and she gave many rebukes to Sir Lancelot, and called him false knight. And then Sir Lancelot told the queen all, and how he was made to lie by her by enchantment in likeness of the queen. So the queen held Sir Lancelot excused.

And as the book saith, King Arthur had been in France, and had made war upon the mighty King Claudas, and had won much of his lands. And when the king was come again he let cry a great feast, that all lords and ladies of all England should be there, but if it were such as were rebellious against him.

And when Dame Elaine, the daughter of King Pelles, heard of this feast, she went to her father and requested him that he would give her leave to ride to that feast.

The king answered and said, 'I will that ye go thither. But in any

Lancelot and Elaine

wise, as ye love me and will have my blessing, look that ye be well beseen in the most richest wise; and look that ye spare not for no cost. Ask and ye shall have all that you needeth.'

Then by the advice of Dame Brisen, her maiden, all thing was apparelled unto the purpose, that there was never no lady richlier beseen. So she rode with twenty knights and ten ladies and gentle-women, to the number of an hundred horses. And when she came to Camelot, King Arthur and Queen Guenever said, with all the knights, that Dame Elaine was the fairest and the best beseen lady that ever was seen in that court.

And anon as King Arthur wist that she was come he met her and saluted her, and so did the most part of all the knights of the Round Table, both Sir Tristram, Sir Bleoberis, and Sir Gawain, and many more that I will not rehearse.

But when Sir Lancelot saw her he was so ashamed, and that because he drew his sword on the morn after that he had lain by her, that he would not salute her nor speak with her. And yet Sir Lancelot thought she was the fairest woman that ever he saw in his life days.

But when Dame Elaine saw Sir Lancelot that would not speak unto her she was so heavy that she weened her heart would have to-brast, for wit you well, out of measure she loved him.

And then Elaine said unto her woman, Dame Brisen, 'The unkindness of Sir Lancelot slayeth my heart near.'

'Ah, peace, madam,' said Dame Brisen, 'I shall undertake that this night shall he lie with you, and he will hold you still.'

'That were me lever,' said Dame Elaine, 'than all the gold that is above earth.'

'Let me deal,' said Dame Brisen.

So when Dame Elaine was brought unto Queen Guenever either made other good cheer as by countenance, but nothing with their hearts. But all men and women spake of the beauty of Dame Elaine, and of her great riches.

Then at night the queen commanded that Dame Elaine should sleep in a chamber nigh her chamber, and all under one roof; and so it was done as the queen commanded. Then the queen sent for Sir Lancelot and bad him come to her chamber that night:

'Or else I am sure,' said the queen, 'that ye will go to your lady's bed, Dame Elaine, by whom ye gat Galahad.'

'Ah, madam,' said Sir Lancelot, 'never say ye so, for that I did was against my will.'

'Then,' said the queen, 'look that ye come to me when I send for you.'

'Madam' said Sir Lancelot, 'I shall not fail you, but I shall be ready at your commandment.'

So this bargain was not so soon done and made between them,

but Dame Brisen knew it by her crafts, and told it to her lady, Dame Elaine.

'Alas,' said she, 'how shall I do?'

'Let me deal,' said Dame Brisen, 'for I shall bring him by the hand even to your bed, and he shall ween that I am Queen Guenever's messenger.'

'Then well were me,' said Dame Elaine, 'for all the world I love not so much as I do Sir Lancelot.'

So when time came that all folks were abed, Dame Brisen came to Sir Lancelot's bed's side and said,

'Sir Lancelot du Lake, sleep you? My lady, Queen Guenever, lieth and awaiteth upon you.'

'O my fair lady,' said Sir Lancelot, 'I am ready to go with you whither ye will have me.'

So Sir Lancelot threw upon him a long gown, and so he took his sword in his hand; and then Dame Brisen took him by the finger and led him to her lady's bed, Dame Elaine; and then she departed and left them there in bed together. And wit ye well the lady was glad, and so was Sir Lancelot, for he weened that he had had another in his arms.

Now leave we them kissing and clipping, as was a kindly thing; and now we speak of Queen Guenever that sent one of her women that she most trusted unto Sir Lancelot's bed. And when she came there she found the bed cold, and he was not therein; and so she came to the queen and told her all.

'Alas,' said the queen, 'where is that false knight become?'

So the queen was nigh out of her wit, and then she writhed and weltered as a mad woman, and might not sleep a four or five hours. Then Sir Lancelot had a condition, that he used of custom to clatter in his sleep, and to speak often of his lady, Queen Guenever. So as Sir Lancelot had awaked as long as it had pleased him, then by course of kind he slept, and Dame Elaine both. And in his sleep he talked and clattered as a jay, of the love that had been betwixt Queen Guenever and him. And so as he talked so loud the queen heard him there as she lay in her chamber; and when she heard him so clatter she was nigh wood and out of her mind, and for anger and pain wist not what to do. And then she coughed so loud that Sir Lancelot awaked, and he knew her heming. And then he knew well that he lay not by the queen; and therewith he leapt out of his bed as he had been a wood man, in his shirt, and the queen met him in the floor; and thus she said:

'Ah, false traitor knight that thou art. Look thou never abide in my court, and lightly that thou avoid my chamber, and not so hardy, thou false traitor knight, that ever more thou come in my sight!'

'Alas,' said Sir Lancelot.

wood: *mad*

heming: *coughing*

And therewith he took such an heartly sorrow at her words that he fell down to the floor in a swoon. And therewithal Queen Guenever departed.

And when Sir Lancelot awoke of his swoon, he leapt out at a bay window into a garden, and there with thorns he was all to-scratched in his visage and his body; and so he ran forth he knew not whither, and was as wild wood as ever was man. And so he ran two year, and never man might have grace to know him.

Now turn we unto Queen Guenever and to the fair Lady Elaine, that when Dame Elaine heard the queen so rebuke Sir Lancelot, and also she saw how he swooned, and how he leapt out at a bay window, then she said unto Queen Guenever,

'Madam, ye are greatly to blame for Sir Lancelot, for now have ye lost him, for I saw and heard by his countenance that he is mad for ever. And therefore, alas, madam, ye have done great sin, and to yourself great dishonour, for ye have a lord royal of your own, and therefore it were your part to love him; for there is no queen in this world hath such another king as ye have. And if ye were not I might have got the love of my lord Sir Lancelot; and a great cause I have to love him, for he had my maidenhood, and by him I have borne a fair son, and his name is Galahad. And he shall be in his time the best knight of the world.'

'Well, Dame Elaine,' said the queen, 'as soon as it is daylight I charge you and command you to avoid my court. And for the love ye owe unto Sir Lancelot discover not his counsel, for and ye do, it will be his death.'

'As for that,' said Dame Elaine, 'I dare undertake he is marred for ever, and that have you made. For neither ye nor I are like to rejoice him, for he made the most piteous groans when he leapt out at yonder bay window that ever I heard man make. Alas,' said fair Elaine, and 'Alas,' said the Queen Guenever, 'for now I wot well that we have lost him for ever.'

So on the morn Dame Elaine took her leave to depart, and would no longer abide. Then King Arthur brought her on her way with more than an hundred knights through a forest. And

RIGHT *Guenever banishes Lancelot*

FAR RIGHT *Lancelot's companions discuss his disappearance*

by the way she told Sir Bors de Ganis all how it betid that same night, and how Sir Lancelot leapt out at a window araged out of his wit.

araged: *enraged*

'Alas,' said Sir Bors, 'Where is my lord, Sir Lancelot, become?'

'Sir,' said Elaine, 'I wot nere.'

'Now alas,' said Sir Bors, 'betwixt you both ye have destroyed that good knight.'

'As for me sir,' said Dame Elaine, 'I said never nor did never thing that should in any wise displease him. But with the rebuke that Queen Guenever gave him I saw him swoon to the earth; and when he awoke he took his sword in his hand, naked save his shirt, and leapt out at a window with the grisliest groan that ever I heard man make.'

'Now farewell, Dame Elaine,' said Sir Bors, 'and hold my lord Arthur with a tale as long as ye can, for I will turn again to Queen Guenever and give her an hete. And I require you, as ever ye will have my service, make good watch and espy if ever ye may see my lord Sir Lancelot.'

hete: *reproach*

'Truly,' said fair Elaine, 'I shall do all that I may do, for as fain would I know and wit where he is become as you, or any of his kin, or Queen Guenever; and cause great enough have I thereto as well as any other. And wit ye well,' said fair Elaine to Sir Bors, 'I would lose my life for him rather than he should be hurt; but alas, I cast me never for to see him, and the chief causer of this is Dame Guenever.'

'Madam,' said Dame Brisen, the which had made the enchantment before betwixt Sir Lancelot and her, 'I pray you heartily, let Sir Bors depart, and hie him with all his might as fast as he may to seek Sir Lancelot, for I warn you he is clean out of his mind; and yet he shall be well holpen and but by miracle.'

Then wept Dame Elaine, and so did Sir Bors de Ganis; and anon they departed. And Sir Bors rode straight unto Queen Guenever. And when she saw Sir Bors she wept as she were wood.

'Now, fie on your weeping,' said Sir Bors de Ganis, 'for ye weep never but when there is no boot. Alas,' said Sir Bors, 'that ever Sir

FAR LEFT *Guenever mourns thinking Lancelot is dead*
LEFT *Lancelot's companions search for him*

Lancelot or any of his blood saw you, for now have ye lost the best knight of our blood, and he that was all our leader and our succour. And I dare say and make it good that all kings, Christian nor heathen, may not find such a knight, for to speak of his nobleness and courtesy, with his beauty and his gentleness. Alas,' said Sir Bors, 'what shall we do that be of his blood?'

'Alas,' said Sir Ector de Maris, and 'Alas,' said Sir Lionel.

And when the queen heard them say so she fell to the earth in a dead swoon. And then Sir Bors took her up, and dawed her; and when she was awaked she kneeled afore those three knights, and held up both her hands, and besought them to seek him. 'And spare not for no goods but that he be founden, for I wot he is out of his mind.'

And Sir Bors, Sir Ector, and Sir Lionel departed from the queen, for they might not abide no longer for sorrow. And then the queen sent them treasure enough for their expenses, and so they took their horses and their armour, and departed. And then they rode from country to country, in forests, and in wilderness, and in wastes; and ever they laid watch both at forests and at all manner of men as they rode, to hearken and spere after him, as he that was a naked man, in his shirt, with a sword in his hand.

And thus they rode nigh a quarter of a year, endlong and overthwart, in many places, forests and wilderness, and oft-times were evil lodged for his sake; and yet for all their labour and seeking could they never hear word of him. And wit you well these three knights were passing sorry.

And now ... speak we of Sir Lancelot that suffered and endured many sharp showers, that ever ran wild wood from place to place, and lived by fruit and such as he might get, and drank water two year; and other clothing had he but little but his shirt and his breeches.

And thus as Sir Lancelot wandered here and there, he came in a fair meadow where he found a pavilion. And thereby upon a tree hung a white shield, and two swords hung thereby, and two spears leaned there by a tree. And when Sir Lancelot saw the swords, anon he leapt to the one sword, and clutched that sword in his hand, and drew it out. And then he lashed at the shield, that all the meadow rang of the dints, that he gave such a noise as ten knights had fought together.

Then came forth a dwarf, and leapt unto Sir Lancelot, and would have had the sword out of his hand. And then Sir Lancelot took him by the both shoulders and threw him to the ground that he fell upon his neck and had nigh broken it. And therewithal the dwarf cried help.

dawed: revived

spere: ask

Then came forth a likely knight, and well apparelled in scarlet furred with minever. And anon as he saw Sir Lancelot he deemed that he should be out of his wit.

And then he said with fair speech, 'Good man, lay down that sword, for as meseemeth thou hadst more need of a sleep and of warm clothes than to wield that sword.'

'As for that,' said Sir Lancelot, 'come not too nigh, for and thou do, wit thou well I will slay thee.'

And when the knight of the pavilion saw that, he start backward into his pavilion. And then the dwarf armed him lightly; and so the knight thought by force and might to have taken the sword from Sir Lancelot. And so he came stepping upon him; and when Sir Lancelot saw him come so all armed with his sword in his hand, then Sir Lancelot flew to him with such a might, and hit him upon the helm such a buffet, that the stroke troubled his brains, and therewith the sword brake in three. And the knight fell to the earth and seemed as he had been dead, the blood brasting out of his mouth, nose, and ears.

Lancelot arrives at the pavilion and draws out the sword

And then Sir Lancelot ran into the pavilion, and rashed even into the warm bed; and there was a lady that lay in that bed, and anon she gat her smock, and ran out of the pavilion. And when she saw her lord lie at the ground like to be dead, then she cried and wept as she had been mad. And so with her noise the knight awaked out of his swoon, and looked up weakly with his eyen. And then he asked her, where was that mad man that had given him such a buffet, 'For such a buffet had I never of man's hand.'

'Sir,' said the dwarf, 'it is not your worship to hurt him, for he is a man out of his wit; and doubt ye not he hath been a man of great worship, and for some heartly sorrow that he hath taken, he is fallen mad; and me, beseemeth,' said the dwarf, 'he resembleth much unto Sir Lancelot, for him I saw at the great tournament beside Lonazep.'

'Jesus defend,' said that knight, 'that ever that noble knight, Sir Lancelot, should be in such a plight; but whatsomever he be,' said that knight, 'harm will I none do him.' And this knight's name was Bliant.

Then he said unto the dwarf, 'Go thou fast on horseback, unto my brother, Sir Selivant, that is in the Castle Blank, and tell him of mine adventure, and bid him bring with him an horse litter, and then will we bear this knight unto my castle.'

So the dwarf rode fast, and he came again and brought Sir Selivant with him, and six men with an horse litter. And so they took up the feather bed with Sir Lancelot, and so carried all away with them unto the Castle Blank, and he never awaked till he was within the castle. And then they bound his hands and his feet, and gave him good meats and good drinks, and brought him again to his strength and his fairness. But in his wit they could not bring him again, nor to know himself. And thus was Sir Lancelot there more than a year and a half, honestly arrayed and fair faren withal.

And then upon a day Sir Lancelot ran his way into the forest; and by adventure he came to the city of Corbin, where Dame Elaine was, that bare Galahad, Sir Lancelot's son. And so when he entered into the town he ran through the town to the castle; and then all the young men of that city ran after Sir Lancelot, and there they threw turves at him, and gave him many sad strokes. And ever as Sir Lancelot might reach any of them, he threw them so that they would never come in his hands no more; for of some he brake the legs and the arms, and so he fled into the castle; and then came out knights and squires and rescued Sir Lancelot.

And when they beheld them and looked upon his person, they thought they saw never so goodly a man. And when they saw so many wounds upon him, they deemed that he had been a man of worship. And then they ordained him clothes to his body, and straw underneath him, and a little house. And so every day they would throw him meat, and set him drink, but there was but few would bring him meat to his hands.

So it befell that King Pelles had a nephew, his name was Castor; and so he desired of the king to be made knight, and at his own request the king made him knight at the feast of Candlemas. And when Sir Castor was made knight, that same day he gave many gowns. And then Sir Castor sent for the fool – that was Sir Lance-lot. And when he was come afore Sir Castor, he gave Sir Lancelot a robe of scarlet and all that longed unto him. And when Sir Lancelot was arrayed like a knight, he was the seemliest man in all the court, and none so well made.

So when he saw his time he went into the garden, and there Sir Lancelot laid him down by a well and slept. And so at after noon Dame Elaine and her maidens came into the garden to sport them; and as they roamed up and down one of Dame Elaine's maidens espied where lay a goodly man by the well sleeping, and anon showed him to Dame Elaine.

'Peace,' said Dame Elaine, 'and say no word, but show me that man, where he lieth.'

And then she brought Dame Elaine where he lay. And when that she beheld him, anon she fell in remembrance of him, and knew him verily for Sir Lancelot; and therewithal she fell on weep-ing so heartily that she sank even to the earth; and when she had thus wept a great while, then she arose and called her maidens and said she was sick.

Lancelot is discovered asleep

And so she yede out of the garden, and she went straight to her father, and there she took him apart by herself; and then she said,

'O my dear father, now have I need of your help, and but if that ye help me now farewell my good days for ever.'

'What is that, daughter?' said King Pelles.

'Sir,' she said, 'thus it is: in your garden I went for to sport me, and there by the well I found Sir Lancelot du Lake sleeping.'

'I may not believe it,' said King Pelles.

'Sir,' she said, 'truly he is there, and meseemeth he should be distract out of his wit.'

'Then hold you still,' said the king, 'and let me deal.'

Then the king called to him such as he most trusted, a four persons, and Dame Elaine, his daughter, and Dame Brisen, her servant. And when they came to the well and beheld Sir Lancelot, anon Dame Brisen knew him.

'Sir,' said Dame Brisen, 'we must be wise how we deal with him, for this knight is out of his mind, and if we awake him rudely what he will do we all know not. And therefore abide ye a while, and I shall throw such an enchantment upon him that he shall not awake within the space of an hour.' And so she did.

Then within a little while after, the king commanded that all people should avoid that none should be in that way there as the king would come. And so when this was done, these four men and these ladies laid hand on Sir Lancelot, and so they bare him into a tower, and so unto a chamber where was the holy vessel of the Sangrail, and before that holy vessel Sir Lancelot was laid. And there came an holy man and unhilled that vessel, and so by miracle and by virtue of that holy vessel Sir Lancelot was healed and recovered.

And as soon as he was awaked he groaned and sighed, and complained him sore of his woodness and strokes that he had had.   woodness: *madness*

And as soon as Sir Lancelot saw King Pelles and Dame Elaine, he waxed ashamed and said thus:

'O Lord Jesu, how I came hither? For God's sake, my lord, let me wit how I came hither.'

'Sir,' said Dame Elaine, 'into this country ye came like a madman, clean out of your wit. And here have ye been kept as a fool; and no creature here knew what ye were, until by fortune a maiden of mine brought me unto you whereas ye lay sleeping by a well. And anon as I verily beheld you I knew you. Then I told my father, and so were ye brought afore this holy vessel, and by the virtue of it thus were ye healed.'

'O Jesu, mercy,' said Sir Lancelot; 'if this be sooth, how many there be that knowen of my woodness?'

Lancelot and Elaine

'So God me help,' said Elaine, 'no more but my father, and I, and Dame Brisen.'

'Now for Christ's love,' said Sir Lancelot, 'keep it in counsel, and let no man know it in the world, for I am sore ashamed that I have been thus misfortuned; for I am banished out of the country of Logris forever.' That is for to say, the country of England.

And so Sir Lancelot lay more than a fortnight or ever that he might stir for soreness. And then upon a day he said unto Dame Elaine these words:

'Fair Lady Elaine, for your sake I have had much travail, care, and anguish, it needeth not to rehearse it, ye know how. Notwith-standing I know well I have done foul to you when that I drew my sword to you, to have slain you, upon the morn after when I had lain with you. And all was for the cause that ye and Dame Brisen made me for to lie by you maugre mine head; and as ye say, that night Galahad your son was begotten.'

Physicians declare Lancelot cured

'That is truth,' said Dame Elaine.

'Now will ye for my sake,' said Sir Lancelot, 'go unto your father and get me a place of him wherein I may dwell? For in the court of King Arthur may I never come.'

'Sir,' said Dame Elaine, 'I will live and die with you, and only for your sake; and if my life might not avail you and my death might avail you, wit you well I would die for your sake. And I will go to my father, and I am right sure there is nothing that I can desire of him but I shall have it. And where ye be, my lord Sir Lancelot, doubt ye not but I will be with you with all the service that I may do.'

So forthwithal she went to her father and said,

'Sir, my lord, Sir Lancelot, desireth to be here by you in some castle of yours.'

'Well daughter,' said the king, 'sith it is his desire to abide in these marches he shall be in the Castle of Bliant, and there shall ye be with him, and twenty of the fairest young ladies that be in this country, and they shall all be of the greatest blood in this country, and ye shall have twenty knights with you. For, daughter, I will that ye wit we all be honoured by the blood of Sir Lancelot.'

Then went Dame Elaine unto Sir Lancelot, and told him all how her father had devised for him and her. Then came the knight Sir Castor, that was nephew unto King Pelles, unto Sir Lancelot, and asked him what was his name.

'Sir,' said Sir Lancelot, 'my name is Le Chevaler Mal Fet, that is to say "the knight that hath trespassed".'

'Sir,' said Sir Castor, 'it may well be so, but ever meseemeth your name should be Sir Lancelot du Lake, for or now I have seen you.'

'Sir,' said Sir Lancelot, 'ye are not as a gentle knight: for I put a case that my name were Sir Lancelot, and that it list me not to discover my name, what should it grieve you here to keep my counsel, and ye not hurt thereby? But wit you well, an ever it lie in my power I shall grieve you, and ever I meet with you in my way.'

Then Sir Castor kneeled down and besought Sir Lancelot of mercy: 'For I shall never utter what ye be while that ye are in these parts.'

Then Sir Lancelot pardoned him.

And then after this King Pelles with twenty knights, and Dame Elaine with her twenty ladies, rode unto the Castle of Bliant that stood in an island beclosed environ with a fair water deep and large. And when they were there Sir Lancelot let call it the Joyous Isle; and there was he called none otherwise but Le Chevaler Mal Fet, 'the knight that hath trespassed'.

Then Sir Lancelot let make him a shield all of sable, and a queen crowned in the midst, all of silver, and a knight clean armed kneeling afore her. And every day once, for any mirths that all the ladies might make him, he would once every day look toward the realm of Logris, where King Arthur and Queen Guenever was. And then would he fall upon a weeping as his heart should tobrast.

And in the meanwhile came Sir Percival de Gales and Sir Ector de Maris under that castle which was called the Joyous Isle. And as they beheld that gay castle they would have gone to that castle, but they might not for the broad water, and bridge could they find none. Then they saw on the other side a lady with a sparhawk in her hand, and Sir Percival called unto her, and asked that lady who was in that castle.

sparhawk: *sparrowhawk*

'Fair knights,' she said, 'here within this castle is the fairest lady in this land, and her name is Dame Elaine. Also we have in this castle one of the fairest knights and the mightiest man that is, I dare say, living. And he calleth himself Le Chevaler Mel Fet.'

'How came he into these marches?' said Sir Percival.

'Truly,' said the damsel, 'he came into this country like a mad man, with dogs and boys chasing him through the city of Corbin, and by the holy vessel of the Sangrail he was brought into his wit again; but he will not do battle with no knight, but by undern or by noon. And if ye list to come into the castle,' said the lady, 'ye must ride unto the further side of the castle, and there shall ye find a vessel that will bear you and your horse.'

Then they departed, and came unto the vessel.

Then came forth Dame Elaine. And she made them great cheer as might be made; and there she told Sir Ector and Sir Percival how and in what manner Sir Lancelot came into that

153

country, and how he was healed. . . . So it befell on a day that Sir Ector and Sir Percival came to Sir Lancelot and asked of him what he would do, and whether he would go with them unto King Arthur or not.

'Nay,' said Sir Lancelot, 'that may I not do by no mean, for I was so vengeably defended at the court that I cast me never to come there more.'

'Sir,' said Sir Ector, 'I am your brother, and ye are the man in the world that I love most. And if I understood that it were your disworship, ye may understand I would never counsel you there- to. But King Arthur and all his knights, and in especial Queen Guenever, make such dole and sorrow for you that it is marvel to hear and see. And ye must remember the great worship and re- nown that ye be of, how that ye have been more spoken of than any other knight that is now living; for there is none that beareth the name now but ye and Sir Tristram. And therefore, brother,' said Sir Ector, 'make you ready to ride to the court with us. And I dare say there was never knight better welcome to the court than ye; and I wot well, and can make it good,' said Sir Ector, 'it hath cost my lady the queen twenty thousand pound, the seeking of you.'

'Well brother,' said Sir Lancelot, 'I will do after your counsel, and ride with you.'

So then they took their horses and made them ready, and anon took their leave at King Pelles and at Dame Elaine. And when Sir Lancelot should depart Dame Elaine made great sorrow.

'My lord, Sir Lancelot,' said Dame Elaine, 'at this same feast of Pentecost shall your son and mine, Galahad, be made knight, for he is fully now fifteen winter old.'

'Madam, do as ye list,' said Sir Lancelot. 'And God give him grace to prove a good knight.'

'As for that,' said Dame Elaine, 'I doubt not he shall prove the best man of his kin except one.'

'Then shall he be a good man enough,' said Sir Lancelot.

So anon they departed, and within five days' journey they came to Camelot, that is in English called Winchester. And when Sir Lancelot was come among them, the king and all the knights made great joy of his homecoming.

And there Sir Percival de Gales and Sir Ector de Maris began and told the whole adventures: how Sir Lancelot had been out of his mind in the time of his absence, and how he called himself Le Chevaler Mal Fet, 'the knight that had trespassed'.

And ever as Sir Ector and Sir Percival told these tales of Sir Lancelot, Queen Guenever wept as she should have died. Then the queen made him great cheer.

'O Jesu,' said King Arthur, 'I marvel for what cause ye, Sir Lancelot, went out of your mind. For I and many other deem it was for the love of fair Elaine, the daughter of King Pelles, by whom ye are noised that ye have gotten a child, and his name is Galahad. And men say that he shall do many marvellous things.'

'My lord,' said Sir Lancelot, 'if I did any folly I have that I sought.'

And therewithal the king spake no more. But all Sir Lancelot's kinsmen knew for whom he went out of his mind.

And then there were made great feasts and great joy was there among them. And all lords and ladies made great joy when they heard how Sir Lancelot was come again to the court.

And here followeth the noble tale of the Sangrail, which called is the holy vessel; and the signification of the blessed blood of Our Lord Jesu Christ, which was brought into this land by Joseph of Arimathea. Therefore on all sinful, blessed Lord, have on thy knight mercy. Amen.

Sauls sire dieux qui de cest
saint vaisset que se toy cy
venir aues fait tant de
miracles en cest pays ete n
autres. Pere regarde moy
en telle maniere q le mal

BOOK 11

The Grail

t the vigil of Pentecost, when all the fellowship of the Round Table were comen unto Camelot and there heard their service, and the tables were set ready to the meat, right so entered into the hall a full fair gentlewoman on horseback, that had ridden full fast, for her horse was all besweat.

Then she there alit, and came before the king and saluted him; and he said, 'Damsel, God thee bless.'

'Sir,' said she, 'for God's sake say me where is Sir Lancelot.'

'He is yonder, ye may see him,' said the king.

Then she went unto Sir Lancelot and said,

'Sir Lancelot, I salute you on King Pelles' behalf, and I also require you come on with me hereby into a forest.'

Then Sir Lancelot asked her with whom she dwelled.

'I dwell,' said she, 'with King Pelles.'

'What will ye with me?' said Sir Lancelot.

'Ye shall know,' said she, 'when ye come thither.'

'Well,' said he, 'I will gladly go with you.'

So Sir Lancelot bad his squire saddle his horse and bring his arms; and in all haste he did his commandment.

Then came the queen unto Sir Lancelot, and said,

'Will ye leave us now alone at this high feast?'

'Madam,' said the gentlewoman, 'wit ye well he shall be with you tomorn by dinner time.'

'If I wist,' said the queen, 'that he should not be here with us tomorn he should not go with you by my good will.'

Right so departed Sir Lancelot with the gentlewoman, and rode until that he came into a forest and into a great valley, where they saw an abbey of nuns. And there was a squire ready, and opened the gates, and so they entered and descended off their horses. And there came a fair fellowship about Sir Lancelot, and welcomed him, and were passing glad of his coming.

And then they led him into the abbess's chamber and unarmed

OPPOSITE
Percival and Galahad
with the Holy Grail

157

him; and right so he was ware upon a bed lying two of his cousins, Sir Bors and Sir Lionel, and then he waked them; and when they saw him they made great joy.

'Sir,' said Sir Bors unto Sir Lancelot, 'what adventure hath brought you hither, for we weened to have found you tomorn at Camelot?'

'As God me help,' said Sir Lancelot, 'a gentlewoman brought me hither, but I know not the cause.'

In the meanwhile that they thus stood talking together, there came in twelve nuns that brought with them Galahad, the which was passing fair and well made, that unnethe in the world men might not find his match. And all those ladies wept.

'Sir,' said they all, 'we bring you here this child the which we have nourished, and we pray you to make him a knight, for of a more worthier man's hand may he not receive the order of knight-hood.'

Sir Lancelot beheld the young squire and saw him seemly and demure as a dove, with all manner of good features, that he weened of his age never to have seen so fair a form of man.

Then said Sir Lancelot, 'Cometh this desire of himself?'

He and all they said 'Yes'.

'Then shall he,' said Sir Lancelot, 'receive the high order of knighthood as tomorn at the reverence of the high feast.'

That night Sir Lancelot had passing good cheer; and on the morn at the hour of prime, at Galahad's desire, he made him knight and said,

'God make you a good man, for of beauty faileth you none as any that is now living.'

'Now fair sir,' said Sir Lancelot, 'will ye come with me unto the court of King Arthur?'

'Nay,' said he, 'I will not go with you as at this time.'

Then he departed from them and took his two cousins with him, and so they came unto Camelot by the hour of undern on Whitsunday. By that time the king and the queen were gone to the minster to hear their service. Then the king and the queen were passing glad of Sir Bors and Sir Lionel, and so was all the fellow-ship.

So when the king and all the knights were come from service, the barons espied in the sieges of the Round Table all about, written with golden letters: HERE OUGHT TO SIT HE, and: HE OUGHT TO SIT HERE.

And thus they went so long till that they came to the Siege Perilous, where they found letters newly written of gold which said: FOUR HUNDRED WINTERS AND FOUR-AND-FIFTY ACCOMPLISHED AFTER THE PASSION OF OUR LORD JESU CHRIST OUGHT THIS SIEGE TO BE FULFILLED.

Then all they said, 'This is a marvellous thing and an adventurous.'

'In the name of God,' said Sir Lancelot; and then accounted the
term of the writing from the birth of Our Lord until that day. 'It
seemeth me,' said Sir Lancelot, 'that this siege ought to be fulfilled
this same day, for this is the feast of Pentecost after the four hundred
and four-and-fifty year; and if it would please all parties, I would
none of these letters were seen this day, till he be come that ought to
achieve this adventure.'

Then made they to ordain a cloth of silk, for to cover these
letters in the Siege Perilous. Then the king bad haste unto dinner.

'Sir,' said Sir Kay the Steward, 'if ye go now to your meat ye
shall break your old custom of your court, for ye have not used on
this day to sit at your meat or that ye have seen some adventure.'

'Ye say sooth,' said the king, 'but I had so great joy of Sir
Lancelot and of his cousins, which be come to the court whole and
sound, that I bethought me not of none old custom.'

So, as they stood speaking, in came a squire and said unto the
king, 'Sir, I bring unto you marvellous tidings.'

'What be they?' said the king.

'Sir, there is here beneath at the river a great stone which I saw
float above the water, and therein I saw sticking a sword.'

The king said, 'I will see that marvel.'

So all the knights went with him, and when they came unto the
river they found there a stone floating, as it were of red marble, and
therein stuck a fair rich sword, and the pommel thereof was of
precious stones wrought with letters of gold subtly. Then the
barons read the letters which said in this wise: NEVER SHALL
MAN TAKE ME HENCE, BUT ONLY HE BY WHOSE SIDE I
OUGHT TO HANG, AND HE SHALL BE THE BEST KNIGHT
OF THE WORLD.

So when the king had seen the letters, he said unto Sir Lancelot,
'Fair sir, this sword ought to be yours, for I am sure ye be the best
knight of the world.'

Then Sir Lancelot answered full soberly,

'Certes sir, it is not my sword; also, sir, wit ye well I have no
hardiness to set my hand thereto, for it longeth not to hang by my
side. Also, who that assayeth to take the sword and faileth of it, he
shall receive a wound by that sword that he shall not be whole
long after. And I will that ye wit that this same day shall the
adventure of the Sangrail begin, that is called the holy vessel.'

'Now, fair nephew,' said the king unto Sir Gawain, 'assay ye,
for my love.'

'Sir,' he said, 'save your good grace, I shall not do that.'

'Sir,' said the king, 'assay to take the sword for my love and at my
commandment.'

'Sir,' said Gawain, 'your commandment I will obey.'

And therewith he took the sword by the handles, but he might not stir it.

'I thank you,' said the king to Sir Gawain.

'My lord Sir Gawain,' said Sir Lancelot, 'now wit ye well this sword shall touch you so sore that ye would not ye had set your hand thereto for the best castle of this realm.'

'Sir,' he said, 'I might not withstay mine uncle's will and commandment.'

But when the king heard this he repented it much, and said unto Sir Percival that he should assay, for his love.

And he assayed gladly, for to bear Sir Gawain fellowship.

And therewith he set his hand on the sword and drew at it strongly, but he might not move it. Then were there no more that durst be so hardy to set their hands thereto.

'Now may ye go to your dinner,' said Sir Kay unto the king, 'for a marvellous adventure have ye seen.'

So the king and all went unto the court, and every knight knew his own place, and set him therein. And young men that were good knights served them.

So when they were served, and all sieges fulfilled save only the Siege Perilous, anon there befell a marvellous adventure, that all the doors and windows of the palace shut by themself. Notforthan the hall was not greatly darked; and therewith they abashed both one and other.

notforthan: nevertheless

Then King Arthur spake first and said,

'By God, fair fellows and lords, we have seen this day marvels. But or night I suppose we shall see greater marvels.'

In the meanwhile came in a good old man, and an ancient, clothed all in white, and there was no knight knew from whence he came. And with him he brought a young knight, and both on foot, in red arms, without sword or shield, save a scabbard hanging by his side. And these words he said:

'Peace be with you, fair lords.'

Then the old man said unto King Arthur, 'Sir, I bring you here a young knight, the which is of kings' lineage, and of the kindred of Joseph of Arimathea, whereby the marvels of this court, and of strange realms, shall be fully accomplished.'

The king was right glad of his words, and said unto the good man,

'Sir, ye be right welcome, and the young knight with you.'

Then the old man made the young man to unarm him. And he was in a coat of red sendal, and bare a mantle upon his shoulder that was furred with ermine, and put that upon him. And the old knight said unto the young knight,

sendal: rich cloth

'Sir, followeth me.'

And anon he led him unto the Siege Perilous, where beside sat Sir Lancelot; and the good man lift up the cloth, and found there letters that said thus:

THIS IS THE SIEGE OF SIR GALAHAD, THE HAUT PRINCE.

'Sir,' said the old knight, 'wit you well that place is yours.'

And then he set him down surely in that siege. And then he said to the old man,

'Sir, ye may now go on your way, for well have ye done that ye were commanded to do; and recommend me unto my grandsire, King Pelles, and unto my lord King Pecchere, and say them on my behalf, I shall come and see them as soon as ever I may.'

So the good man departed; and there met him twenty noble squires, and so took their horses and went their way.

Then all the knights of the Table Round marvelled greatly of Sir Galahad, that he durst sit there in that Siege Perilous, and was so tender of age; and wist not from whence he came but all only by God. All they said,

'This is he by whom the Sangrail shall be achieved, for there sat none but he there, but he were mischieved.'

Then Sir Lancelot beheld his son and had great joy of him. Then Bors told his fellows,

'Upon pain of my life this young knight shall come to great worship.'

So this noise was great in all the court, so that it came to the queen. Then she had marvel what knight it might be that durst adventure him to sit in that Siege Perilous. Many said unto the queen he resembled much unto Sir Lancelot.

'I may well suppose,' said the queen, 'that Sir Lancelot begat him on King Pelles' daughter, by the which he was made to lie by, by enchantment, and his name is Galahad. I would fain see him,' said the queen, 'for he must needs be a noble man, for so is his father that him begat, I report me unto all the Table Round.'

So when the meat was done, that the king and all were risen, the king yede to the Siege Perilous and lift up the cloth, and found there the name of Sir Galahad; and then he showed it unto Sir Gawain, and said,

'Fair nephew, now have we among us Sir Galahad, the good knight that shall worship us all. And upon pain of my life he shall achieve the Sangrail, right as Sir Lancelot had done us to under-stand.'

Then came King Arthur unto Sir Galahad and said,

'Sir, ye be right welcome, for ye shall move many good knights to the quest of the Sangrail, and ye shall achieve that many other knights might never bring to an end.'

Then the king took him by the hand, and went down from the palace to show Galahad the adventures of the stone.

The queen heard thereof, and came after with many ladies, and they showed her the stone where it hoved on the water.

'Sir,' said the king unto Sir Galahad, 'here is a great marvel as ever I saw, and right good knights have assayed and failed.'

'Sir,' said Sir Galahad, 'it is no marvel, for this adventure is not theirs but mine. And for the surety of this sword I brought none with me, for here by my side hangeth the scabbard.'

And anon he laid his hand on the sword, and lightly drew it out of the stone, and put it in the sheath, and said unto the king, 'Now it goeth better than it did aforehand.'

'Sir,' said the king, 'a shield God may send you.'

So therewith the king and all espied where came riding down the river a lady on a white palfrey a great pace toward them. Then she saluted the king and the queen, and asked if that Sir Lancelot was there.

And then he answered himself, and said, 'I am here, my fair lady.'

Then she said all with weeping, 'Ah, Sir Lancelot, how your great doing is changed sith this day in the morn.'

'Damsel, why say ye so?' said Lancelot.

'Sir, I say you sooth,' said the damsel, 'for ye were this day in the morn the best knight of the world. But who should say so now, he should be a liar, for there is now one better than ye, and well it is proved by the adventure of the sword whereto ye durst not set to your hand; and that is the change of your name and living. Wherefore I make unto you a remembrance, that ye shall not ween from henceforth that ye be the best knight of the world.'

'As touching unto that,' said Sir Lancelot, 'I know well I was never none of the best.'

'Yes,' said the damsel, 'that were ye, and are yet, of any sinful man of the world. And sir king, Nacien, the hermit, sendeth thee word, that thee shall befall the greatest worship that ever befell king in Britain; and I say you wherefore: for this day the Sangrail appeared in thy house and fed thee and all thy fellowship of the Round Table.'

So she departed and went that same way that she came.

'Now,' said the king, 'I am sure at this quest of the Sangrail shall all ye of the Round Table depart, and never shall I see you again wholly together; therefore once shall I see you all whole together in the meadow of Camelot, to joust and to tourney, that after your death men may speak of it that such good knights were here such a day wholly together.'

OPPOSITE ABOVE
*Lancelot approaches
a lady in bed*

OPPOSITE BELOW
*Lancelot travels with
Elaine and Galahad*

OVERLEAF LEFT
ABOVE
*Lancelot is given
directions by an
old woman*

OVERLEAF LEFT
BELOW
*A lady and her squire
asking for news
of Lancelot after
his disappearance*

OVERLEAF RIGHT
*Scenes from the life
of Galahad*

Il dit ly comptes
que asa veille de
pentecoste que celle
grant assemblee
fut faicte dedens
kamaaloiht. se la
feussies seigneur

cheualiers asses p
euissies bcoir hon
neur et prie et
cheualerie et haul
teste et gloire de
tous biens. Carbie
sachies que acelle

En ceste ystoire dñt auous paint et pron
de maint vmeil ala riue de la mer et
vne espee fichie dedens que nul ne pot
auoir ostee du pron mais galaad losta
et le chainst

en la forest. Sile metent elgrant
chemin et esterent lamoitie dune
liewe tant quil vindrent enune va

As unto that counsel and at the king's request they accorded all, and took on their harness that longed unto jousting. But all this moving of the king was for this intent, for to see Galahad proved; for the king deemed he should not lightly come again unto the court after this departing. So were they assembled in the meadow, both more and less.

Then Sir Galahad, by the prayer of the king and the queen, did upon him a noble jesseraunce, and also he did on his helm, but shield would he take none for no prayer of the king.

jesseraunce: coat of armour

So then Sir Gawain and other knights prayed him to take a spear. Right so he did. So the queen was in a tower with all her ladies, for to behold that tournament.

Then Sir Galahad dressed him in midst of the meadow, and began to break spears marvellously, that all men had wonder of him; for he there surmounted all other knights. For within a while he had defouled many good knights of the Table Round save all only twain, that was Sir Lancelot and Sir Percival.

Then the king, at the queen's desire, made him to alight and to unlace his helm, that the queen might see him in the visage. When she beheld him she said,

'I dare well say soothly that Sir Lancelot begat him, for never two men resembled more in likeness. Therefore it is no marvel though he be of great prowess.'

So a lady that stood by the queen said,

'Madam, for God's sake ought he of right to be so good a knight?'

'Yea, forsooth,' said the queen, 'for he is of all parties come of the best knights of the world, and of the highest lineage; for Sir Lancelot is come but of the eighth degree from Our Lord Jesu Christ, and this Sir Galahad is of the ninth degree from Our Lord Jesu Christ. Therefore I dare say they be the greatest gentlemen of the world.'

And then the king and all estates went home unto Camelot, and so went to evensong to the great minster. And so after upon that to supper, and every knight sat in his own place as they were tofore-hand.

Then anon they heard cracking and crying of thunder, that them thought the palace should all to-drive. So in the midst of the blast entered a sunbeam more clearer by seven times than ever they saw day, and all they were alighted of the grace of the Holy Ghost. Then began every knight to behold other, and either saw other, by their seeming, fairer than ever they were before. Notforthan there was no knight might speak one word a great while, and so they looked every man on other as they had been dumb.

Then there entered into the hall the Holy Grail covered with

OPPOSITE
Galahad draws the sword from the stone in the river

163

*Arthur and his
knights at table*

forthinketh: *grieves*

white samite, but there was none might see it, nor who that bare it. And there was all the hall fulfilled with good odours, and every knight had such meats and drinks as he best loved in this world. And when the Holy Grail had been borne through the hall, then the holy vessel departed suddenly, that they wist not where it became. Then had they all breath to speak. And then the king yielded thankings to God, of His good grace that he had sent them.

'Certes,' said the king, 'we ought to thank Our Lord Jesu greatly for that he hath showed us this day, at the reverence of this high feast of Pentecost.'

'Now,' said Sir Gawain, 'we have been served this day of what meats and drinks we thought on. But one thing beguiled us, we might not see the Holy Grail, it was so preciously covered. Wherefore I will make here a vow, that tomorn, without longer abiding, I shall labour in the quest of the Sangrail, and that I shall hold me out a twelvemonth and a day, or more if need be, and never shall I return unto the court again, till I have seen it more openly than it hath been showed here. And if I may not speed I shall return again as he that may not be against the will of God.'

So when they of the Table Round heard Sir Gawain say so, they arose up the most part and made such avows as Sir Gawain had made. Anon as King Arthur heard this he was greatly displeased, for he wist well they might not again-say their avows.

'Alas,' said King Arthur unto Sir Gawain, 'ye have nigh slain me with the avow and promise that ye have made. For through you ye have bereft me the fairest fellowship and the truest of knighthood that ever were seen together in any realm of the world. For when they depart from hence I am sure they all shall never meet more together in this world, for they shall die many in the quest. And so it forthinketh me a little, for I have loved them as well as my life. Wherefore it shall grieve me right sore, the departition of this fellowship; for I have had an old custom to have them in my fellowship.'

And therewith the tears fell in his eyen. And then he said,

'Gawain, Gawain, ye have set me in great sorrow, for I have great doubt that my true fellowship shall never meet here more again.'

'Ah, sir,' said Sir Lancelot, 'comfort yourself; for it shall be unto us a great honour, and much more than if we died in any other places, for of death we be siker.'

'Ah, Lancelot,' said the king, 'the great love that I have had unto you all the days of my life maketh me to say such doleful words; for there was never Christian king that ever had never so many worthy men at his table as I have had this day at the Round Table. And that is my great sorrow.'

Arthur in discussion with one of his knights

When the queen, ladies, and gentlewomen knew of these tidings, they had such sorrow and heaviness that there might no tongue tell, for those knights had held them in honour and charity. But above all other Queen Guenever made great sorrow.

'I marvel,' said she, 'that my lord would suffer them to depart from him.'

Thus was all the court troubled for the love of the departing of those knights. And many of those ladies that loved knights would have gone with their lovers; and so had they done, had not an old knight come among them in religious clothing and spake all on high and said:

'Fair lords, which have sworn in the quest of the Sangrail, thus sendeth you Nacien, the hermit, word, that none in this quest lead lady nor gentlewoman with him, for it is not to do in so high a service as they labour in; for I warn you plain, he that is not clean of his sins he shall not see the mysteries of Our Lord Jesus Christ.'

And for this cause they left these ladies and gentlewomen. So after this the queen came unto Sir Galahad and asked him of whence he was, and of what country. Then he told her of whence

he was. And son unto Lancelot, she said he was. As to that, he said neither yea or nay.

'So God me help,' said the queen, 'of your father, ye need not to shame you, for he is the goodliest knight, and of the best men of the world comen, and of the strain, of all parties, of kings. Wherefore ye ought of right to be, of your deeds, a passing good man; and certainly,' she said, 'ye resemble him much.'

Then Sir Galahad was a little ashamed and said,

'Madam, sith ye know in certain, wherefore do ye ask it me? For he that is my father shall be known openly and all betimes.'

And then they went to rest them. And in the honour of the highness of knighthood of Galahad he was led into King Arthur's chamber, and there rested in his own bed.

And as soon as it was day the king arose, for he had no rest of all that night for sorrow. Then he went unto Sir Gawain and to Sir Lancelot that were arisen for to hear mass. And then the king again said,

'Ah Gawain, Gawain, ye have betrayed me; for never shall my court be amended by you. But ye will never be sorry for me as I am for you.' And therewith the tears began to run down by his visage. And therewith the king said,

'Ah, courteous knight, Sir Lancelot, I require you that ye counsel me, for I would that this quest were at an end and it might be.'

'Sir,' said Sir Lancelot, 'ye saw yesterday so many worthy knights there were sworn that they may not leave it in no manner of wise.'

'That wot I well,' said the king, 'but it shall so heavy me at their departing that I wot well there shall no manner of joy remedy me.'

And then the king and the queen went unto the minster.

So anon Sir Lancelot and Sir Gawain commanded their men to bring their arms. And when they all were armed save their shields and their helms, then they came to their fellowship, which were all ready in the same wise, for to go to the minster to hear their service.

Then after the service was done the king would wit how many had undertake the quest of the Holy Grail; and to account them he prayed them all. Then found they by tally an hundred and fifty, and all those were knights of the Round Table. And then they put on their helms and departed, and commended them all wholly unto the king and queen. And there was weeping and great sorrow.

Then the queen departed into her chamber and held her there, that no man should perceive her great sorrows. When Sir Lancelot missed the queen he went till her chamber, and when she saw him she cried aloud and said,

'O Sir Lancelot, Lancelot, ye have betrayed me and put me to the death, for to leave thus my lord.'

OPPOSITE
*Gawain takes his leave
of Arthur and Guenever*

167

The Grail

FAR RIGHT
*Lancelot and his
companions ride out
on the quest*

RIGHT *The knights
hear mass before
setting out*

'Ah, madam, I pray you be not displeased, for I shall come again as soon as I may with my worship.'

'Alas,' said she, 'that ever I saw you. But he that suffered death upon the cross for all mankind, He be unto you good conduct and safety, and all the whole fellowship.'

Right so departed Sir Lancelot, and found his fellowship that abode his coming. And then they took their horses and rode through the street of Camelot. And there was weeping of rich and poor, and the king turned away and might not speak for weeping.

So within a while they rode all together till they came to a city, and a castle that hight Vagon. And so they entered into the castle, and the lord thereof was an old man that hight Vagon, and he was a good man of his living, and set open the gates, and made them all the cheer that he might.

And so on the morn they were all accorded that they should depart every each from other. And on the morn they departed with weeping cheer, and every knight took the way that him liked best.

Galahad

Now rideth Galahad yet withouten shield, and so rode four days without any adventure. And at the fourth day after evensong he came to a white abbey. And there was he received with great rever-ence, and led unto a chamber, and there he was unarmed. And then was he ware of two knights of the Table Round, one was Sir Bagdemagus, and Sir Uwain. And when they saw him they went unto Galahad and made of him great solace, and so they went unto supper.

'Sirs,' said Sir Galahad, 'what adventure brought you hither?'

'Sir,' they said all, 'it is told us that within this place is a shield that no man may bear about his neck but he be mischieved other dead within three days, or maimed for ever.'

'But sir,' said King Bagdemagus, 'I shall bear it tomorn for to assay this adventure.'

'In the name of God,' said Sir Galahad.

'Sir,' said Bagdemagus, 'and I may not achieve the adventure of this shield ye shall take it upon you, for I am sure ye shall not fail.'

'Sir,' said Sir Galahad, 'I right well agree me thereto, for I have no shield.'

So on the morn they arose and heard mass. Then Sir Bagdemagus asked where the adventurous shield was. Anon a monk led him behind an altar where the shield hung as white as any snow, but in the midst was a red cross.

'Sirs,' said the monk, 'this shield ought not to be hanged about the neck of a knight but he be the worthiest knight of the world. Therefore I counsel you knights to be well advised.'

'Well,' said Sir Bagdemagus, 'I wot well I am not the best knight of the world, but I shall assay to bear it,' and so bare it out of the monastery. Then he said unto Sir Galahad, 'And it please you to abide here still, till that ye wit how that I speed.'

'Sir, I shall abide you,' said Sir Galahad.

Then King Bagdemagus took with him a good squire, to bring tidings unto Sir Galahad how he sped. Then they rode two mile and came to a fair valley before an hermitage, and then they saw a knight come from that part in white armour, horse and all; and he came as fast as his horse might run, with his spear in his rest. Then Sir Bagdemagus dressed his spear against him and brake it upon the white knight. But the other struck him so hard that he brast the mails, and thrust him through the right shoulder, for the shield covered him not as at that time. And so he bare him from his horse. And therewith he alit and took the white shield from him, saying,

'Knight, thou hast done thyself great folly, for this shield ought not to be borne but by him that shall have no peer that liveth.'

And then he came to Bagdemagus' squire and bad him,

'Bear this shield unto the good knight Sir Galahad, that thou left in the abbey, and greet him well by me.'

'Sir,' said the squire, 'what is your name?'

'Take thou no heed of my name,' said the knight, 'for it is not for thee to know nor for none earthly man.'

'Now, fair sir,' said the squire, 'at the reverence of Jesu Christ, tell me by what cause this shield may not be borne, but if the bearer thereof be mischieved.'

'Now sith thou hast conjured me so,' said the knight, 'this shield behoveth unto no man but unto Sir Galahad.'

Then the squire went unto Bagdemagus and asked whether he were sore wounded or not.

'Yea forsooth,' said he, 'I shall escape hard from the death.'

Then he fetched his horse, and led him with great pain till they came unto the abbey. Then he was taken down softly and unarmed, and laid in his bed, and there was looked to his wounds. And as

Sir Galahad bearing the shield with the red cross

The Grail

the book telleth, he lay there long, and escaped hard with the life.

'Sir Galahad,' said the squire, 'that knight that wounded Sir Bagdemagus sendeth you greeting, and bad that ye should bear this shield, wherethrough great adventures should befall.'

'Now blessed be good and fortune,' said Sir Galahad.

And then he asked his arms, and mounted upon his horse, and hung the white shield about his neck, and commended them unto God.

Then within a while came Sir Galahad thereas the white knight abode him by the hermitage, and every each saluted other courteously.

'Sir,' said Sir Galahad, 'by this shield be many marvels fallen?'

'Sir,' said the knight, 'it befell after the passion of Our Lord Jesu Christ thirty-two year, that Joseph of Arimathea, that gentle knight the which took down Our Lord off the holy Cross, at that time he departed from Jerusalem with a great party of his kindred with him. And so he laboured till that they came to a city that hight Sarras. And at that same hour that Joseph came to Sarras there was a king that hight Evelake, that had great war against the Saracens, and in especial against one Saracen, the which was King Evelake's cousin, a rich king and a mighty, which marched nigh this land, and his name was called Tolleme la Feintes. So on a day these two met to do battle.

'Then Joseph, the son of Joseph of Arimathea, went to King Evelake and told him he should be discomfit and slain, but if he left his belief of the old law and believe upon the new law. And then there he showed him the right belief of the Holy Trinity, for the which he agreed unto with all his heart. And there this shield was made for King Evelake, in the name of Him that died upon the Cross. And then through his good belief he had the better of King Tolleme. For when Evelake was in the battle there was a cloth set afore the shield, and when he was in the greatest peril he let put away the cloth, and then his enemies saw a figure of a man on the cross, wherethrough they all were discomfit.

'And so it befell that a man of King Evelake's was smitten his hand off, and bare that hand in his other hand. And Joseph called that man unto him and bad him go with good devotion touch the cross. And as soon as that man had touched the cross with his hand it was as whole as ever it was tofore. Then soon after there fell a great marvel, that the cross of the shield at one time vanished away that no man wist where it became. And then King Evelake was baptised, and for the most part all the people of that city.

'So, soon after Joseph would depart, and King Evelake would go with him whether he would or nold. And so by fortune they came into this land, that at that time was called Great Britain.'

'So not long after that Joseph was laid in his deadly bed. And when King Evelake saw that, he made much sorrow, and said,

' "For thy love I have left my country, and sith ye shall depart out of this world, leave me some token that I may think on you."

'Then Joseph said, "that will I do full gladly. Now bring me your shield that I took you when ye went into battle against King Tolleme."

'Then Joseph bled sore at the nose, that he might not by no mean be staunched. And there upon that shield he made a cross of his own blood, and said,

' "Now may ye see a remembrance that I love you, for ye shall never see this shield but ye shall think on me, and it shall be always as fresh as it is now. And never shall no man bear this shield about his neck but he shall repent it, unto the time that Galahad, the good knight, bear it. And the last of my lineage shall have it about his neck, that shall do many marvellous deeds."

' "Now," said King Evelake, "where shall I put this shield, that this worthy knight may have it?"

' "Sir, ye shall leave it thereas Nacien, the hermit, shall put it after his death; for thither shall that good knight come the fifteenth day after that he shall receive the order of knighthood."

'And so that day that they set is this time that he have his shield. And in the same abbey lieth Nacien, the hermit.'

And then the white knight vanished away.

Lancelot

So when Sir Galahad was departed . . . he rode till he came to a waste forest, and there he met with Sir Lancelot and Sir Percival. But they knew him not, for he was new disguised. Right so his father, Sir Lancelot, dressed his spear and brake it upon Sir Galahad, and Sir Galahad smote him so again that he bare down horse and man. And then he drew his sword, and dressed him unto Sir Percival, and smote him so on the helm, that it rove to the coif of steel and had not the sword swerved Sir Percival had been slain. And with the stroke he fell out of his saddle.

So this joust was done tofore the hermitage where a recluse dwelled. And when she saw Sir Galahad ride, she said,

'God be with thee, best knight of the world. Ah certes,' said she, all aloud, that Lancelot and Percival might hear it, 'and yonder two knights had known thee as well as I do they would not have encountered with thee.'

When Sir Galahad heard her say so, he was adread to be known; and therewith he smote his horse with his spurs and rode a great pace toward them.

The Grail

Then perceived they both that he was Galahad; and up they gat on their horses, and rode fast after him. But within a while he was out of their sight. And then they turned again with heavy cheer, and said,

'Let us spere some tidings,' said Percival, 'at yonder recluse.'

'Do as ye list,' said Sir Lancelot.

When Sir Percival came to the recluse she knew him well enough, and Sir Lancelot both.

But Sir Lancelot rode overthwart and endlong a wild forest, and held no path but as wild adventure led him. And at the last he came to a stony cross which departed two ways in waste land; and by the cross was a stone that was of marble, but it was so dark that Sir Lancelot might not wit what it was.

Then Sir Lancelot looked by him, and saw an old chapel, and there he weened to have found people; and Sir Lancelot tied his horse till a tree, and there he did off his shield and hung it upon a tree. And then he went to the chapel door, and found it waste and broken. And within he found a fair altar, full richly arrayed with cloth of clean silk, and there stood a fair clean candlestick, which bare six great candles, and the candlestick was of silver. And when Sir Lancelot saw this light he had great will for to enter into the chapel, but he could find no place where he might enter. Then was he passing heavy and dismayed, and returned again and came to his horse, and did off his saddle and bridle, and let him pasture him, and unlaced his helm, and ungirt his sword, and laid him down to sleep upon his shield tofore the cross.

And so he fell asleep; and half waking and sleeping he saw come by him two palfreys all fair and white, which bare a litter, therein lying a sick knight. And when he was nigh the cross he there abode still. All this Sir Lancelot saw and beheld, for he slept not verily; and he heard him say,

'O sweet Lord, when shall this sorrow leave me? And when shall the holy vessel come by me, wherethrough I shall be healed? For I have endured thus long, for little trespass, a full great while.'

Thus complained the knight thus, and always Sir Lancelot heard it.

So with that Sir Lancelot saw the candlestick with the six tapers come before the cross, and he saw nobody that brought it. Also there came a table of silver, and the holy vessel of the Sangrail, which Sir Lancelot had seen aforetime in King Pecchere's house. And therewith the sick knight sat him up, and held up both his hands, and said, 'Fair sweet Lord, which is here within this holy vessel, take heed unto me that I may be whole of this malady.'

And therewith on his hands and knees he went so nigh that he touched the holy vessel and kissed it, and anon he was whole. And then he said,

'Lord God, I thank Thee, for I am healed of this sickness.'

So when the holy vessel had been there a great while it went unto the chapel with the chandelier and the light, so that Sir Lancelot wist not where it was become; for he was overtaken with sin that he had no power to rise against the holy vessel. Wherefore after that many men said of him shame, but he took repentance after that.

Then the sick knight dressed him up and kissed the cross. Anon his squire brought him his arms, and asked his lord how he did.

'Certes,' said he, 'I thank God right well. Through the holy vessel I am healed. But I have marvel of this sleeping knight that he had no power to awake when this holy vessel was brought hither.'

'I dare right well say,' said the squire, 'that he dwelleth in some deadly sin whereof he was never confessed.'

'By my faith,' said the knight, 'whatsomever he be he is unhappy. For as I deem he is of the fellowship of the Round Table, which is entered into the quest of the Sangrail.'

'Sir,' said the squire, 'here I have brought you all your arms save your helm and your sword, and therefore by mine assent now may ye take this knight's helm and his sword': and so he did. And when he was clean armed he took Sir Lancelot's horse, for it was better than his; and so departed they from the cross.

Then anon Sir Lancelot waked, and sat him up, and bethought him what he had seen there, and whether it were dreams or not. Right so heard he a voice that said,

'Sir Lancelot, more harder than is the stone, and more bitter than is the wood, and more naked and barer than is the leaf of the fig tree; therefore go thou from hence, and withdraw thee from this holy place.'

And when Sir Lancelot heard this he was passing heavy and wist not what to do. And so departed sore weeping, and cursed the time that he was born. For then he seemed never to have worship more. For those words went to his heart, till that he knew wherefore he was called so.

Then Sir Lancelot went to the cross and found his helm, his sword, and his horse taken away. And then he called himself a very wretch, and most unhappy of all knights; and there he said,

'My sin and my wickedness have brought me unto great dishonour. For when I sought worldly adventures for worldly desires, I ever achieved them and had the better in every place, and never was I discomfit in no quarrel, were it right or wrong. And now I take upon me the adventures to seek of holy things, now I see and understand that mine old sin hindereth me and shameth me, that I had no power to stir nor speak when the holy blood appeared before me.'

So thus he sorrowed till it was day, and heard the fowls sing; then somewhat he was comforted. But when Sir Lancelot missed his horse and his harness than he wist well God was displeased with him. And so he departed from the cross on foot into a fair forest; and so by prime he came to an high hill, and found an hermitage and a hermit therein which was going unto mass.

And then Lancelot kneeled down and cried on Our Lord mercy for his wicked works. So when mass was done Lancelot called him, and prayed him for saint charity for to hear his life.

'With a good will,' said the good man. 'Sir,' said he, 'be ye of King Arthur's court and of the fellowship of the Round Table?'

'Yea forsooth, sir, and my name is Sir Lancelot du Lake that hath been right well said of. And now my good fortune is changed, for I am the most wretch of the world.'

The hermit beheld him and had marvel why he was so abashed.

'Sir,' said the hermit, 'ye ought to thank God more than any knight living, for He hath caused you to have more worldly worship than any knight that now liveth. And for your presumption to take upon you in deadly sin for to be in His presence, where His flesh and His blood was, that caused you ye might not see it with your worldly eyen; for He will not appear where such sinners be, but if it be unto their great hurt, or unto their great shame. And there is no knight now living that ought to yield God so great thank as ye, for He hath given you beauty, bounty, seemliness, and great strength over all other knights. And therefore ye are the more beholden unto God than any other man, to love Him and dread Him, for your strength and manhood will little avail you and God be against you.'

Then Sir Lancelot wept with heavy heart, and said,

'Now I know well ye say me sooth.'

'Sir,' said the good man, 'hide none old sin from me.'

'Truly,' said Sir Lancelot, 'that were me full loth to discover. For this fourteen year I never discovered one thing that I have used, and that may I now wit my shame and my disadventure.'

And then he told there that good man all his life. And how he had loved a queen unmeasurably and out of measure long. 'And all my great deeds of arms that I have done, I did for the most part for the queen's sake, and for her sake would I do battle were it right or wrong. And never did I battle all only for God's sake, but for to win worship and to cause me the better to be loved, and little or nought I thanked never God of it.'

Then Sir Lancelot said, 'Sir, I pray you counsel me.'

'Sir, I will counsel you,' said the hermit, 'if ye will ensure me, by your knighthood, that ye will never come in that queen's fellow-ship as much as ye may forbear.'

And then Sir Lancelot promised him he nold, by the faith of his body.

nold: *would not*

'Sir, look that your heart and your mouth accord,' said the good man, 'and I shall ensure you ye shall have more worship than ever ye had.'

'Holy father,' said Sir Lancelot, 'I marvel of the voice that said to me marvellous words, as ye have heard toforehand.'

'Have ye no marvel,' said the good man, 'thereof, for it seemeth well God loveth you. For men may understand a stone is hard of kind, and namely one more than another; and that is to understand by thee, Sir Lancelot, for thou wilt not leave thy sin for no goodness that God hath sent thee; therefore thou art more harder than any stone, and never wouldst thou be made nesh nor by water nor by fire, and that is the heat of the Holy Ghost may not enter in thee.

nesh: *soft (word still in dialect use)*

'Now take heed, in all the world men shall not find one knight to whom Our Lord hath given so much of grace as He hath given you, for He hath given you fairness with seemliness; also He hath given thee wit, discretion to know good from evil; He hath also given thee prowess and hardiness, and given thee to work so largely that thou hast had the better all the days of thy life, wheresomever thou came. And now Our Lord will suffer thee no longer, but that thou shalt know Him whether thou wilt or nilt. And why the voice called thee bitterer than wood, for wheresomever much sin dwelleth, there may be but little sweetness; wherefore thou art likened to an old rotten tree.

'Now have I showed thee why thou art harder than the stone and bitterer than the tree. Now shall I show thee why thou art more naked and barer than the fig tree. It befell that Our Lord on Palm Sunday preached in Jerusalem, and there He found in the people that all hardness was harboured in them, and there He found in all the town not one that would harbour him. And then He went out of the town, and found in the midst of the way a fig tree, the which was right fair and well garnished of leaves, but fruit had it none. Then Our Lord cursed the tree that bare no fruit; that betokeneth the fig tree unto Jerusalem, that had leaves and no fruit. So thou, Sir Lancelot, when the Holy Grail was brought afore thee, He found in thee no fruit, nor good thought nor good will, and defouled with lechery.'

'Certes,' said Sir Lancelot, 'all that you have said is true, and from henceforward I cast me, by the grace of God, never to be so wicked as I have been, but as to follow knighthood and to do feats of arms.'

Then this good man joined Sir Lancelot such penance as he might do and to sue knighthood, and so assoiled him, and prayed Sir Lancelot to abide with him all that day.

'I will well,' said Sir Lancelot, 'for I have neither helm, ne horse, ne sword.'

'As for that,' said the good man, 'I shall help you or tomorn at even of an horse, and all that longeth unto you.'

And then Sir Lancelot repented him greatly of his misdeeds.

Here leaveth the tale of Sir Lancelot, and beginneth of Sir Percival de Gales.

Percival

Now saith the tale, that when Sir Lancelot was ridden after Sir Galahad, the which had all these adventures above said, Sir Percival turned again unto the recluse, where he deemed to have tidings of that knight that Sir Lancelot followed. And so he kneeled at her window, and the recluse opened it and asked Sir Percival what he would.

'Madam,' he said, 'I am a knight of King Arthur's court, and my name is Sir Percival de Gales.'

When the recluse heard his name she had great joy of him, for mickle she had loved him tofore passing any other knight; for she ought to do so, for she was his aunt. And then she commanded the gates to be opened, and there he had all the cheer that she might make him, and all that was in her power was at his commandment.

So on the morn Sir Percival went to the recluse and asked her if she knew that knight with the white shield.

'Sir,' said she, 'why would ye wit?'

'Truly, madam,' said Sir Percival, 'I shall never be well at ease till that I know of that knight's fellowship, and that I may fight

assoiled: *absolved*

with him, for I may not leave him so lightly, for I have the shame yet.'

'Ah, Sir Percival,' said she, 'would ye fight with him? I see well ye have great will to be slain, as your father was through out
rageousness slain.'

'Madam,' said Sir Percival, 'it seemeth by your words that ye know me.'

'Yea,' said she, 'I well ought to know you, for I am your aunt, although I be in a poor place. For some called me sometime the Queen of the Waste Lands, and I was called the queen of most riches in the world; and it pleased me never so much my riches as doth my poverty.'

Then Sir Percival wept for very pity when that he knew it was his aunt.

'Ah, fair nephew,' said she, 'when heard ye tidings of your mother?'

'Truly,' said he, 'I heard none of her, but I dream of her much in my sleep; and therefore I wot not whether she be dead or alive.'

'Certes, fair nephew,' said she, 'your mother is dead, for after your departing from her she took such a sorrow that anon, after she was confessed, she died.'

'Now, God have mercy on her soul,' said Sir Percival. 'It sore forthinketh me; but all we must change the life. Now, fair aunt, tell me what is the knight? I deem it be he that bare the red arms on Whitsunday.'

'Wit you well,' said she, 'that this is he, for otherwise ought he not to do, but to go in red arms. And that same knight hath no peer, for he worketh all by miracle, and he shall never be overcome of none earthly man's hand.

'Also Merlin made the Round Table in tokening of roundness of the world, for by the Round Table is the world signified by right; for all the world, Christian and heathen repaireth unto the Round Table; and when they are chosen to be of the fellowship of the Round Table they think them more blessed and more in wor
ship than if they had gotten half the world. And ye have seen that they have lost their fathers and their mothers, and all their kin, and their wives and their children, for to be of your fellowship. It is well seen by you; for since ye departed from your mother ye would never see her, ye found such fellowship at the Round Table.

'When Merlin had ordained the Round Table he said, by them which should be fellows of the Round Table the truth of the Sangrail should be well known. And men asked him how they might know them that should best do and to achieve the Sangrail. Then he said there should be three white bulls that should achieve it, and the two should be maidens, and the third should be chaste. And that one of the three should pass his father as much as the lion passeth the leopard, both of strength and hardiness. They that heard Merlin say so said thus unto Merlin:

' "Sithen there shall be such a knight, thou shouldest ordain by thy crafts a siege, that no man should sit in it but he all only that shall pass all other knights."

'Then Merlin answered that he would do so. And then he made the Siege Perilous, in the which Galahad sat at his meat on Whitsunday last past.'

'Now, madam,' said Sir Percival, 'so much have I heard of you that by my good will I will never have ado with Sir Galahad but by way of kindness; and for God's love, fair aunt, can ye teach me where I might find him? For much would I love the fellowship of him.'

'Fair nephew,' said she, 'ye must ride unto a castle the which is called Goothe, where he hath a cousin-germain, and there may ye be lodged this night. And as he teacheth you, sueth after as fast as ye can; and if he can tell you no tidings of him, ride straight unto the Castle of Carbonek, where the Maimed King is lying, for there shall ye hear true tidings of him.'

Then departed Sir Percival from his aunt, either making great sorrow. And so he rode till after evensong; and then he heard a clock smite. And anon he was ware of an house closed well with walls and deep ditches, and there he knocked at the gate, and was let in, and he alit and was led unto a chamber, and soon he was unarmed. And there he had right good cheer all that night.

And on the morn he heard his mass, and in the monastery he found a priest ready at the altar. And on the right side he saw a pew closed with iron, and behind the altar he saw a rich bed and a fair, as of cloth of silk and gold. Then Sir Percival espied that therein was a man or a woman, for the visage was covered; then he left off his looking and heard his service.

And when it came to the sacring, he that lay within that perclose dressed him up, and uncovered his head; and then him beseemed a passing old man, and he had a crown of gold upon his head, and his shoulders were naked and unhilled unto his navel. And then Sir Percival espied his body was full of great wounds, both on the shoulders, arms, and visage. And ever he held up his hands against Our Lord's body, and cried,

'Fair, sweet Lord, Jesu Christ, forget not me.'

And so he lay not down, but was always in his prayers and orisons; and him seemed to be of the age of three hundred winter.

And when the mass was done the priest took Our Lord's body and bare it to the sick king. And when he had used it he did off his crown, and commanded the crown to be set on the altar. Then Sir Percival asked one of the brethren what he was.

A knight takes leave of an old woman

'Sir,' said the good man, 'ye have heard much of Joseph of Arimathea, how he was sent by Jesu Christ into this land for to teach and preach the holy Christian faith; and therefore he suffered many persecutions the which the enemies of Christ did unto him. And in the city of Sarras he converted a king whose name was Evelake. And so this king came with Joseph into this land, and ever he was busy to be thereas the Sangrail was; and on a time he nighed it so nigh that Our Lord was displeased with him, but ever he followed it more and more, till God struck him almost blind. Then this king cried mercy, and said, "Fair Lord, let me never die till the good knight of my blood and of the ninth degree be come, that I may see him openly that shall achieve the Sangrail, and that I might kiss him."

'When the king thus had made his prayers he heard a voice that said,

'"Heard be thy prayers, for thou shalt not die till he have kissed thee. And when that knight shall come the clearness of your eyen shall come again, and thou shalt see openly, and thy wounds shall be healed, and erst shall they never close."

'And this befell of King Evelake, and this same king hath lived four hundred years this holy life, and men say the knight is in this court that shall heal him. Sir,' said the good man, 'I pray you tell me what knight that ye be, and if ye be of King Arthur's court and of the Table Round.'

'Yea, forsooth,' said he, 'and my name is Sir Percival de Gales.'

And when the good man understood his name he made great joy of him.

And then Sir Percival departed and rode till the hour of noon. And he met in a valley about twenty men of arms, which bare in a bier a knight deadly slain. And when they saw Sir Percival they asked him of whence he was.

And he answered, 'Of the court of King Arthur.'

Then they cried all at once, 'Slay him!'

Then Sir Percival smote the first to the earth and his horse upon him. And then seven of the knights smote upon his shield all at once, and the remnant slew his horse so that he fell to the earth. So had they slain him or taken him had not the good knight Sir Galahad, with the red arms, come there by adventure into those parts.

And when he saw all those knights upon one knight, he cried, 'Save me that knight's life.'

And then he dressed him toward the twenty men of arms as fast as his horse might drive, with his spear in the rest, and smote the foremost horse and man to the earth. And when his spear was broken he set his hand to his sword, and smote on the right hand

and on the left hand that it was marvel to see, and at every stroke
he smote down one or put him to a rebuke, so that they would
fight no more but fled to a thick forest, and Sir Galahad followed
them. And when Sir Percival saw him chase them so, he made
great sorrow that his horse was away. And then he wist well it was
Sir Galahad. And then he cried aloud, and said, 'Ah fair knight,
abide and suffer me to do you thankings, for much have ye done for
me.'

But ever Sir Galahad rode so fast that at the last he passed out
of his sight. And as fast as Sir Percival might he went after him
on foot, crying . . . and anon he saw that he was in a wild mountain the which was closed with the sea nigh all about that he
might see no land about him which might relieve him, but wild
beasts.

By that Sir Percival had abiden there till mid-day he saw a ship
come sailing in the sea as all the wind of the world had driven
it. And so it landed under that rock. And when Sir Percival saw
this he hied him thither, and found the ship covered with silk
more blacker than any bier, and therein was a gentlewoman of
great beauty, and she was clothed richly, there might be none
better.

And when she saw Sir Percival she said, 'Who brought you
into this wilderness where ye be never like to pass hence, for ye shall
die here for hunger and mischief?'

'Damsel,' said Sir Percival, 'I serve the best man of the world,
and in his service he will not suffer me to die, for who that knocketh
shall enter, and who that asketh shall have, and who seeketh him
he hideth him not.'

But then she said, 'Sir Percival, wot ye what I am?'

'Now who taught you my name?' said Sir Percival.

'I know you better than ye ween. I came but late out of the
Waste Forest, where I found the red knight with the white shield,'
said the damsel.

'Ah, damsel,' said he, 'that knight would I fain meet withal.'

'Sir knight,' said she, 'and ye will ensure me by the faith that
ye owe unto knighthood that ye shall do my will what time I summon you, and I shall bring you unto that knight.'

'Yea,' said he, 'I shall promise you to fulfil your desire.'

'Well,' said she, 'now shall I tell you. I saw him in the forest
chasing two knights unto the water, which is called Mortaise; and
they drove into that water for dread of death. And the two knights
passed over, and the red knight passed after, and there his horse
was drowned, and he, through great strength, escaped unto the
land.'

Thus she told him, and Sir Percival was passing glad thereof.

Then Sir Percival promised her all the help that he might; and then she thanked him.

And at that time the weather was hot. Then she called unto her a gentlewoman and bad her bring forth a pavilion; and so she did, and pitched it upon the gravel.

'Sir,' said she, 'now may ye rest you in this heat of the day.'

Then he thanked her, and she put off his helm and his shield, and there he slept a great while.

And then he awoke and asked her if she had any meat, and she said,

'Yea, also ye shall have enough.'

And so there was laid the table, and so much meat was set thereon that he had marvel, for there was all manner of meats that he could think on. Also he drank there the strongest wine that ever he drank, him thought, and therewith he was chafed a little more than he ought to be. With that he beheld that gentlewoman, and him thought she was the fairest creature that ever he saw.

And then Sir Percival proffered her love, and prayed her that she would be his. Then she refused him, in a manner, when he required her, for the cause he should be the more ardent on her. And ever he ceased not to pray her of love. And when she saw him well enchafed, then she said,

'Sir Percival, wit you well I shall not fulfil your will but if ye swear from henceforth ye shall be my true servant, and to do nothing but that I shall command you. Will ye ensure me this as ye be a true knight?'

'Yea,' said he, 'fair lady, by the faith of my body.'

'Well,' said she, 'now shall ye do with me what ye will; and now, wit ye well, ye are the knight in the world that I have most desire to.'

And then two squires were commanded to make a bed in midst of the pavilion. And anon she was unclothed and laid therein. And then Sir Percival laid him down by her naked; and by adventure and grace he saw his sword lie on the ground naked, in whose pommel was a red cross and the sign of the crucifix therein, and bethought him on his knighthood and his promise made toforehand unto the good man; then he made a sign of the cross in his forehead. And therewith the pavilion turned up-so-down, and then it changed unto a smoke, and a black cloud. And then he was adread and cried aloud:

'Fair sweet Lord, Jesu Christ, ne let me not be shamed, the which was nigh lost had not Thy good grace been.'

And then he looked unto her ship, and saw her enter therein, which said,

'Sir Percival, ye have betrayed me.'

And so she went with the wind roaring and yelling, that it seemed all the water burnt after her.

Then Sir Percival made great sorrow, and drew his sword unto him, and said,

'Sithen my flesh will be my master I shall punish it.'

And therewith he rove himself through the thigh, that the blood start about him, and said,

'O good Lord, take this in recompensation of that I have done against Thee, my Lord.'

So then he clothed him and armed him, and called himself wretch of all wretches, saying,

'How nigh was I lost, and to have lost that I should never have gotten again, that was my virginity, for that may never be recovered after it is once lost.'

And then he stopped his bleeding wound with a piece of his shirt.

Gawain

When Sir Gawain was departed from his fellowship he rode long without any adventure. For he found not the tenth part of adventure as he was wont to do. For Sir Gawain rode from Whitsuntide until Michaelmas and found none adventure that pleased him.

So on a day it befell that Gawain met with Sir Ector de Maris, and either made great joy of other that it were marvel to tell. And so they told every each other, and complained them greatly that they could find none adventure.

'Truly,' said Sir Gawain unto Sir Ector, 'I am nigh weary of this quest, and loth I am to follow further in strange countries.'

'One thing marvelleth me,' said Sir Ector, 'I have met with twenty knights that be fellows of mine, and all they complain as I do.'

'I have marvel,' said Sir Gawain, 'where Sir Lancelot, your brother, is.'

'Truly,' said Sir Ector, 'I cannot hear of him, nor of Sir Galahad, Sir Percival, nor Sir Bors.'

'Let them be,' said Sir Gawain, 'for they four have no peers. And if one thing were not in Sir Lancelot he had no fellow of none earthly man; but he is as we be, but if he took more pain upon him. But and these four be met together they will be loth that any man meet with them; for and they fail of the Sangrail it is in waste of all the remnant to recover it.'

Thus Sir Ector and Sir Gawain rode more than eight days, and on a Saturday they found an ancient chapel, which was wasted

FAR LEFT
*Gawain rides on his
quest through a forest*

LEFT *Gawain arrives
at a monastery*

that there seemed no man nor woman thither repaired; and there they alit, and set their spears at the door. And so they entered into the chapel, and there made their orisons a great while. And then sat them down in the sieges of the chapel. And as they spake of one thing and other, for heaviness they fell asleep. And there befell them both marvellous adventures.

Sir Gawain him seemed he came into a meadow full of herbs and flowers, and there he saw a rack of bulls, an hundred and fifty, that were proud and black, save three of them were all white, and one had a black spot, and the other two were so fair and so white that they might be no whiter. And these three bulls which were so fair were tied with two strong cords. And the remnant of the bulls said among them,

'Go we hence to seek better pasture.'

And so some went, and some came again, but they were so lean that they might not stand upright; and of the bulls that were so white, that one came again and no more. But when this white bull was come again among these other there rose up a great cry for lack of viande that failed them; and so they departed one here and another there. This advision befell Gawain that night.

But to Ector de Maris befell another vision, the contrary. For it seemed to him that his brother, Sir Lancelot, and he alit out of a chair and leapt upon two horses. And the one said to the other,

'Go we seek that we shall not find.'

And him thought that a man beat Sir Lancelot, and despoiled him, and clothed him in another array, which was all full of knots, and set him upon an ass. And so he rode till he came to the fairest well that ever he saw. And there Sir Lancelot alit and would have drunk of that well. And when he stooped to drink of the water the water sank from him. And when Sir Lancelot saw that, he turned and went thither as he had come from.

And in the meanwhile he trowed that himself, Sir Ector, rode till that he came to a rich man's house where there was a wedding. And there he saw a king which said,

'Sir knight, here is no place for you.'

And then he turned again unto the chair that he came from.

Thus within a while both Sir Gawain and Sir Ector awaked, and either told other of their advision, which marvelled them greatly.

'Truly,' said Sir Ector, 'I shall never be merry till I hear tidings of my brother Lancelot.'

Now as they sat thus talking they saw an hand showing unto the elbow, and was covered with red samite, and upon that hung a bridle not right rich, and held within the fist a great candle which burned right clear; and so passed before them, and entered into the chapel, and then vanished away they wist not where.

And anon came down a voice which said,

'Knights full of evil faith and of poor belief, these two things have failed you, and therefore ye may not come to the adventures of the Sangrail.'

Then first spake Sir Gawain and said, 'Sir Ector, have ye heard these words?'

'Yea truly,' said Sir Ector, 'I heard all. Now go we,' said Sir Ector, 'unto some hermit that will tell us of our advision, for it seemeth me we labour all in vain.'

And so they departed and rode into a valley, and there met with a squire which rode on an hackney, and they saluted him fair.

'Sir,' said Sir Gawain, 'can thou teach us to any hermit?'

'Here is one in a little mountain, but it is so rough there may no horse go thither. And therefore ye must go on foot, and there shall ye find a poor house, and there is Nacien the hermit, which is the holiest man in this country.'

And so they departed either from other, . . . and so rode till they came to the rough mountain, and there they tied their horses and went on foot to the hermitage.

And when they were come up they saw a poor house, and beside the chapel a little courtelage, where Nacien the hermit gathered worts, as he which had tasted none other meat of a great while. And when he saw the errant knights he came toward them and saluted them, and they him again.

'Fair lords,' said he, 'what adventure brought you hither?'

'Sir,' said Sir Gawain, 'to speak with you for to be confessed.'

'Sir,' said the hermit, 'I am ready.'

Then they told him so much that he wist well what they were. And then he thought to counsel them if he might.

Then began Sir Gawain first and told him of his advision that he had had in the chapel, and Sir Ector told him all as it is afore rehearsed.

'Sir,' said the hermit unto Sir Gawain, 'the fair meadow and the rack therein ought to be understand the Round Table, and by the

worts: *roots*

meadow ought to be understand humility and patience, those be
the things which be always green and quick; for men may no time
overcome humility and patience, therefore was the Round Table
founden; and the chivalry hath been at all times so high, by the
fraternity which was there, that she might not be overcomen; for
men said she was founded in patience and in humility. At the
rack ate an hundred and fifty bulls; but they ate not in the meadow,
for if they had, their hearts should be set in humility and patience;
and the bulls were proud and black save only three.

'And by the bulls is to understand the fellowship of the Round
Table, which for their sin and their wickedness be black. Black-
ness is as much to say: without good virtues or works. And the
three bulls which were white save only one that was spotted: and
two white betokenen Sir Galahad and Sir Percival, for they be
maidens clean and without spot; and the third that had a spot
signifieth Sir Bors de Ganis, which trespassed but once in his
virginity. But sithen he kept himself so well in chastity that all is
forgiven him and his misdeeds. And why those three were tied
by the necks: they be three knights in virginity and chastity, and
there is no pride smitten in them.

'And the black bulls which said, "Go we hence," they were
those which at Pentecost at the high feast took upon them to go
in the quest of the Sangrail without confession: they might not
enter in the meadow of humility and patience. And therefore they
returned into waste countries, that signifieth death, for there shall
die many of them. For every each of them shall slay other for sin,
and they that shall escape shall be so lean that it shall be marvel
to see them. And of the three bulls without spot, the one shall come
again and the other two never.'

Then spake Nacien unto Sir Ector: 'Sooth it is that Sir Lancelot
and ye came down off one chair: the chair betokeneth mastership
and lordship which ye came down from. But ye two knights,' said
the hermit, 'ye go to seek that ye shall never find, that is the
Sangrail; for it is the secret thing of Our Lord Jesu Christ. But
what is to mean that Sir Lancelot fell down off his horse? He hath
left his pride and taken to humility, for he hath cried mercy loud for
his sin, and sore repented him, and Our Lord hath clothed him in
his clothing which is full of knots, that is the hair that he weareth
daily. And the ass that he rideth upon is a beast of humility, for
God would not ride upon no steed, nor upon no palfrey; so in
example that an ass betokeneth meekness, thou that sawest Sir
Lancelot ride on in thy sleep.

'And the well whereas the water sank from him when he should
have taken thereof, and when he saw he might not have it, he returned thither from whence he came: for the well betokeneth the

high grace of God, the more men desire it to take it, the more shall be their desire. So when he came nigh the Sangrail, he meeked him that he held him not a man worthy to be so nigh the holy vessel, for he had been so defouled in deadly sin by the space of many years; yet when he kneeled to drink of the well, there he saw great providence of the Sangrail. And for he had served so long the devil, he shall have vengeance four and twenty days long, for that he hath been the devil's servant four and twenty years. And then soon after he shall return unto Camelot out of this country, and he shall say a part of such things as he hath found.

'Now will I tell you what betokeneth the hand with the candle and the bridle: that is to understand the holy ghost where charity is ever, and the bridle signifieth abstinence. For when she is bridled in a Christian man's heart she holdeth him so short that he falleth not in deadly sin. And the candle which showeth clearness and light signifieth the right way of Jesu Christ. And when He went He said, "Knights of poor faith and of wicked belief, these three things failed: charity, abstinence, and truth;" therefore ye may not attain that high adventure of the Sangrail.'

'Certes,' said Sir Gawain, 'soothly have ye said, that I see it openly. Now, I pray you, good man and holy father, tell me why we met not with so many adventures as we were wont to do?'

'I shall tell you gladly,' said the good man: 'the adventure of the Sangrail which ye and many other have undertake the quest of it and find it not, the cause is for it appeareth not to sinners. Wherefore marvel not though ye fail thereof, and many other. For ye be an untrue knight, and a great murderer, and to good men signifieth other things than murder. For I dare say as sinful as Sir Lancelot hath been, sith that he went into the quest of the Sangrail he slew never man, nor nought shall, till that he come unto Camelot again, for he hath taken upon him for to forsake sin. And nere were that he is not stable, but by his thought he is likely to turn again, he should be next to achieve it save Galahad, his son. But God knoweth his thought and his unstableness. And yet shall he die right an holy man, and no doubt he hath no fellow of no earthly sinful man living.'

'Sir,' said Sir Gawain, 'it seemeth me by your words that for our sins it will not avail us to travel in this quest.'

'Truly,' said the good man, 'there be an hundred such as ye be that never shall prevail, but to have shame.'

And when they had heard these voices they commended him unto God. Then the good man called Gawain, and said,

'It is long time passed sith that ye were made knight, and never since served thou thy Maker, and now thou art so old a tree that in thee is neither leaf nor fruit. Wherefore bethink thee that thou

nere were: were it not

yield to Our Lord the bare rind, sith the fiend hath the leaves and the fruit.'

'Sir,' said Sir Gawain, 'and I had leisure I would speak with you, but my fellow here, Sir Ector, is gone, and abideth me yonder beneath the hill.'

'Well,' said the good man, 'thou were better to be counselled.'

Then departed Sir Gawain and came to Sir Ector, and so took their horses and rode till they came to a forester's house, which harboured them right well. And on the morn they departed from their host, and rode long or they could find any adventure.

Now turneth this tale unto Sir Bors de Ganis.

Bors

When Bors was departed from Camelot he met with a religious man riding on an ass, and anon Sir Bors saluted him. Anon the good man knew him that he was one of the knights errant that was in the quest of the Sangrail.

'What are ye?' said the good man.

'Sir,' said he, 'I am a knight that fain would be counselled, that is entered into the quest of the Sangrail. For he shall have much earthly worship that may bring it to an end.'

'Certes,' said the good man, 'that is sooth without fail, for he shall be the best knight of the world, and the fairest of all the fellowship. But wit ye well there shall none attain it but by cleanness, that is pure confession.'

So rode they together till that they came to an hermitage. And there he prayed Sir Bors to dwell all that night with him. And so he alit and put away his armour, and prayed him that he might be confessed; and so they went into the chapel, and there he was clean confessed. And so they ate bread and drank water together.

'Now,' said the good man, 'I pray thee that thou eat none other till that thou sit at the table where the Sangrail shall be.'

'Sir,' said he, 'I agree me thereto. But how wit ye that I shall sit there?'

'Yes,' said the good man, 'that know I well, but there shall be but few of your fellows with you.'

'All is welcome,' said Sir Bors, 'that God sendeth me.'

'Also,' said the good man, 'instead of a shirt, and in sign of chastisement, ye shall wear a garment; therefore I pray you do off all your clothes and your shirt.'

And so he did. And then he took him a scarlet coat, so that should be his instead of his shirt till he had fulfilled the quest of the Sangrail; and this good man found him in so marvellous a life and so stable, that he felt he was never greatly corrupt in fleshly lusts, but in one time that he begat Elaine le Blank. Then he armed him, and took his leave, and so departed.

And at the last by fortune he came to an abbey which was nigh the sea, and that night Sir Bors rested him there.

And as he slept, there came a voice to him and bad him go to the sea. Then he start up and made a sign of the cross in the midst of his forehead, and took his harness, and made ready his horse, and mounted upon him. And at a broken wall he rode out, and rode so long till that he came to the sea.

And upon the sea-strand he found a ship that was covered all with white samite. Then he alit, and betook him to Jesu Christ. And as soon as he entered into the ship, the ship departed into the sea, and went so fast that him seemed the ship went flying, but it was soon dark so that he might know no man. Then he laid him downward and slept till it was day.

And when he was awaked, he saw in midst of the ship a knight lie all armed save his helm. Then knew he it was Sir Percival of Wales, and then he made of him right great joy; but Sir Percival was abashed of him, and asked him what he was.

'Ah, fair sir,' said Sir Bors, 'know ye me not?'

'Certes,' said he, 'I marvel how ye came hither, but if Our Lord brought you hither Himself.'

Then Sir Bors smiled, and did off his helm. Then Sir Percival knew him, and either made great joy of each other, that it was marvel to hear.

Then Sir Bors told him how he came into the ship . . . . So went they downward in the sea, one while backward, another while forward, and every each comforted other, and oft were in their prayers.

Then said Sir Percival, 'We lack nothing but Sir Galahad, the good knight.'

Now turneth the tale unto Sir Galahad.

The Three Companions

Now saith the tale when Sir Galahad had rescued Sir Percival from the twenty knights, he rode then into a waste forest wherein he did many journeys and found many adventures, which he brought all to an end, whereof the tale maketh here no mention.

Then he took his way to the sea; and on a day, as it befell as he passed by a castle, there was a wonder tournament. But they without had done so much that they within were put to the worse, and yet were they within good knights enough.

So when Sir Galahad saw that those within were at so great a mischief that men slew them at the entry of the castle, then he thought to help them, and put a spear forth and smote the first that he flew to the earth, and the spear brake to pieces. Then he drew his sword and smote thereas they were thickest and so he did wonderful deeds of arms, that all they marvelled.

And so it happened that Sir Gawain and Sir Ector de Maris were with the knights without. But when they espied the white shield with the red cross the one said to the other,

'Yonder is the good knight, Sir Galahad, the Haut Prince. Now, forsooth, me thinketh he shall be a great fool that shall meet with him to fight.'

But at the last by adventure he came by Sir Gawain, and smote him so hard that he clave his helm and the coif of iron unto his head, so that Sir Gawain fell to the earth; but the stroke was so great that it slanted down and cut the horse's shoulder in two. So when Sir Ector saw Sir Gawain down, he drew him aside, and thought it no wisdom for to abide him, and also for natural love, for because he was his uncle.

Thus through his great hardiness he beat aback all the knights without. And then they within came out and chased them all about. But when Sir Galahad saw there would none turn again, he stole away privily so that none wist where he was become.

'Now by my head,' said Sir Gawain to Sir Ector, 'now are the wonders true that were said of Lancelot du Lake, that the sword which stuck in the stone should give me such a buffet that I would not have it for the best castle in the world. And soothly now it is proved true, for never ere had I such a stroke of man's hand.'

'Sir,' said Sir Ector, 'meseemeth your quest is done, and mine is not done.'

'Well,' said he, 'I shall seek no further.'

Then was Sir Gawain borne into the castle and unarmed him, and laid him in a rich bed, and a leech was found that he might live, and to be whole within a month. Thus Sir Gawain and Sir Ector abode together, for Sir Ector would not away till Sir Gawain were whole.

And so this good knight, Sir Galahad, rode so fast th͏ that night to the Castle of Carbonek. And it be͏ he was benighted and came unto in an hermitage. ͏ was fain when he saw he was a knight errant.

Then when they were at rest there came a gentl͏ knocked at the door, and called Sir Galahad. And man came to the door to wit what she would.

Then she called the hermit, 'Sir Ulfin, I am a gentlew͏ would speak with the knight which is with you.'

Then the good man awaked Sir Galahad, and bad him: 'Arise, and speak with a gentle woman that seemeth hath great need of you.'

Then Sir Galahad went to her and asked her what she would.

'Sir Galahad,' said she, 'I will that ye arm you, and mount upon your horse and follow me, for I shall show you within these three days the highest adventure that ever any knight saw.'

So anon Sir Galahad armed him, and took his horse, and commended the hermit to God, and bad the gentlewoman to ride, and he would follow thereas she liked.

So she rode as fast as her palfrey might bear her, till that she came to the sea, which was called Collibe. And by night they came unto a castle in a valley, closed with a running water, and with strong walls and high; and so she entered into the castle with Sir Galahad, and there had he great cheer, for the lady of that castle was the damsel's lady. So when he was unarmed, then said the damsel,

'Madam, shall we abide here all this day?'

'Nay,' said she, 'but till he hath dined and slept a little.'

And so he ate and slept a while till that the maid called him, and armed him by torchlight. And when the maiden was horsed and he both, the lady took Sir Galahad a fair shield and rich; and so they departed from the castle till they came to the seaside. And there they found the ship where Sir Bors and Sir Percival were in, which said on the ship-board,

'Sir Galahad, ye be welcome, we have abiden you long.'

And when he heard them he asked them what they were.

'Sir,' said she, 'leave your horse here, and I shall leave mine also;' and took their saddles and their bridles with them, and made a cross on them, and so entered into the ship.

And the two knights received them both with great joy, and every each knew other. And so the wind arose, and drove them through the sea into a marvellous place. And within a while it dawed. Then did Galahad off his helm and his sword, and asked of his fellows from whence came that fair ship.

'Truly,' said they, 'ye wot as well as we but it come of God's grace.' And then they told every each to other of all their hard adventures, and of their great temptations.

'Truly,' said Sir Galahad, 'ye are much bounden to God, for ye have escaped great adventures; and had not the gentlewoman been I had not comen hither at this time. For as for you two, I weened never to have found you in these strange countries.'

'Ah, Sir Galahad,' said Sir Bors, 'if Sir Lancelot, your father, were here then were we well at ease, for then meseemed we failed nothing.'

The three companions
on board the ship

'That may not be,' said Sir Galahad, 'but it if pleased Our Lord.'

By then the ship had run from the land of Logris many miles, so by adventure it arrived up betwixt two rocks passing great and marvellous; but there they might not land, for there was a swallow of the sea, save there was another ship, and upon it they might go without danger.

'Now, go we thither,' said the gentlewoman, 'and there shall we see adventures, for so is Our Lord's will.'

And when they came thither they found the ship rich enough, but they found neither man ne woman therein. But they found in the end of the ship two fair letters written, which said a dreadful word and a marvellous:

'Thou man, which shall enter into this ship, beware that thou be in steadfast belief, for I am Faith, And therefore beware how thou enterest, but if thou be steadfast. For and thou fail I shall not help thee.'

And then said the gentlewoman, 'Sir Percival, wot ye what ' am?'

'Certes,' said he, 'nay. To my witting, I saw you

'Wit you well,' said she, 'I am thy sister, which King Pellinor, and therefore wit ye well ye are the m. that I most love. And if ye be not in perfect belief o. enter not in no manner of wise, for then should ye per for he is so perfect he will suffer no sinner within him.'

So when Sir Percival understood that she was his ve. was inwardly glad, and said,

'Fair sister, I shall enter in, for if I be a miscreature or an untrue knight there shall I perish.'

So in the meanwhile Sir Galahad blessed him, and entered therein; and then next the gentlewoman, and then Sir Bors and then Sir Percival. And when they were in, it was so marvellous fair and rich that they marvelled; and in midst of the ship was a fair bed. And anon Sir Galahad went thereto, and found there a crown of silk. And at the feet was a sword, rich and fair, and it was drawn out of the sheath half a foot and more. And the sword was of divers fashions, and the pommel was of stone, and there was in him all manner of colours that any man might find, and every each of the colours had divers virtues. And the scales of the haft were of two ribs of divers beasts, the one beast was a serpent which is conversant in Caledonia, and is called there the serpent of the fiend; and the bone of him is of such a virtue that there is no hand that handleth him shall never be weary nor hurt. And the other bone is of a fish which is not right great, and haunteth the flood of Euphrates; and that fish is called Ertanax, and his bones be of such a manner of kind that who that handleth them shall have so much will that he shall never be weary, and he shall not think on joy nor sorrow that he hath had, but only that thing that he beholdeth before him.

Galahad, Percival, and Bors gaze on the sword

AND AS FOR THIS SWORD THERE SHALL NEVER MAN BEGRIP HIM AT THE HANDLES BUT ONE, BUT HE SHALL PASS ALL OTHER.

'In the name of God,' said Sir Percival, 'I shall assay to handle it.'

So he set his hand to the sword, but he might not begrip it.

'By my faith,' said he, 'now have I failed.'

Then Sir Bors set his hand thereto and failed.

Then Sir Galahad beheld the sword and saw letters like blood that said:

LET SEE WHO SHALL ASSAY TO DRAW ME OUT OF MY SHEATH, BUT IF HE BE MORE HARDIER THAN ANY OTHER; AND WHO THAT DRAWETH ME, WIT YE WELL THAT HE SHALL NEVER FAIL OF SHAME OF HIS BODY, OR BE WOUNDED TO THE DEATH.

'By my faith,' said Sir Galahad, 'I would draw this sword out of the sheath, but the offending is so great that I shall not set my hand thereto.'

'Now sirs,' said the gentlewoman, 'wit ye well that the drawing of this sword is warned to all men save all only to you. Also this ship arrived in the realm of Logris; and that time was deadly war between King Labor, which was father unto the Maimed King, and King Hurlame, which was a Saracen. But then was he newly christened, so that men held him afterward one of the wittiest men of the world.

'And so upon a day it befell that King Labor and King Hurlame had assembled their folk upon the sea where this ship was arrived; and there King Hurlame was discomfit, and his men slain; and he was afeared to be dead, and fled to his ship, and there found this sword and drew it, and came out and found King Labor, the man in the world of all Christendom in whom was then the greatest faith. And when King Hurlame saw King Labor he dressed his sword, and smote him upon the helm so hard that he clave him and his horse to the earth with the first stroke of his sword.

'And it was in the realm of Logris; and so befell great pestilence and great harm to both realms. For sithen increased neither corn, ne grass, nor well-nigh no fruit, ne in the water was no fish; wherefore men callen it, the lands of the two marches, the Waste Land, for that dolorous stroke.

'And when King Hurlame saw this sword so carving, he turned again to fetch the scabbard, and so came into this ship and entered, and put up the sword in the sheath. And as soon as he had done it he fell down dead afore the bed. Thus was the sword proved, that none ne drew it but he were dead or maimed. So lay he there till a maiden came into the ship and cast him out, for there was no man so hardy of the world to enter into that ship for the defence.'

And then beheld they the scabbard, it seemed to be of a serpent's skin, and thereon were letters of gold and silver. And the girdle was but poorly to come to, and not able to sustain such a rich sword. And the letters said:

'He which shall wield me ought to be more hardy than any other, if he bear me as truly as me ought to be borne. For the body of him which I ought to hang by, he shall not be shamed in no place while he is girt with this girdle; nor never none be so hardy to do away this girdle; for it ought not to be done away but by the hands of a maid, and that she be a king's daughter and queen's, and she must be a maid all the days of her life, both in will and in deed. And if she break her virginity she shall die the most villain-ous death that ever died any woman.'

'Sir,' said Sir Percival, 'turn this sword that we may see what is on the other side.' And it was red as blood, with black letters as any coal, which said:

'He that shall praise me most, most shall he find me to blame at a great need; and to whom I should be most debonair shall I be most felon. And that shall be at one time only.'

'Sir,' said she, 'there was a king that hight Pelles, which men called the Maimed King. And while he might ride he sup-ported much Christendom and Holy Church. So upon a day he

The Grail

hunted in a wood of his own which lasted unto the sea; and at the last he lost his hounds and his knights save only one. And there he and his knight went till that they came toward Ireland, and there he found the ship.

'And when he saw the letters and understood them, yet he entered, for he was right perfect of his life, but his knight had none hardiness to enter; and there found he this sword, and drew it out as much as ye may see. So therewith entered a spear wherewith he was smit him through both the thighs. And never sith might he be healed, ne nought shall tofore we come to him. Thus,' said she, 'was King Pelles, your grandsire, maimed for his hardiness.'

'In the name of God, damsel,' said Sir Galahad.

So they went toward the bed to behold all about it, and above the bed there hung two swords. Also there were two spindles which were as white as any snow, and other that were as red as blood, and other above green as any emerald: of these three colours were the spindles, and of natural colour within, and without any painting.

'These spindles,' said the damsel, 'were when sinful Eve came to gather fruit, for which Adam and she were put out of paradise. She took with her the bough which the apple hung on. Then perceived she that the branch was fresh and green, and she remembered of the loss which came of the tree. Then she thought to keep the branch as long as she might. And for she had no coffer to keep it in, she put it in the earth. So by the will of Our Lord the branch grew to a great tree within a little while, and was as white as any snow, branches, boughs, and leaves: that was a token that a maiden planted it. But after that God came to Adam, and bad him know his wife fleshly as nature required. So lay Adam with his wife under the same tree; and anon the tree which was white fell to green as any grass, and all that came out of it; and in the same time that they meddled together there was Abel begotten. Thus was the tree long of green colour.

'And so it befell many days after, under the same tree, Cain slew Abel; whereof befell great marvel. For anon as Abel had received the death under the green tree, he lost the green colour and became red; and that was in tokening of blood. And anon all the plants died thereof, but the tree grew and waxed marvellously fair, and it was the most fairest tree and the most delectable that any man might behold and see; and so died the plants that grew out of it tofore that Abel was slain under it.

'And so long dured the tree till that Solomon, King David's son, reigned, and held the land after his father. This Solomon was wise, and knew all the virtues of stones and trees, and knew the course of the stars and many other divers things. This Solomon had an evil

OPPOSITE
*Galahad is presented
to Arthur and his
knights at the
Round Table*

OVERLEAF LEFT
*Arthur rides out
with his knights and
takes leave of them as
they set out
on the quest*

OVERLEAF RIGHT
*Watched by Arthur
and Guenever, Galahad
sheathes the sword
after removing it from
the stone*

te famar. qi prrent sor ses espaules. apar
de dunz estoit fozes une biane samit.

Jant il la uestu et appreilie se li dit. ue
nes. aps moi sur. chr. et il li fist et ille
meme tot droit au siege pilleus. de le en
taint. se seont. et leue le pra dont il estoit
couers. qe lanc. ua uoit fere ment. se troue
les lettres qi disoit a est la siege galahz.
I prenrens regarde les lettres si les
troue eicetes le noms se lit. qil i auoit se
escit de leen sont. Sur chr. ascer no
au est leu enit. Se ci si siet tot seur.
ment. a dit apstome. Que uos uoil p
et alsi qe bien aues fet ce qe len uos co
manda. a saluec moi en ces a tou celles
del saint ostel. a mon auid. le roi palu

et mon besaucel le roi pescheor. et li dites
de par moi qe le li uni ueou au plus tost
qe ge porr et qe ge en aui loisir.
Tant se pur li pucees. de leenz a coma
de ateu mte seigneu. le roi a toute sa g
pigme. et qnt il uonstret de matre. qil
estoit. sine tuit onqucs pler aaui. auis le
ar respont tot plenemant. qil ne lor uiu
cr en pr cu il le sauoict bien en cor uoi a
tant fil lossoet demanda. Si uieir au me
stre bns. uni pain. qi dom estoit si le o
uir. a siseie dual le chi gret. ille conr q
troue. chra. qi si est dire qe uot le ru
uoient. et fozete uir a. la celi e u. n
e une q nel menace o l ne souit t..
efon chir. a ule forte.

plus qe li uenus air trop a en m̄ me · · · · · repart deuos. Oies puis qe qe uos qe
feir li conuent si me retorncrc·:·

li fois cleiz uos en noient deus au came
part ansi com il afet espre. Lors regardet
ners lanne ᵹtreual et uoit uenu ansi
come abesoing une damoiselle monte
seur un palefroi blác et uenoit ners
aus grnz aleure.

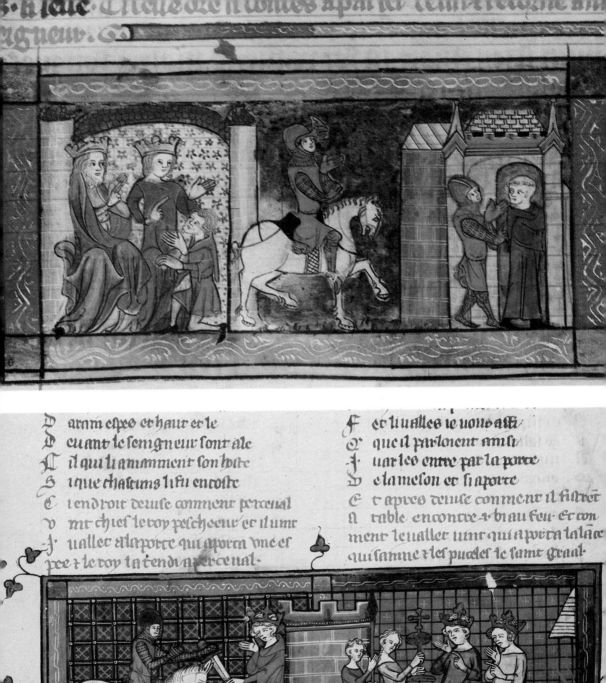

arm espes et haut et le
euant le seigneur sont ale
il qui li amaimment son hoste
s ique chascuns li fu encoste
e tendroit deuise comment perceual
u mt chies le roy pescheeur et il umt
f ualler alaporte qui aporta une es
pee et le roy ta tendi aperceual

et li uallies ie uous assi
que il parloient ainsi
uar leo entre par la porte
e la meson et si aporte
et apres deuise comment il fistret
a table encontre et biau feu et con
ment leualler umt qui aporta la lace
qui saune et les pucles le sunt graal

wife, wherethrough he weened that there had be no good woman born, and so he despised them in his books. So there answered a voice that said to him thus:

'"Solomon, if heaviness come to a man by a woman, ne reck thou never; for yet shall there come a woman whereof there shall come greater joy to man an hundred times more than this heaviness giveth sorrow; and that woman shall be born of thy lineage."

'So when Solomon heard these words he held himself but a fool, and the truth he perceived by old books. Also the Holy Ghost showed him the coming of the glorious Virgin Mary. Then asked he of the voice, if it should be in the yard of his lineage.

yard: *branch*

'"Nay," said the voice, "but there shall come a man which shall be a maid, and the last of your blood, and he shall be as good a knight as Duke Joshua, thy brother-in-law.

'"Now have I certified thee of that thou stoodest in doubt."

'Then was Solomon glad that there should come any such of his lineage; but ever he marvelled and studied who that should be, and what his name might be. So his wife perceived that he studied, and thought she would know it at some season. And so she waited her time, and asked of him the cause of his studying; and there he told her altogether how the voice told him.

'"Well," said she, "I shall let make a ship of the best wood and most durable that any man may find."

'So Solomon sent for all the carpenters, of all the land the best. And when they had made the ship the lady said to Solomon:

'"Sir," said she, "since it is so that this knight ought to pass all knights of chivalry which have been tofore him and shall come after him, moreover I shall learn you," said she, "ye shall go into Our Lord's temple, where is King David's sword, your father, which is the marvelloust and the sharpest that ever was taken in any knight's hand. Therefore take ye that, and take off the pommel, and thereto make ye a pommel of precious stones; let it be so subtly made that no man perceive it but that they be all one; and after make there an hilt so marvellously and wonderly that no man may know it; and after that make a marvellous sheath. And when ye have made all this I shall let make a girdle thereto, such one as shall please me."

'All this King Solomon did let make as she devised, both the ship and all the remnant. And when the ship was ready in the sea to sail, the lady let make a great bed and marvellous rich, and set her upon the bed's head, covered with silk, and laid the sword at the feet, and the girdles were of hemp, and therewith the king was right angry.

'"Sir, wit ye well," said she, "that I have none so high a thing which were worthy to sustain so high a sword. And a maid shall

OPPOSITE ABOVE
*Gawain leaves Arthur
and Guenever, rides on
his quest, and arrives
at a monastery*

OPPOSITE BELOW
*In the castle of the
Holy Grail, the Grail
is carried to a table while
Percival is presented
with a sword by the
Maimed King*

bring other knights hereto, but I wot not when it shall be, ne what time."

'And there she let make a covering to the ship, of cloth of silk that should never rot for no manner of weather. Then this lady went and made a carpenter to come to the tree which Abel was slain under.

'"Now," said she, "carve me out of this tree as much wood as will make me a spindle."

'"Ah madam," said he, "this is the tree the which our first mother planted."

'"Do it," said she, "or else I shall destroy thee."

'Anon as he began to work there came out drops of blood; and then would he have left, but she would not suffer him, and so he took as much wood as he might make a spindle: and so she made him to take as much of the green tree and of the white tree. And when these three spindles were shapen she made them to be fastened upon the selar of the bed. So when Solomon saw this, he said to his wife,

'"Ye have done marvellously, for though all the world were here right now, they could not devise wherefore all this was made, but Our Lord Himself; and thou that hast done it wotest not what it shall betoken."

'"Now let it be," said she, "for ye shall hear peradventure tidings sooner than ye ween."

'Now here is a wonderful tale of King Solomon and his wife.

'That night lay Solomon before the ship with little fellowship. And when he was asleep him thought there come from heaven a great company of angels, and alit into the ship, and took water which was brought by an angel, in a vessel of silver, and sprent all the ship. And after he came to the sword, and drew letters on the hilt. And after went to the ship-board, and wrote there other letters which said: "Thou man that wilt enter within me, beware that thou be full in the faith, for I ne am but Faith and Belief."

'When Solomon espied these letters he was so abashed that he durst not enter, and so he drew him aback; and the ship was anon shoven in the sea. He went so fast that he lost sight of him within a little while.

'And then a voice said, "Solomon, the last knight of thy lineage shall rest in this bed."

'Then went Solomon and awaked his wife, and told her of the adventures of the ship.'

Now saith the tale that a great while the three fellows beheld the bed and the three spindles. Then they were at certain that they were of natural colours without any painting. Then they lift up a cloth which was above the ground, and there found a rich purse by seem-

selar: *canopy*

sprent: *sprinkled*

196

ing. And Sir Percival took it, and found therein a writ, and so he read it, and devised the manner of the spindles and of the ship, whence it came, and by whom it was made.

'Now,' said Sir Galahad, 'where shall we find the gentlewoman that shall make new girdles to the sword?'

'Fair sir,' said Sir Percival's sister, 'dismay you not, for by the leave of God I shall let make a girdle to the sword, such one as should long thereto.'

And then she opened a box, and took out girdles which were seemly wrought with golden threads, and upon that were set full precious stones, and a rich buckle of gold.

'Lo, lords,' said she, 'here is a girdle that ought to be set about the sword. And wit ye well the greatest part of this girdle was made of my hair, which sometime I loved well while that I was a woman of the world. But as soon as I wist that this adventure was ordained me I clipped off my hair, and made this girdle.'

'In the name of God, ye be well found,' said Sir Bors, 'for certes ye have put us out of great pain, wherein we should have entered ne had your tidings been.'

Then went the gentlewoman and set it on the girdle of the sword.

'Now,' said the fellowship, 'what is the name of the sword, and what shall we call it?'

'Truly,' said she, 'the name of the sword is the Sword with the Strange Girdles; and the sheath, Mover of Blood; for no man that hath blood in him ne shall never see the one part of the sheath which was made of the tree of life.'

Then they said to Sir Galahad, 'In the name of Jesu Christ, and pray you that ye gird you with this sword which hath been desired so much in the realm of Logris.'

'Now let me begin,' said Sir Galahad, 'to grip this sword for to give you courage; but wit ye well it longeth no more to me than it doth to you.'

And then he gripped about it with his fingers a great deal; and then she girt him about the middle with the sword.

'Now reck I not though I die, for now I hold me one of the blessed maidens of the world, which hath made the worthiest knight of the world.'

'Damsel,' said Sir Galahad, 'ye have done so much that I shall be your knight all the days of my life.'

Then they went from that ship, and went to the other. And anon the wind drove them into the sea a great pace, but they had no victual: but it befell that they came on the morn to a castle that men call Carteloise, that was in the marches of Scotland. And when they had passed the port, the gentlewoman said,

'Lords, here be men arriven that, and they wist that ye were of King Arthur's court, ye should be assailed anon.'

'Well, damsel, dismay you not,' said Sir Galahad, 'He that cast us out of the rock shall deliver us from them.'

(And upon the morn, when they had heard mass, they departed ... and so they came to a castle and passed by.

So there came a knight armed after them and said,

'Lords, this gentlewoman that ye lead with you, is she a maid?'

'Sir,' said she, 'a maid I am.'

Then he took her by the bridle and said,

'By the Holy Cross, ye shall not escape me tofore ye have yielden the custom of this castle.'

'Let her go,' said Sir Percival, 'ye be not wise, for a maid in what place she cometh is free.'

So in the meanwhile there came out a ten or twelve knights armed, out of the castle, and with them came gentlewomen which held a dish of silver. And then they said,

'This gentlewoman must yield us the custom of this castle.'

'Why,' said Sir Galahad, 'what is the custom of this castle?'

'Sir,' said a knight, 'what maid passeth hereby shall give this dish full of blood of her right arm.'

'Blame have he,' said Sir Galahad, 'that brought up such customs. And so God me save, also sure may ye be that this gentlewoman shall ye fail while that I live.'

'So God me help,' said Sir Percival, 'I had lever be slain.'

'And I also,' said Sir Bors.

'By my faith,' said the knight, 'then shall ye die, for ye may not endure against us, though ye were the best knights of the world.'

Then let they run each horse to other, and these three knights beat the ten knights, and then set their hands to their swords and beat them down and slew them. Then there came out of the castle a sixty knights armed.

'Now, fair lords,' said these three knights, 'have mercy on yourself and have not ado with us.'

'Nay, fair lords,' said the knights of the castle, 'we counsel you to withdraw you, for ye be the best knights of the world, and therefore do no more, for ye have done enough. We will let you go with this harm, but we must needs have the custom.'

'Certes,' said Sir Galahad, 'for nought speak ye.'

'Well,' said they, 'will ye die?'

'Sir, we be not yet come thereto,' said Sir Galahad.

Then began they to meddle together. And Sir Galahad, with the strange girdles, drew his sword, and smote on the right hand and on the left hand, and slew whom that ever abode him, and did so marvellously that there was none that saw him they weened he had been none earthly man, but a monster. And his two fellows halp him passing well, and so they held their journey every each in like hard till it was night: then must they needs depart.

So there came a good knight, and said to these three knights,

'If ye will come in tonight and take such harbour as here is ye shall be right welcome. And we shall ensure you by the faith of our bodies, and as we be true knights, to leave you in such estate tomorrow as here we find you, without any falsehood. And as soon as ye know of the custom, we dare say ye will accord therefore.'

'For God's love,' said the gentlewoman, 'go we thither and spare not for me.'

'Well, go we,' said Sir Galahad.

And so they entered into the castle. And when they were alit they made great joy of them. So within a while the three knights asked the custom of the castle and wherefore it was.

'Sir, what it is,' said they, 'we will say you sooth: There is in this castle a gentlewoman which both we and this castle is hers, and many other. So it befell many years agone there fell upon her a malady; and when she had lain a great while she fell unto a mesel. And no leech could remedy her. But at the last an old man said and she might have a dish full of blood of a maiden and a clean virgin in will and in work, and a king's daughter, that blood should be her health, and for to anoint her withal; and for this thing was this custom made.'

mesel: *bad illness*

'Now,' said Sir Percival's sister, 'fair knights, I see well that this gentlewoman is but dead without help, and therefore let me bleed.'

'Certes,' said Sir Galahad, 'and ye bleed so much ye may die.'

'Truly,' said she, 'and I die for her to heal her I shall get me great worship and soul's health, and worship to my lineage, and better is one harm than twain. And therefore there shall be no more battle, but tomorn I shall yield you your custom of this castle.'

And then there was great joy more than there was tofore. For else had there been mortal war upon the morn; notwithstanding she would none other, whether they would or nold. So that night were these three fellows eased with the best; and on the morn they heard mass. And Sir Percival's sister bad them bring forth the sick lady. So she was brought forth, the which was evil at ease.

Then said she, 'Who shall let me blood?'

So one came forth and let her blood, and she bled so much that the dish was full. Then she lift up her hand and blessed her; and then she said to the lady,

'Madam, I am come to the death for to make you whole. Therefore for God's love pray for me.'

With that she fell in a swoon. Then Sir Galahad and his two fellows start up to her, and lift her up and staunched her blood, but she had bled so much that she might not live.

Then she said when she was awaked,

The Grail

'Fair brother, Sir Percival, I die for the healing of this lady. And when I am dead I require you that ye bury me not in this country, but as soon as I am dead put me in a boat at the next haven, and let me go as adventure will lead me. And as soon as ye three come to the City of Sarras, there to achieve the Holy Grail, ye shall find me under a tower arrived. And there bury me in the spiritual palace. For I shall tell you for truth, there Sir Galahad shall be buried, and ye both, in the same place.'

When Sir Percival understood these words, he granted it her, weeping. And then said a voice unto them,

'Lords and fellows, tomorrow at the hour of prime ye three shall depart every each from other, till the adventure bring you to the Maimed King.'

Then asked she her Saviour; and as soon as she had received it the soul departed from the body.

So the same day was the lady healed, when she was anointed withal. Then Sir Percival made a letter of all that she had holpen them as in strange adventures, and put it in her right hand, and so laid her in a barge, and covered it with black silk; and so the wind arose, and drove the barge from the land, and all knights beheld it till it was out of their sight.

Then they drew all to the castle, and so forthwith there fell a sudden tempest and a thunder, lait, and rain, as all the earth would have broken. So half the castle turned up-so-down. So it passed evensong or the tempest was ceased.

'Now,' said Sir Percival unto Sir Galahad, 'we must depart, and therefore pray we Our Lord that we may meet together in short time; then they did off their helms and kissed together, and sore wept at their departing.

Now turneth this tale unto Sir Lancelot.

Lancelot

Now saith the tale, that when Sir Lancelot was come to the water of Mortaise, as it is rehearsed before, he was in great peril. And so he laid him down and slept and took the adventure that God would send him. So when he was asleep there came a vision unto him that said,

'Sir Lancelot, arise up and take thine armour, and enter into the first ship that thou shalt find.'

And when he heard these words he start up and saw great clear-ness about him. And then he lift up his hand and blessed him, and so took his arms and made him ready. And at the last he came by a strand, and found a ship, without sail or oar.

And as soon as he was within the ship there he felt the most sweetness that ever he felt, and he was fulfilled with all thing that he thought on or desired. Then he said,

'Fair sweet Father, Jesu Christ, I wot not in what joy I am, for this joy passeth all earthly joys that ever I was in.'

And so in this joy he laid him down to the ship-board, and slept till day. And when he awoke he found there a fair bed, and therein lying a gentlewoman dead, the which was Sir Percival's sister.

And as Sir Lancelot avised her, he espied in her right hand a writ, which he read, that told him all the adventures that ye have heard before, and of what lineage she was come.

So with this gentlewoman Sir Lancelot was a month and more. If ye would ask how he lived, He that fed the people of Israel with manna in desert, so was he fed; for every day when he had said his prayers he was sustained with the grace of the Holy Ghost.

So on a night he went to play him by the water side, for he was somewhat weary of the ship. And then he listened and heard an horse come, and one riding upon him. And when he came nigh he seemed a knight. And so he let him pass, and went thereas the ship was; and there he alit, and took the saddle and the bridle and put the horse from him, and so went into the ship.

And then Sir Lancelot dressed unto him, and said, 'Sir, ye be welcome.'

And he answered and saluted him again, and asked him, 'What is your name? For much my heart giveth unto you.'

'Truly,' said he, 'my name is Sir Lancelot du Lake.'

'Sir,' said he, 'then be ye welcome, for ye were the beginner of me in this world.'

'Ah,' said he, 'are ye Sir Galahad?'

'Yea, forsooth,' said he; and so he kneeled down and asked him his blessing, and after took off his helm and kissed him. And there was great joy between them, for there is no tongue can tell the joy that they made either of other, and many a friendly word spoken between, as kind would, the which is no need here to be rehearsed. And there every each told other of their adventures and marvels that were befallen to them in many journeys sith that they departed from the court.

And anon, as Sir Galahad saw the gentlewoman dead in the bed, he knew her well enough, and said great worship of her, that she was one of the best maidens living, and it was great pity of her death. But when Sir Lancelot heard how the marvellous sword was gotten, and who made it, and all the marvels rehearsed afore, then he prayed Sir Galahad, his son, that he would show him the sword. And so he brought it forth and kissed the pommel, and the hilts, and the scabbard.

'Truly,' said Sir Lancelot, 'never erst knew I of so high adventures done, and so marvellous and strange.'

So dwelt Sir Lancelot and Sir Galahad within that ship half a year, and served God daily and nightly with all their power; and often they arrived in isles far from folk, where there repaired none but wild beasts, and there they found many strange adventures and perilous, which they brought to an end. But for those adventures were with wild beasts, and not in the quest of the Sangrail, therefore the tale maketh here no mention thereof; for it would be too long to tell of all those adventures that befell them.

So after, on a Monday, it befell that they arrived in the edge of a forest tofore a cross. And then saw they a knight armed all in white, and was richly horsed, and led in his right hand a white horse; and so he came to the ship, and saluted the two knights on the High Lord's behalf, and said unto Sir Galahad,

'Sir, ye have been long enough with your father. Therefore come out of the ship, and take this horse, and go where adventures shall lead you in the quest of the Sangrail.'

Then he went to his father and kissed him sweetly, and said,

'Fair sweet father, I wot not when I shall see you more till I see the body of Jesu Christ.'

'Now, for God's love,' said Sir Lancelot, 'pray to the Father that He hold me still in His service.'

And so he took his horse, and there they heard a voice that said,

'Every of you think for to do well; for the one shall never see the other before the dreadful day of doom.'

'Now, my son Sir Galahad,' said Sir Lancelot, 'since we shall depart, and neither of us see other more, I pray to the High Father to conserve me and you both.'

'Sir,' said Sir Galahad, 'no prayer availeth so much as yours.'

And therewith Sir Galahad entered into the forest. And the wind arose, and drove Sir Lancelot more than a month throughout the sea, where he slept but little, but prayed to God that he might see some tidings of the Sangrail.

So it befell on a night, at midnight, he arrived before a castle, on the back side, which was rich and fair, and there was a postern opened toward the sea, and was open without any keeping, save two lions kept the entry; and the moon shone clear.

Anon Sir Lancelot heard a voice that said,

'Lancelot, go out of this ship and enter into the castle, where thou shalt see a great part of thy desire.'

Then he ran to his arms, and so armed him, and so went to the gate and saw the lions. Then set he hand to his sword and drew it. Then there came a dwarf suddenly, and smote him on the arm so sore that the sword fell out of his hand.

Lancelot arrives at a castle

Then heard he a voice say,

'O man of evil faith and poor belief! Wherefore trustest thou more on thy harness than in thy Maker? For he might more avail thee than thine armour, in what service that thou art set in.'

Then said Sir Lancelot, 'Fair Father, Jesu Christ, I thank thee of Thy great mercy that Thou reprovest me of my misdeed; now see I well that Thou holdest me for Thy servant.'

*Lancelot is
confronted by lions*

Then took he his sword again and put it up in his sheath, and made a cross in his forehead, and came to the lions. And they made semblant to do him harm. Notwithstanding he passed by them without hurt, and entered into the castle to the chief fortress. And there were they all at rest.

Then Sir Lancelot entered in so armed, for he found no gate nor door but it was open. And at the last he found a chamber whereof the door was shut, and he set his hand thereto to have opened it, but he might not.

Then he enforced him mickle to undo the door. Then he listened and heard a voice which sang so sweetly that it seemed none earthly thing; and him thought the voice said,

'Joy and honour be to the Father of Heaven.'

Then Sir Lancelot kneeled down tofore the chamber door, for well wist he that there was the Sangrail within that chamber. Then said he,

'Fair sweet Father, Jesu Christ, if ever I did thing that pleased Thee, Lord for Thy pity ne have me not in despite for my sins done beforetime, and that Thou show me something of that I seek.'

And with that he saw the chamber door open, and there came out a great clearness, that the house was as bright as all the torches of the world had been there. So came he to the chamber door, and would have entered. And anon a voice said to him,

'Flee, Sir Lancelot, and enter not, for thou ought not to do it. For and if thou enter thou shalt forthink it.'

Then he withdrew him aback right heavy. Then looked he up in the midst of the chamber, and saw a table of silver, and the holy vessel, covered with red samite, and many angels about it – whereof one held a candle of wax burning, and the other held a cross – and the ornaments of an altar. And before the holy vessel he saw a good man clothed as a priest. And it seemed that he was at the sacring of the mass. And it seemed to Sir Lancelot that above the priest's hands were three men, whereof the two put the youngest by likeness between the priest's hands; and so he lift it up right high, and it seemed to show so to the people. And then Sir Lancelot marvelled not a little, for him thought the priest was so greatly charged of the figure that him seemed that he should fall to the earth.

And when he saw none about him that would help him, then came he to the door a great pace, and said,

'Fair Father Jesu Christ, ne take it for no sin if I help the good man which hath great need of help.'

Right so entered he into the chamber, and came toward the table of silver; and when he came nigh it he felt a breath that him thought it was intermeddled with fire, which smote him so sore in the visage that him thought it burnt his visage. And therewith he fell to the earth, and had no power to arise, as he that was so araged, that had lost the power of his body, and his hearing, and his sight. Then felt he many hands about him, which took him up and bare him out of the chamber door, without any amending of his swoon, and left him there, seeming dead to all people.

So upon the morrow when it was fair day, they within were risen and found Sir Lancelot lying before the chamber door. All they marvelled how that he came in. And so they looked upon him, and felt his pulse to wit whether there were any life in him; and so they found life in him, but he might not stand nor stir no member that he had. And so they took him by every part of the body, and bare him into a chamber, and laid him in a rich bed, far from all folk; and so he lay four days. Then the one said he was alive, and the other said nay, he was dead.

'In the name of God,' said an old man, 'I do you verily to wit he is not dead, but he is so full of life as the strongest of you all. Therefore I counsel you all that he be well kept till God send life in him again.'

So in such manner they kept Sir Lancelot four and twenty days and all so many nights, that ever he lay still as a dead man. And at the twenty-fifth day befell him after midday that he opened his eyen. And when he saw folk he made great sorrow, and said,

'Why have ye awaked me, for I was more at ease than I am now. O Jesu Christ, who might be so blessed that might see openly Thy great marvels of secretness there where no sinner may be!'

'What have ye seen?' said they about him.

'I have seen,' said he, 'so great marvels that no tongue may tell, and more than any heart can think. And had not my sin been beforetime I had seen much more.'

Lancelot recovering in bed talks with his attendants

Then they told him how he had lain there four and twenty days and nights. Then him thought it was punishment for the four and twenty years that he had been a sinner, wherefore Our Lord put him in penance four and twenty days and nights. . . . . Then they asked how it stood with him.

'Forsooth,' said he, 'I am whole of body, thanked be Our Lord; therefore, sirs, for God's love tell me where I am.'

Then said they all that he was in the Castle of Carbonek.

'Sir,' said they, 'the quest of the Sangrail is achieved now right in you, that never shall ye see of the Sangrail no more than ye have seen.'

'Now I thank God,' said Sir Lancelot, 'for His great mercy, of that I have seen, for it sufficeth me; for as I suppose no man in this world hath lived better than I have done to achieve that I have done.'

Then came word to King Pelles that the knight that had lain so long dead was the noble knight Sir Lancelot. Then was the king right glad, and went to see him. And when Sir Lancelot saw him come he dressed him against him, and then made the king great joy of him. And there the king told him tidings that his fair daughter was dead. Then Sir Lancelot was right heavy of it, and said,

'Sir, me forthinketh of the death of your daughter, for she was a full fair lady, fresh and young. And well I wot she bare the best knight that is now on earth, or that ever was sith God was born.'

So the king held him there four days, and on the morrow he took his leave at King Pelles and at all the fellowship, and thanked them of the great labour.

Right so as they sat at their dinner in the chief hall, then it so befell that the Sangrail had fulfilled the tables with all manner of meats that any heart might think. So as they sat they saw all the doors and the windows of the palace were shut without man's hand, whereof they were all abashed, and none wist what to do.

And then it happed suddenly that a knight which was all armed came to the chief door and knocked, and cried, 'Undo the door.'

But they would not.

And ever he cried, 'Undo!' but they would not.

And at last it noyed them so much that the king himself arose and came to a window there where the knight called.

Then he said, 'Sir knight, ye shall not enter at this time while the Sangrail is here. And therefore go ye into another fortress for ye be none of the knights of the Quest, but one of them which hath served the fiend, and hast left the service of Our Lord.'

Then was he passing wroth at the king's words.

'Sir knight,' said the king, 'since ye would so fain enter, say me of what country ye be.'

'Sir,' said he, 'I am of the realm of Logris, and my name is Sir Ector de Maris, brother unto my lord Sir Lancelot.'

'In the name of God,' said the king, 'me forthinketh of that I have said, for your brother is here within.'

When Sir Ector de Maris understood that his brother was there

– for he was the man in the world that he most dread and loved –
then he said,

'Ah, good Lord, now doubleth my sorrow and shame. Full
truly said the good man of the hill unto Sir Gawain and to me of
our dreams.'

Then went he out of the court as fast as his horse might, and so
throughout the castle.

Then King Pelles came to Sir Lancelot and told him tidings of
his brother, whereof he was sorry, that he wist not what to do.

So Sir Lancelot departed, and took his arms, and said he would
go see the realm of Logris, 'which I have not seen in a twelvemonth.' And therewith he commended the king to God. And so
rode through many realms.

And [then] he turned unto Camelot, where he found King
Arthur and the queen. But many of the knights of the Round
Table were slain and destroyed, more than half. And so three
were come home, Sir Ector, Sir Gawain and Sir Lionel, and
many other that needen now not to rehearse. And all the court was
passing glad of Sir Lancelot, and the king asked him many tidings
of his son Sir Galahad.

And there Sir Lancelot told the king of his adventures that had
befallen him since he departed. And also he told him of the adventures of Sir Galahad, Sir Percival, and Sir Bors, which that he
knew by the letter of the dead maiden, and as Sir Galahad had
told him.

'Now God would,' said the king, 'that they were all three here.'

'That shall never be,' said Sir Lancelot, 'for two of them shall
ye never see. But one of them shall come again.'

Now leave we this tale and speak of Sir Galahad.

*Lancelot and his
companions tell Arthur
of their quest*

The Grail Achieved

Now saith the tale that Sir Galahad rode many journeys in vain
. . . and so he rode . . . till that he came to the Maimed King. And
ever followed Sir Percival . . . asking where he had been; and so
one told him how the adventures of Logris were achieved.

So on a day it befell that he came out of a great forest, and there
they met at traverse with Sir Bors, which rode alone. It is none
need to ask if they were glad! And so he saluted, and they yielded
him honour and good adventure, and every each told other how
they had sped.

Then said Sir Bors, 'It is more than a year and an half that I ne
lay ten times where men dwelled, but in wild forests and in mountains, but God was ever my comfort.'

Then rode they a great while till that they came to the Castle of
Carbonek. And when they were entered within the castle King
Pelles knew them; then there was great joy, for he wist well by
their coming that they had fulfilled the quest of the Sangrail.

Then Eliazar, King Pelles' son, brought tofore them the broken
sword wherewith Joseph was stricken through the thigh. Then
Sir Bors set his hand thereto, to assay if that he might have soldered
it again; but it would not be. Then he took it to Sir Percival, but
he had no more power thereto than he.

'Now have ye it again,' said Sir Percival to Sir Galahad, 'for
and it be ever achieved by any bodily man ye must do it.'

And then he took the pieces and set them together, and they
seemed that they had never been broken, and as well as it had been
first forged. And when they within espied that the adventure of the
sword was achieved, then they gave the sword to Sir Bors, for it
might not be better set; for he was a good knight and a worthy
man.

And a little before even the sword arose great and marvellous,
and was full of great heat that many men fell for dread. And anon
alit a voice among them, and said:

Galahad and Percival
arrive at a castle

The Grail

'They that ought not to sit at the table of Our Lord Jesu Christ arise, avoid hence, for now shall very knights be fed.'

So they went thence, all save King Pelles and Eliazar, his son, which were holy men, and a maid which was his niece. And so these three knights and they three were there, no more.

And so as they sat thus, there came out a bed of tree, of a chamber, the which four gentlewomen brought; and in the bed lay a good man sick, and a crown of gold upon his head; and there in the midst of the palace they set him down, and went again. Then he lift up his head, and said,

'Sir Galahad, knight, ye be right welcome, for much have I desired your coming. For in such pain and anguish I have suffered long. But now I trust to God the term is come that my pain shall be allayed, that I shall pass out of this world, so as it was promised me long ago.'

And therewith a voice said, 'There be two among you that be not in the quest of the Sangrail, and therefore depart ye.'

Then King Pelles and his son departed. And therewithal beseemed them that there came a man, and four angels from heaven, clothed in likeness of a bishop, and had a cross in his hand. And these four angels bare him up in a chair, and set him down before the table of silver whereupon the Sangrail was. And it seemed that he had in the midst of his forehead letters the which said, 'See ye here Joseph, the first bishop of Christendom, the same which Our Lord succoured in the city of Sarras, in the spiritual palace.'

Then the knights marvelled, for that bishop was dead more than three hundred year tofore.

'O knights,' said he, 'marvel not, for I was sometime an earthly man.'

With that they heard the chamber door open, and there they saw angels; and two bare candles of wax, and the third bare a towel, and the fourth a spear which bled marvellously, that three drops fell within a box which he held with his other hand. And they set the candles upon the table, and the third the towel upon the vessel, and the fourth the holy spear even upright upon the vessel.

obley: wafer

And then the bishop made semblant as though he would have gone to the sacring of the mass. And then he took an obley which was made in likeness of bread. And at the lifting up there came a figure in likeness of a child, and the visage was as red and as bright as any fire, and smote himself into the bread, so that they all saw it that the bread was formed of a fleshly man; and then he put it into the holy vessel again, and then he did that longed to a priest to do mass.

And then he went to Sir Galahad and kissed him, and bad him go and kiss his fellows: and so he did anon.

'Now,' said he, 'servants of Jesu Christ, ye shall be fed afore this table with sweetmeats that never knights yet tasted.'

And when he had said, he vanished away. And they set them at the table in great dread, and made their prayers.

Then looked they and saw a man come out of the holy vessel, that had all the signs of the passion of Jesu Christ, bleeding all openly, and said,

'My knights, and my servants, and my true children, which be come out of deadly life into spiritual life, I will now no longer hide me from you, but ye shall see now a part of my secrets and of my hid things. Now holdeth and receiveth the high meat which ye have so much desired.'

Then took he himself the holy vessel and came to Sir Galahad; and he kneeled down, and there he received his Saviour, and after him so received all his fellows; and they thought it so sweet that it was marvellous to tell.

Then said he to Sir Galahad, 'Son, wotest thou what I hold betwixt my hands?'

'Nay,' said he, 'but if Ye will tell me.'

'This is,' said He, 'the holy dish wherein I ate the lamb on Easter Day. And now hast thou seen that thou most desired to see, but yet hast thou not seen it so openly as thou shalt see it in the city of Sarras in the spiritual palace. Therefore thou must go hence and bear with thee this holy vessel; for this night it shall depart from the realm of Logris, and it shall never more be seen here. And knowest thou wherefore? For he is not served nor worshipped to his right by them of this land, for they be turned to evil living; and therefore I shall disherit them of the honour which I have done them. And therefore go ye three tomorrow unto the sea, where ye shall find your ship ready, and with you take the sword with the strange girdles, and no more with you but Sir Percival and Sir Bors. Also I will that ye take with you of this blood of this spear for to anoint the Maimed King, both his legs and all his body, and he shall have his health.'

Galahad with the Maimed King

'Sir,' said Sir Galahad, 'why shall not these other fellows go with us?'

'For this cause: for right as I departed my apostles one here and another there, so I will that ye depart; and two of you shall die in my service, but one of you shall come again and tell tidings.'

Then gave He them his blessing and vanished away.

And Sir Galahad went anon to the spear which lay upon the table, and touched the blood with his fingers, and came after to the Maimed King and anointed his legs and his body.

And therewith he clothed him anon, and start upon his feet out of his bed as an whole man, and thanked Our Lord that He had healed him. And anon he left the world, and he yielded him to a place of religion of white monks, and was a full holy man.

That same night about midnight came a voice among them which said, 'My sons and not my chief sons, my friends and not my warriors, go ye hence where ye hope best to do and as I bad you do.'

'Ah, thanked be Thou, Lord, that Thou wilt vouchsafe to call us, Thy sinners. Now may we well prove that we have not lost our pains.'

And anon in all haste they took their harness and departed.

Right so departed Sir Galahad, and Sir Percival and Sir Bors with him; and so they rode three days, and then they came to a rivage, and found the ship whereof the tale speaketh of tofore. And when they came to the board they found in the midst the table of silver which they had left with the Maimed King, and the Sangrail which was covered with red samite.

Then were they glad to have such things in their fellowship; and so they entered and made great reverence thereto; and Sir Galahad fell on his knees and prayed long time to Our Lord, that at what time he asked, he might pass out of this world. And so long he prayed, till a voice said:

'Sir Galahad, thou shalt have thy request; and when thou askest the death of thy body thou shalt have it, and then shalt thou have the life of thy soul.'

Then Sir Percival heard this, and prayed him, of fellowship that was between them, to tell him wherefore he asked such things.

'Sir that shall I tell you,' said Sir Galahad. 'This other day when we saw a part of the adventures of the Sangrail, I was in such a joy of heart, that I trow never man was that was earthly. And therefore I wot well, when my body is dead my soul shall be in great joy to see the Blessed Trinity every day, and the majesty of Our Lord, Jesu Christ.'

And so long were they in the ship that they said to Sir Galahad, 'Sir, in this bed ye ought to lie, for so saith the letter.'

And so he laid him down and slept a great while; and when he awaked he looked afore him and saw the city of Sarras. And as they would have landed they saw the ship wherein Sir Percival had put his sister in.

'Truly,' said Sir Percival, 'in the name of God, well hath my sister holden us covenant.'

Then took they out of the ship the table of silver, and he took it to Sir Percival and to Sir Bors, to go tofore, and Sir Galahad came behind. And right so they went to the city, and at the gate of the city they saw an old man crooked, and anon Sir Galahad called him and bad him help to bear this heavy thing.

'Truly,' said the old man, 'it is ten year ago that I might not go but with crutches.'

'Care thou not,' said Sir Galahad, 'arise up and show thy good will.'

And so he assayed, and found himself as whole as ever he was. Then ran he to the table, and took one part against Sir Galahad. And anon rose there a great noise in the city, that a cripple was made whole by knights marvellous that entered into the city.

Then anon after, the three knights went to the water, and brought up into the palace Sir Percival's sister, and buried her as richly as they ought a king's daughter.

And when the king of that country (whose name was Estorause) knew that and saw the fellowship, he asked them of whence they were, and what thing it was that they had brought upon the table of silver. And they told him the truth of the Sangrail, and the power which that God had set there.

Then this king was a tyrant, and was come of the line of pay-nims, and took them and put them in prison in a deep hole. But as soon as they were there Our Lord sent them the Sangrail, through whose grace they were always fulfilled while that they were in prison.

So at the year's end it befell that this King Estorause lay sick, and felt that he should die. Then he sent for the three knights, and they came afore him; and he cried them mercy of that he had done to them, and they forgave it him goodly; and he died anon.

When the king was dead all the city stood dismayed, and wist not who might be their king. Right so as they were in counsel there came a voice down among them, and bad them choose the young-est knight of them three to be their king: 'For he shall well main-tain you and all yours.'

So they made Sir Galahad king by all the assent of the whole city, and else they would have slain him. And when he was come to behold his land, he let make above the table of silver a chest of gold and of precious stones, that covered the holy vessel. And every day early the three fellows would come before it, and make their prayers.

Now at the year's end, and the self Sunday after that Sir Galahad had borne the crown of gold, he arose up early and his fellows, and came to the palace, and saw tofore them the holy vessel, and a man kneeling on his knees in likeness of a bishop, that had about him a great fellowship of angels as it had been Jesu Christ Himself. And then he arose and began a mass of Our Lady.

And when he came to the sacrament of the mass, and had done, anon he called Sir Galahad, and said to him,

'Come forth the servant of Jesu Christ, and thou shalt see that thou hast much desired to see.'

And then he began to tremble right hard when the deadly flesh began to behold the spiritual things. Then he held up his hands toward heaven and said,

'Lord, I thank Thee, for now I see that that hath been my desire many a day. Now, my blessed Lord, would I not live in this wretched world longer, if it might please Thee, Lord.'

And therewith the good man took Our Lord's body betwixt his hands, and proffered it to Sir Galahad, and he received it right gladly and meekly.

'Now wotest thou what I am?' said the good man.

'Nay,' said Sir Galahad.

'I am Joseph, the son of Joseph of Arimathea, which Our Lord hath sent here to thee to bear thee fellowship; and wotest thou wherefore that He hath sent me more than any other? For thou hast resembled [me] in two things; in that thou hast seen the marvels of the Sangrail, in that thou hast been a clean maiden, as I have been and am.'

And when he had said these words Sir Galahad went to Sir Percival and kissed him, and commended him to God; and so he went to Sir Bors and kissed him, and commended him to God, and said,

'My fair lord, salute me to my lord, Sir Lancelot, my father, and as soon as ye see him, bid him remember of this unstable world.'

And therewith he kneeled down tofore the table and made his prayers. And then suddenly his soul departed to Jesu Christ, and a great multitude of angels bare his soul up to heaven, even in the sight of his two fellows. Also these two knights saw come from heaven an hand, but they saw not the body. And then it came right to the vessel, and took it and the spear, and so bare it up into heaven. Sithen was there never man so hardy to say that he had seen the Sangrail.

So when Sir Percival and Sir Bors saw Sir Galahad dead they made as much sorrow as ever did two men. And if they had not been good men they might lightly have fallen in despair. And so the people of the country and of the city were right heavy. And then he was buried; and as soon as he was buried Sir Percival yielded him to an hermitage out of the city, and took religious clothing. And Sir Bors was alway with him, but never changed he his secular clothing, for that he purposed him to go again into the realm of Logris.

Thus a year and two months lived Sir Percival in the hermitage a full holy life, and then passed out of this world. Then Sir Bors let bury him by his sister and by Sir Galahad in the spiritualities.

So when Sir Bors saw that he was in so far countries as in the parts of Babylon, he departed from the city of Sarras, and armed him and came to the sea, and entered into a ship. And so it befell him, by good adventure he came into the realm of Logris; and he rode so fast till he came to Camelot where the king was.

And then was there made great joy of him in the court, for they weened all he had been dead, forasmuch as he had been so long out of the country.

And when they had eaten, the king made great clerks to come before him, that they should chronicle of the high adventures of the good knights. When Sir Bors had told him of the high adventures of the Sangrail, such as had befall him and his three fellows, that was Sir Lancelot, Sir Percival, and Sir Galahad, and himself, then Sir Lancelot told the adventures of the Sangrail that he had seen. All this was made in great books, and put up in almeries at Salisbury.

Arthur listens to the adventures of the knights

And anon Sir Bors said to Sir Lancelot, 'Sir Galahad, your own son, saluted you by me, and after you my lord King Arthur and all the whole court, and so did Sir Percival. For I buried them with mine own hands in the city of Sarras. Also, Sir Lancelot, Sir Galahad prayed you to remember of this unsiker world as ye benight him when ye were together more than half a year.'

'This is true,' said Sir Lancelot; 'now I trust to God his prayer shall avail me.'

Then Sir Lancelot took Sir Bors in his arms, and said,

'Gentle cousin, ye are right welcome to me, and all that ever I may do for you and for yours ye shall find my poor body ready at all times, whiles the spirit is in it, and that I promise you faithfully, and never to fail. And wit ye well, gentle cousin, Sir Bors, that ye and I will never depart in sunder whilst our lives may last.'

'Sir,' said he, 'as ye will, so will I.'

Thus endeth the tale of the Sangrail, that was briefly drawn out of French into English, which is a tale chronicled for one of the truest and the holiest that is in this world, by Sir Thomas Malory, knight.

O blessed Jesu help him, through His might. AMEN.

riche tresoz ne pourt tous anne complecte tesoz
fait elle ie le scay bien et ien feray quanq tous
men comanderes Dame fait galaot grut mas
et ie tous pri que tous li tonnes bie amour
et que tous le premes a bie chlr a tousiours et
treneres sa loyal dame a tous les iours de bie bie
Et puis si laires fait plus riche q se to li aires
comme tout le monde . Coment . Lancelot baile

la royne greneme la premiere fois.

ansi fait elle loctroy ie que bier
que il soit tout unen et ie tou
sienne et que par tous soient
amendes tous les messais et
les trespas des couuenances .
Dame fait galaot grut merus
auais ore y couuient commeucement de seurte
tous nen teuiseres ia chose fait elle que ie ne

BOOK 12

Lancelot and Guenever

S o after the quest of the Sangrail was fulfilled, and all knights that were left alive were comen home again unto the Table Round, as the Book of the Sangrail maketh mention, then was there great joy in the court; and in especial King Arthur and Queen Guenever made great joy of the remnant that were comen home. And passing glad was the king and the queen of Sir Lancelot and of Sir Bors, for they had been passing long away in the quest of the Sangrail.

Then, as the book saith, Sir Lancelot began to resort unto Queen Guenever again, and forgat the promise and the perfection that he made in the quest. For, as the book saith, had not Sir Lancelot been in his privy thoughts and in his minds so set in-wardly to the queen as he was in seeming outward to God, there had no knight passed him in the quest of the Sangrail. But ever his thoughts were privily on the queen, and so they loved together more hotter than they did toforehand, and had many such privy draughts together, that many in the court spake of it, and in es-pecial Sir Agravain, Sir Gawain's brother, for he was ever open-mouthed.

So it befell that Sir Lancelot had many resorts of ladies and damsels that daily resorted unto him, that besought him to be their champion. In all such matters of right Sir Lancelot applied him daily to do for the pleasure of Our Lord, Jesu Christ. And ever as much as he might he withdrew him from the company and fellowship of Queen Guenever, for to eschew the slander and noise; wherefore the queen waxed wroth with Sir Lancelot.

And upon a day she called Sir Lancelot unto her chamber, and said thus:

'Sir Lancelot, I see and feel daily that thy love beginneth to slake, for thou hast no joy to be in my presence, but ever thou art out of this court, and quarrels and matters thou hast nowadays for

OPPOSITE
Lancelot kisses Guenever for the first time

ladies, maidens and gentlewomen more than ever thou were wont to have aforehand.'

'Ah madam,' said Sir Lancelot, 'in this ye must hold me excused for divers causes; one is, I was but late in the quest of the Sangrail; and I thank God of His great mercy, and never of my deserving, that I saw in that my quest as much as ever saw any sinful man, and so was it told me. And if I had not had my privy thoughts to return your love again as I do, I had seen as great mysteries as ever saw my son Sir Galahad, Sir Percival, or Sir Bors; and therefore, madam, I was but late in that quest. Wit ye well, madam, it may not be yet lightly forgotten, the high service in whom I did my diligent labour.

'Also, madam, wit ye well that there be many men speaken of our love in this court, and have you and me greatly in a-wait, as Sir Agravain and Sir Mordred. And, madam, wit ye well I dread them more for your sake than for any fear I have of them myself, for I may happen to escape and rid myself in a great need, where, madam, ye must abide all that will be said unto you. And then if that ye fall in any distress through wilful folly, then is there none other remedy or help but by me and my blood.

'And wit ye well, madam, the boldness of you and me will bring us to great shame and slander; and that were me loth to see you dishonoured. And that is the cause I take upon me more for to do for damsels and maidens than ever I did tofore, that men should understand my joy and my delight is my pleasure to have ado for damsels and maidens.'

All this while the queen stood still and let Sir Lancelot say what he would. And when he had all said she brast out on weeping, and so she sobbed and wept a great while. And when she might speak she said,

'Sir Lancelot, now I well understand that thou art a false rec-reant knight, and a common lecher, and lovest and holdest other ladies, and of me thou hast disdain and scorn. For wit thou well,' she said, 'now I understand thy falsehood, I shall never love thee more. And look thou be never so hardy to come in my sight. And right here I discharge thee this court, that thou never come within it; and I forfend thee my fellowship, and upon pain of thy head that thou see me never more.'

forfend: *deny*

Right so Sir Lancelot departed with great heaviness, that un-nethe he might sustain himself for great dole-making. Then he called Sir Bors, Sir Ector de Maris, and Sir Lionel, and told them how the queen had forfended him the court, and so he was in will to depart into his own country.

'Fair sir,' said Sir Bors de Ganis, 'ye shall not depart out of this land by mine advice. Ye must remember in what honour ye are renowned, and called the noblest knight of the world; and many great matters ye have in hand. And women in their hastiness will do oftentimes that, after, them sore repenteth. And therefore, by mine advice, ye shall take your horse, and ride to the good hermitage here beside Windsor, that sometime was a good knight, his name is Sir Brastias. And there shall ye abide till I send you word of better tidings.'

'Brother,' said Sir Lancelot, 'wit ye well I am full loth to depart out of this realm, but the queen hath defended me so highly, that meseemeth she will never be my good lady as she hath been.'

'Say ye never so,' said Sir Bors, 'for many times or this she hath been wroth with you, and after it she was the first that repented it.'

'Ye say well,' said Sir Lancelot, 'for now will I do by your counsel, and take mine horses and my harness, and ride to the hermit, Sir Brastias, and there will I repose me until I hear some manner of tidings from you. But, fair brother, I pray you get me the love of my lady, Queen Guenever, and ye may.'

'Sir,' said Sir Bors, 'ye need not to move me of such matters, for well ye wot I will do what I may to please you.'

And then the noble knight, Sir Lancelot, departed with right heavy cheer suddenly, that none earthly creature wist of him, nor where he was become, but Sir Bors. So when Sir Lancelot was departed, the queen outward made no manner of sorrow in showing to none of his blood nor to none other. But wit ye well, inwardly, as the book saith, she took great thought, but she bare it out with a proud countenance as though she felt no thought nor danger.

And then the queen let make a privy dinner in London unto the knights of the Round Table. And all was for to show outward that she had as great joy in all other knights of the Table Round as she had in Sir Lancelot. So there was all only at that dinner she had Sir Gawain and his brethren, that is for to say Sir Agravain, Sir Gaheris, Sir Gareth, and Sir Mordred. Also there was Sir Bors de Ganis, Sir Blamor de Ganis, Sir Bleoberis de Ganis, Sir Galihud, Sir Galihodin, Sir Ector de Maris, Sir Lionel, Sir Palomides, Sir Safer his brother, Sir La Cote Male Taile, Sir Persant, Sir Ironside, Sir Brandiles, Sir Kay le Seneschal, Sir Mador de la Porte, Sir Patrise, a knight of Ireland, Sir Aliduke, Sir Astamore, and Sir Pinel le Savage, the which was cousin to Sir Lamorak de Gales, the good knight that Sir Gawain and his brethren slew by treason.

Arthur's knights dining

And so these four and twenty knights should dine with the queen in a privy place by themself, and there was made a great feast of all manner of dainties. But Sir Gawain had a custom that he used daily at dinner and at supper, that he loved well all manner of fruit, and in especial apples and pears. And therefore whosomever dined or feasted Sir Gawain would commonly purvey for good fruit for him. And so did the queen; for to please Sir Gawain she let purvey for him all manner of fruit. For Sir Gawain was a passing hot knight of nature, and this Pinel hated Sir Gawain because of his kinsman Sir Lamorak's death; and therefore, for pure envy and hate, Sir Pinel enpoisoned certain apples for to enpoison Sir Gawain.

And so this was well unto the end of the meat; and so it befell by misfortune a good knight named Patrise, cousin unto Sir Mador de la Porte, took an apple, for he was enchafed with heat of wine. And it mishapped him to take a poisoned apple. And when he had eaten it he swelled so till he brast, and there Sir Patrise fell down suddenly dead among them.

Then every knight leapt from the board ashamed, and araged for wrath, nigh out of their wits. For they wist not what to say; considering Queen Guenever made the feast and dinner, they all had suspicion unto her.

'My lady, the queen,' said Sir Gawain, 'wit ye well, madam, that this dinner was made for me and my fellows, for all folks that knowen my condition understand that I love well fruit. And now I see well I had near been slain; therefore, madam, I dread me lest ye will be shamed.'

Then the queen stood still and was sore abashed, that she nist not what to say.

'This shall not so be ended,' said Sir Mador de la Porte, 'for here have I lost a full noble knight of my blood; and therefore upon this shame and despite I will be revenged to the utterance.'

And there openly Sir Mador appelled the queen of the death of his cousin, Sir Patrise.

Then stood they all still, that none would speak a word against him, for they all had great suspicion unto the queen because she let make that dinner. And the queen was so abashed that she could none other ways do, but wept so heartily that she fell in a swoon. With this noise and cry came to them King Arthur, and when he wist of that trouble he was a passing heavy man.

And ever Sir Mador stood still afore the king, and ever he appelled the queen of treason; for the custom was such that time that all manner of shameful death was called treason.

'Fair lords,' said King Arthur, 'me repenteth of this trouble, but the case is so I may not have ado in this matter, for I must be a rightful judge. And that repenteth me that I may not do battle for my wife: for, as I deem, this deed came never by her. And therefore I suppose she shall not be all distained, but that some good knight shall put his body in jeopardy for my queen rather than she shall be burnt in a wrong quarrel. And therefore Sir Mador, be not so hasty, for it may happen she shall not be all friendless. And therefore desire thou thy day of battle, and she shall purvey her of some good knight that shall answer you, or else it were to me great shame, and to all my court.'

'My gracious lord,' said Sir Mador, 'ye must hold me excused, for though ye be our king, in that degree ye are but a knight as we are, and ye are sworn unto knighthood as well as we be. And therefore I beseech you that ye be not displeased, for there is none of the four and twenty knights that were bidden to this dinner but all they have great suspicion unto the queen. What say ye all, my lords?' said Sir Mador.

Then they answered by and by that they could not excuse the queen; for why she made the dinner, and other it must come by her or by her servants.

'Alas,' said the queen, 'I made this dinner for a good intent, and never for none evil, so Almighty Jesu me help in my right, as I was never purposed to do such evil deeds, and that I report me unto God.'

'My lord, the king,' said Sir Mador, 'I require you as ye be a righteous king give me a day that I may have justice.'

'Well,' said the king, 'I give the day this day fifteen days that thou be ready armed on horseback in the meadow beside Winchester. And if it so fall that there be any knight to encounter with you, there may you do your best, and God speed the right. And if it so fall that there be no knight ready at that day, then must my queen be burnt, and there she shall be ready to have her judge' ment.'

'I am answered,' said Sir Mador.

And every knight went where it liked them. So when the king and the queen were together the king asked the queen how this case befell.

The queen answered, 'Sir, as Jesu be my help, I wot not how nor in what manner.'

'Where is Sir Lancelot?' said King Arthur; 'And he were here he would not grudge to do battle for you.'

'Sir,' said the queen, 'I wot not where he is, but his brother and his kinsmen deem that he be not within this realm.'

'That me repenteth,' said King Arthur, 'for and he were here he would soon stint this strife. Then I will counsel you,' said the king, 'that ye go unto Sir Bors, and pray him to do battle for you for Sir Lancelot's sake, and upon my life he will not refuse you. For well I see,' said the king, 'that none of these four and twenty knights that were with you at your dinner where Sir Patrise was slain, that will do battle for you, nor none of them will say well of you, and that shall be a great slander for you in this court.'

'Alas,' said the queen, 'and I may not do withal, but now I miss Sir Lancelot, for and he were here he would put me soon in my heart's ease.'

'What aileth you,' said the king, 'that ye cannot keep Sir Lancelot upon your side? For wit ye well,' said the king, 'who that hath Sir Lancelot upon his part hath the most man of worship in this world upon his side. Now go your way,' said the king unto the queen, 'and require Sir Bors to do battle for you for Sir Lancelot's sake.'

So the queen departed from the king, and sent for Sir Bors into her chamber. And when he was come she besought him of succour.

'Madam,' said he, 'what would ye that I did? For I may not with my worship have ado in this matter, because I was at the same dinner, for dread that any of those knights would have me in suspicion. Also, Madam,' said Sir Bors, 'now miss ye Sir Lancelot, for he would not have failed you neither in right nor in wrong, as ye have well proved, for when ye have been in right great danger he hath succoured you and now ye have driven him out of this country, by whom ye and all we were daily worshipped by; therefore, madam, I marvel how ye dare for shame require me to do any thing for you, in so much ye have chased him out of your country by whom we were borne up and honoured.'

'Alas, fair knight,' said the queen, 'I put me wholly in your grace, and all that is done amiss I will amend as ye will counsel me.' And therewith she kneeled down upon both her knees, and besought Sir Bors to have mercy upon her: 'Other eles I shall have a shameful death, and thereto I never offended.'

Right so came King Arthur, and found the queen kneeling afore Sir Bors; then Sir Bors pulled her up and said,

'Madam, ye do me great dishonour.'

'Ah, gentle knight,' said the king, 'have mercy upon my queen, courteous knight, for I am now in certain she is untruly defamed. And therefore, courteous knight,' said the king, 'promise her to do battle for her, I require you for the love of Sir Lancelot.'

'My lord,' said Sir Bors, 'ye require me the greatest thing that any man may require me; and wit ye well if I grant to do battle for the queen I shall wrath many of my fellowship of the Table Round. But as for that,' said Sir Bors, 'I will grant my lord that for my lord Sir Lancelot's sake, and for your sake I will at that day be the queen's champion unless that there come by adventure a better knight than I am to do battle for her.'

'Will ye promise me this,' said the king, 'by your faith?'

'Yea sir,' said Sir Bors, 'of that I will not fail you, nor her both, but if there came a better knight than I am, and then shall he have the battle.'

Then was the king and the queen passing glad, and so departed, and thanked him heartily. Then Sir Bors departed secretly upon a day, and rode unto Sir Lancelot thereas he was with the hermit, Sir Brastias, and told him of all this adventure.

'Ah Jesu,' Sir Lancelot said, 'this is come happily as I would have it, and therefore I pray you make you ready to do battle, but look that ye tarry till ye see me come, as long as ye may. For I am sure Sir Mador is an hot knight when he is enchafed, for the more ye suffer him the hastier will he be to battle.'

'Sir,' said Sir Bors, 'let me deal with him. Doubt ye not ye shall have all your will.'

So then departed Sir Bors from him and came to the court again. Then was it noised in all the court that Sir Bors should do battle for the queen; wherefore many knights were displeased with him, that he would take upon him to do battle in the queen's quarrel; for there were but few knights in all the court but they deemed the queen was in the wrong, and that she had done that treason. So Sir Bors answered thus to his fellows of the Table Round:

'Wit ye well, my fair lords, it were shame to us all and we suffered to see the most noble queen of the world to be shamed openly, considering her lord and our lord is the man of most worship christened, and he hath ever worshipped us all in all places.'

Many answered him again: 'As for our most noble King Arthur, we love him and honour him as well as ye do, but as for Queen Guenever, we love her not, because she is a destroyer of good knights.'

'Fair lords,' said Sir Bors, 'meseemeth ye say not as ye should say, for never yet in my days knew I never nor heard say that ever she was a destroyer of any good knight. But at all times as far as ever I could know, she was a maintainer of good knights; and ever she hath been large and free of her goods to all good knights, and the most bounteous lady of her gifts and her good grace, that ever I saw or heard speak of. And therefore it were shame,' said Sir Bors, 'to us all to our most noble king's wife, whom we serve, and we suffered her to be shamefully slain. And wit ye well,' said Sir Bors, 'I will not suffer it, for I dare say so much, the queen is not guilty of Sir Patrise's death, for she owed him never none ill will, nor none of the four and twenty knights that were at that dinner; for I dare say for good love she bad us to dinner, and not for no mal engine. And that, I doubt not, shall be proved hereafter, for howsomever the game goeth, there was treason among us.'

Then some said to Sir Bors, 'We may well believe your words.'

And so some of them were well pleased, and some were not.

So the day came on fast until the even that the battle should be. Then the queen sent for Sir Bors and asked him how he was disposed.

'Truly madam,' said he, 'I am disposed in likewise as I promised you, that is for to say I shall not fail you, unless by adventure there come a better knight than I am to do battle for you. Then, madam, am I discharged of my promise.'

'Will ye,' said the queen, 'that I tell my lord Arthur thus?'

'Do as it shall please you, madam.'

Then the queen went unto the king and told him the answer of Sir Bors.

'Have ye no doubt,' said the king, 'of Sir Bors, for I call him now one of the best knights of the world, and the most perfectest man.'

And thus it passed on till the morn, and so the king and the queen and all manner of knights that were there at that time drew them unto the meadow beside Winchester where the battle should be. And so when the king was come with the queen and many knights of the Round Table, then the queen was put there in the constabie's ward, and a great fire made about an iron stake, that and Sir Mador de la Porte had the better, she should be burnt: for such custom was used in those days, that neither for favour, love nor affinity, there should be none other but righteous judgement, as well upon a king as upon a knight, and as well upon a queen as upon another poor lady.

So in this meanwhile came in Sir Mador de la Porte, and took his oath afore the king, how that the queen did this treason until his cousin Sir Patrise, and unto his oath he would prove it with his body, hand for hand, who that would say the contrary.

Right so came in Sir Bors de Ganis, and said that as for Queen Guenever, 'She is in the right, and that will I make good with my hands, that she is not culpable of this treason that is put upon her.'

'Then make thee ready,' said Sir Mador, 'and we shall prove whether thou be in the right or I.'

'Sir Mador,' said Sir Bors, 'wit thou well I know you for a good knight, Notforthan I shall not fear you so greatly, but I trust to God I shall be able to withstand your malice. But thus much have I promised my lord Arthur and my lady the queen, that I shall do battle for her in this case to the uttermost, unless that there come a better knight than I am and discharge me.'

'Is that all?' said Sir Mador, 'other come thou off and do battle with me, or else say nay.'

'Take your horse,' said Sir Bors, 'and as I suppose, I shall not tarry long but ye shall be answered.'

Then either departed to their tents and made them ready to horseback as they thought best. And anon Sir Mador came into the field with his shield on his shoulder and his spear in his hand; and so rode about the place crying unto Arthur: 'Bid your champion come forth and he dare.'

Then was Sir Bors ashamed and took his horse and came to the list's end.

And then was he ware where came from a wood there fast by a knight all armed, upon a white horse, with a strange shield of strange arms; and he came riding all that he might run, and so he came to Sir Bors, and said thus:

'Fair knight, I pray you be not displeased, for here must a better knight than ye are have this battle. Therefore I pray you withdraw you. For wit ye well I have had this day a right great journey, and this battle ought to be mine. And so I promised you when I spake with you last, and with all my heart I thank you of your good will.'

Then Sir Bors rode unto King Arthur and told him how there was a knight come that would have the battle for to fight for the queen.

'What knight is he?' said the king.

'I wot not,' said Sir Bors, 'but such covenant he made with me to be here this day. Now my lord,' said Sir Bors, 'here am I discharged.'

Then the king called to that knight, and asked him if he would fight for the queen.

Then he answered to the king, 'Sir, therefore came I hither. And therefore, sir king,' he said, 'tarry me no longer, for I may not tarry. For anon as I have finished this battle I must depart hence, for I have ado many matters elsewhere. For wit you well,' said that knight, 'this is dishonour to you and to all knights of the Round Table, to see and know so noble a lady and so courteous a queen as Queen Guenever is, thus to be rebuked and shamed amongst you.'

Then they all marvelled what knight that might be that so took the battle upon him. For there was not one that knew him, but if it were Sir Bors.

Then said Sir Mador de la Porte unto the king, 'Now let me with with whom I shall have ado.'

And then they rode to the list's end, and there they couched their spears, and ran together with all their mights. And Sir Mador's spear brake all to pieces, but the other's spear held, and bare Sir Mador's horse and all backward to the earth a great fall. But mightily and suddenly he avoided his horse and put his shield before him, and then drew his sword, and bad the other knight alight and do battle with him on foot.

Lancelot and Guenever

Then that knight descended down from his horse lightly like a valiant man, and put his shield before him and drew his sword; and so they came eagerly unto battle, and either gave other many great strokes, tracing and traversing, rasing and foining, and hurtling together with their swords as it were wild boars. Thus were they fighting nigh an hour, for this Sir Mador was a strong knight, and mightily proved in many strong battles. But at the last this knight smote Sir Mador grovelling upon the earth, and the knight stepped near him to have pulled Sir Mador flatling upon the ground; and therewith suddenly Sir Mador arose, and in his rising he smote that knight through the thick of the thighs that the blood burst out fiercely.

And when he felt himself so wounded, and saw his blood, he let him arise upon his feet. And then he gave him such a buffet upon the helm that he fell to the earth flatling. And therewith he strode to him to have pulled off his helm off his head. And so Sir Mador prayed that knight to save his life. And so he yielded him as overcome, and released the queen of his quarrel.

'I will not grant thee thy life,' said that knight, 'only that thou freely release the queen for ever, and that no mention be made upon Sir Patrise's tomb that ever Queen Guenever consented to that treason.'

'All this shall be done,' said Sir Mador, 'I clearly discharge my quarrel for ever.'

Then the knights parters of the lists took up Sir Mador, and led him to his tent. And the other knight went straight to the stairfoot where sat King Arthur; and by that time was the queen come to the king, and either kissed other heartily.

And when the king saw that knight, he stooped down to him, and thanked him, and in likewise did the queen. And the king prayed him to put off his helmet, and to repose him, and to take a sop of wine. And then he put off his helmet to drink and then every knight knew him that it was Sir Lancelot du Lake.

Anon as the king wist that, he took the queen in his hand, and yode unto Sir Lancelot, and said, 'Sir, gramercy of your great travail that ye have had this day for me and for my queen.'

'My lord,' said Sir Lancelot, 'wit ye well I ought of right ever to be in your quarrel, and in my lady's the queen's quarrel, to do battle; for ye are the man that gave me the high order of knighthood, and that day my lady, your queen, did me great worship. And else I had been shamed; for that same day ye made me knight, through my hastiness I lost my sword, and my lady, your queen, found it, and lapped it in her train, and gave me my sword when I had need thereto, and else had I been shamed among all knights. And therefore, my lord Arthur, I promised her at that day ever to be her knight in right other in wrong.'

OPPOSITE
*Knights in combat
before Arthur.
Another example of
the medieval interest
in the testing of
knightly valour*

plaiſt et bel du chaſtel de
ſombre et ce vous deviſera
liſtoire tout au long

comment le roy utherpen
dragon tint court ouuerte
et moult grant feſte le xij.

chk quel part quil soit ne ou monde na chk q
ra maffe meuto a Resambler moult sa mess
Gauain senou chk et quant tous en orent
sa parole laisse sila reprist Galaot et dist au
roy sire ses ses conbutas plus baillant chk de li

Ertes fait le Roy Jene bionese
cheualier de qui re bouk sterme
auoir sacomtante pour chk
qui en liu fust non fait Galaot
or me dites par la soy q bous
deues a madam sa Roynt qui
est ne a mess Gauain bre nepieu que bous
bes a combien bouldies bous auoir done pour
auoir sa compartme a tousiouis Se maist die
fait le Roy quiesi bouldroie auoir parti mon
Roiaume et quaque re pouroie auoir sors seu

'Gramercy,' said the king, 'for this journey; and wit ye well,' said the king, 'I shall acquit your goodness.'

And ever the queen beheld Sir Lancelot, and wept so tenderly that she sank almost to the ground for sorrow that he had done to her so great goodness where she showed him great unkindness.

Then the knights of his blood drew unto him, and there either of them made great joy of other. And so came all the knights of the Table Round that were there at that time, and welcomed him. And then Sir Mador was had to leech craft, and Sir Lancelot was healed of his wound. And then there was made great joy and mirths in that court.

And so it befell that the Damsel of the Lake, her name was Nimue, which wedded the good knight Sir Pelleas, and so she came to the court; for ever she did great goodness unto King Arthur and to all his knights through her sorcery and enchantments. And so when she heard how the queen was grieved for the death of Sir Patrise, then she told it openly that she was never guilty; and there she disclosed by whom it was done, and named him, Sir Pinel; and for what cause he did it. There it was openly disclosed; and so the queen was excused. And the knight Sir Pinel fled into his country.

Then was it openly known that Sir Pinel enpoisoned the apples at that feast to that intent to have destroyed Sir Gawain, because Sir Gawain and his brethren destroyed Sir Lamorak de Gales, which Sir Pinel was cousin unto.

Then was Sir Patrise buried in the church of Westminster in a tomb, and thereupon was written: HERE LIETH SIR PATRISE OF IRELAND, SLAIN BY SIR PINEL LE SAVAGE, THAT ENPOISONED APPLES TO HAVE SLAIN SIR GAWAIN, AND BY MISFORTUNE SIR PATRISE ATE ONE OF THOSE APPLES AND THEN SUDDENLY HE BRAST. Also there was written upon the tomb that Queen Guenever was appelled of treason of the death of Sir Patrise, by Sir Mador de la Porte; and there was made mention how Sir Lancelot fought with him for Queen Guenever, and overcame him in plain battle. All this was written upon the tomb of Sir Patrise in excusing of the queen.

And then Sir Mador sued daily and long, to have the queen's good grace; and so by means of Sir Lancelot he caused him to stand in the queen's good grace, and all was forgiven.

Thus it passed on till Our Lady Day, Assumption. Within a fifteen days of that feast the king let cry a great jousts and a tournament that should be at that day at Camelot, otherwise called Winchester; and the king let cry that he and the King of Scots would joust against all that would come against them.

And when this cry was made, thither came many knights.

OPPOSITE
Arthur sits with Guenever and his advisers

227

That is to say, the King of Northgales, and King Anguish of Ireland, and the King with the Hundred Knights, and Galahaut, the Haut Prince, and the King of Northumberland, and many other noble dukes and earls of divers countries.

So King Arthur made him ready to depart to these jousts, and would have had the queen with him, but at that time she would not, she said, for she was sick and might not ride at that time.

'That me repenteth,' said the king, 'for this seven year ye saw not such a noble fellowship together, except the Whitsuntide when Sir Galahad departed from the court.'

'Truly,' said the queen to the king, 'ye must hold me excused. I may not be there, and that me repenteth.'

And many deemed the queen would not be there because of Sir Lancelot du Lake, for Sir Lancelot would not ride with the king; for he said that he was not whole of the wound the which Sir Mador had given him; wherefore the king was heavy and passing wroth.

And so he departed toward Winchester with his fellowship. And so by the way the king lodged in a town called Astolat, that is now in English called Guildford, and there the king lay in the castle. So when the king was departed the queen called Sir Lancelot to her, and said thus:

'Sir, ye are greatly to blame thus to hold you behind my lord; what, trow ye, what will your enemies and mine say and deem? Nought else but, "See how Sir Lancelot holdeth him ever behind the king, and so the queen doth also, for that they would have their pleasure together." And thus will they say,' said the queen to Sir Lancelot.

'Have ye no doubt thereof, madam,' said Sir Lancelot. 'I allow your wit. It is of late come since ye were waxen so wise. And therefore, madam, at this time I will be ruled by your counsel, and this night I will take my rest, and tomorrow betime I will take my way toward Winchester. But wit you well,' said Sir Lancelot to the queen, 'that at that jousts I will be against the king, and against all his fellowship.'

'Sir, ye may there do as ye list,' said the queen, 'but by my counsel ye shall not be against your king, and your fellowship. For therein be full many hardy knights of your blood, as ye wot well enough, it needeth not to rehearse them.'

'Madam,' said Sir Lancelot, 'I pray you that ye be not displeased with me, for I shall take the adventure that God will give me.'

And so upon the morn early Sir Lancelot heard mass and brake his fast, and so took his leave of the queen and departed. And then he rode so much until he came to Astolat, that is Guildford; and

Sir Lancelot hears mass

there it happed him in the eventide he came to an old baron's place that hight Sir Bernard of Astolat. And as Sir Lancelot entered into his lodging, King Arthur espied him as he did walk in a garden beside the castle; he knew him full well enough.

'Well, sirs,' said King Arthur unto the knights that were by him beside the castle, 'I have now espied one knight that will play his play at the jousts to the which we be gone toward; I undertake he will do marvels.'

'Who is that, we pray you tell us?' said many knights that were there at that time.

'Ye shall not wit for me,' said the king, 'as at this time.' And so the king smiled, and went to his lodging.

So when Sir Lancelot was in his lodging, and unarmed him in his chamber, the old baron, Sir Bernard, came to him making his reverence, and welcomed him in the best manner; but the old knight knew not Sir Lancelot.

'Fair sir,' said Sir Lancelot to his host, 'I would pray you to lend me a shield that were not openly known, for mine is well known.'

'Sir,' said his host, 'ye shall have your desire, for meseemeth ye be one of the likeliest knights of the world, and therefore, sir, I shall show you friendship. Sir, wit you well I have two sons that were but late made knights, and the eldest hight Sir Tirre, and he was hurt that same day he was made knight, that he may not ride. And his shield ye shall have; for that is not known, I dare say, but here, and in no place else. And my youngest son hight Sir Lavaine; and if it please you, he shall ride with you unto that jousts, for he is of his age strong and wight. For much my heart giveth unto you that ye should be a noble knight, and therefore I pray you, tell me your name,' said Sir Bernard.

'As for that,' said Sir Lancelot, 'ye must hold me excused as at this time. And if God give me grace to speed well at the jousts I shall come again and tell you my name. But I pray you,' said Sir Lancelot, 'in any wise let me have your son, Sir Lavaine, with me, and that I may have his brother's shield.'

'Sir, all this shall be done,' said Sir Bernard.

So this old baron had a daughter that was called that time the Fair Maiden of Astolat. And ever she beheld Sir Lancelot wonderfully; and as the book saith, she cast such a love unto Sir Lancelot that she could never withdraw her love, wherefore she died, and her name was Elaine le Blank. So thus as she came to and fro she was so hot in her love that she besought Sir Lancelot to wear upon him at the jousts a token of hers.

'Fair damsel,' said Sir Lancelot, 'and if I grant you that, ye may say I do more for your love than ever I did for lady or gentlewoman.'

Lancelot and Guenever

Then he remembered him he would go to the jousts disguised. And because he had never afore that time borne no manner of token of no damsel, he bethought him to bear a token of hers, that none of his blood thereby might know him. And then he said,

'Fair maiden, I will grant you to wear a token of yours upon mine helmet. And therefore what is it? Show it me.'

'Sir,' she said, 'it is a red sleeve of mine, of scarlet, well em-broidered with great pearls:' and so she brought it him.

So Sir Lancelot received it, and said, 'Never did I erst so much for no damsel.'

And then Sir Lancelot betook the fair maiden his shield in keeping, and prayed her to keep that until time that he came again; and so that night he had merry rest and great cheer, for the damsel Elaine was ever about Sir Lancelot all the while she might be suffered.

So upon a day, on the morn, King Arthur and all his knights departed, for there the king had tarried three days to abide his noble knights. And so when the king was ridden, Sir Lancelot and Sir Lavaine made them ready to ride, and either of them had white shields, and the red sleeve Sir Lancelot let carry with him.

And so they took their leave at Sir Bernard, the old baron, and at his daughter, the Fair Maiden of Astolat. And then they rode so long till that they came to Camelot, that time called Winchester; and there was great press of kings, dukes, earls, and barons, and many noble knights. But there Sir Lancelot was lodged privily by the means of Sir Lavaine with a rich burgess, that no man in that town was ware what they were. And so they reposed them there till Our Lady Day, Assumption, that the great jousts should be.

So then trumpets blew unto the field, and King Arthur was set on high upon a scaffold to behold who did best. But as the French book saith, the king would not suffer Sir Gawain to go from him, for never had Sir Gawain the better and Sir Lancelot were in the field; and many times was Sir Gawain rebuked when Lancelot came into any jousts disguised. Then some of the kings, as King Anguish of Ireland and the King of Scots, were that time turned upon the side of King Arthur. And then on the other party was the King of Northgales, and the King with the Hundred Knights, and the King of Northumberland, and Sir Galahaut, the Haut Prince. But these three kings and this duke were passing weak to hold against King Arthur's party, for with him were the noblest knights of the world.

So then they withdrew them either party from other, and every man made him ready in his best manner to do what he might. Then Sir Lancelot made him ready, and put the red sleeve upon his head, and fastened it fast; and so Sir Lancelot and Sir Lavaine

*Arthur in company
with his knights*

departed out of Winchester privily, and rode until a little leaved
wood behind the party that held against King Arthur's party, and
there they held them still till the parties smote together. And then
came in the King of Scots and the King of Ireland on Arthur's
party. . . . .So there began a strong assail upon both parties.

When Sir Lancelot saw this, as he hoved in the little leaved
wood, then he said unto Sir Lavaine,

'See yonder is a company of good knights, and they hold them
together as boars that were chased with dogs.'

'That is truth,' said Sir Lavaine.

'Now,' said Sir Lancelot, 'and ye will help me a little, ye shall
see yonder fellowship that chaseth now these men in our side that
they shall go as fast backwards as they went forward.'

'Sir, spare ye not for my part,' said Sir Lavaine, 'for I shall do
what I may.'

Then Sir Lancelot and Sir Lavaine came in at the thickest of
the press, and there Sir Lancelot smote down Sir Brandiles, Sir
Sagramore, Sir Dodinas, Sir Kay, Sir Griflet and all this he did
with one spear; and Sir Lavaine smote down Sir Lucan the
Butler and Sir Bedevere. And then Sir Lancelot gat another great
spear and there he smote down Sir Agravain, Sir Gaheris, and
Sir Mordred, and Sir Meliot de Logris; and Sir Lavaine smote
Ozanna le Cure Hardy. And then Sir Lancelot drew his sword,
and there he smote on the right hand and on the left hand, and by
great force he unhorsed Sir Safer, Sir Epinogrus, and Sir Galleron.
And then the knights of the Table Round withdrew them aback,
after they had gotten their horses as well as they might.

*Lancelot riding
with his squire*

'O mercy Jesu,' said Sir Gawain, 'what knight is yonder that
doth so marvellous deeds of arms in that field?'

'I wot what he is,' said King Arthur, 'but as at this time I will
not name him.'

'Sir,' said Sir Gawain, 'I would say it were Sir Lancelot by his
riding and his buffets that I see him deal. But ever meseemeth it
should not be he for that he beareth the red sleeve upon his helmet,
for I wist him never bear token at no jousts of lady nor gentlewoman.'

'Let him be,' said King Arthur, 'he will be better known and
do more or ever he depart.'

Then the party that was against King Arthur were well comforted, and then they held them together that beforehand were sore
rebuked. Then Sir Bors, Sir Ector de Maris, and Sir Lionel
called unto them the knights of their blood, as Sir Blamor de Ganis,
Sir Bleoberis, Sir Aliduke, Sir Galihud, Sir Galihodin, Sir
Bellengerus le Beuse. So these nine knights of Sir Lancelot's kin
thrust in mightily, for they were all noble knights; and they, of

great hate and despite that they had unto him, thought to rebuke that noble knight Sir Lancelot, and Sir Lavaine, for they knew them not. And so they came hurling together, and smote down many knights of Northgales and of Northumberland.

And when Sir Lancelot saw them fare so, he gat a great spear in his hand and there encountered with him all at once Sir Bors, Sir Ector, and Sir Lionel, and all they three smote him at once with their spears. And with force of themself they smote Sir Lancelot's horse to the earth; and by misfortune Sir Bors smote Sir Lancelot through the shield into the side, and the spear brake, and the head left still in his side.

When Sir Lavaine saw his master lie on the ground, he ran to the King of Scots and smote him to the earth; and by great force he took his horse, and brought him to Sir Lancelot, and maugre of them all he made him to mount upon that horse. And then Sir Lancelot gat a spear in his hand, and there he smote Sir Bors, horse and man, to the earth. And in the same wise he served Sir Ector and Sir Lionel; and Sir Lavaine smote down Sir Blamor de Ganis. And then Sir Lancelot drew his sword, for he felt himself so sore hurt that he weened there to have had his death. And then he smote Sir Bleoberis such a buffet on the helmet that he fell down to the earth in a swoon. And in the same wise he served Sir Aliduke and Sir Galihud. And Sir Lavaine smote down Sir Bellengerus, that was the son of Alisander le Orphelin.

And by this was done, was Sir Bors horsed again, and then he came with Sir Ector and Sir Lionel, and all they three smote with their swords upon Sir Lancelot's helmet. And when he felt their buffets, and with that his wound grieved him grievously, then he thought to do what he might while he could endure. And then he gave Sir Bors such a buffet that made him bow his head passing low; and therewithal raced off his helm, and might have slain him; and so pulled him down. And in the same wise he served Sir Ector and Sir Lionel. For as the book saith he might have slain them, but when he saw their visages his heart might not serve him thereto, but left them there. And then afterward he hurled into the thickest press of them all, and did there the marvelloust deeds of arms that ever man saw or heard speak of, and ever Sir Lavaine, the good knight, with him. And there Sir Lancelot with his sword smote down and pulled down, as the French book maketh mention, more than thirty knights, and the most part were of the Table Round. And there Sir Lavaine did full well that day, for he smote down ten knights of the Table Round.

'Mercy Jesu,' said Sir Gawain to King Arthur, 'I marvel what knight that he is with the red sleeve.'

'Sir,' said King Arthur, 'he will be known or ever he depart.'

And then the king blew unto lodging, and the prize was given by heralds unto the knight with the white shield that bare the red sleeve.

Then came the King with the Hundred Knights, the King of Northgales, and the King of Northumberland, and Sir Galahaut, the Haut Prince, and said unto Sir Lancelot,

'Fair knight, God thee bless, for much have ye done for us this day, and therefore we pray you that ye will come with us that ye may receive the honour and the prize as ye have worshipfully deserved it.'

'My fair lords,' said Sir Lancelot, 'wit you well if I have deserved thank I have sore bought it, and that me repenteth, for I am like never to escape with my life. Therefore, fair lords, I pray you that ye will suffer me to depart where me liketh, for I am sore hurt. And I take no force of none honour, for I had lever to repose me than to be lord of all the world.'

And therewithal he groaned piteously, and rode a great wallop away-ward from them until he came under a wood's side. And when he saw that he was from the field nigh a mile, that he was sure he might not be seen, then he said with an high voice, and with a great groan,

'O gentle knight, Sir Lavaine, help me that this truncheon were out of my side, for it sticketh so sore that it nigh slayeth me.'

'O mine own lord,' said Sir Lavaine, 'I would fain do that might please you, but I dread me sore and I pull out the truncheon, that ye shall be in peril of death.'

'I charge you,' said Sir Lancelot, 'as ye love me, draw it out.'

And therewithal he descended from his horse, and right so did Sir Lavaine. And forthwithal Sir Lavaine drew the truncheon out of his side, and gave a great shriek and a marvellous grisly groan, and the blood brast out nigh a pint at once, that at the last he sank down upon his arse, and so swooned down pale and deadly.

'Alas,' said Sir Lavaine, 'what shall I do?'

And then he turned Sir Lancelot into the wind, but so he lay there nigh half an hour as he had been dead.

And so at the last Sir Lancelot cast up his eyen, and said, 'O Sir Lavaine, help me that I were on my horse. For here is fast by, within this two mile, a gentle hermit that sometime was a full noble knight and a great lord of possessions. And for great goodness he hath taken him to wilful poverty, and forsaken many lands. And his name is Sir Baudwin of Britain, and he is a full noble surgeon and a good leech. Now let see, and help me up that I were there, for ever my heart giveth me that I shall never die of my cousin-germain's hands.'

And then with great pain Sir Lavaine halp him upon his

horse. And then they rode a great wallop together, and ever Sir Lancelot bled that it ran down to the earth; and so by fortune they came to that hermitage the which was under a wood, and a great cliff on the other side, and a fair water running under it. And then Sir Lavaine beat on the gate with the butt of his spear, and cried fast,

'Let in, for Jesu's sake!'

And anon there came a fair child to them, and asked them what they would.

'Fair son,' said Sir Lavaine, 'go and pray thy lord, the hermit, for God's sake to let in here a knight that is full sore wounded; and this day, tell thy lord, I saw him do more deeds of arms than ever I heard say that any man did,'

So the child went in lightly, and then he brought the hermit, which was a passing good man. When Sir Lavaine saw him he prayed him for God's sake of succour.

'What knight is he?' said the hermit. 'Is he of the house of King Arthur, or not?'

'I wot not,' said Sir Lavaine, 'what is he, nor what is his name, but well I wot I saw him do marvellously this day as of deeds of arms.'

'On whose party was he?' said the hermit.

'Sir,' said Sir Lavaine, 'he was this day against King Arthur, and there he won the prize of all the knights of the Round Table.'

'I have seen the day,' said the hermit, 'I would have loved him the worse because he was against my lord, King Arthur, for sometime I was one of the fellowship of the Round Table. But I thank God now I am otherwise disposed. But where is he? Let me see him.'

Then Sir Lavaine brought the hermit to him. And when the hermit beheld him, as he sat leaning upon his saddle bow ever bleeding piteously, and ever the knight hermit thought that he should know him, but he could not bring him to knowledge because he was so pale for bleeding.

'What knight are ye,' said the hermit, 'and where were ye born?'

'My fair lord,' said Sir Lancelot, 'I am a stranger and a knight adventurous, that laboureth throughout many realms for to win worship.'

Then the hermit advised him better, and saw by a wound on his cheek that he was Sir Lancelot.

layne: *conceal*

'Alas,' said the hermit, 'mine own lord! Why layne you your name from me? Pardie, I ought to know you of right, for ye are the most noblest knight of the world. For well I know you for Sir Lancelot.'

'Sir,' said he, 'sith ye know me help me and ye may, for God's sake. For I would be out of this pain at once, other to death or to life.'

'Have ye no doubt,' said the hermit, 'ye shall live and fare right well.'

And so the hermit called to him two of his servants, and so he and his servants bare him into the hermitage, and lightly unarmed him, and laid him in his bed. And then anon the hermit staunched his blood, and made him to drink good wine, so that Sir Lancelot was well refreshed and knew himself; for in these days it was not the guise of hermits as is nowadays, for there were none hermits in those days but that they had been men of worship and of prowess; and those hermits held great household, and refreshed people that were in distress.

Now turn we unto King Arthur, and leave we Sir Lancelot in the hermitage. So when the kings were comen together on both parties, and the great feast should be holden, King Arthur asked the King of Northgales and their fellowship, where was that knight that bare the red sleeve:

'Bring him before me, that he may have his laud, and honour, and the prize, as it is right.'

Then spake Sir Galahaut, the Haut Prince, and the King with the Hundred Knights, and said,

'We suppose that knight is mischieved, and that he is never like to see you nor none of us all, and that is the greatest pity that ever we wist of any knight.'

'Alas,' said Arthur, 'how may this be? Is he so sore hurt? But what is his name?' said King Arthur.

'Truly,' said they all, 'we know not his name, nor from whence he came, nor whither he would.'

'Alas,' said the king, 'these be to me the worst tidings that came to me this seven year. For I would not for all the lands I wield to know and wit it were so, that that noble knight were slain.'

'Sir, know ye ought of him?' said they all.

'As for that,' said Arthur, 'whether I know him or know him not, ye shall not know for me what man he is, but Almighty Jesu send me good tidings of him.'

And so said they all.

'By my head,' said Sir Gawain, 'if it so be that the good knight be so sore hurt, it is great damage and pity to all this land, for he is one of the noblest knights that ever I saw in a field handle a spear or a sword. And if he may be found I shall find him, for I am sure he nis not far from this town.'

'Sir, ye bear you well,' said King Arthur, 'and ye may find him, unless that he be in such a plight that he may not wield himself.'

'Jesu defend,' said Sir Gawain, 'but wit well, I shall know what he is, and I may find him.'

Right so Sir Gawain took a squire with him upon hackneys, and rode all about Camelot within six or seven mile, but so he came again and could hear no word of him.

Then within two days King Arthur and all the fellowship returned unto London again. And so as they rode by the way it happened Sir Gawain at Astolat to lodge with Sir Bernard thereas was Sir Lancelot lodged. And so as Sir Gawain was in his chamber to repose him Sir Bernard, the old baron, came into him, and his daughter Elaine, to cheer him and to ask him what tidings, and who did best at that tournament of Winchester.

'So God me help,' said Sir Gawain, 'there were two knights that bare two white shields, but the one of them bare a red sleeve upon his head, and certainly he was one of the best knights that ever I saw joust in field. For I dare say,' said Sir Gawain, 'that one knight with the red sleeve smote down forty knights of the Round Table, and his fellow did right well and worshipfully.'

'Now blessed be God,' said this Fair Maiden of Astolat, 'that that knight sped so well! For he is the man in the world that I first loved, and truly he shall be last that ever I shall love.'

'Now, fair maiden,' said Sir Gawain, 'is that good knight your love?'

'Certainly sir,' said she, 'wit ye well he is my love.'

'Then know ye his name?' said Sir Gawain.

'Nay truly sir,' said the damsel, 'I know not his name nor from whence he come, but to say that I love him, I promise you and God that I love him.'

'How had ye knowledge of him first?' said Sir Gawain.

Then she told him as ye have heard before, and how her father betook him her brother to do him service, and how her father lent him her brother's, Sir Tirre's, shield: 'And here with me he left his own shield.'

'For what cause did he so?' said Sir Gawain.

'For this cause,' said the damsel, 'for his shield was too well known among many noble knights.'

'Ah fair damsel,' said Sir Gawain, 'please it you to let me have a sight of that shield.'

'Sir,' said she, 'it is in my chamber, covered with a case, and if ye will come with me ye shall see it.'

'Not so,' said Sir Bernard till his daughter, 'let send for it.'

So when the shield was come, Sir Gawain took off the case, and when he beheld that shield he knew it anon, that it was Sir Lancelot's shield, and his own arms.

'Ah Jesu mercy,' said Sir Gawain, 'now is my heart more heavier than ever it was tofore.'

'Why?' said this maid Elaine.

'For I have a great cause,' said Sir Gawain. 'Is that knight that oweth this shield your love?'

'Yea truly,' said she, 'my love he is. God would that I were his love.'

'So God me speed,' said Sir Gawain, 'fair damsel ye have right, for and he be your love ye love the most honourable knight of the world, and the man of most worship.'

'So me thought ever,' said the damsel, 'for never or that time, for no knight that ever I saw, loved I never none erst.'

'God grant,' said Sir Gawain, 'that either of you may rejoice other, but that is in a great adventure. But truly,' said Sir Gawain unto the damsel, 'ye may say ye have a fair grace, for why I have known that noble knight this four and twenty year, and never or that day, I nor none other knight, I dare make good, saw never nor heard say that ever he bare token or sign of no lady, gentlewoman, nor maiden, at no jousts nor tournament. And therefore, fair maiden,' said Sir Gawain, 'ye are much beholden to him to give him thanks. But I dread me,' said Sir Gawain, 'that ye shall never see him in this world, and that is as great pity as ever was of any earthly man.'

'Alas,' said she, 'how may this be? Is he slain?'

'I say not so,' said Sir Gawain, 'but wit ye well he is grievously wounded, by all manner of signs, and by men's sight more likelier to be dead than to be alive; and wit ye well he is the noble knight, Sir Lancelot, for by this shield I know him.'

'Alas,' said the Fair Maiden of Astolat, 'how may this be? And what was his hurt?'

'Truly,' said Sir Gawain, 'the man in the world that loved him best hurt him so; and I dare say,' said Sir Gawain, 'and that knight that hurt him knew the very certainty that he had hurt Sir Lancelot, it would be the most sorrow that ever came to his heart.'

'Now fair father,' said then Elaine, 'I require you give me leave to ride and seek him, or else I wot well I shall go out of my mind. For I shall never stint till that I find him and my brother, Sir Lavaine.'

'Do as it liketh you,' said her father, 'for me sore repenteth of the hurt of that noble knight.'

Right so the maid made her ready, and departed before Sir Gawain, making great dole.

Then on the morn Sir Gawain came to King Arthur, and told him how he had found Sir Lancelot's shield in the keeping of the Fair Maiden of Astolat.

'All that knew I aforehand,' said King Arthur, 'and that caused me I would not suffer you to have ado at the great jousts. For I espied him,' said King Arthur, 'when he came in till his lodging, full late in the evening, into Astolat. But great marvel have I,' said King Arthur, 'that ever he would bear any sign of any damsel, for or now I never heard say nor knew that ever he bare any token of none earthly woman.'

'By my head sir,' said Sir Gawain, 'the Fair Maiden of Astolat loveth him marvellously well. What it meaneth I cannot say. And she is ridden after to seek him.'

So the king and all came to London, and there Sir Gawain all openly disclosed it to all the court, that it was Sir Lancelot that jousted best.

And when Sir Bors heard that, wit ye well he was an heavy man, and so were all his kinsmen. But when Queen Guenever wist that Sir Lancelot that bare the red sleeve of the Fair Maiden of Astolat, she was nigh out of her mind for wrath. And then she sent for Sir Bors de Ganis in all the haste that might be. So when Sir Bors was come tofore the queen, she said,

'Ah Sir Bors, have ye heard say how falsely Sir Lancelot hath betrayed me?'

'Alas madam,' said Sir Bors, 'I am afeared he hath betrayed himself and us all.'

'No force,' said the queen, 'though he be destroyed, for he is a false traitor knight.'

'Madam,' said Sir Bors, 'I pray you say ye no more so, for wit you well I may not hear no such language of him.'

'Why so, Sir Bors?' said she. 'Should I not call him traitor when he bare the red sleeve upon his head at Winchester, at the great jousts?'

'Madam,' said Sir Bors, 'that sleeve-bearing repenteth me sore, but I dare say he did bear it to none evil intent, but for this cause he bare the red sleeve that none of his blood should know him. For or then we nor none of us all never knew that ever he bare token or sign of maiden, lady, neither gentlewoman.'

'Fie on him!' said the queen. 'Yet for all his pride and bobaunce there ye proved yourself better man than he.'

'Nay madam, say ye never more so, for he beat me and my fellows, and might have slain us and he had would.'

'Fie on him,' said the queen, 'for I heard Sir Gawain say before my lord Arthur that it were marvel to tell the great love that is between the Fair Maiden of Astolat and him.'

'Madam,' said Sir Bors, 'I may not warn Sir Gawain to say what it pleaseth him; but I dare say, as for my lord, Sir Lancelot, that he loveth no lady, gentlewoman, nor maiden, but all he loveth in like much. And therefore madam,' said Sir Bors, 'ye may say what ye will, but wit ye I will haste me to seek him, and find him wheresomever he be, and God send me good tidings of him.'

And so leave we them there, and speak we of Sir Lancelot that lay in great peril.

And so as this fair maiden Elaine came to Winchester she sought there all about, and by fortune Sir Lavaine, her brother, was ridden to sport him, to enchafe his horse. And anon as this maiden Elaine saw him she knew him, and then she cried aloud till him. And when he heard her anon he came to her. And anon, with that, she asked her brother,

'How doth my lord, Sir Lancelot.'

'Who told you, sister, that my lord's name was Sir Lancelot?'

Then she told him how Sir Gawain by his shield knew him. So they rode together till that they came to the hermitage, and anon she alit. So Sir Lavaine brought her in to Sir Lancelot; and when she saw him lie so sick and pale in his bed she might not speak, but suddenly she fell down to the earth in a swoon. And there she lay a great while.

And when she was relieved, she shrieked and said, 'My lord, Sir Lancelot, alas why lie ye in this plight?' And then she swooned again.

And then Sir Lancelot prayed Sir Lavaine to take her up: 'And bring her hither to me.'

And when she came to herself Sir Lancelot kissed her, and said,

'Fair maiden, why fare ye thus? For ye put me to more pain; wherefore make ye no more such cheer, for and ye be come to comfort me ye be right welcome; and of this little hurt that I have I shall be right hastily whole, by the grace of God. But I marvel,' said Sir Lancelot, 'who told you my name?'

And so this maiden told him all how Sir Gawain was lodged with her father: 'And there by your shield he discovered your name.'

'Alas,' said Sir Lancelot, 'that me repenteth that my name is known, for I am sure it will turn unto anger.'

And then Sir Lancelot compassed in his mind that Sir Gawain would tell Queen Guenever how he bare the red sleeve, and for whom; that he wist well would turn into great anger.

So this maiden Elaine never went from Sir Lancelot, but watched him day and night, and did such attendance to him, that the French book saith there was never woman did more kindlier for man than she.

Then Sir Lancelot prayed Sir Lavaine to make aspies in Winchester for Sir Bors if he came there, and told him by what tokens he should know him, by a wound in his forehead.

'For well I am sure,' said Sir Lancelot, 'that Sir Bors will seek me, for he is the same good knight that hurt me.'

Now turn we unto Sir Bors de Ganis, that came unto Winchester to seek after his cousin Sir Lancelot. And so when he came to Winchester, anon there were men that Sir Lavaine had made to lie in a watch for such a man, and anon Sir Lavaine had warning; and then Sir Lavaine came to Winchester and found Sir Bors, and there he told him what he was, and with whom he was, and what was his name.

'Now fair knight,' said Sir Bors, 'ye be welcome. And I require you that ye will bring me to my lord, Sir Lancelot.'

'Sir,' said Sir Lavaine, 'take your horse, and within this hour ye shall see him.'

And so they departed, and came to the hermitage. And when Sir Bors saw Sir Lancelot lie in his bed, dead pale and discoloured, anon Sir Bors lost his countenance, and for kindness and pity he might not speak, but wept tenderly a great while. And then when he might speak he said thus:

'O my lord, Sir Lancelot, God you bless, and send you hasty recovering. For full heavy am I of my misfortune and of mine unhappiness. For now I may call myself unhappy. And I dread me that God is greatly displeased with me, that He would suffer me to have such a shame for to hurt you that are all our leader, and all our worship; and therefore I call myself unhappy. Alas that ever such a caitiff knight as I am should have power by unhappiness to hurt the most noblest knight of the world. Where I so shamefully set upon you and overcharged you, and where ye might have slain me, ye saved me; and so did not I, for I and all our blood did to you our utterance. I marvel,' said Sir Bors, 'that my heart or my blood would serve me, wherefore my lord, Sir Lancelot, I ask your mercy.'

'Fair cousin,' said Sir Lancelot, 'ye be right welcome; and wit ye well, overmuch ye say for to please me the which pleaseth me not, for why I have the same sought; for I would with pride have overcome you all, and there in my pride I was near slain, and that was in mine own default, for I might have give you warning of my being there. And then had I had no hurt. For it is an old-said saw, there is hard battle thereas kin and friends do battle either against other, for there may be no mercy but mortal war. Therefore, fair cousin,' said Sir Lancelot, 'let this speech overpass, and all shall be welcome that God sendeth. And let us leave off this matter and let us speak of some rejoicing, for this that is done may not be undone; and let us find a remedy how soon that I may be whole.'

Then Sir Bors leaned upon his bedside, and told Sir Lancelot how the queen was passing wroth with him, because he wore the red sleeve at the great jousts; and there Sir Bors told him all how

caitiff: *miserable*

Sir Gawain discovered it: 'By your shield that ye left with the Fair Maiden of Astolat.'

'Then is the queen wroth?' said Sir Lancelot. 'And therefore am I right heavy, for I deserved no wrath, for all that I did was because I would not be known.'

'Sir, right so excused I you,' said Sir Bors, 'but all was in vain, for she said more largelier to me than I to you say now. But, sir, is this she,' said Sir Bors, 'that is so busy about you, that men call the Fair Maiden of Astolat?'

'Forsooth, she it is,' said Sir Lancelot, 'that by no means I cannot put her from me.'

'Why should ye put her from you?' said Sir Bors, 'For she is a passing fair damsel, and well beseen, and well taught; and God would, fair cousin,' said Sir Bors, 'that ye could love her, but as to that I may not, nor I dare not, counsel you. But I see well,' said Sir Bors, 'by her diligence about you that she loveth you entirely.'

'That me repenteth,' said Sir Lancelot.

'Sir,' said Sir Bors, 'she is not the first that hath lost her pain upon you, and that is the more pity.'

And so they talked of many more things. And so within three or four days Sir Lancelot was big and strong again.

So then they made them ready to depart from the hermitage. And so upon a morn they took their horses and Elaine le Blank with them; and when they came to Astolat there were they well lodged, and had great cheer of Sir Bernard, the old baron, and of Sir Tirre, his son. And so upon the morn when Sir Lancelot should depart, fair Elaine brought her father with her, and Sir Lavaine, and Sir Tirre, and thus she said:

'My lord, Sir Lancelot, now I see ye will depart from me. Now fair knight and courteous knight,' said she, 'have mercy upon me, and suffer me not to die for your love.'

'Why, what would ye that I did?' said Sir Lancelot.

'Sir, I would have you to my husband,' said Elaine.

'Fair damsel, I thank you heartily,' said Sir Lancelot, 'but truly,' said he, 'I cast me never to be wedded man.'

'Then, fair knight,' said she, 'will ye be my paramour?'

'Jesu defend me,' said Sir Lancelot, 'for then I rewarded your father and your brother full evil for their great goodness.'

'Alas,' said she, 'then must I die for your love.'

'Ye shall not do so,' said Sir Lancelot, 'for wit ye well, fair maiden, I might have been married and I had would, but I never applied me yet to be married. But because, fair damsel, that ye love me as ye say ye do, I will for your good will and kindness show you some goodness, and that is this, that wheresomever ye will beset your heart upon some good knight that will wed you, I shall give you together a thousand pound yearly to you and to your heirs; thus much will I give you, fair madam, for your kindness, and always, while I live, to be your own knight.'

'Sir, of all this,' said the maiden, 'I will none, for but if ye will wed me, or else be my paramour at the least, wit ye well, Sir Lancelot, my good days are done.'

'Fair damsel,' said Sir Lancelot, 'of these two things ye must pardon me.'

Then she shrieked shrilly, and fell down in a swoon; and then women bare her into her chamber, and there she made over much sorrow. And then Sir Lancelot would depart, and there he asked Sir Lavaine what he would do.

'Sir, what should I do,' said Sir Lavaine, 'but follow you, but if ye drive me from you, or command me to go from you.'

Then came Sir Bernard to Sir Lancelot and said to him, 'I cannot see but that my daughter Elaine will die for your sake.'

'Sir, I may not do withal,' said Sir Lancelot, 'for that me sore repenteth, for I report me to yourself, that my proffer is fair; and me repenteth,' said Sir Lancelot, 'that she loveth me as she doth, for I was never the causer of it. For I report me to your son, I never early ne late proffered her bounty nor fair behests; and as for me,' said Sir Lancelot, 'I dare do all that a knight should do and say that she is a clean maiden for me, both for deed and for will. And I am right heavy of her distress. For she is a full fair maiden, good and gentle, and well taught.'

'Father,' said Sir Lavaine, 'I dare make good she is a clean maiden as for my lord Sir Lancelot; but she doth as I do, for sithen I first saw my lord Sir Lancelot, I could never depart from him, nor nought I will and I may follow him.'

Then Sir Lancelot took his leave, and so they departed, and came unto Winchester. And when King Arthur wist that Sir Lancelot was come whole and sound, the king made great joy of him; and so did Sir Gawain and all the knights of the Round Table except Sir Agravain and Sir Mordred. Also Queen Guenever was wood wroth with Sir Lancelot, and would by no means speak with him, but estranged herself from him. And Sir Lancelot made all the means that he might for to speak with the queen, but it would not be.

Now speak we of the Fair Maiden of Astolat that made such sorrow day and night that she never slept, ate, nor drank, and ever she made her complaint unto Sir Lancelot. So when she had thus endured a ten days, that she feebled so, that she must needs pass out of this world, then she shrived her clean, and received her Creator. And ever she complained still upon Sir Lancelot. Then her ghostly father bad her leave such thoughts. Then she said,

'Why should I leave such thoughts? Am I not an earthly

woman? And all the while the breath is in my body I may complain me, for my belief is I do none offence though I love an earthly
man unto God, for He formed me thereto, and all manner of good
love cometh of God. And other than good love loved I never Sir
Lancelot du Lake. And I take God to my record I loved never
none but Sir Lancelot du Lake, nor never shall, of earthly creature;
and a clean maiden I am for him and for all other. And sithen it
is the sufferance of God that I shall die for the love of so noble a
knight, I beseech the High Father of Heaven to have mercy upon
me and my soul, and upon mine innumerable pains that I suffer
may be allegiance of part of my sins. For sweet Lord Jesu,' said the
fair maiden, 'I take Thee to record, I was never to Thee great offen-
cer, neither against Thy laws; but that I loved this noble knight, Sir
Lancelot, out of measure. And of myself, good lord, I had no
might to withstand the fervent love wherefore I have my death.'

And then she called her father, Sir Bernard, and her brother
Sir Tirre, and heartily she prayed her father that her brother might
write a letter like as she did indite it; and so her father granted her.

And when the letter was written word by word like as she devised it then she prayed her father that she might be watched until
she were dead.

'And while my body is hot let this letter be put in my right
hand, and my hand bound fast with the letter until that I be cold.
And let me be put in a fair bed with all the richest clothes that
I have about me, and so let my bed and all my richest clothes be
laid with me in a chariot unto the next place where the Thames is;
and there let me be put within a barget, and but one man with me,
such as ye trust, to steer me thither, and that my barget be covered
with black samite over and over: thus father I beseech you let it be
done.'

So her father granted it her faithfully, all thing should be done
like as she had devised. Then her father and her brother made great
dole for her. And when this was done anon she died.

And so when she was dead the corpse and the bed all was led
the next way unto the Thames, and there a man, and the corpse,
and all, were put into Thames; and so the man steered the barget
unto Westminster, and there it rubbed and rolled to and fro a
great while or any man espied it.

So by fortune King Arthur and the Queen Guenever were
talking together at a window, and so as they looked unto the
Thames they espied this black barget, and had marvel what it
meant. Then the king called Sir Kay, and showed it him.

'Sir,' said Sir Kay, 'wit you well there is some new tidings.'

'Go thither,' said the king to Sir Kay, 'and take with you Sir
Brandiles and Sir Agravain, and bring me ready word what is
there.'

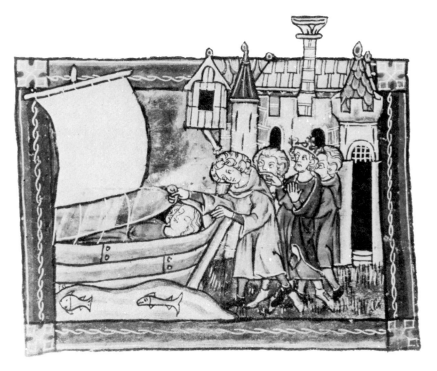

*The body of the
Maid of Astolat is
placed in a barge*

Then these three knights departed and came to the barget and
went in. And there they found the fairest corpse lying in a rich
bed that ever ye saw, and a poor man sitting in the barget's end,
and no word would he speak. So these three knights returned unto
the king again, and told him what they found.

'That fair corpse will I see,' said the king.

And so then the king took the queen by the hand, and went
thither. Then the king made the barget to be holden fast, and then
the king and the queen went in with certain knights with them;
and there he saw the fairest woman lie in a rich bed, covered unto
her middle with many rich clothes, and all was of cloth of gold.
And she lay as though she had smiled. Then the queen espied a
letter in her right hand, and told the king. Then the king took it
and said,

'Now am I sure this letter will tell what she was, and why she is
come hither.'

So the king and the queen went out of the barget, and so commanded a certain to await upon the barget. And so when the king
was come within his chamber, he called many knights about him,
and said that he would wit openly what was written within that
letter. Then the king brake it, and made a clerk to read it, and this
was the intent of the letter:

'Most noble knight, my lord Sir Lancelot, now hath death made
us two at debate for your love. And I was your lover, that men
called the Fair Maiden of Astolat. Therefore unto all ladies I
make my moan, yet for my soul ye pray and bury me at the least,

and offer ye my mass-penny; this is my last request. And a clean maiden I died, I take God to witness. And pray for my soul, Sir Lancelot, as thou art peerless.'

This was all the substance in the letter. And when it was read, the king, the queen, and all the knights wept for pity of the doleful complaints. Then was Sir Lancelot sent for; and when he was come King Arthur made the letter to be read to him. And when Sir Lancelot heard it word by word, he said,

'My lord Arthur, wit ye well I am right heavy of the death of this fair lady. And God knoweth I was never causer of her death by my willing, and that will I report me to her own brother that here is, Sir Lavaine. I will not say nay,' said Sir Lancelot, 'but that she was both fair and good, and much I was beholden unto her, but she loved me out of measure.'

'Sir,' said the queen, 'ye might have showed her some bounty and gentleness that might have preserved her life.'

'Madam,' said Sir Lancelot, 'she would none other ways be answered but that she would be my wife, other else my paramour; and of these two I would not grant her. But I proffered her, for her good love that she showed me, a thousand pound yearly to her, and to her heirs, and to wed any manner knight that she could find best to love in her heart. For madam,' said Sir Lancelot, 'I love not to be constrained to love; for love must arise of the heart, and not by no constraint.'

'That is truth,' said the king, 'and many knight's love is free in himself, and never will be bound; for where he is bounden he looseth himself.' Then said the king unto Sir Lancelot, 'Sir, it will be your worship that ye oversee that she be interred worship-fully.'

'Sir,' said Sir Lancelot, 'that shall be done as I can best devise.'

And so many knights yede thither to behold that fair dead maiden. And so upon the morn she was interred richly, and Sir Lancelot offered her mass-penny; and all the knights of the Table Round that were there at that time offered with Sir Lancelot. And then the poor man went again with the barget.

Then the queen sent for Sir Lancelot, and prayed him of mercy, for why that she had been wroth with him causeless.

'This is not the first time,' said Sir Lancelot, 'that ye had been displeased with me causeless. But, madam, ever I must suffer you, but what sorrow I endure ye take no force.'

So this passed on all that winter, with all manner of hunting and hawking; and jousts and tourneys were many betwixt many great lords. And ever in all places Sir Lavaine gat great worship, so that he was nobly renowned among many knights of the Table Round.

And thus it passed on from Candlemas until after Easter, that the month of May was come, when ever lusty heart beginneth to blossom, and to bring forth fruit. For like as herbs and trees bringen forth fruit and flourish in May, in likewise every lusty heart that is in any manner a lover, springeth, burgeoneth, buddeth, and flourisheth in lusty deeds. For it giveth unto all lovers courage, that lusty month of May, in something to constrain him to some manner of thing more in that month than in any other month, for diverse causes. For then all herbs and trees renewen a man and woman, and in likewise lovers callen again to their mind old gentleness and old service, and many kind deeds that were forgotten by negligence.

For like as winter rasure doth alway erase and deface green summer, so fareth it by unstable love in man and woman. For in many persons there is no stability; for we may see all day, for a little blast of winter's rasure, anon we shall deface and lay apart true love for little or nought, that cost much thing; this is no wisdom nor stability, but it is feebleness of nature and great disworship, whomsoever useth this.

Therefore, like as May month flowereth and flourisheth in every man's garden, so in likewise let every man of worship flourish his heart in this world: first unto God, and next unto the joy of them that he promised his faith unto; for there was never worshipful man nor worshipful woman, but they loved one better than another; and worship in arms may never be foiled, but first reserve the honour to God, and secondly the quarrel must come of thy lady. And such love I call virtuous love.

But nowadays men cannot love seven night but they must have all their desires. That love may not endure by reason; for where they be soon accorded and hasty, heat soon it cooleth. And right so fareth love nowadays, soon hot soon cold: this is no stability. But the old love was not so. For men and women could love together seven years, and no licours lusts were between them, and then was love truth and faithfulness: and lo, in likewise was used such love in King Arthur's days.

Wherefore I liken love nowadays unto summer and winter; for like as the one is hot and the other cold, so fareth love nowadays. And therefore all ye that be lovers, call unto your remembrance the month of May, like as did Queen Guenever, for whom I make here a little mention, that while she lived she was a true lover, and therefore she had a good end.

So it befell in the month of May, Queen Guenever called unto her ten knights of the Table Round; and she gave them warning that early upon the morrow she would ride on Maying into woods and fields beside Westminster:

'And I warn you that there be none of you but that he be well horsed, and that ye all be clothed in green, other in silk other in cloth; and I shall bring with me ten ladies, and every knight shall have a lady by him. And every knight shall have a squire and two yeoman, and I will that all be well horsed.'

So they made them ready in the freshest manner. And these were the names of the knights: Sir Kay le Seneschal, Sir Agravain, Sir Brandiles, Sir Sagramore le Desirous, Sir Dodinas le Savage, Sir Ozanna le Cure Hardy, Sir Ladinas of the Forest Savage, Sir Persant of Inde, Sir Ironside, that was called the Knight of the Red Launds, and Sir Pelleas, the lover. And these ten knights made them ready in the freshest manner to ride with the queen.

And so upon the morn ere it were day, in a May morning, they took their horses with the queen, and rode on Maying in woods and meadows as it pleased them, in great joy and delights. For the queen had cast to have been again with King Arthur at the furthest by ten of the clock, and so was that time her purpose.

Then there was a knight that hight Sir Meliagaunt, and he was son unto King Bagdemagus, and this knight had at that time a castle of the gift of King Arthur within seven mile of Westminster. And this knight, Sir Meliagaunt, loved passing well Queen Guenever, and so had he done long and many years. And the book saith he had lain in a wait for to steal away the queen, but evermore he forbare for because of Sir Lancelot; for in no wise he would meddle with the queen and Sir Lancelot were in her company, other else and he were near hand her.

And that time was such a custom, that the queen rode never without a great fellowship of men of arms about her. And they were many good knights, and the most part were young men that would have worship; and they were called the Queen's Knights. And never in no battle, tournament, nor jousts, they bare none of them no manner of knowledging of their own arms, but plain white shields, and thereby they were called the Queen's Knights. And then it happed any of them to be of great worship by his noble deeds, then at the next feast of Pentecost, if there were any slain or dead, as there was none year that there failed but there were some dead, then was there chosen in his stead that was dead, the most men of worship that were called the Queen's Knights. And thus they came up first, or they were renowned men of worship, both Sir Lancelot and all the remnant of them.

But this knight Sir Meliagaunt, had espied the queen well and her purpose, and how Sir Lancelot was not with her, and how she had no man of arms with her but the ten noble knights all arrayed in green for Maying. Then he purveyed him a twenty men of arms and an hundred archers for to destroy the queen and her knights, for he thought that time was best season to take the queen.

So as the queen was out on Maying, with all her knights which were bedashed with herbs, mosses and flowers, in the best manner and freshest; right so came out of a wood Sir Meliagaunt with an eight score men, all harnessed as they should fight in a battle of arrest, and bad the queen and her knights abide, for maugre their heads they should abide.

'Traitor knight,' said Queen Guenever, 'what cast thou to do? Wilt thou shame thyself? Bethink thee how thou art a king's son, and knight of the Table Round, and thou thus to be about to dishonour the noble king that made thee knight; thou shamest all knighthood and thyself, and me. And I let thee wit shalt thou never shame, for I had lever cut mine own throat in twain rather than thou shouldest dishonour me.'

'As for all this language,' said Meliagaunt, 'be it as it be may. For wit you well, madam, I have loved you many a year, and never ere now could I get you at such an advantage as I do now. And therefore I will take you as I find you.'

Then spake all the ten noble knights at once and said, 'Sir Meliagaunt, wit thou well ye are about to jeopard thy worship to dishonour, and also ye cast to jeopard our persons. Howbeit we be unarmed, and ye have us at a great advantage, for it seemeth by you that ye have laid watch upon us; but rather than ye should put the queen to a shame and us all, we had as leve to depart from our lives, for and if we other ways did, we were shamed for ever.'

Then said Sir Meliagaunt, 'Dress you as well ye can, and keep the queen.'

Then the ten knights of the Table Round drew their swords, and the other let run at them with their spears, and the ten knights manly abode them, and smote away their spears, that no spear did them no harm. Then they lashed together with swords, and anon Sir Kay, Sir Sagramore, Sir Agravain, Sir Dodinas, Sir Ladinas, and Sir Ozanna were smitten to the earth with grimly wounds. Then Sir Brandiles, and Sir Persant, Sir Ironside and Sir Pelleas fought long, and they were sore wounded, for these ten knights, or ever they were laid to the ground, slew forty men of the boldest and the best of them.

So when the queen saw her knights thus dolefully wounded, and needs must be slain at the last, then for very pity and sorrow she cried and said,

'Sir Meliagaunt, slay not my noble knights, and I will go with thee upon this covenant: that thou save them, and suffer them no more to be hurt, with this, that they be led with me wheresomever thou leadest me. For I will rather slay myself than I will go with thee, unless that these my noble knights may be in my presence.'

'Madam,' said Sir Meliagaunt, 'for your sake they shall be led with you into mine own castle, with that ye will be ruled, and ride with me.'

Then the queen prayed the four knights to leave their fighting, and she and they would not depart.

'Madam,' said Sir Pelleas, 'we will do as ye do, for as for me I take no force of my life nor death.'

For as the French book saith, Sir Pelleas gave such buffets there that none armour might hold him.

Then by the queen's commandment they left battle, and dressed the wounded knights on horseback, some sitting, some overthwart their horses, that it was pity to behold them. And then Sir Meliagaunt charged the queen and all her knights that none of all her fellowship should depart from her; for full sore he dread Sir Lancelot du Lake, lest he should have any knowledging.

All this espied the queen, and privily she called unto her a child of her chamber that was swiftly horsed, to whom she said, 'Go thou, when thou seest thy time, and bear this ring unto Sir Lancelot du Lake, and pray him as he loveth me that he will see me and rescue me, if ever he will have joy of me; and spare not thy horse,' said the queen, 'neither for water, neither for land.'

So the child espied his time, and lightly he took his horse with the spurs, and departed as fast as he might. And when Sir Meliagaunt saw him so flee, he understood that it was by the queen's commandment for to warn Sir Lancelot. Then they that were best horsed chased him and shot at him, but from them all the child went suddenly.

And then Sir Meliagaunt said to the queen, 'Madam, ye are about to betray me, but I shall ordain for Sir Lancelot that he shall not come lightly at you.'

And then he rode with her, and they all, to his castle, in all the haste that they might. And by the way Sir Meliagaunt laid in an ambushment the best archers that he might get in his country, to the number of thirty, to await upon Sir Lancelot, charging them that if they saw such a manner of knight come by the way upon a white horse, that in any wise they slay his horse, 'but in no manner of wise have not ado with him bodily, for he is over-hardy to be overcome.' So this was done, and they were come to his castle, but in no wise the queen would never let none of the ten knights and her ladies out of her sight, but always they were in her presence. For the book saith, Sir Meliagaunt durst make no masteries, for dread of Sir Lancelot, insomuch he deemed that he had warning.

So when the child was departed from the fellowship of Sir Meliagaunt, within a while he came to Westminster, and anon he found Sir Lancelot. And when he had told his message, and de-livered him the queen's ring,

RIGHT *Guenever being taken prisoner*

FAR RIGHT
Lancelot receives a message from the queen

'Alas,' said Sir Lancelot, 'now am I shamed for ever, unless that I may rescue that noble lady from dishonour.'

Then eagerly he asked his armour; and ever the child told Sir Lancelot how the ten knights fought marvellously, and how Sir Pelleas, and Sir Ironside, and Sir Brandiles, and Sir Persant of Inde, fought strongly, but namely Sir Pelleas, there might none withstand him; and how they all fought till at the last they were laid to the earth; and how the queen made appointment for to save their lives, and go with Sir Meliagaunt.

'Alas,' said Sir Lancelot, 'that most noble lady, that she should be so destroyed; I had lever,' said Sir Lancelot, 'than all France, that I had been there well armed.'

So when Sir Lancelot was armed and upon his horse, he prayed the child of the queen's chamber to warn Sir Lavaine how suddenly he was departed, and for what cause.

'And pray him as he loveth me, that he will hie him after me, and that he stint not until he come to the castle where Sir Meliagaunt abideth, or dwelleth; for there,' said Sir Lancelot, 'he shall hear of me and I be a man living, and rescue the queen and the ten knights the which he traitorously hath taken, and that shall I prove upon his head, and all them that hold with him.'

Then Sir Lancelot rode as fast as he might, and the book saith he took the water at Westminster Bridge, and made his horse swim over the Thames unto Lambeth. And so within a while he came to the same place whereas the ten noble knights fought with Sir Meliagaunt. And then Sir Lancelot followed the track until that he came to a wood, and there was a strait way, and there the thirty archers bad Sir Lancelot turn again, and follow no longer that track.

'What commandment have ye,' said Sir Lancelot, 'to cause me that am a knight of the Round Table, to leave my right way?'

'This way shalt thou leave other else thou shalt go it on thy foot, for wit thou well thy horse shall be slain.'

'That is little mastery,' said Sir Lancelot, 'to slay mine horse; but as for myself, when my horse is slain, I give right nought for you, not and ye were five hundred more.'

So then they shot Sir Lancelot's horse, and smote him with many arrows; and then Sir Lancelot avoided his horse, and went on foot; but there were so many ditches and hedges betwixt them and him that he might not meddle with none of them.

'Alas for shame,' said Sir Lancelot, 'that ever one knight should betray another knight; but it is an old-said saw, "A good man is never in danger but when he is in the danger of a coward."'

Then Sir Lancelot walked on a while, and then he was foul cumbered of his armour, his shield, and his spear, and all that longed unto him. Wit ye well he was full sore annoyed, and full loth he was for to leave anything that longed unto him, for he dread sore the treason of Sir Meliagaunt. Then by fortune there came by him a chariot that came thither to fetch wood.

'Say me, carter,' said Sir Lancelot, 'what shall I give thee to suffer me to leap into thy chariot, and that thou bring me unto a castle within this two mile?'

'Thou shalt not come within my chariot,' said the carter, 'for I am sent for to fetch wood.'

'Unto whom?' said Sir Lancelot.

'Unto my lord, Sir Meliagaunt,' said the carter.

'And with him would I speak,' said Sir Lancelot.

'Thou shalt not go with me,' said the carter.

Then Sir Lancelot leapt to him, and gave him backward with his gauntlet a rear-main, that he fell to the earth stark dead. Then the other carter, his fellow, was afeared, and weened to have gone the same way. And then he cried,

rear-main: *backhanded stroke*

'Fair lord, save my life, and I shall bring you where ye will.'

'Then I charge thee,' said Sir Lancelot, 'that thou drive me and this chariot even unto Sir Meliagaunt's gate.'

'Then leap ye up into the chariot,' said the carter, 'and ye shall be there anon.'

Lancelot is driven in a cart

So the carter drove on a great wallop, and Sir Lancelot's horse

followed the chariot, with more than a forty arrows broad and rough in him.

And more than an hour and an half Dame Guenever was awaiting in a bay window. Then one of her ladies espied an armed knight standing in a chariot.

'See madam,' said the lady, 'where rides in a chariot a goodly armed knight; I suppose he rideth unto hanging.'

'Where?' said the queen.

Then she espied by his shield that he was there himself, Sir Lancelot du Lake. And then she was ware where came his horse after that chariot, and ever he trod his guts and his paunch under his feet.

'Alas,' said the queen, 'now I see well and prove, that well is him that hath a trusty friend. Ha, most noble knight,' said Queen Guenever, 'I see well that ye were hard bestad when ye ride in a chariot.'

Then she rebuked that lady that likened Sir Lancelot to ride in a chariot to hanging.

'It was foul mouthed,' said the queen, 'and evil likened, so for to liken the most noble knight of the world unto such a shameful death. O Jesu defend him and keep him,' said the queen, 'from all mischievous end.'

By this was Sir Lancelot comen to the gates of that castle, and there he descended down, and cried, that all the castle rang of it,

'Where art thou, thou false traitor, Sir Meliagaunt, and knight of the Table Round? Now come forth here, thou traitor knight, thou and thy fellowship with thee; for here I am, Sir Lancelot du Lake, that shall fight with you.'

And therewithal he bare the gate wide open upon the porter, and smote him under his ear with his gauntlet, that his neck brast in two pieces.

When Sir Meliagaunt heard that Sir Lancelot was come he ran unto Queen Guenever, and fell upon his knee, and said,

'Mercy, madam, now I put me wholly into your good grace.'

'What ails you now?' said Queen Guenever. 'Pardie, I might well wit some good knight would revenge me, though my lord King Arthur wist not of this your work.'

'Madam,' said Sir Meliagaunt, 'all this that is amiss on my part shall be amended right as yourself will devise, and wholly I put me in your grace.'

'What would ye that I did?' said the queen.

'Madam, I would no more,' said Sir Meliagaunt, 'but that ye would take all in your own hands, and that ye will rule my lord Sir Lancelot; and such cheer as may be made him in this poor castle ye and he shall have unto to-morn, and then may ye and all

BELOW *A knight begs forgiveness of Guenever*

they return again unto Westminster. And my body and all that I have I shall put in your rule.'

'Ye say well,' said the queen, 'and better is peace than evermore war, and the less noise the more is my worship.'

Then the queen and her ladies went down unto the knight, Sir Lancelot, that stood wood wroth out of measure in the inner court, to abide battle; and ever he said:

'Thou traitor knight come forth.'

Then the queen came to him and said, 'Sir Lancelot, why be ye so moved?'

'Ha, madam,' said Sir Lancelot, 'why ask ye me that question? Meseemeth,' said Sir Lancelot, 'ye ought to be more wroth than I am, for ye have the hurt and the dishonour. For wit ye well, madam, my hurt is but little for the killing of a mare's son, but the despite grieveth me much more than all my hurt.'

'Truly,' said the queen, 'ye say truth; but heartily I thank you,' said the queen. 'But ye must come in with me peaceable, for all thing that is put in my hand, and all that is amiss be amended, for the knight full sore repenteth him of the misadventure that is befallen him.'

'Madam,' said Sir Lancelot, 'sith it is so that ye be accorded with him, as for me I may not gainsay it, howbeit Sir Meliagaunt hath done full shamefully to me, and cowardly. And madam,' said Sir Lancelot, 'and I had wist ye would have been so lightly accorded with him I would not have made such haste unto you.'

'Why say ye so?' said the queen, 'Do ye forthink yourself of your good deeds? Wit you well,' said the queen, 'I accorded never unto him for no favour nor love that I had unto him, but for to lay down every shameful noise.'

'Madam,' said Sir Lancelot, 'ye understand full well I was never willing nor glad of shameful slander nor noise; and there is neither king, queen, ne knight, that beareth the life, except my lord King Arthur, and you, madam should let me but I should make Sir Meliagaunt's heart full cold or ever I departed from hence.'

'That wot I well,' said the queen, 'but what will ye more? Ye shall have all thing ruled as ye list to have it.'

'Madam,' said Sir Lancelot, 'so ye be pleased I care not, as for my part ye shall soon please.'

Right so the queen took Sir Lancelot by the bare hand, for he had put off his gauntlet, and so she went with him till her chamber; and then she commanded him to be unarmed. And then Sir Lancelot asked where were her ten knights that were wounded sore; so she showed them unto Sir Lancelot, and there they made great joy of the coming of him, and Sir Lancelot made great dole of their hurts, and bewailed them greatly. And there Sir Lancelot

BELOW
Arthur welcomes Guenever back after her rescue

told them how cowardly and traitorly Meliagaunt set archers to slay his horse, and how he was fain to put himself in a chariot. Thus they complained every each to other; and full fain they would have been revenged, but they kept the peace because of the queen.

Then, as the French book saith, Sir Lancelot was called many a day after 'le Chevaler du Chariot', and did many deeds, and great adventures he had. And so leave we off here of 'le Chevaler du Chariot', and turn we to this tale.

So Sir Lancelot had great cheer with the queen. And then he made a promise with the queen that the same night he should come to a window outward toward a garden; and that window was barred with iron, and there Sir Lancelot promised to meet her when all folks were asleep.

So then came Sir Lavaine driving to the gates, crying, 'Where is my lord, Sir Lancelot du Lake?'

And anon he was sent for, and when Sir Lavaine saw Sir Lancelot, he said, 'My lord, I found how ye were hard bestad, for I have found your horse that is slain with arrows.'

'As for that,' said Sir Lancelot, 'I pray you, Sir Lavaine, speak ye of other matters, and let ye this pass, and we shall right it another time when we best may.'

Then the knights that were hurt were searched, and soft salves were laid to their wounds; and so it passed on till supper time. And all the cheer that might be made them there was done unto the queen and all her knights. Then when season was, they went unto their chambers, but in no wise the queen would not suffer the wounded knights to be from her, but that they were laid within draughts by her chamber, upon beds and pallets, that she herself might see to them, that they wanted nothing.

draughts: *recesses*

So when Sir Lancelot was in his chamber that was assigned unto him, he called unto him Sir Lavaine, and told him that night he must go speak with his lady, Dame Guenever.

'Sir,' said Sir Lavaine, 'let me go with you and it please you, for I dread me sore of the treason of Sir Meliagaunt.'

'Nay,' said Sir Lancelot, 'I thank you, but I will have nobody with me.'

Then Sir Lancelot took his sword in his hand, and privily went to a place where he had spied a ladder toforehand, and then he took under his arm, and bare it though the garden, and set it up to the window. And anon the queen was there ready to meet him. And then they made either to other their complaints of many diverse things, and then Sir Lancelot wished that he might have comen in to her.

'Wit ye well,' said the queen, 'I would fain as ye, that ye might come in to me.'

'Would ye so, madam,' said Sir Lancelot, 'with your heart that I were with you?'

'Yea, truly,' said the queen.

'Then shall I prove my might,' said Sir Lancelot, 'for your love.'

And then he set his hands upon the bars of iron, and he pulled at them with such a might that he brast them clean out of the stone walls. And therewithal one of the bars of iron cut the brawn of his hands throughout to the bone; and then he leapt into the chamber to the queen.

'Make ye no noise,' said the queen, 'for my wounded knights lie here fast by me.'

So, to pass upon this tale, Sir Lancelot went unto bed with the queen, and he took no force of his hurt hand, but took his pleasance and his liking until it was in the dawning of the day; and wit ye well he slept not but watched. And when he saw his time that he might tarry no longer he took his leave and departed at the window, and put it together as well as he might again, and so departed unto his own chamber. And there he told Sir Lavaine how he was hurt.

Then Sir Lavaine dressed his hand and staunched it, and put upon it a glove, that it should not be espied; and so the queen lay long a-bed in the morning till it was nine of the clock.

Then Sir Meliagaunt went to the queen's chamber, and found her ladies there ready clothed.

'Jesu mercy,' said Sir Meliagaunt, 'what ails you, madam, that ye sleep this long?'

And right therewithal he opened the curtain for to behold her. And then was he ware where she lay, and all the head-sheet, pillow, and over-sheet was be-bled with the blood of Sir Lancelot and of his hurt hand. When Sir Meliagaunt espied that blood, then he deemed in her that she was false to the king, and that some of the wounded knights had lain by her all that night.

'Ah, madam,' said Sir Meliagaunt, 'now I have founden you a false traitress unto my lord Arthur; for now I prove well it was not for nought that ye laid these wounded knights within the bounds of your chamber. Therefore I will call you of treason before my lord, King Arthur. And now I have proved you, madam, with a shameful deed; and that they be all false, or some of them, I will make it good; for a wounded knight this night hath lain by you.'

'That is false,' said the queen, 'and that I will report me unto them all.'

Then when the ten knights heard Sir Meliagaunt's words, they spake all at once and said to Sir Meliagaunt,

'Thou sayest falsely, and wrongfully puttest upon us such a deed, and that we will make good upon thee, any of us; now choose which thou list of us when we are whole of the wounds thou gavest us.'

'Ye shall not,' said Sir Meliagaunt. 'Away with your proud language. For here ye may all see,' said Sir Meliagaunt, 'that by the queen this night a wounded knight hath lain.'

Then they all looked, and were sore ashamed when they saw that blood. And wit you well Sir Meliagaunt was passing glad that he had the queen at such an advantage, for he deemed by that to hide his own treason. So with this rumour came in Sir Lancelot, and found them all at a great affray.

'What array is this?' said Sir Lancelot.

Then Sir Meliagaunt told them what he had found, and showed them the queen's bed.

'Now truly,' said Sir Lancelot, 'ye did not your part nor knightly, to touch a queen's bed while it was drawn, and she lying therein. For I dare say my lord King Arthur himself would not have displayed her curtains, she being within her bed, unless that it had pleased him to have lain down by her. And therefore ye have done unworshipfully and shamefully to yourself.'

'Sir, I wot not what ye mean,' said Sir Meliagaunt, 'but well I am sure there hath one of her wounded knights lain with her this night. And therefore I will prove with my hands that she is a traitress unto my lord King Arthur.'

'Beware what ye do,' said Sir Lancelot, 'for and ye say so, and ye will prove it, it will be taken at your hands.'

'My lord Sir Lancelot,' said Sir Meliagaunt, 'I rede you beware what ye do; for though ye are never so good a knight, as I wot well ye are renowned the best knight of the world, yet should ye be advised to do battle in a wrong quarrel; for God will have a stroke in every battle.'

'As for that,' said Sir Lancelot, 'God is to be dread; but as to that I say plainly, that this night there lay none of these ten wounded knights with my lady Queen Guenever, and that will I prove with my hands, that ye say untruly in that. Now, what say ye?' said Sir Lancelot.

'Thus I say,' said Sir Meliagaunt, 'here is my glove that she is traitress unto my lord, King Arthur, and that this night one of the wounded knights lay with her.'

'Well, sir, and I receive your glove,' said Sir Lancelot.

And so they were sealed with their signets, and delivered unto the ten knights.

'At what day shall we do battle together?' said Sir Lancelot.

'This day eight days,' said Sir Meliagaunt, 'in the field beside Westminster.'

'I am agreed,' said Sir Lancelot.

'But now,' said Sir Meliagaunt, 'sithen it is so that we must needs fight together, I pray you, as ye be a noble knight, await me with no treason, nor none villainy the meanwhile, nor none for you.'

'So God me help,' said Sir Lancelot, 'ye shall right well wit I was never of no such conditions. For I report me to all knights that ever have known me, I fared never with no treason, nor I loved never the fellowship of no man that fared with treason.'

'Then let us go to dinner,' said Sir Meliagaunt, 'and after dinner the queen and ye may ride all to Westminster.'

'I will well,' said Sir Lancelot.

Then Sir Meliagaunt said to Sir Lancelot, 'Sir, pleaseth you to see the esturies of this castle?'

esturies: *fish ponds*

'With a good will,' said Sir Lancelot.

And then they went together from chamber to chamber, for Sir Lancelot dread no perils; for ever a man of worship and of prowess dreads but little of perils, for they ween that every man be as they be. But ever he that fareth with treason putteth often a true man in great danger. And so it befell upon Sir Lancelot, that no peril dread, as he went with Sir Meliagaunt he trod on a trap, and the board rolled, and there Sir Lancelot fell down more than ten fathom into a cave full of straw.

And then Sir Meliagaunt departed and made no fare, no more than that he wist not where he was. And when Sir Lancelot was thus missed they marvelled where he was become; and then the queen and many of them deemed that he was departed, as he was wont to do, suddenly. For Sir Meliagaunt made suddenly to put away aside Sir Lavaine's horse, that they might all understand that Sir Lancelot was departed suddenly.

So then it passed on till after dinner; and then Sir Lavaine would not stint until that he had litters for the wounded knights, that they might be carried in them; and so with the queen and them all, both ladies and gentlewomen and other, rode unto Westminster; and there the knights told King Arthur how Sir Meliagaunt had appelled the queen of high treason, and how Sir Lancelot had received the glove of him; 'and this day eight days they shall do battle afore you.'

'By my head,' said King Arthur, 'I am afeared Sir Meliagaunt hath taken upon him a great charge; but where is Sir Lancelot?' said the king.

'Sir,' said they all, 'we wot not where he is, but we deem he is ridden to some adventure, as he is oftentimes wont to do, for he hath Sir Lavaine's horse.'

'Let him be,' said the king, 'he will be founden, but if he be betrapped with some treason.'

So leave we Sir Lancelot lying within that cave in great pain;

and every day there came a lady and brought him his meat and his drink, and wooed him every day, to have lain by her; and ever the noble knight, Sir Lancelot, said her nay.

'Sir Lancelot,' said she, 'ye are not wise, for ye may never out of this prison, but if ye have my help; and also your lady, Queen Guenever, shall be burnt in your default, unless that ye be there at the day of battle.'

'God defend,' said Sir Lancelot, 'that she should be burnt in my default; and if it be so,' said Sir Lancelot, 'that I may not be there, it shall be well understand, both at the king and at the queen, and with all men of worship, that I am dead, sick, other in prison. For all men that know me will say for me that I am in some evil case and I be not there that day. And well I wot there is some good knight, other of my blood, or some other that loveth me, that will take my quarrel in hand; and therefore,' said Sir Lancelot, 'wit you well, ye shall not fear me; and if there were no more women in all this land but ye, yet I shall not have ado with you.'

'Then art ye shamed,' said the lady, 'and destroyed for ever.'

'As for world's shame, now Jesu defend me. And as for my distress, it is welcome whatsoever it be that God sends me.'

So she came to him the same day that the battle should be, and said,

'Sir Lancelot, methinketh ye are too hard-hearted. But would ye but once kiss me I should deliver you, and your armour, and the best horse that is within Sir Meliagaunt's stable.'

'As for to kiss you,' said Sir Lancelot, 'I may do that and lose no worship; and wit ye well, and I understood there were any disworship for to kiss you, I would not do it.'

Then he kissed her. And anon she gat him up into his armour. And when he was armed, she brought him to a stable, where stood twelve good coursers, and bad him choose the best. Then Sir Lancelot looked upon a white courser, and that liked him best; and anon he commanded the keepers fast to saddle him with the best saddle of war that there was; and so it was done as he bad.

Then gat he his own spear in his hand, and his sword by his side, and commended the lady unto God, and said,

'Lady, for this day's deed I shall do you service, if ever it lie in my power.'

Now leave we Sir Lancelot, all that ever he might wallop, and speak we of Queen Guenever that was brought to a fire to be burnt; for Sir Meliagaunt was sure, him thought, that Sir Lancelot should not be at that battle; therefore he ever cried upon King Arthur to do him justice, other else bring forth Sir Lancelot du Lake.

OPPOSITE
Scenes from the life of Lancelot; his birth; boyhood; jousting; and quest for the Grail

OVERLEAF
Guenever watches Lancelot taking part in a mêlée

Cest le liure de messire lancelot du lac ou
quel liure sont contenus tous les fais et les che
ualeries du dit messire lancelot et la queste du
saint graal fait p le dit mess lancelor le roy
artus gauand le bon chlr tristan pceual palame
des et les autres compaignons de la table reonde.

Il qui se tient et iuste
au plus petit et au plus
pecheur de tous man
de salut au commen
cement de ceste histoi
re a tous ceulx qui
leur cuer ont et leur
creance en la sainte
trinite cest ou pere et
ou filz et ou saint es
prit. Ou pere par qui toutes choses sont establiez
et recoiuent commencement de bie. Ou filz par
qui toutes choses sont deliurez des paines dinfer

et ramenees a la ioie pardurable. Ou saint esprit
par qui toutes choses sont mises hors des mains
au maligne esprit et remplie de ioie par le sainte
ment de lieu qui est bien enlumineux et bien
confort. le nom de celui qui ceste histoire fist nest
me nomme au commencement mais p les pa
roles qui ci apres sont dites pourres bien aper
ceuoir le nom de lu et le pays dont il fu ne et bne
ptie partie de son lignaige. Mais au commence
ment ne se veult pas desouurir et si y a trois
raisons pour quoi. La pmiere est pour ce que sil
se nommast et il deist que dieu lui eust descouur
te si haulte histoire les felons et les enuieux le
tenoient en bieulte. la secode raison si est pour
ce que se se sauoit son non tel le pourroit oir no
mer quil le cognoistroit si en priseroit moins lis
tone pour ce que par tant petite personne eust
este mise en escript. La tierce raison si est que sil
eust mis son nom en lhistoire et on trouuast autre
fiz

ſle on̄ qſ lanc̄ dou lac̄ ſie tiet
au milior eſlir dou mōde · ſle fut
li morte & proeſce que en alui
fut par ſō cors · car il ne fina hui
& ferir ne puis ne recrure ne qui

gn̄ perte euc̄
ne; plꝰ voltiz
qui bn̄ ont ceſ p
z qui vont auſi
maudient riz·

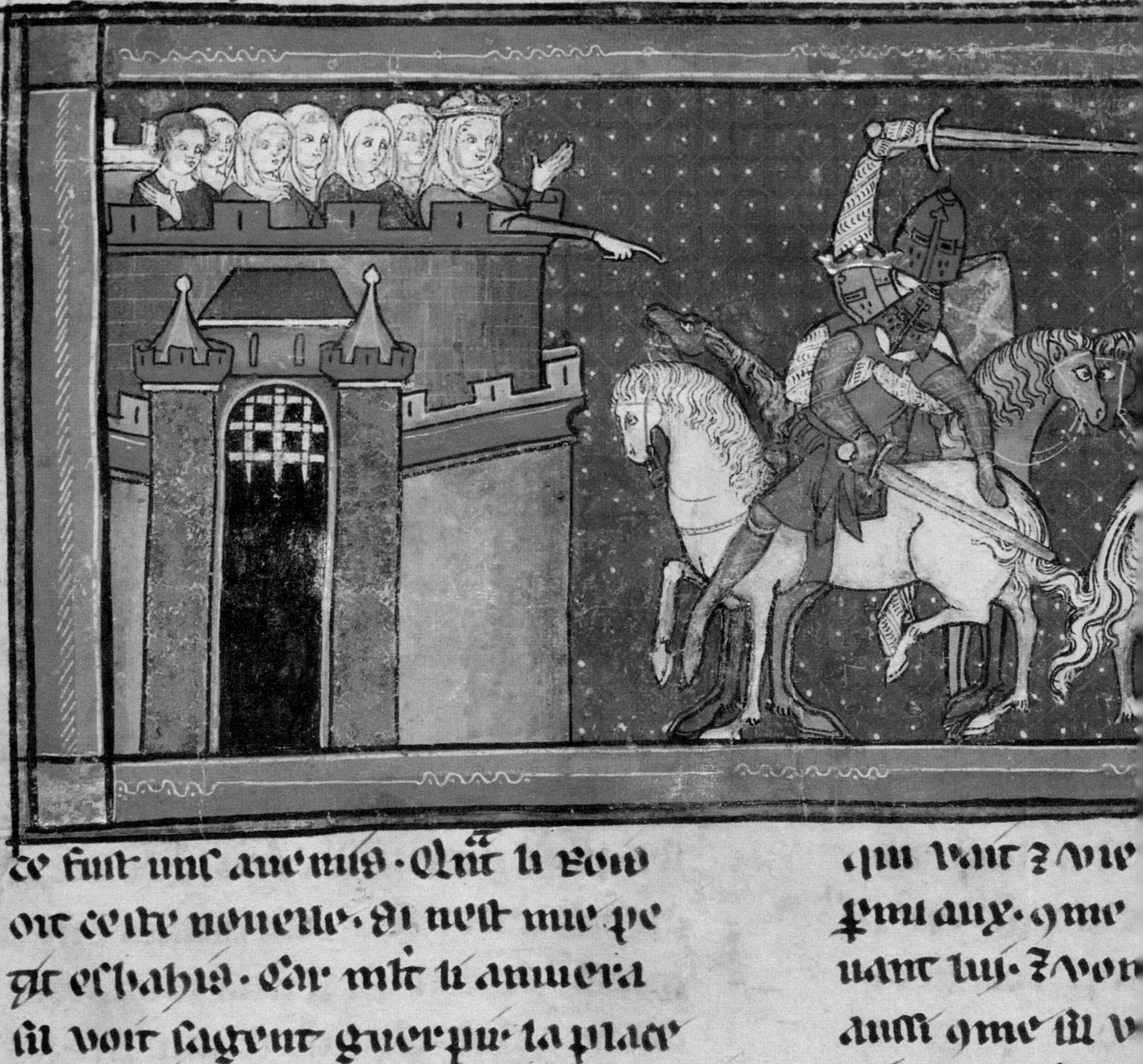

ce fut une auenture · chant li roiz
oit ceſte nouelle · ſi neſt mie pe
gn̄ eſbahiz · car mlt li auuiera
ſil voit ſagent guerpir la place
ꝓ poon aller auenture. Lorſ regrette
lanc̄ z dit mlt dolanz · z mlt corre
ciez; Ha lanc̄ bliaus douz amiſ·
ơ vogre bn̄ go eſt ma maiſons
vn̄ & preudomeſ · qn̄ vol ni en̄

qn̄ uant z me
ꝓmaux· qme
uant luy· z uon
auſi qme ſil v
nir· z il atāt a
duant leſ au
ꝛls euuid qn
qul eſt venir
ou la roine eu

le Abor ne retor

ort. Et la roine

ner. ? cof regart

lu eu ellec

eigart com amt

cheoir le gmeur. Si na qui le

tiegne. Si regarde derrer lui.

z voit le Boy bandemagu. ch dut

Que p dieu teue. mol cur vos

bras. car vos me vire. ja cheoir

ant ligieremt

eut ame de

ut le fuient

t la mort. ve

grat z chataît

housi ettoient

ore ne toient

at ter logreo

qui le regar

acre. le le vat aut. car ie me ser

si malade or endroit que ie croi

bîe morir en ceste place. Quant

Bous oit ceste pole. Sil a pate qui

ne son naure. amort. sil le prit

entre ses bras mlt doucemem.

z gmêce afaire tp grant duel. z

li demaï. Ha sire p dieu etre v

naure. dite le nouo. Qar il na

Then was the king and all the court full sore abashed and shamed that the queen should be burnt in the default of Sir Lancelot.

'My lord Arthur,' said Sir Lavaine, 'ye may understand that it is not well with my lord Sir Lancelot, for and he were alive, so he be not sick other in prison, wit ye well he would have been here. For never heard ye that ever he failed yet his part for whom he should do battle for. And therefore,' said Sir Lavaine, 'my lord King Arthur, I beseech you that ye will give me licence to do battle here this day for my lord and master, and for to save my lady, the queen.'

'Gramercy gentle Sir Lavaine,' said King Arthur, 'for I dare say all that Sir Meliagaunt putteth upon my lady the queen is wrong. For I have spoken with all the ten wounded knights, and there is not one of them, and he were whole and able to do battle, but he would prove upon Sir Meliagaunt's body that it is false that he putteth upon my queen.'

'And so shall I,' said Sir Lavaine, 'in the defence of my lord Sir Lancelot, and ye will give me leave.'

'Now I give you leave,' said King Arthur, 'and do your best, for I dare well say there is some treason done to Sir Lancelot.'

Then was Sir Lavaine armed and horsed, and suddenly at the lists' end he rode to perform this battle; and right as the heralds should cry, 'Lesses les aler,' right so came in Sir Lancelot driving with all the might of his horse.

And then King Arthur cried, 'Whoa!' and 'Abide!'

And then was Sir Lancelot called on horseback tofore King Arthur, and there he told openly tofore the king and all, how Sir Meliagaunt had served him first and last. And when the king, and the queen, and all the lords, knew of the treason of Sir Meliagaunt they were all ashamed on his behalf. Then was Queen Guenever sent for, and set by the king in the great trust of her champion.

And then there was no more else to say, but Sir Lancelot and Sir Meliagaunt dressed them unto battle, and took their spears; and so they came together as thunder, and there Sir Lancelot bare him down quite over his horse's croup. And then Sir Lancelot alit and dressed his shield on his shoulder, with his sword in his hand, and Sir Meliagaunt in the same wise dressed him unto him, and there they smote many great strokes together. And at the last Sir Lancelot smote him such a buffet upon the helmet that he fell on the one side to the earth.

And then he cried upon him aloud, and said, 'Most noble knight, Sir Lancelot du Lake, save my life. For I yield me unto you, and I require you, as ye be a knight and fellow of the Table

OPPOSITE ABOVE
Guenever sends her ring to Lancelot

OPPOSITE BELOW
Arthur and Guenever at a feast

Round, slay me not, for I yield me as overcomen; and whether I shall live or die, I put me in the king's hands and yours.'

Then Sir Lancelot wist not what to do, for he had lever than all the good of the world he might have been revenged upon Sir Meliagaunt; and Sir Lancelot looked up to the queen Guenever, if he might espy by any sign or countenance what she would have done. And then the queen wagged her head upon Sir Lancelot, as though she would say, 'Slay him.' Full well knew Sir Lancelot by the wagging of her head that she would have him dead. Then Sir Lancelot bad him rise for shame and perform that battle to the utterance.

'Nay,' said Sir Meliagaunt, 'I will never arise until ye take me as yielden and recreant.'

'Well, I shall proffer you large proffers,' said Sir Lancelot, 'that is for to say, I shall unarm my head and my left quarter of my body, all that may be unarmed, as for that quarter, and I will let bind my left hand behind me, so that it shall not help me, and right so I shall do battle with you.'

Then Sir Meliagaunt start up upon his legs, and said on high, 'My lord Arthur, take heed to this proffer, for I will take it. And let him be disarmed and bounden according to his proffer.'

'What say ye,' said King Arthur unto Sir Lancelot, 'will ye abide by your proffer?'

'Yea, my lord,' said Sir Lancelot, 'for I will never go from that I have once said.'

Then the knights parters of the field disarmed Sir Lancelot, first his head, and sithen his left arm, and his left side, and they bound his left arm to his left side fast behind his back, without shield or anything, and then they were put together. Wit you well there was many a lady and many a knight marvelled that Sir Lancelot would jeopardy himself in such wise.

Then Sir Meliagaunt came with his sword all on high, and Sir Lancelot showed him openly his bare head and the bare left side; and when he weened to have smitten him upon the bare head, then lightly he avoided the left leg and the left side, and put his right hand and his sword to that stroke, and put it aside with great sleight. And then with such great force Sir Lancelot smote him on the helmet such a buffet that the stroke carved the head in two parts.

Then there was no more to do, but he was drawn out of the field. And at the great instance of the knights of the Table Round, the king suffered him to be interred, and the mention made upon him, who slew him, and for what cause he was slain.

And then the king and the queen made more of Sir Lancelot du Lake, and more he was cherished, than ever he was aforehand.

But every night and day Sir Agravain, Sir Gawain's brother, awaited Queen Guenever and Sir Lancelot du Lake to put them both to a rebuke and shame.

And so I leave here of this tale, and overleap great books of Sir Lancelot du Lake, what great adventures he did when he was called 'le Chevaler du Chariot'. For as the French book saith, because of despite that knights and ladies called him 'the knight that rode in the chariot' like as he were judged to the gallows, therefore in despite of all them that named him so, he was carried in a chariot a twelvemonth; for, but little after that he had slain Sir Meliagaunt in the queen's quarrel, he never in a twelvemonth came on horseback. And as the French book saith, he did that twelvemonth more than forty battles.

And because I have lost the very matter of 'le Chevaler du Chariot', I depart from the tale of Sir Lancelot, and here I go unto the 'Morte Arthur'; and that caused Sir Agravain.

And here on the other side followeth the most piteous tale of the Morte Arthur sans guerdon, par le chevalier Sir Thomas Malory, knight.   guerdon: *reward*

Jesu aide le, pour votre bonne merci! AMEN.

BOOK 13

The Death of Arthur

In May, when every lusty heart flourisheth and burgeoneth – for as the season is lusty to behold and comfortable, so man and woman rejoicen and gladden of summer coming with his fresh flowers: for winter with his rough winds and blasts causeth lusty men and women to cower, and to sit fast by the fire – so in this season as in the month of May, it befell a great anger and unhap that stinted not till the flower of chivalry of all the world was destroyed and slain.

And all was long upon two unhappy knights, which were named Sir Agravain and Sir Mordred, that were brethren unto Sir Gawain. For this Sir Agravain and Sir Mordred had ever a privy hate unto the queen, Dame Guenever, and to Sir Lancelot; and daily and nightly they ever watched upon Sir Lancelot.

So it mishapped, Sir Gawain and all his brethren were in King Arthur's chamber; and then Sir Agravain said thus openly, and not in no counsel, that many knights might hear it,

'I marvel that we all be not ashamed both to see and to know how Sir Lancelot lieth daily and nightly by the queen. And all we know it is so; and it is shamefully suffered of us all, that we should suffer so noble a king as King Arthur is so to be shamed.'

Then spake Sir Gawain, and said, 'Brother Sir Agravain, I pray you and charge you move no such matters no more afore me, for wit you well,' said Sir Gawain, 'I will not be of your counsel.'

'So God me help,' said Sir Gaheris and Sir Gareth, 'we will not be knowing, brother Agravain, of your deeds.'

'Then will I,' said Sir Mordred.

'I leve well that,' said Sir Gawain, 'for ever unto all unhappiness, brother Sir Mordred, thereto will ye grant; and I would that ye left all this, and made you not so busy, for I know,' said Sir Gawain, 'what will fall of it.'

'Fall of it what fall may,' said Sir Agravain, 'I will disclose it to the king.'

OPPOSITE
*Mordred and Arthur
meet on the field
of battle*

hen Arthur had
Retaken hrs reame
of gret Brutayne
vnto a ndred hxt

The Death of Arthur

'Not by my counsel,' said Sir Gawain, 'for and there arise war and wrack betwixt Sir Lancelot and us, wit you well brother, there will many knights and great lords hold with Sir Lancelot. Also, brother Sir Agravain,' said Sir Gawain, 'ye must remember how oftentimes Sir Lancelot hath rescued the king and the queen; and the best of us all had been full cold at the heart root had not Sir Lancelot been better than we, and that hath he proved himself full oft. And as for my part,' said Sir Gawain, 'I will never be against Sir Lancelot for one day's deed, when he rescued me from King Carados of the Dolorous Tower, and slew him, and saved my life. Also, brother Sir Agravain and Sir Mordred, in like wise Sir Lancelot rescued you both, and threescore and two, from Sir Turquin. Methinketh brother, such kind deeds and kindness should be remembered.'

'Do as ye list,' said Sir Agravain, 'for I will layne it no longer.'

With these words came to them King Arthur.

'Now brother, stint your noise,' said Sir Gawain.

'We will not,' said Sir Agravain and Sir Mordred.

'Well, will ye so?' said Sir Gawain. 'Then God speed you, for I will not hear your tales, neither be of your counsel.'

'No more will I,' said Sir Gareth and Sir Gaheris, 'for we will never say evil by that man; for because,' said Sir Gareth, 'Sir Lancelot made me knight, by no manner owe I to say ill of him.' And therewithal they three departed, making great dole.

'Alas,' said Sir Gawain and Sir Gareth, 'now is this realm wholly destroyed and mischieved, and the noble fellowship of the Round Table shall be disparbeled.'

disparbeled: *dispersed*

So they departed. And then King Arthur asked them what noise they made.

'My lord,' said Sir Agravain, 'I shall tell you, for I may keep it no longer. Here is I, and my brother Sir Mordred, brake unto my brother Sir Gawain, Sir Gaheris, and to Sir Gareth – for this is all, to make it short – how this we know all, that Sir Lancelot holdeth your queen, and hath done long; and we be your sister's sons, and we may suffer it no longer. And all we wot that ye should be above Sir Lancelot; and ye are the king that made him knight, and therefore we will prove it, that he is a traitor to your person.'

'If it be so,' said the king, 'wit you well he is none other. But I would be loth to begin such a thing but I might have proofs of it; for Sir Lancelot is an hardy knight, and all ye know he is the best knight among us all; and but if he be taken with the deed, he will fight with him that bringeth up the noise, and I know no knight that is able to match him. Therefore and it be sooth as ye say, I would that he were taken with the deed.'

For as the French book saith, the king was full loth thereto, that such a noise should be upon Sir Lancelot and his queen; for the king had a deeming of it, but he would not hear of it, for Sir Lancelot had done so much for him and for the queen so many times, that wit ye well the king loved him passingly well.

'My lord,' said Sir Agravain, 'ye shall ride to⁄morn an⁄hunting, and doubt ye not Sir Lancelot will not go with you. And when it draweth toward night, ye may send the queen word that ye will lie out all that night, and so may ye send for your cooks. And then upon pain of death we shall take him that night with the queen, and other we shall bring him to you quick or dead.'

'I will well,' said the king. 'Then I counsel you to take with you sure fellowship.'

'Sir,' said Sir Agravain, 'my brother, Sir Mordred, and I, will take with us twelve knights of the Round Table.'

'Beware,' said King Arthur, 'for I warn you ye shall find him wight.'

'Let us deal,' said Sir Agravain and Sir Mordred.

So on the morn King Arthur rode an⁄hunting, and sent word to the queen that he would be out all that night. Then Sir Agravain and Sir Mordred gat to them twelve knights, and hid themself in a chamber in the Castle of Carlisle. And these were their names: Sir Colgrevaunce, Sir Mador de la Porte, Sir Gingalin, Sir Meliot de Logris, Sir Petipase of Winchelsea, Sir Galleron of Galway, Sir Melion of the Mountain, Sir Astamore, Sir Gromore Somir Jaure, Sir Curselaine, Sir Florence and Sir Lovel. So these twelve knights were with Sir Mordred and Sir Agravain, and all they were of Scotland, other of Sir Gawain's kin, other well⁄willers to his brethren.

So when the night came, Sir Lancelot told Sir Bors how he would go that night and speak with the queen.

'Sir,' said Sir Bors, 'ye shall not go this night by my counsel.'

'Why?' said Sir Lancelot.

'Sir,' said Sir Bors, 'I dread me ever of Sir Agravain, that waiteth upon you daily to do you shame and us all. And never gave my heart against no going, that ever ye went to the queen, so much as now. For I mistrust that the king is out of this night from the queen because peradventure he hath lain some watch for you and the queen, and therefore I dread me sore of some treason.'

'Have ye no dread,' said Sir Lancelot, 'for I shall go and come again, and make no tarrying.'

'Sir,' said Sir Bors, 'that me repenteth, for I dread me sore that your going out this night shall wrath us all.'

'Fair nephew,' said Sir Lancelot, 'I marvel much why ye say thus, sithen the queen hath sent for me. And wit ye well I will not be so much a coward, but she shall understand I will see her good grace.'

'God speed you well,' said Sir Bors, 'and send you sound and safe again.'

So Sir Lancelot departed, and took his sword under his arm, and so in his mantle, that noble knight, and put himself in great jeopardy. And so he passed till he came to the queen's chamber, and then Sir Lancelot was lightly had into the chamber.

And then, as the French book saith, the queen and Sir Lancelot were together. And whether they were abed or at other manner of disports, me list not thereof make no mention, for love that time was not as love is nowadays.

But thus as they were together, there came Sir Agravain and Sir Mordred, with twelve knights with them of the Round Table, and they said with great crying and scaring voice,

'Traitor knight, Sir Lancelot du Lake, now art thou taken.'

And thus they cried with a loud voice, that all the court might hear it; and they all fourteen were armed at all points as they should fight a battle.

'Alas,' said Queen Guenever, 'now are we mischieved both.'

'Madam,' said Sir Lancelot, 'is there here any armour within your chamber, that I might cover my poor body withal? And if there be any give it me, and I shall soon stint their malice, by the grace of God.'

'Truly,' said the queen, 'I have none armour, neither helm, shield, sword, nor spear; wherefore I dread me sore our long love is come to a mischievous end. For I hear by their noise there be many noble knights, and well I wot they be surely armed; and against them ye may make no resistance. Wherefore ye are likely to be slain, and then shall I be burnt. For and ye might escape them,' said the queen, 'I would not doubt but that ye would rescue me in what danger that ever I stood in.'

'Alas,' said Sir Lancelot, 'in all my life thus was I never bestad, that I should be thus shamefully slain for lack of mine armour.'

But ever in one Sir Agravain and Sir Mordred cried, 'Traitor knight, come out of the queen' chamber, for wit thou well thou art so beset that thou shalt not escape.'

'O Jesu mercy,' said Sir Lancelot, 'this shameful cry and noise I may not suffer, for better were death at once than thus to endure this pain.'

Then he took the queen in his arms, and kissed her, and said,

'Most noble Christian queen, I beseech you, as ye have been ever my special good lady, and I at all times your true poor knight and true unto my power, and as I never failed you in right nor in wrong, sithen the first day King Arthur made me knight, that ye will pray for my soul if that I here be slain. For well I am assured that Sir Bors, my nephew, and all the remnant of my kin, with Sir Lavaine and Sir Urré, that they will not fail you to rescue you from the fire. And therefore, mine own lady, recomfort yourself, whatsomever come of me, that ye go with Sir Bors, my nephew, and Sir Urré, and they all will do you all the pleasure that they can or may, and ye shall live like a queen upon my lands.'

'Nay, Sir Lancelot, nay' said the queen. 'Wit thou well I will never live after thy days. But and thou be slain I will take my death as meekly as ever did any martyr take his death for Jesus Christ's sake.'

'Well, madam,' said Sir Lancelot, 'sith it is so that the day is come that our love must depart, wit you well I shall sell my life as dear as I may. And a thousandfold,' said Sir Lancelot, 'I am more heavier for you than for myself. And now I had lever than to be lord of all Christendom, that I had sure armour upon me, that men might speak of my deeds or ever I were slain.'

'Truly,' said the queen. 'And it might please God, I would that they would take me and slay me, and suffer you to escape.'

'That shall never be,' said Sir Lancelot, 'God defend me from such a shame. But Jesu Christ be Thou my shield and mine armour!'

And therewith Sir Lancelot wrapped his mantle about his arm well and surely; and by then they had gotten a great form out of the hall, and therewithal they all rushed at the door.

'Now, fair lords,' said Sir Lancelot, 'leave your noise and your rashing, and I shall set open this door, and then may ye do with me what it liketh you.'

'Come off then,' said they all, 'and do it, for it availeth thee not to strive against us all. And therefore let us into this chamber, and we shall save thy life until thou come to King Arthur.'

Then Sir Lancelot unbarred the door, and with his left hand he held it open a little, so that but one man might come in at once. And so there came striding a good knight, a much man and a large, and his name was Sir Colgrevaunce of Gore. And he with a sword struck at Sir Lancelot mightily; and he put aside the stroke and gave him such a buffet upon the helmet, that he fell grovelling dead within the chamber door.

And then Sir Lancelot with great might drew that dead knight within the chamber door; and Sir Lancelot with help of the queen and her ladies was lightly armed in Sir Colgrevaunce's armour.

And ever stood Sir Agravain and Sir Mordred crying, 'Traitor knight, come out of the queen's chamber.'

'Sirs, leave your noise,' said Sir Lancelot unto Sir Agravain, 'for wit ye well, Sir Agravain, ye shall not prison me this night. And therefore and ye do my counsel, go ye all from this chamber door, and make not such crying and such manner of slander as ye do. For I promise you by my knighthood, and ye will depart and make no more noise, I shall as to-morn appear afore you all and before the king, and then let it be seen which of you all, other else ye all, that will accuse me of treason. And there I shall answer you as a knight should, that hither I came to the queen for no manner of mal engine, and that will I prove and make it good upon you within my hands.'

'Fie on thee, traitor,' said Sir Agravain and Sir Mordred, 'for we will have thee maugre thy head, and slay thee if we list for we let thee wit we have the choice of King Arthur to save thee or to slay thee.'

'Ah sirs,' said Sir Lancelot, 'is there none other grace with you? Then keep yourself.'

So then Sir Lancelot set all open the chamber door, and mightily and knightily he strode in amongst them; and anon at the first buffet he slew Sir Agravain, and anon after twelve of his fellows. Within a little while he had lain them cold to the earth, and there was none of the twelve that might stand Sir Lancelot one buffet. Also Sir Lancelot wounded Sir Mordred, and he fled with all his might. And then Sir Lancelot returned again unto the queen, and said,

'Madam, now wit you well all our true love is brought to an end, for now will King Arthur ever be my foe. And therefore, madam, and it like you that I have you with me, I shall save you from all manner adventures dangerous.'

'Sir, that is not best,' said the queen. 'Meseemeth now ye have done so much harm, it will be best ye hold you still with this. And if ye see that as to-morn they will put me unto the death, then may ye rescue me as ye think best.'

'I will well,' said Sir Lancelot, 'for have ye no doubt, while I am a man living I shall rescue you.'

And then he kissed her, and either of them gave other a ring; and so there he left the queen, and went until his lodging.

When Sir Bors saw Sir Lancelot he was never so glad of his home coming as he was then.

'Jesu mercy,' said Sir Lancelot, 'why be ye all armed? What meaneth this?'

'Sir,' said Sir Bors, 'after ye were departed from us, we all that be of your blood and your well-willers were so dretched that some of us leapt out of our beds naked, and some in their dreams caught naked swords in their hands. And therefore,' said Sir Bors, 'we deemed there was some great strife at hand; and then we all deemed that ye were betrapped with some treason, and therefore we made us ready, what need that ever ye were in.'

268

'My fair nephew,' said Sir Lancelot unto Sir Bors, 'now shall ye wit all, that this night I was more harder bestad than ever I was in my life; and thanked be God, I am myself escaped their danger.' And so he told them all how and in what manner, as ye have heard tofore. 'And therefore, my fellows,' said Sir Lancelot, 'I pray you all that ye will be of good heart, and help me in what need that ever I stand, for now is war come to us all.'

'Sir,' said Sir Bors, 'all is welcome that God sendeth us, and we have had much weal with you and much worship, and therefore we will take the woe with you as we have taken the weal.'

'And therefore,' they said all, all the good knights, 'look ye take no discomfort, for there nis no bands of knights under heaven but we shall be able to grieve them as much as they may us. And therefore discomfort not yourself by no manner. And we shall gather together all that we love, and that loveth us, and what that ye will have done shall be done. And therefore, Sir Lancelot,' said they, 'we will take the woe with the weal.'

'Gramercy,' said Sir Lancelot, 'of your good comfort, for in my great distress, my fair nephew, ye comfort me greatly. And much I am beholding unto you. But this, my fair nephew, I would that ye did in all haste that ye may, or it is far days past: that ye will look in their lodging that be lodged here nigh about the king, which will hold with me, and which will not. For now I would know which were my friends from my foes.'

'Sir,' said Sir Bors, 'I shall do my pain, and or it be seven of the clock I shall wit of such as ye have doubt for, who will hold with you.'

Then Sir Bors called unto him Sir Lionel, Sir Ector de Maris, Sir Blamor de Ganis, Sir Bleoberis de Ganis, Sir Gahalantine, Sir Galihodin, Sir Galihud, Sir Menaduke, Sir Villiars the Valiant, Sir Hebes le Renoumes, Sir Lavaine, Sir Urré of Hungary, Sir Nerovens, Sir Plenorious (these two were knights Sir Lancelot made, and the one he won upon a bridge, and therefore they would never be against him), and Sir Harry le Fise du Lake, and Sir Selises of the Dolorous Tower, and Sir Melias de Lile, and Sir Bellengerus le Beuse, that was Sir Alisander's son le Orphelin, because his mother Alice la Beale Pellerin and she was kin unto Sir Lancelot, and he held with him. So there came Sir Palomides and Sir Safer, his brother, to hold with Sir Lancelot, and Sir Clegis, Sir Sadok, and Sir Dinas, Sir Clarrus of Cleremont.

So these two-and-twenty knights drew them together, and by then they were armed on horseback, and promised Sir Lancelot to do what he would. Then there fell to them, what of North Wales and of Cornwall, for Sir Lamorak's sake and for Sir Tristram's sake, to the number of a four-score knights.

'My lords,' said Sir Lancelot, 'wit you well I have been ever since I came into this country well willed unto my lord, King Arthur, and unto my lady, Queen Guenever, unto my power; and this night because my lady the queen sent for me to speak with her, I suppose it was made by treason, howbeit I dare largely excuse her person, notwithstanding I was there by a forecast near slain, but as Jesu provided me I escaped all their malice and treason.'

And then that noble knight Sir Lancelot told them all how he was hard bestad in the queen's chamber, and how and in what manner he escaped from them.

'And therefore,' said Sir Lancelot, 'wit you well, my fair lords, I am sure there nis but war unto me and mine. And for because I have slain this night these knights, I wot well, as is Sir Agravain Sir Gawain's brother, and at the least twelve of his fellows, for this cause now I am sure of mortal war. For these knights were sent and ordained by King Arthur to betray me. And therefore the king will in his heat and malice judge the queen to the fire, and that may not I suffer, that she should be burnt for my sake. For and I may be heard and suffered and so taken, I will fight for the queen, that she is a true lady unto her lord. But the king in his heat, I dread me, will not take me as I ought to be taken.'

'My lord, Sir Lancelot,' said Sir Bors, 'by mine advice ye shall take the woe with the weal, and take it in patience, and thank God of it. And sithen it is fallen as it is, I counsel you to keep yourself, for and ye will yourself, there is no fellowship of knights christened that shall do you wrong. Also I will counsel you my lord, Sir Lancelot, that and my lady, Queen Guenever, be in distress, insomuch as she is in pain for your sake, that ye knightly rescue her; for and ye did otherwise, all the world will speak of you shame to the world's end. Insomuch as ye were taken with her, whether ye did right or wrong, it is now your part to hold with the queen, that she be not slain and put to a mischievous death, for and she so die the shame shall be yours.'

'Now Jesu defend me from shame,' said Sir Lancelot, 'and keep and save my lady the queen from villainy and shameful death, and that she never be destroyed in my default; wherefore my fair lords, my kin, and my friends,' said Sir Lancelot, 'what will ye do?'

Then they said all with one voice, 'We will do as ye will do.'

'Then I put this case to you,' said Sir Lancelot, 'that if my lord Arthur by evil counsel will to-morn in his heat put my lady the queen to the fire there to be burnt; then I pray you, counsel me what is best for me to do.'

Then they said all at once with one voice,

'Sir, us thinketh best that ye knightly rescue the queen. Insomuch as she shall be burnt, it is for your sake; and it is to suppose, and ye might be handled, ye should have the same death, or a more shamefuller death. And sir, we say all, that ye have many times rescued her from death for other men's quarrels, therefore us seemeth it is more your worship that ye rescue the queen from this peril, insomuch that she hath it for your sake.'

Then Sir Lancelot stood still, and said, 'My fair lords, wit you well I would be loth to do that thing that should dishonour you or my blood; and wit you well I would be loth that my lady, the queen, should die such a shameful death; but and it be so that ye will counsel me to rescue her, I must do much harm or I rescue her; and peradventure I shall there destroy some of my best friends, that should much repent me; and peradventure there be some, and they could well bring it about, or disobey my lord King Arthur, they would soon come to me, the which I were loth to hurt. And if so be that I rescue her, where shall I keep her?'

'Sir, that shall be the least care of us all,' said Sir Bors. 'How did the noble knight Sir Tristram? By your good will kept not he with him La Beale Isoud near three year in Joyous Gard? The which was done by your althers advice? And that same place is your own; and in likewise may ye do and ye list, and take the queen lightly away, if it so be the king will judge her to be burnt. And in Joyous Gard ye may keep her long enough until the heat of the king be past. And then it may fortune you to bring again the queen to the king with great worship; and then peradventure ye shall have thank for her bringing home, and love and thank where other shall have maugre.'

'That is hard to do,' said Sir Lancelot, 'for by Sir Tristram I may have a warning, for when by means of treaties, Sir Tristram brought again La Beale Isoud unto King Mark from Joyous Gard, look ye now what befell on the end, how shamefully that false traitor King Mark slew him as he sat harping afore his lady La Beale Isoud. With a grounden glaive he thrust him in behind to the heart. It grieveth me,' said Sir Lancelot, 'to speak of his death, for all the world may not find such another knight.'

'All this is truth,' said Sir Bors, 'but there is one thing shall courage you and us all: ye know well King Arthur and King Mark were never like of conditions, for there was never yet man could prove King Arthur untrue of his promise.'

So to make short tale, they were all consented that, for better other for worse, if so were that the queen were on that morn brought to the fire, shortly they all would rescue her. And so by the advice of Sir Lancelot, they put them all in an ambushment in a wood, as nigh Carlisle as they might, and there they abode still, to wit what the king would do.

Now turn we again unto Sir Mordred, that when he was escaped

from the noble knight, Sir Lancelot, he anon gat his horse and mounted upon him, and rode unto King Arthur, sore wounded and smitten, and all forbled; and there he told the king all how it was, and how they were all slain save himself alone.

'Jesu mercy, how may this be?' said the king. 'Took ye him in the queen's chamber?'

'Yea, so God me help,' said Sir Mordred, 'there we found him unarmed, and there he slew Sir Colgrevaunce, and armed him in his armour.'

And all this he told the king from the beginning to the ending.

'Jesu mercy,' said the king, 'he is a marvellous knight of prowess. Alas, me sore repenteth,' said the king, 'that ever Sir Lancelot should be against me. Now I am sure the noble fellowship of the Round Table is broken for ever, for with him will many a noble knight hold. And now it is fallen so,' said the king, 'that I may not with my worship but the queen must suffer the death,' and was sore amoved.

So then there was made great ordinance in this ire, that the queen must be judged to the death. And the law was such in those days that whatsomever they were, of what estate or degree, if they were found guilty of treason, there should be none other remedy but death; and either the menour or the taking with the deed should be causer of their hasty judgement. And right so it was ordained for Queen Guenever, because Sir Mordred was escaped sore wounded, and the death of thirteen knights of the Round Table, these proofs and experiences caused King Arthur to command the queen to the fire and there to be burnt.

menour: behaviour

Then spake Sir Gawain, and said,

'My lord Arthur, I would counsel you not to be over-hasty, but that ye would put it in respite, this judgement of my lady the queen, for many causes. One is this, though it were so that Sir Lancelot were found in the queen's chamber, yet it might be so that he came thither for none evil. For ye know my lord,' said Sir Gawain, 'that the queen has oftentimes been much beholden unto Sir Lancelot, more than unto any other knight, for oftentimes he hath saved her life, and done battle for her when all the court refused the queen. And peradventure she sent for him for goodness and for none evil, to reward him for his good deeds that he had done to her in times past. And peradventure my lady, the queen, sent for him to that intent, that Sir Lancelot should come to her good grace privily and secretly, weening to her that it was best so to do, in eschewing and dreading of slander; for oftentimes we do many things that we ween it be for the best, and yet peradventure it turneth to the worst. For I dare say,' said Sir Gawain, 'my lady, your queen, is to you both good and true. And as for SirLancelot,' said Sir Gawain, 'I dare say he will make it good upon any knight living that will put upon himself villainy or shame, and in like wise he will make good for my lady the queen.'

'That I believe well,' said King Arthur, 'but I will not that way work with Sir Lancelot, for he trusteth so much upon his hands and his might that he doubteth no man. And therefore for my queen he shall never fight more, for she shall have the law. And if I may get Sir Lancelot, wit you well he shall have as shameful a death.'

'Jesu defend,' said Sir Gawain, 'that I may never see it nor know it.'

'Why say ye so?' said King Arthur. 'Pardie, ye have no cause to love Sir Lancelot, for this night last past he slew your brother, Sir Agravain, a full good knight, and almost he had slain your other brother, Sir Mordred, and also there he slew thirteen noble knights. And also, Sir Gawain, remember ye he slew two sons of yours, Sir Florence and Sir Lovel.'

'My lord,' said Sir Gawain, 'of all this I have knowledge, of whose deaths I repent me sore; but insomuch as I gave them warning, and told my brethren and my sons aforehand what would fall in the end, and insomuch as they would not do by my counsel, I will not meddle me thereof, nor revenge me nothing of their deaths; for I told them there was no boot to strive with Sir Lancelot. Howbeit I am sorry of the death of my brethren and of my two sons; but they are the causers of their own death; for oftentimes I warned my brother Sir Agravain, and I told him the perils the which be now fallen.'

Then said the noble King Arthur to Sir Gawain,

'Dear nephew, I pray you make you ready in your best armour, with your brethren, Sir Gaheris and Sir Gareth, to bring my queen to the fire, there to have her judgement and receive the death.'

'Nay, my most noble king,' said Sir Gawain, 'that will I never do; for wit you well I will never be in that place where so noble a queen as is my lady, Dame Guenever, shall take such a shameful end. For wit ye well,' said Sir Gawain, 'my heart will never serve me to see her die; and it shall never be said that ever I was of your counsel of her death.'

Then said the king to Sir Gawain, 'Suffer your brethren Sir Gaheris and Sir Gareth to be there.'

'My lord,' said Sir Gawain, 'wit you well they will be loth to be there present, because of many adventures that is like there to fall, but they are young and full unable to say you nay.'

Then spake Sir Gaheris, and the good knight Sir Gareth, unto King Arthur:

'Sir, ye may well command us to be there, but wit you well it shall be sore against our will; but and we be there by your straight commandment ye shall plainly hold us there excused: we will be there in peaceable wise, and bear none harness of war upon us.'

'In the name of God,' said the king, 'then make you ready, for she shall soon have her judgement.'

'Alas,' said Sir Gawain, 'that ever I should endure to see this woeful day.'

So Sir Gawain turned him and wept heartily, and so he went into his chamber.

And then the queen was led forth without Carlisle, and there she was despoiled into her smock. And so then her ghostly father was brought to her, to be shriven of her misdeeds. Then was there weeping, and wailing, and wringing of hands, of many lords and ladies, but there were but few in comparison that would bear any armour for to strength the death of the queen.

Then was there one that Sir Lancelot had sent unto that place for to espy what time the queen should go unto her death; and anon as he saw the queen despoiled into her smock, and so shriven, then he gave Sir Lancelot warning.

Then was there but spurring and plucking up of horses, and right so they came to the fire. And who that stood against them, there were they slain; there might none withstand Sir Lancelot. So all that bare arms and withstood them, there were they slain, full many a noble knight.

And so in this rushing and hurling, as Sir Lancelot thrang here and there, it mishapped him to slay Sir Gaheris and Sir Gareth, the noble knight, for they were unarmed and unware. For as the French book saith, Sir Lancelot smote Sir Gareth and Sir Gaheris upon the brainpans, wherethrough they were slain in the field. Howbeit in very truth Sir Lancelot saw them not. And so were they found dead among the thickest of the press.

Then when Sir Lancelot had thus done, and slain and put to flight all that would withstand him, then he rode straight unto Queen Guenever, and made a kirtle and a gown to be cast upon her; and then he made her to set behind him, and prayed her to be of good cheer.

Now wit ye well the queen was glad that she was escaped from the death. And then she thanked God and Sir Lancelot. And so he rode his way with the queen, as the French book saith, unto Joyous Gard, and there he kept her as a noble knight should. And many great lords and some kings sent Sir Lancelot many good knights, and many noble knights drew unto Sir Lancelot. When this was known openly, that King Arthur and Sir Lancelot were at debate, many knights were glad, and many were sorry of their debate.

OPPOSITE
*Sir Lancelot
and other knights
in combat*

ce feust mess Gauain et se cest il sile soit tou
toit te suoies ne en peut il auoir se ho meur non
sil iouste a lui car maintes fois auoit desire
quil peust a lui iouster ainz quil ne feust cōgne

Ore huvta le cheual des espo
et mist lestur a son senestur cos
et laissa couure contre mess
Gauain si tost come le cheual
li pot aler. Et messire Gauain
le vit venir. Or aduint que
cestoit le chlr quil auoit veu tout seul em le
prez. Et sadreca. et sentre feruent et thars a leu
sur les estur, si durement quil ny ot si fort aqui
lestur ne fendist. et la lance Lancelos cola main
tenant en pieces. Et mess Gauain lem paw

The Death of Arthur

Now turn we again unto King Arthur, that when it was told him how and in what manner the queen was taken away from the fire, and when he heard of the death of his noble knights, and in especial for Sir Gaheris' and Sir Gareth's death, then the king swooned for pure sorrow. And when he awoke of his swoon, then he said,

'Alas, that ever I bare crown upon my head! For now have I lost the fairest fellowship of noble knights that ever held Christian king together. Alas, my good knights be slain and gone away from me: now within these two days I have lost forty knights, and also the noble fellowship of Sir Lancelot and his blood, for now I may never more hold them together with my worship. Alas that ever this war began.

'Now fair fellows,' said the king, 'I charge you that no man tell Sir Gawain of the death of his two brethren; for I am sure,' said the king, 'when Sir Gawain heareth tell that Sir Gareth is dead he will go nigh out of his mind. Mercy Jesu,' said the king, 'why slew he Sir Gareth and Sir Gaheris? For I dare say as for Sir Gareth he loved Sir Lancelot above all men earthly.'

'That is truth,' said some knights, 'but they were slain in the hurtling as Sir Lancelot thrang in the thick of the press; and as they were unarmed he smote them and wist not whom that he smote, and so unhappily they were slain.'

'The death of them,' said Arthur, 'will cause the greatest mortal war that ever was; for I am sure that when Sir Gawain knoweth hereof, that Sir Gareth is slain, I should never have rest of him till I have destroyed Sir Lancelot's kin and himself both, other else he to destroy me. And therefore,' said the king, 'wit you well my heart was never so heavy as it is now, and much more I am sorrier for my good knights' loss than for the loss of my fair queen; for queens I might have enow, but such a fellowship of good knights shall never be together in no company. And now I dare say,' said King Arthur, 'there was never Christian king that ever held such a fellowship together. And alas, that ever Sir Lancelot and I should be at debate. Ah Agravain, Agravain,' said the king, 'Jesu forgive it thy soul, for thine evil will that thou and thy brother Sir Mordred hadst unto Sir Lancelot hath caused all this sorrow.'

And ever among these complaints the king wept and swooned.

Then there came one unto Sir Gawain, and told him how the queen was led away with Sir Lancelot, and nigh a twenty-four knights slain.

'O Jesu, save me my two brethren,' said Sir Gawain. 'For full well wist I that Sir Lancelot would rescue her, other else he would die in that field; and to say the truth he had not been a man of worship had he not rescued the queen that day, insomuch as she should have been burnt for his sake. And as in that,' said Sir Gawain, 'he hath done but knightly, and as I would have done myself and I had stand in like case. But where are my brethren?' said Sir Gawain, 'I marvel I hear not of them.'

Then said that man, 'Truly Sir Gareth and Sir Gaheris be slain.'

'Jesu defend!' said Sir Gawain. 'For all this world I would not that they were slain, and in especial my good brother, Sir Gareth.'

'Sir,' said the man, 'he is slain, and that is great pity.'

'Who slew him?' said Sir Gawain.

'Sir,' said the man, 'Sir Lancelot slew them both.'

'That may I not believe,' said Sir Gawain, 'that ever he slew my good brother, Sir Gareth; for I dare say my brother Sir Gareth loved him better than me, and all his brethren, and the king both. Also I dare say, and Sir Lancelot had desired my brother, Sir Gareth, with him he would have been with him against the king and us all. And therefore I may never believe that Sir Lancelot slew my brother.'

'Verily, sir,' said this man, 'it is noised that he slew him.'

'Alas,' said Sir Gawain, 'now is my joy gone.'

And then he fell down and swooned, and long he lay there as he had been dead. And then, when he arose of his swoon, he cried out sorrowfully, and said, 'Alas!'

And right so Sir Gawain ran to the king, crying and weeping, and said:

'O King Arthur, mine uncle, my good brother Sir Gareth is slain, and so is my brother Sir Gaheris, the which were two noble knights.'

Then the king wept, and he both; and so they fell on swooning.

And when they were revived then spake Sir Gawain: 'Sir, I will go see my brother, Sir Gareth.'

'Sir, ye may not see him,' said the king, 'for I caused him to be interred, and Sir Gaheris both; for I well understood that ye would make over-much sorrow, and the sight of Sir Gareth should have caused your double sorrow.'

'Alas, my lord,' said Sir Gawain, 'how slew he my brother, Sir Gareth? Mine own good lord I pray you tell me.'

'Truly,' said the king, 'I shall tell you as it hath been told me: Sir Lancelot slew him and Sir Gaheris both.'

'Alas,' said Sir Gawain, 'they bare none arms against him, neither of them both.'

'I wot not how it was,' said the king, 'but as it is said, Sir Lancelot slew them both in the thickest of the press and knew them not; and therefore let us shape a remedy for to revenge their deaths.'

'My king, my lord, and mine uncle,' said Sir Gawain, 'wit you well, now I shall make you a promise that I shall hold by my knighthood, that from this day forward I shall never fail Sir Lancelot until the one of us have slain the other. And therefore I require you, my lord and king, dress you to the war, for wit you well I will be revenged upon Sir Lancelot; and therefore, as ye will have my service and my love, now haste you thereto, and assay your friends. For I promise unto God,' said Sir Gawain, 'for the death of my brother, Sir Gareth, I shall seek Sir Lancelot through-out seven kings' realms, but I shall slay him or else he shall slay me.'

'Ye shall not need to seek him so far,' said the king, 'for as I hear say, Sir Lancelot will abide me and us all in the castle of Joyous Gard. And much people draweth unto him, as I hear say.'

'That may I right well believe,' said Sir Gawain. 'But my lord,' he said, 'assay your friends, and I will assay mine.'

'It shall be done,' said the king, 'and as I suppose I shall be big enough to draw him out of the biggest tower of his castle.'

So then the king sent letters and writs throughout all England, both the length and breadth, for to assummon all his knights. And so unto King Arthur drew many knights, dukes, and earls, so that he had a great host. And when they were assembled, the king in-formed them how Sir Lancelot had bereft him his queen. Then the king and all his host made them ready to lay siege about Sir Lancelot, where he lay within Joyous Gard.

And anon Sir Lancelot heard thereof, and purveyed him of many good knights, for with him held many knights; and some for his own sake, and some for the queen's sake. Thus they were on both parties well furnished and garnished of all manner of thing that longed to the war. But King Arthur's host was so big that Sir Lancelot would not abide him in the field. For he was full loth to do battle against the king; but Sir Lancelot drew him to his strong castle with all manner of victual plenty, and as many noble men as he might suffice within the town and the castle.

Then came King Arthur with Sir Gawain with an huge host, and laid a siege all about Joyous Gard, both the town and the castle. And there they made strong war on both parties. But in no wise Sir Lancelot would ride out, nor go out of his castle, of long time; neither he would not suffer none of his good knights to issue out, neither none of the town nor of the castle, until fifteen weeks were past.

Then it befell upon a day in harvest time, Sir Lancelot looked over the walls and spake on high unto King Arthur and Sir Gawain:

'My lords both, wit ye well all is in vain that ye make at this siege, for here win ye no worship but maugre and dishonour; for

Arthur leads his knights to war against Lancelot

maugre: *ill-will*

and it list me to come myself out and my good knights, I should full soon make an end of this war.'

'Come forth,' said King Arthur unto Sir Lancelot, 'and thou darst, and I promise thee I shall meet thee in midst of the field.'

'God defend me,' said Sir Lancelot, 'that ever I should encounter with the most noble king that made me knight.'

Lancelot's castle is besieged by Arthur's forces

'Fie upon thy fair language,' said the king, 'for wit thou well and trust it, I am thy mortal foe, and ever will to my death day; for thou hast slain my good knights, and full noble men of my blood, that I shall never recover again. Also thou hast lain by my queen, and holden her many winters, and sithen, like a traitor, taken her from me by force.'

'My most noble lord and king,' said Sir Lancelot, 'ye may say what ye will, for ye wot well with yourself I will not strive; but thereas ye say I have slain your good knights, I wot well that I have done so, and that me sore repenteth; but I was enforced to do battle with them in saving of my life, or else I must have suffered them to have slain me. And as for my lady, Queen Guenever, except your person of your highness, and my lord Sir Gawain, there is no knight under heaven that dare make it good upon me that ever I was traitor unto your person. And where it please you to say that I have holden my lady your queen years and winters, unto that I shall ever make a large answer, and prove it upon any knight that beareth the life, except your person and Sir Gawain, that my lady, Queen Guenever, is as a true lady unto your person as is any lady living unto her lord, and that will I make good with my hands. Howbeit it hath liked her good grace to have me in favour, and cherish me more than any other knight; and unto my power I again have deserved her love, for oftentimes, my lord, ye have consented that she should have been burnt and destroyed, in your heat, and then it fortuned me to do battle for her, and or I departed from her adversary they confessed their untruth, and she full worshipfully excused. And at such times, my lord King Arthur,' said Sir Lancelot, 'ye loved me, and thanked me when I saved your queen from the fire; and then ye promised me for ever to be my good lord. And now methinketh ye reward me full ill for my good service. And, my good lord, meseemeth I had lost a great part of my worship in my knighthood and I had suffered my lady, your queen, to have been burnt, and insomuch as she should have been burnt for my sake. For sithen I have done battles for your queen in other quarrels than in mine own, meseemeth now I had more right to do battle for her in her right quarrel. And therefore my good and gracious lord,' said Sir Lancelot, 'take your queen unto your good grace; for she is both fair, true, and good.'

'Fie on thee, false recreant knight,' said Sir Gawain. 'For I let thee wit: my lord, mine uncle, King Arthur, shall have his queen and thee both, maugre thy visage, and slay you both and save you, whether it please him.'

'It may well be,' said Sir Lancelot, 'but wit you well, my lord Sir Gawain, and me list to come out of this castle ye should win me and the queen more harder than ever ye won a strong battle.'

'Fie on thy proud words,' said Sir Gawain; 'as for my lady, the queen, I will never say of her shame. But thou, false and recreant knight,' said Sir Gawain, 'what cause hadst thou to slay my good brother Sir Gareth, that loved thee more than me and all my kin? And alas thou madest him knight thine own hands; why slew thou him that loved thee so well?'

'For to excuse me,' said Sir Lancelot, 'it helpeth me not, but by Jesu, and by the faith that I owe to the high order of knighthood, I should with as good a will have slain my nephew, Sir Bors de Ganis, at that time. But alas that ever I was so unhappy,' said Sir Lancelot, 'that I had not seen Sir Gareth and Sir Gaheris.'

'Thou liest, recreant knight,' said Sir Gawain, 'thou slewest him in despite of me; and therefore, wit thou well I shall make war to thee, and all the while that I may live be thine enemy.'

'That me repenteth,' said Sir Lancelot; 'for well I understand it helpeth not to seek none accordment while ye Sir Gawain, are so mischievously set. And if ye were not, I would not doubt to have the good grace of my lord King Arthur.'

'I believe it well, false recreant knight,' said Sir Gawain; 'for thou hast many long days overlead me and us all, and destroyed many of our good knights .... Wit thou well I shall never leave thee till I have thee at such avail that thou shalt not escape my hands.'

'I trust you well enough,' said Sir Lancelot, 'and ye may get me I get but little mercy.'

But as the French book saith, the noble King Arthur would have taken his queen again, and have been accorded with Sir Lancelot, but Sir Gawain would not suffer him by no manner of mean. And so Sir Gawain made many men to blow upon Sir Lancelot; and all at once they called him false recreant knight.

Then when Sir Bors de Ganis, Sir Ector de Maris, and Sir Lionel, heard this outcry, they called to them Sir Palomides, and Sir Lavaine, with many more knights of their blood, and all they went unto Sir Lancelot, and said thus:

'My lord Sir Lancelot, wit ye well we have great scorn of the great rebukes that we heard Sir Gawain say to you; wherefore we pray you, and charge you as ye will have our service, keep us no longer within these walls; for we let you wit plainly, we will ride into the field and do battle with them. For ye fare as a man that were afeared, and for all your fair speech it will not avail you. For wit you well Sir Gawain will never suffer you to be accorded with King Arthur, and therefore fight for your life and your right, and ye dare.'

'Alas,' said Sir Lancelot, 'for to ride out of this castle, and to do battle, I am full loth.'

Then Sir Lancelot spake on high unto Sir Arthur and Sir Gawain:

'My lords, I require you and beseech you, sithen that I am thus required and conjured to ride into the field, that neither you, my lord King Arthur, nor you Sir Gawain, come not into the field.'

'What shall we do then?' said Sir Gawain. 'Is not this the king's quarrel to fight with thee? And also it is my quarrel to fight with thee, Sir Lancelot, because of the death of my brother Sir Gareth.'

'Then must I needs unto battle,' said Sir Lancelot. 'Now wit you well, my lord King Arthur and Sir Gawain, ye will repent it whensomever I do battle with you.'

And so then they departed either from other; and then either party made them ready on the morn for to do battle, and great pur, veyance was made on both sides. And Sir Gawain let purvey many knights for to wait upon Sir Lancelot, for to overset him and to slay him.

And on the morn at undern King Arthur was ready in the field with three great hosts. And then Sir Lancelot's fellowship came out at three gates, in a full good array; and Sir Lionel came in the fore, most battle, and Sir Lancelot came in the middle, and Sir Bors came out at the third gate. Thus they came in order and rule, as full noble knights; and always Sir Lancelot charged all his knights in any wise to save King Arthur and Sir Gawain.

Then came forth Sir Gawain from the king's host, and he came before and proffered to joust. And Sir Lionel was a fierce knight, and lightly he encountered with Sir Gawain; and there Sir Gawain smote Sir Lionel throughout the body, that he dashed to the earth like as he had been dead; and then Sir Ector de Maris and other bare him into the castle.

Then there began a great stour, and much people were slain; and ever Sir Lancelot did what he might to save the people on King Arthur's party. For Sir Palomides, and Sir Bors, and Sir Safer overthrew many knights, for they were deadly knights. And Sir Blamor de Ganis, and Sir Bleoberis de Ganis, with Sir Bellengerus le Beuse, these six knights did much harm; and ever King Arthur was nigh about Sir Lancelot to have slain him, and ever Sir Lancelot suffered him, and would not strike again.

So Sir Bors encountered with King Arthur, and there with a

stour: *battle*

spear Sir Bors smote him down; and so he alit and drew his sword, and said to Sir Lancelot,

'Shall I make an end of this war?' And that he meant to have slain King Arthur.

'Not so hardy,' said Sir Lancelot, 'upon pain of thy head, that thou touch him no more. For I will never see that most noble king that made me knight neither slain ne shamed.'

And therewithal Sir Lancelot alit off his horse and took up the king and horsed him again, and said thus:

'My lord Arthur, for God's love stint this strife, for ye get here no worship, and I would do mine utterance; but always I forbear you, and ye nor none of yours forbeareth me. And therefore, my lord, I pray you remember what I have done in many places and now I am evil rewarded.'

Then when King Arthur was on horseback, he looked upon Sir Lancelot, and then the tears brast out of his eyen, thinking on the great courtesy that was in Sir Lancelot more than in any other man. And therewith the king rode his way, and might no longer behold him, saying to himself,

'Alas, alas, that ever this war began.'

And then either parties of the battles withdrew them to repose them, and buried the dead, and to the wounded men laid soft salves to their wounds; and thus they endured that night till on the morn.

And on the morn by undern they made them ready to do battle. And then Sir Bors led the forward. So upon the morn there came Sir Gawain as brim as any boar, with a great spear in his hand. And when Sir Bors saw him he thought to revenge his brother Sir Lionel of the despite that Sir Gawain gave him the other day. And so, as they knew either other fewtered their spears, and with all their mights of their horses and themself, so fiercely they met together and so feloniously that either bare other through, and so they fell both to the bare earth. And then the battles joined, and there was much slaughter on both parties.

Then Sir Lancelot rescued Sir Bors, and sent him into the castle; but neither Sir Gawain nor Sir Bors died not of their wounds, for they were well holpen. Then Sir Lavaine and Sir Urré prayed Sir Lancelot to do his pain, and fight as they had done:

'For we see that ye forbear and spare, and that doth us much harm. And therefore we pray you spare not your enemies no more than they do you.'

'Alas,' said Sir Lancelot, 'I have no heart to fight against my lord King Arthur, for ever meseemeth I do not as I ought to do.'

'My lord,' said Sir Palomides, 'though ye spare them never so much all this day they will never can you thank; and if they may get you at avail ye are but dead.'

So then Sir Lancelot understood that they said him truth; and then he strained himself more than he did aforehand, and because his nephew Sir Bors was sore wounded he pained himself the more.

And then within a little while, by evensong time, Sir Lancelot's party the better stood, for their horses went in blood past the fet⁄locks, there were so many people slain. And then for very pity Sir Lancelot withheld his knights, and suffered King Arthur's party for to withdraw them aside. And then Sir Lancelot's party with⁄drew them into his castle, and either parties buried the dead, and put salve unto the wounded men. So when Sir Gawain was hurt, they on King Arthur's party were not so orgulous as they were tofore⁄hand to do battle.

orgulous: *proud*

Of this war that was between King Arthur and Sir Lancelot it was noised through all Christendom, and so it came at the last by relation unto the Pope. And then the Pope took a consideration of the great goodness of King Arthur, and the high prowess of Sir Lancelot, that was called the most noblest knights of the world. Wherefore the Pope called unto him a noble clerk that at that time was there present (the French book saith, it was the Bishop of Rochester), and the Pope gave him bulls under lead and sent them unto King Arthur of England, charging him upon pain of inter⁄dicting of all England, that he take his queen Dame Guenever unto him again, and accord with Sir Lancelot.

So when this Bishop was come to Carlisle he showed the king these bulls. And when the king understood these bulls he nist what to do: full fain he would have been accorded with Sir Lancelot, but Sir Gawain would not suffer him; but as for to have the queen, thereto he agreed. But in nowise Sir Gawain would not suffer the king to accord with Sir Lancelot; but as for the queen he consented. And then the Bishop had of the king his great seal, and his assurance as he was a true and anointed king that Sir Lancelot should come safe, and go safe, and that the queen should not be spoken unto of the king, nor of none other, for no thing done of time past; and of all these appointments the Bishop brought with him sure assurance and writing, to show Sir Lancelot.

So when the Bishop was come to Joyous Gard, there he showed Sir Lancelot how the Pope had written to King Arthur and unto him. And there he told him the perils if he withheld the queen from the king.

'It was never in my thought,' said Sir Lancelot, 'to withhold the queen from my lord King Arthur; but I kept her for this cause: insomuch as she should have been burnt for my sake, me⁄seemed it was my part to save her life, and put her from that danger, till better recover might come. And now I thank God,' said Sir Lancelot, 'that the Pope hath made her peace; for God knoweth,' said Sir Lancelot, 'I will be a thousandfold more gladder to bring her again, than ever I was of taking her away; with this, I may be sure to come safe and go safe, and that the queen shall have her liberty as she had before; and never for no thing that hath been surmised afore this time, that she never from this day stand in no peril. For else,' said Sir Lancelot, 'I dare adventure me to keep her from an harder shower than ever I kept her.'

'Sir, it shall not need you,' said the Bishop, 'to dread so much; for wit ye well, the Pope must be obeyed, and it were not the Pope's worship nor my poor honesty to know you distressed, neither the queen, neither in peril, nor shamed.'

And then he showed Sir Lancelot all his writing, both from the Pope and from King Arthur.

'This is sure enough,' said Sir Lancelot, 'for full well I dare trust my lord's own writing and his seal, for he was never shamed of his promise. Therefore,' said Sir Lancelot unto the Bishop, 'ye shall ride unto the king afore, and recommend me unto his good grace, and let him have knowledging that this same day eight days, by the grace of God, I myself shall bring my lady, Queen Guenever, unto him. And then say ye unto my most redoubted king, that I will say largely for the queen, that I shall none except for dread nor fear, but the king himself, and my lord Sir Gawain – and that is more for the king's love than for himself.'

So the Bishop departed and came to the king at Carlisle, and told him all how Sir Lancelot answered him; and then the tears brast out of the king's eyen.

Then Sir Lancelot purveyed him an hundred knights, and all were clothed in green velvet, and their horses trapped in the same to their heels; and every knight held a branch of olive in his hand, in tokening of peace. And the queen had four and twenty gentle-women following her in the same wise; and Sir Lancelot had twelve coursers following him, and on every courser sat a young gentleman, and all they were arrayed in white velvet, with sarpes of gold about their quarters, and the horse trapped in the same wise down to the heels, with many ouches, set with stones and pearls in gold, to the number of a thousand. And she and Sir Lancelot were clothed in white cloth of gold tissue. And right so as ye have heard, as the French book maketh mention, he rode with the queen from Joyous Gard to Carlisle.

And so Sir Lancelot rode throughout Carlisle, and so into the castle, that all men might behold them. And wit you well there was many a weeping eyen. And then Sir Lancelot himself alit and voided his horse, and took adown the queen, and so led her

sarpes: *chains*

ouches: *ornaments*

where King Arthur was in his seat; and Sir Gawain sat afore him, and many other great lords.

So when Sir Lancelot saw the king and Sir Gawain, then he led the queen by the arm, and then he kneeled down, and the queen both. Wit you well then was there many a bold knight there with King Arthur that wept as tenderly as though they had seen all their kin dead afore them.

So the king sat still, and said no word. And when Sir Lancelot saw his countenance, he arose up and pulled up the queen with him, and thus he spake full knightly:

Arthur in discussion with Gawain and Lancelot

'My most redoubted king, ye shall understand, by the Pope's commandment and yours, I have brought to you my lady the queen, as right requireth. And if there be any knight, of whatsomever degree that he be, except your person, that will say or dare say but that she is true and clean to you, I here myself, Sir Lancelot du Lake, will make it good upon his body, that she is a true lady unto you. But, sir, liars ye have listened, and that hath caused great debate betwixt you and me. For time hath been, my lord Arthur, that ye have been greatly pleased with me when I did battle for my lady, your queen; and full well ye know, my most noble king, that she hath been put to great wrong or this time; and sithen it pleased you at many times that I should fight for her, therefore meseemeth, my good lord, I had more cause to rescue her from the fire when she should have been burnt for my sake. For they that told you those tales were liars, and so it fell upon them; for by likelihood had not the might of God been with me, I might never have endured fourteen knights, and they armed, and afore purposed, and I unarmed and not purposed. For I was sent for unto my lady your queen, I wot not for what cause; but I was not so soon within the chamber door, but anon Sir Agravain and Sir Mordred called me traitor and false recreant knight.'

'By my faith, they called thee right,' said Sir Gawain.

'My lord Sir Gawain,' said Sir Lancelot, 'in their quarrel they proved themself not in the right.'

'Well, well, Sir Lancelot,' said the king, 'I have given you no cause to do to me as ye hast done, for I have worshipped you and yours more than any of all my knights.'

'My good lord,' said Sir Lancelot, 'so ye be not displeased, ye shall understand that I and mine have done you oft better service than any other knights have done, in many diverse places; and where ye have been full hard bestad divers times, I have myself rescued you from many dangers; and ever unto my power I was glad to please you, and my lord Sir Gawain. Both in jousts and, tournaments, and in battles set, both on horseback and on foot, I have often rescued you, and my lord Sir Gawain, and many more of your knights in many diverse places. For now I will make avaunt,' said Sir Lancelot, 'I will that ye all wit that yet I found never no manner of knight but that I was overhard for him, and I had done my utterance, thanked be God; howbeit I have been matched with good knights, as Sir Tristram and Sir Lamorak, but ever I had a favour unto them and a deeming what they were. And I take God to record,' said Sir Lancelot, 'I never was wroth nor greatly heavy with no good knight and I saw him busy about to win worship; and glad I was ever when I found good knight that might endure me on horseback and on foot. Howbeit Sir Carados of the Dolorous Tower was a full noble knight and a passing strong man, and that wot ye, my lord Sir Gawain; for he might well be called a noble knight when he by fine force pulled you out of your saddle, and bound you overthwart afore him to his saddle bow. And there, my lord Sir Gawain, I rescued you, and slew him afore your sight. Also I found his brother, Sir Turquin, in likewise leading Sir Gaheris, your brother, bounden afore him; and there also I rescued your brother and slew that Turquin, and delivered three-score-and-four of my lord Arthur's knights out of his prison. And now I dare say,' said Sir Lancelot, 'I met never with so strong knights, nor so well fighting, as was Sir Carados and Sir Turquin, for I fought with them to the uttermost. And therefore,' said Sir Lancelot unto Sir Gawain, 'meseemeth ye ought of right to remember this; for, and I might have your good will, I would trust to God to have my lord Arthur's good grace.'

'Sir, the king may do as he will,' said Sir Gawain, 'but wit thou well, Sir Lancelot, thou and I shall never be accorded while we live, for thou hast slain three of my brethren; and two of them thou slew traitorly and piteously, for they bare none harness against thee, nor none would bear.'

'Sir, God would they had been armed,' said Sir Lancelot, 'for then had they been alive. And wit ye well Sir Gawain, as for Sir Gareth, I love none of my kinsmen so much as I did him; and ever while I live,' said Sir Lancelot, 'I will bewail Sir Gareth's death, not all only for the great fear I have of you, but many causes which causen me to be sorrowful. One is that I made him knight; another is, I wot well he loved me above all other knights; and the third is, he was passing noble, true, courteous and gentle, and well conditioned. The fourth is, I wist well, anon as I heard that Sir Gareth was dead, I should never after have your love, my lord Sir Gawain, but everlasting war betwixt us. And also I wist well that ye would cause my noble lord King Arthur for ever to be my mortal foe. And as Jesu be my help,' said Sir Lancelot, 'and by my knighthood, I slew never Sir Gareth nor Sir Gaheris by my will; but alas that ever they were unarmed that unhappy day.

'But thus much I shall offer me,' said Sir Lancelot, 'if it may please the king's good grace, and you, my lord Sir Gawain: I shall first begin at Sandwich, and there I shall go in my shirt, bare foot; and at every ten miles' end I will found and gar make an house of religion, of what order that ye will assign me, with an whole convent, to sing and read, day and night, in especial for Sir Gareth's sake and Sir Gaheris. And this shall I perform from Sandwich unto Carlisle; and every house shall have sufficient livelihood. And this shall I perform while I have any livelihood in Christendom; and there nis none of all these religious places, but they shall be performed, furnished and garnished in all things as an holy place ought to be, I promise you faithfully. And this, Sir Gawain, methinketh were more fairer, holier, and more perfect to their souls, than ye, my most noble king, and you, Sir Gawain, to war upon me, for thereby shall ye get none avail.'

gar: command

Then all knights and ladies that were there wept as they were mad, and the tears fell on King Arthur's cheeks.

'Sir Lancelot,' said Sir Gawain, 'I have right well heard thy speech, and thy great proffers. But wit thou well, let the king do as it pleaseth him, I will never forgive my brothers' death, and in especial the death of my brother, Sir Gareth. And if mine uncle, King Arthur, will accord with thee, he shall lose my service, for wit thou well thou art both false to the king and to me.'

'Sir,' said Sir Lancelot, 'he beareth not the life that may make that good; and if ye, Sir Gawain, will charge me with so high a thing, ye must pardon me, for then needs must I answer you.'

'Nay, nay,' said Sir Gawain, 'we are past that at this time, and that caused the Pope, for he hath charged mine uncle, the king, that he shall take his queen again, and to accord with thee, Sir Lancelot, as for this season, and therefore thou shalt go safe as thou camest. But in this land thou shalt not abide past fifteen days, such summons I give thee; so the king and we were consented and accorded ere thou came. And else,' said Sir Gawain, 'wit thou well thou shouldst not have comen here, but if it were maugre thy head. And if it were not for the Pope's commandment,' said Sir Gawain, 'I should do battle with mine own body against thy body, and prove it upon thee, that thou hast been both false unto mine uncle King Arthur, and to me both; and that shall I prove upon thy body, when thou art departed from hence, wheresomever I find thee.'

Then Sir Lancelot sighed, and therewith the tears fell on his cheeks, and then he said thus:

'Alas, most noble Christian realm, whom I have loved above

all other realms, and in thee I have gotten a great part of my worship, and now I shall depart in this wise. Truly me repenteth that ever I came in this realm, that should be thus shamefully banished undeserved and causeless: but fortune is so variant, and the wheel so moveable, there nis none constant abiding, and that may be proved by many old chronicles, of noble Ector, and Troilus, and Alisander, the mighty Conqueror, and many more other; when they were most in their royalty, they alit lowest. And so fareth it by me,' said Sir Lancelot, 'for in this realm I had worship, and by me and mine all the whole Round Table hath been increased more in worship by me and mine blood than by any other. And therefore wit thou well, Sir Gawain, I may live upon my lands as well as any knight that here is. And if ye, most redoubted king, will come upon my lands with Sir Gawain to war upon me, I must endure you as well as I may. But as to you, Sir Gawain, if that ye come there, I pray you charge me not with treason nor felony, for and ye do, I must answer you.'

'Do thou thy best,' said Sir Gawain; 'therefore hie thee fast that thou were gone, and wit thou well we shall soon come after, and break the strongest castle that thou hast, upon thy head.'

'It shall not need that,' said Sir Lancelot, 'for and I were as orgulous set as ye are, wit you well I should meet you in the midst of the field.'

'Make thou no more language,' said Sir Gawain, 'but deliver the queen from thee, and pick thee lightly out of this court.'

'Well,' said Sir Lancelot, 'and I had wist of this shortcoming, I would have advised me twice or that I had come here. For and the queen had been so dear to me as ye noise her, I durst have kept her from the fellowship of the best knights under heaven.'

And then Sir Lancelot said unto Queen Guenever, in hearing of the king and them all,

'Madam, now I must depart from you and this noble fellowship for ever. And sithen it is so, I beseech you to pray for me, and I shall pray for you. And if ye be hard bestad by any false tongues, lightly my lady send me word, and if any knight's hands may deliver you by battle, I shall deliver you.'

And therewithal Sir Lancelot kissed the queen: and then he said all openly,

'Now let see what he be in this place that dare say the queen is not true unto my lord King Arthur, let see who will speak and he dare speak.'

And therewith he brought the queen to the king, and then Sir Lancelot took his leave and departed. And there was neither king, duke, ne earl, baron nor knight, lady nor gentlewoman, but all they wept as people out of their mind, except Sir Gawain.

And when the noble Sir Lancelot took his horse to ride out of Carlisle, there was sobbing and weeping for pure dole of his departing. And so he took his way unto Joyous Gard. And then ever after he called it the Dolorous Gard. And thus departed Sir Lancelot from the court for ever.

And so when he came to Joyous Gard he called his fellowship unto him, and asked them what they would do. Then they answered all wholly together with one voice, they would do as he would do.

'Then, my fair fellows,' said Sir Lancelot, 'I must depart out of this most noble realm. And now I shall depart it grieveth me sore, for I shall depart with no worship; for a flemed man departed never out of a realm with no worship. And that is to me great heaviness, for ever I fear after my days that men shall chronicle upon me that I was flemed out of this land; and else, my fair lords, be ye sure, and I had not dread shame, my lady Queen Guenever and I should never have departed.'

flemed: *banished*

Then spake many noble knights, as Sir Palomides, Sir Safer his brother, and Sir Bellengerus le Beuse, and Sir Urré, with Sir Lavaine, with many other:

'Sir, and ye be so disposed to abide in this land we will never fail you; and if ye list not to abide in this land there nis none of the good knights that here be will fail you, for many causes. One is, all we that be not of your blood shall never be welcome to the court. And sithen it liked us to take a part with you in your distress and heaviness in this realm, wit you well it shall like us as well to go in other countries with you, and there to take such part as ye do.'

'My fair lords,' said Sir Lancelot, 'I well understand you, and as I can, I thank you; and ye shall understand, such livelihood as I am born unto I shall depart with you in this manner of wise: that is for to say I shall depart all my livelihood and all my lands freely among you, and I myself will have as little as any of you, for have I sufficient that may long to my person, I will ask none other riches nother array; and I trust to God to maintain you on my lands as well as ever were maintained any knights.'

Then spake all the knights at once: 'He have shame that will leave you; for we all understand, in this realm will be now no quiet, but ever strife and debate, now the fellowship of the Round Table is broken. For by the noble fellowship of the Round Table was King Arthur upborne, and by their noblesse the king and all his realm was in quiet and rest. And a great part,' they said all, 'was because of your noblesse.'

'Now truly,' said Sir Lancelot, 'I thank you all of your good saying; howbeit, I wot well, in me was not all the stability of this realm, but in that I might I did my devoir; and well I am sure I knew how many rebellions in my days that by me were peaced, and I trow we all shall hear of them in short space, and that sore me repenteth. For ever I dread me,' said Sir Lancelot, 'that Sir Mordred will make trouble, for he is passing envious and applieth him much to trouble.'

So they were accorded to depart with Sir Lancelot to his lands; and to make short tale, they trussed and paid all that would ask them; and wholly an hundred knights departed with Sir Lancelot at once, and made their avows they would never leave him for weal nor for woe.

And so they shipped at Cardiff, and sailed unto Benwick: some men call it Bayonne, and some men call it Beaune, where the wine of Beaune is. But to say the sooth, Sir Lancelot and his nephews were lords of all France, and of all the lands that longed unto France; he and his kindred rejoiced it all through Sir Lancelot's noble prowess.

And then Sir Lancelot stuffed and furnished and garnished all his noble towns and castles.

So leave we Sir Lancelot in his lands, and his noble knights with him, and return we again unto King Arthur and to Sir Gawain, that made a great host ready, to the number of threescore thousand. And all thing was made ready for their shipping to pass over the sea, to war upon Sir Lancelot and upon his lands. And so they shipped at Cardiff.

And there King Arthur made Sir Mordred chief ruler of all England, and also he put Queen Guenever under his governance; because Sir Mordred was King Arthur's son, he gave him the rule of his land, and of his wife. And so the king passed the sea and landed upon Sir Lancelot's lands, and there he burnt and wasted, through the vengeance of Sir Gawain, all that they might overrun.

When this word came to Sir Lancelot, that King Arthur and Sir Gawain were landed upon his lands, and made a full great destruction and waste, then spake Sir Bors, and said:

'My lord Sir Lancelot, it is shame that we suffer them thus to ride over our lands. For wit you well, suffer ye them as long as ye will, they will do you no favour and they may handle you.'

Then said Sir Lionel that was ware and wise, 'My lord Sir Lancelot, I will give you this counsel: let us keep our strong walled towns until they have hunger and cold, and blow on their nails; and then let us freshly set upon him, and shred them down as sheep in a fold, that aliens may take example for ever how they land upon our lands.'

Then spake King Bagdemagus to Sir Lancelot and said: 'Sir, your courtesy will shend us all, and your courtesy hath waked

OPPOSITE
Malory reveals a deep sense of regret at the destruction of what he evidently regarded as the 'golden age' of chivalry

Here Arthur's court watches a tournament held outside the walls of Camelot

OVERLEAF LEFT
Two knights in the lists from a fifteenth-century manuscript

OVERLEAF RIGHT
One version of this element of the Arthurian legend has Arthur discovering paintings by Lancelot which reveal his love for Guenever

te bretaigne fu et estoit alore
ŋ grant habondance de tous
e z de toutes richesses et en si
ꝛ superfluite de adournemes
relation des habitans ꝗ elle
oit et surmontoit tous ault
realmes car tous les cheua
renommez de proesse estoit

armeures pareilles les vnes de
aultres. pareillement les courtoi
ses dames de la court la roynne
se abilloient lune come laultre
ne ne daugnassent recheuoir le
amour daulcun cheualier se am
chois ne se fuist esprouuez en fait

N celle saison et
entretant que les

que le puit Sauuertyne en re
uoit les plantes en xenoient

Comment le Roy artus trouua en la chambre
de moꝛtram liſtoire de lancelot doꝛt/ꝯe ſe doubter
fort de lamo de la Royne gemeure et de lancelot

Vant gyfles voit que
faire li couient . sire
uient arriere la ou let
pee estoit si la prent & la recome
ce a regarder & a plaindze mlt
durement & dist tot en plozant .
ha . espee boine & bele plus que nu
le autre tant est sñs damages

all this sorrow; for and they thus over our lands ride, they shall by process bring us all to nought whilst we thus in holes us hide.'

Then said Sir Galihud unto Sir Lancelot, 'Sir, here be knights come of kings' blood, that will not long droop and dare within these walls; therefore give us leave, like as we be knights, to meet them in the field, and we shall slay them, that they shall curse the time that ever they came into this country.'

Then spake seven brethren of North Wales and they were seven noble knights; a man might seek in seven kings' lands or he might find such seven knights. Then they all said at once,

'Sir Lancelot, for Christ's sake let us out ride with Sir Galihud, for we be never wont to cower in castles nor in noble towns.'

Then spake Sir Lancelot, that was master and governor of them all:

'My fair lords, wit you well I am full loth to ride out with my knights for shedding of Christian blood; and yet my lands I understand be full bare for to sustain any host awhile, for the mighty wars that whilom made King Claudas upon this country, and upon my father King Ban, and on mine uncle King Bors; howbeit we will as at this time keep our strong walls, and I shall send a messenger unto my lord Arthur, a treaty for to take; for better is peace than always war.'

So Sir Lancelot sent forth a damsel with a dwarf with her, requiring King Arthur to leave his warring upon his lands; and so she start upon a palfrey, and the dwarf ran by her side.

And when she came to the pavilion of King Arthur, there she alit; and there met her a gentle knight, Sir Lucan the Butler, and said, 'Fair damsel, come ye from Sir Lancelot du Lake?'

'Yea sir,' she said, 'therefore I come hither to speak with my lord the king.'

'Alas,' said Sir Lucan, 'my lord Arthur would accord with Sir Lancelot, but Sir Gawain will not suffer him.' And then he said, 'I pray to God, damsel, ye may speed well, for all we that be about the king would that Sir Lancelot did best of any knight living.'

And so with this Lucan led the damsel unto the king where he sat with Sir Gawain, for to hear what she would say. So when she had told her tale, the water ran out of the king's eyen, and all the lords were full glad for to advise the king as to be accorded with Sir Lancelot, save all only Sir Gawain. And he said,

'My lord mine uncle, what will ye do? Will ye now turn again now ye are passed this far upon your journey? All the world will speak of you villainy and shame.'

'Nay,' said King Arthur, 'wit thou well, Sir Gawain, I will do as ye will advise me; and yet meseemeth,' said King Arthur, 'his fair proffers were not good to be refused; but sithen I am comen so far upon this journey, I will that ye give the damsel her answer, for I may not speak to her for pity, for her proffers be so large.'

Then Sir Gawain said to the damsel thus:

'Damsel, say ye to Sir Lancelot that it is waste labour now to sue to mine uncle; for tell him, and he would have made any labour for peace, he should have made it or this time, for I tell him now it is too late; and say that I, Sir Gawain, so send him word, that I promise him by the faith I owe unto God and to knighthood, I shall never leave him till he have slain me or I him.'

So the damsel wept and departed, and there was many a weeping eye; and so Sir Lucan brought the damsel to her palfrey, and so she came to Sir Lancelot where he was among all his knights.

And when Sir Lancelot had heard this answer, then the tears ran down by his cheeks. And then his noble knights strode about him, and said,

'Sir Lancelot, wherefore make ye such cheer. Think what ye are, and what men we are, and let us noble knights match them in midst of the field.'

'That may be lightly done,' said Sir Lancelot, 'but I was never so loth to do battle. And therefore I pray you, fair sirs, as ye love me be ruled at this time as I will have you. For I will always flee that noble king that made me knight. And when I may no further, I must needs defend me, and that will be more worship for me and us all than to compare with that noble king whom we have all served.'

Then they held their language, and as that night they took their rest. And upon the morn early, in the dawning of the day, as knights looked out, they saw the city of Benwick besieged round about. And fast they began to set up ladders, and they within kept them out of the town, and beat them mightily from the walls.

Then came forth Sir Gawain well armed upon a stiff steed, and he came before the chief gate, with his spear in his hand, crying,

'Sir Lancelot, where art thou? Is there none of you proud knights dare break a spear with me?'

Then Sir Bors made him ready, and came forth out of the town, and there Sir Gawain encountered with Sir Bors. And at that time he smote Sir Bors down from his horse, and almost he had slain him; and so Sir Bors was rescued and borne into the town.

Then came forth Sir Lionel, brother to Sir Bors, and thought to revenge him; and either fewtered their spears, and ran together; and there they met spitefully, but Sir Gawain had such a grace that he smote Sir Lionel down, and wounded him there passing sore; and then Sir Lionel was rescued and borne into the town.

And thus this Sir Gawain came every day, and he failed not but that he smote down one knight or other. So thus they endured half a year, and much slaughter was of people on both parties.

Then it befell upon a day, Sir Gawain came afore the gates armed at all pieces on a noble horse, with a great spear in his hand; and then he cried with a loud voice, and said,

'Where art thou now, thou false traitor, Sir Lancelot? Why hidest thou thyself within holes and walls like a coward? Look out now, thou false traitor knight, and here I shall revenge upon thy body the death of my three brethren.'

All this language heard Sir Lancelot every deal. Then his kin and his knights drew about him, and all they said at once to Sir Lancelot,

'Sir Lancelot, now must you defend you like a knight, or else ye be shamed for ever; for, now ye be called upon treason, it is time for you to stir. For ye have slept overlong and suffered over-much.'

'So God me help,' said Sir Lancelot, 'I am right heavy at Sir Gawain's words, for now he charged me with a great charge. And therefore I wot it as well as ye, that I must defend me, or else to be recreant.'

Then Sir Lancelot bad saddle his strongest horse, and bad let fetch his arms, and bring all unto the tower of the gate; and then Sir Lancelot spake on high unto King Arthur, and said,

'My lord Arthur, and noble king that made me knight, wit you well I am right heavy for your sake, that ye thus sue upon me. And always I forbare you, for and I would have been vengeable, I might have met you in midst of the field, and there to have made your boldest knights full tame. And now I have forborne you half a year, and suffered you and Sir Gawain to do what ye would do. And now may I endure it no longer, but now must I needs defend myself, insomuch as Sir Gawain hath appelled me of treason; which is greatly against my will, that ever I should fight against any of your blood, but now I may not forsake it. For I am driven thereto as a beast till a bay.'

Then Sir Gawain said, 'Sir Lancelot, and thou darst do battle, leave thy babbling and come off, and let us ease our hearts.'

Then Sir Lancelot armed him, and mounted upon his horse, and either of the knights gat great spears in their hands. And the host without stood still all apart, and the noble knights came out of the city by a great number insomuch that when Arthur saw the number of men and knights, he marvelled, and said to himelf,

'Alas, that ever Sir Lancelot was against me. For now I see that he hath forborne me.'

And so the covenant was made, there should no man nigh them, nor deal with them, till the one were dead or yielden.

Then Sir Gawain and Sir Lancelot departed a great way in

sunder, and then they came together with all their horses' might as fast as they might run, and either smote other in midst of their shields. But the knights were so strong, and their spears so big, that their horses might not endure their buffets, and so their horses fell to the earth; and then they avoided their horses, and dressed their shields afore them. Then they came together and gave many sad strokes on divers places of their bodies, that the blood brast out on many sides.

Then had Sir Gawain such a grace and gift that an holy man had given to him, that every day in the year, from undern till high noon, his might increased those three hours as much as thrice his strength. And that caused Sir Gawain to win great honour. And for his sake King Arthur made an ordinance, that all manner of battles for any quarrels that should be done afore King Arthur should begin at undern; and all was done for Sir Gawain's love, that by likelihood, if Sir Gawain were on the one part, he should have the better in battle while his strength endured three hours; but there were but few knights that time living that knew this advantage that Sir Gawain had, but King Arthur all only.

So thus Sir Lancelot fought with Sir Gawain, and when Sir Lancelot felt his might evermore increase, Sir Lancelot wondered and dread him sore to be shamed. For as the French book saith, Sir Lancelot weened, when he felt Sir Gawain double his strength, that he had been a fiend and none earthly man; wherefore Sir Lancelot traced and traversed, and covered himself with his shield, and kept his might and his breath during three hours. And that while Sir Gawain gave him many sad brunts, and many sad strokes, that all the knights that beheld Sir Lancelot marvelled how that he might endure him; but full little understood they that travail that Sir Lancelot had to endure him.

And then when it was past noon Sir Gawain's strength was gone, and he had no more but his own might. When Sir Lancelot felt him so come down, then he stretched him up, and strode near Sir Gawain, and said thus:

'My lord Sir Gawain, now I feel ye have done your worst, and now my lord Sir Gawain, I must do my part, for many great and grievous strokes I have endured you this day with great pain.'

Then Sir Lancelot doubled his strokes and gave Sir Gawain such a buffet on the helmet that sidelong he fell down on his one side. And Sir Lancelot withdrew him from him.

'Why withdrawest thou thee?' said Sir Gawain. 'Now turn again, false traitor knight, and slay me, for and thou leave me thus, when I am whole I shall do battle with thee again.'

'Sir,' said Sir Lancelot, 'I shall endure you, by God's grace. But wit thou well, Sir Gawain, I will never smite a felled knight.'

And so Sir Lancelot departed and went into the city. And Sir Gawain was borne into King Arthur's pavilion, and anon leeches were brought to him of the best, and searched and salved with soft ointments.

And then Sir Lancelot said, 'Now have good day, my lord the king, for wit you well ye win no worship at these walls; for if I would my knights outbring, there should many a doughty man die. Therefore, my lord Arthur, remember you of old kindness; and however I fare, Jesu be your guide in all places.'

'Alas,' said the king, 'that ever this unhappy war was begun; for ever Sir Lancelot forbeareth me in all places, and in likewise my kin, and that is seen well this day, what courtesy he showed my nephew Sir Gawain.'

Then King Arthur fell sick for sorrow of Sir Gawain, that he was so sore hurt, and because of the war betwixt him and Sir Lancelot. So after that they on King Arthur's part kept the siege with little war withoutforth; and they withinforth kept their walls, and defended them when need was.

Thus Sir Gawain lay sick and unsound three weeks in his tents, with all manner of leechcraft that might be had. And as soon as Sir Gawain might go and ride, he armed him at all points, and bestrode a stiff courser, and gat a great spear in his hand, and so he came riding afore the chief gate of Benwick. And there he cried on height and said,

'Where art thou, Sir Lancelot? Come forth, thou false traitor knight and recreant, for I am here, Sir Gawain, that will prove this that I say on thee.'

All this language Sir Lancelot heard, and said thus:

'Sir Gawain, me repents of your foul saying, that ye will not cease of your language. For you wot well, Sir Gawain, I know your might and all that ye may do; and well ye wot, Sir Gawain, ye may not greatly hurt me.'

'Come down, traitor knight,' said he, 'and make it good the contrary with thy hands. For it mishapped me the last battle to be hurt of thy hands; therefore wit thou well I am come this day to make amends, for I ween this day to lay thee as low as thou laidest me.'

'Jesu defend me,' said Sir Lancelot, 'that ever I be so far in your danger as ye have been in mine, for then my days were done. But Sir Gawain,' said Sir Lancelot, 'ye shall not think that I tarry long, but sithen that ye so unknightly call me thus of treason, ye shall have both your hands full of me.'

And then Sir Lancelot armed him at all points, and mounted upon his horse, and gat a great spear in his hand, and rode out at the gate. And both the hosts were assembled, of them without and of them within, and stood in array full manly. And both parties were charged to hold them still, to see and behold the battle of these two noble knights.

And then they laid their spears in their rests, and they came together as thunder. And Sir Gawain brake his spear upon Sir Lancelot in a hundred pieces unto his hand; and Sir Lancelot smote him with a greater might, that Sir Gawain's horse's feet raised, and so the horse and he fell to the earth. Then Sir Gawain deliverly devoided his horse, and put his shield afore him, and eagerly drew his sword, and bad Sir Lancelot: 'Alight, traitor knight, for if this mare's son hath failed me wit thou well a king's son and a queen's son shall not fail thee.'

Then Sir Lancelot devoided his horse, and dressed his shield afore him, and drew his sword; and so came they together and gave many sad strokes, that all men on both parties had thereof passing great wonder.

But when Sir Lancelot felt Sir Gawain's might so marvellously increase, he then withheld his courage and his wind, and kept himself under covert of his might and of his shield. He traced and traversed here and there, to break Sir Gawain's strokes and his courage. And Sir Gawain enforced himself with all his might and power to destroy Sir Lancelot; for as the French book saith, ever as Sir Gawain's might increased, right so increased his wind and his evil will. Thus Sir Gawain did great pain unto Sir Lancelot three hours, that he had right great pain for to defend him.

And when the three hours were passed, that Sir Lancelot felt that Sir Gawain was come home to his own proper strength, then Sir Lancelot said unto Sir Gawain,

'Now have I proved you twice, that ye are a full dangerous knight, and a wonderful man of your might; and many wonderful deeds have ye done in your days, for by your might increasing you have deceived many a full noble and valiant knight; and, now I feel that ye have done your mighty deeds, now wit you well I must do my deeds.'

And then Sir Lancelot strode near Sir Gawain, and then Sir Lancelot doubled his strokes; and ever Sir Gawain defended him mightily, but nevertheless Sir Lancelot smote such a stroke upon Sir Gawain's helm, and upon the old wound, that Sir Gawain sank down upon his one side in a swoon.

And anon as he did awake he waved and foined at Sir Lancelot as he lay, and said,

'Traitor knight, wit thou well I am not yet slain. Therefore come thou near me and perform this battle unto the uttermost.'

'I will no more do than I have done,' said Sir Lancelot, 'for when I see you on foot I will do battle upon you all the while I see you stand on your feet; but for to smite a wounded man that may not stand, God defend me from such a shame.'

And then he turned him and went his way toward the city, and Sir Gawain evermore calling him traitor knight, and said,

'Wit thou well Sir Lancelot, when I am whole I shall do battle with thee again, for I shall never leave thee till that one of us be slain.'

Thus as this siege endured, and as Sir Gawain lay sick near a month, and when he was well recovered and ready within three days to do battle again with Sir Lancelot, right so came tidings unto King Arthur from England that made King Arthur and all his host to remove.

As Sir Mordred was ruler of all England, he let make letters as though that they came from beyond the sea, and the letters specified that King Arthur was slain in battle with Sir Lancelot. Wherefore Sir Mordred made a parliament, and called the lords together, and there he made them to choose him king; and so was he crowned at Canterbury, and held a feast there fifteen days.

And afterward he drew him unto Winchester, and there he took the queen Guenever, and said plainly that he would wed her, which was his uncle's wife and his father's wife. And so he made ready for the feast, and a day prefixed that they should be wedded; wherefore Queen Guenever was passing heavy. But she durst not discover her heart, but spake fair, and agreed to Sir Mordred's will.

And anon she desired of Sir Mordred for to go to London, to buy all manner of things that longed unto the wedding. And because of her fair speech Sir Mordred trusted her well enough, and gave her leave to go. And so when she came to London she took the Tower of London, and suddenly in all haste possible she stuffed it with all manner of victual, and well garnished it with men, and kept it.

Then when Sir Mordred wist and understood how he was beguiled, he was passing wroth out of measure. And a short tale to make, he went and laid a mighty siege about the Tower of London, and made many great assaults thereat, and threw many great engines unto them, and shot great guns. But all might not prevail, for Queen Guenever would never for fair speech nor for foul, would never trust to come in his hands again.

Then came the Bishop of Canterbury, which was a noble clerk and an holy man, and thus he said to Sir Mordred:

Mordred besieges Guenever in the Tower of London

'Sir, what will do? Will ye first displease God and sithen shame yourself, and all knighthood? For is not King Arthur your uncle, no farther but your mother's brother, and on her himself King Arthur begat you, upon his own sister? Therefore how may you wed your own father's wife? Sir,' said the noble clerk, 'leave this opinion or I shall curse you with book, bell and candle.'

'Do thou thy worst,' said Sir Mordred, 'wit thou well I shall defy thee.'

'Sir,' said the Bishop, 'and wit you well I shall not fear me to do that me ought to do. Also where ye noise that my lord Arthur is slain, and that is not so, and therefore ye will make a foul work in this land.'

'Peace, thou false priest,' said Sir Mordred, 'for and thou chafe me any more, I shall make strike off thy head.'

orgulest: proudest

So the Bishop departed and did the cursing in the most orgulest wise that might be done. And then Sir Mordred sought the Bishop of Canterbury, for to have slain him. Then the Bishop fled, and took part of his goods with him, and went nigh unto Glastonbury; and there he was a priest-hermit in a chapel, and lived in poverty and in holy prayers; for well he understood that mischievous war was at hand.

Then Sir Mordred sought on Queen Guenever by letters and

sondes, and by fair means and foul means, to have her to come out of the Tower of London; but all this availed not, for she answered him shortly, openly and privily, that she had lever slay herself than to be married with him.

sondes: *messengers*

Then came word to Sir Mordred that King Arthur had araised the siege from Sir Lancelot, and he was coming homeward with a great host, to be avenged upon Sir Mordred; wherefore Sir Mordred made write writs to all the barony of this land, and much people drew to him. For then was the common voice among them that with King Arthur was never none other life but war and strife, and with Sir Mordred was great joy and bliss. Thus was King Arthur depraved, and evil said of. And many there were that King Arthur had brought up of nought, and given them lands, might not then say him a good word.

Lo ye all Englishmen, see ye not what a mischief here was? For he that was the most king and noblest knight of the world, and most loved the fellowship of noble knights, and by him they were all upholden, now might not these Englishmen hold them content with him. Lo thus was the old custom and usage of this land; and also men say that we of this land have not yet lost ne forgotten that custom and usage. Alas, this is a great default of us English-men, for there may nothing please us no term.

And so fared the people at that time, they were better pleased with Sir Mordred than they were with the noble King Arthur; and much people drew unto Sir Mordred, and said they would abide with him for better and for worse. And so Sir Mordred drew with a great host to Dover, for there he heard say that King Arthur would arrive, and so he thought to beat his own father from his own lands; and the most part of all England held with Sir Mordred, for the people were so new fangle.

And so as Sir Mordred was at Dover with his host, there came King Arthur with a great navy of ships, and galleys, and carracks. And there was Sir Mordred ready awaiting upon his landing, to let his own father to land up the land that he was king over.

Then there was launching of great boats and small, and full of noble men of arms; and there was much slaughter of gentle knights, and many a full bold baron was laid full low, on both parties.

But King Arthur was so courageous that there might be no manner of knights let him to land, and his knights fiercely followed him; and so they landed maugre Sir Mordred's head and all his power, and put Sir Mordred aback, that he fled and all his people.

So when the battle was done, King Arthur let bury his people that were dead. And then was noble Sir Gawain found in a great boat, lying more than half dead. When King Arthur wist that Sir

Gawain was laid so low, he went unto him, and so found him. And there the king made great sorrow out of measure, and took Sir Gawain in his arms, and thrice he there swooned. And then when he awaked King Arthur said,

'Alas, Sir Gawain, my sister's son, here now thou liest, the man in the world that I loved most. And now is my joy gone; for now, my nephew Sir Gawain, I will discover me unto you; that in your person and in Sir Lancelot and you I most had my joy, and mine affiance. And now have I lost my joy of you both; wherefore all mine earthly joy is gone from me.'

'Mine uncle King Arthur,' said Sir Gawain, 'now I will that ye wit my death day is come, and all is through mine own hastiness and wilfulness; for through my wilfulness I was causer of my own death. For I am smitten upon my old wound that Sir Lancelot gave me, and I feel myself that I must needs be dead by the hour of noon. And through me and my pride ye have all this shame and disease. For had that noble knight Sir Lancelot been with you, as he was and would have been, this unhappy war had been never begun; and of all this am I causer, for Sir Lancelot through his noble knighthood and his noble blood, held all your cankered enemies in subjection and danger. And now,' said Sir Gawain, 'ye shall miss Sir Lancelot. But alas, I would not accord with him. And therefore,' said Sir Gawain, 'I pray you, fair uncle, that I may have paper, pen and ink, that I may write to Sir Lancelot a letter written with mine own hands.'

And then when paper and ink was brought, then Sir Gawain was set up weakly by King Arthur, for he was shriven a little afore; and then he took his pen and wrote thus, as the French book maketh mention:

'Unto thee Sir Lancelot, flower of all noble knights that ever I heard of or saw by my days: I, Sir Gawain, King Lot's son of Orkney, sister's son unto the noble King Arthur, send thee greeting, and let thee have knowledge that the tenth day of May I was smitten upon the old wound that thou gavest me afore the city of Benwick, and through the same wound that thou gavest me I am come to my death day. And I will that all the world wit, that I, Sir Gawain, knight of the Table Round, sought my death, and not through thy deserving, but it was mine own seeking. Wherefore I beseech thee, Sir Lancelot, to return again unto this realm, and see my tomb, and pray some prayer more or less for my soul. And this same day that I wrote this cedle, I was hurt to the death in the same wound, the which I had of thy hand, Sir Lancelot; for of a more nobler man might I not be slain.

'Also Sir Lancelot, for all the love that ever was betwixt us, make no tarrying, but come over the sea in all goodly haste that

cedle: *letter*

300

thou mayst, with thy noble knights, and rescue that noble king that made thee knight, that is my lord Arthur, for he is full straitly bestad with a false traitor, that is my half-brother, Sir Mordred. For he hath crowned himself king, and would have wedded my lady Queen Guenever, and so had he done had she not kept the Tower of London with strong hand. And so the tenth day of May last past, my lord Arthur and we all landed upon them at Dover; and there we put that false traitor Sir Mordred, to flight, and there it misfortuned me to be stricken upon thy stroke. And at the date of this letter was written, but two hours and a half afore my death, written with mine own hand, and so subscribed with part of my heart's blood. And therefore I require thee, most famous knight of the world, that thou wilt see my tomb.'

And then Sir Gawain wept, and King Arthur wept; and then they swooned both. And when they awaked both, the king made Sir Gawain to receive his Saviour. And then Sir Gawain prayed the king for to send for Sir Lancelot, and to cherish him above all other knights.

And so at the hour of noon Sir Gawain yielded up the ghost. And then the king let inter him in a chapel within Dover Castle; and there yet all men may see the skull of him, and the same wound is seen that Sir Lancelot gave him in battle.

Then was it told the king that Sir Mordred had pitched a new field upon Barham Down. And upon the morn the king rode thither to him, and there was a great battle betwixt them, and much people was slain on both parties; but at the last Sir Arthur's party stood best, and Sir Mordred and his party fled unto Canterbury.

And then the king let search all the downs for his knights that were slain, and interred them; and salved them with soft salves that so sore were wounded.

Then much people drew unto King Arthur. And then they said that Sir Mordred warred upon King Arthur with wrong. And then King Arthur drew him with his host down by the seaside westward toward Salisbury; and there was a day assigned betwixt King Arthur and Sir Mordred, that they should meet upon a down beside Salisbury, and not far from the seaside; and this day was assigned on Monday after Trinity Sunday; whereof King Arthur was passing glad, that he might be avenged upon Sir Mordred.

Then Sir Mordred araised much people about London, for they of Kent, Sussex and Surrey, Essex, Suffolk and Norfolk, held the most part with Sir Mordred; and many a full noble knight drew unto Sir Mordred, and also to the king; but they that loved Sir Lancelot drew unto Sir Mordred.

chaflet: *platform*

So upon Trinity Sunday at night, King Arthur dreamed a wonderful dream, and that was this: that him seemed he saw upon a chaflet, a chair, and the chair was fast to a wheel, and thereupon sat King Arthur in the richest cloth of a gold that might be made. And the king thought there was under him, far from him, an hideous deep black water, and therein were all manner of serpents, and worms, and wild beasts, foul and horrible; and suddenly the king thought the wheel turned up-so-down, and he fell among the serpents, and every beast took him by a limb; and then the king cried as he lay in his bed and slept, 'Help, help.'

And then knights, squires, and yeomen, awaked the king; and then he was so amazed that he wist not where he was. And then so he awaked until it was nigh day. And then he fell on slumbering again, not sleeping nor thoroughly waking.

So the king seemed verily that there came Sir Gawain unto him, with a number of fair ladies with him. And when King Arthur saw him, then he said,

'Welcome my sister's son; I weened thou hadst been dead, and now I see thee alive, much am I beholding unto Almighty Jesu. O fair nephew and my sisters' son, what be these ladies that hither be come with you?'

'Sir,' said Sir Gawain, 'all these be ladies for whom I have foughten when I was man living, and all these are those that I did battle for in righteous quarrel; and God hath given them that grace at their great prayer, because I did battle for them, that they should bring me hither unto you: thus much hath God given me leave, for to warn you of your death. For and ye fight as tomorn with Sir Mordred, as ye both have assigned, doubt ye not ye must be slain, and the most part of your people on both parties. And for the great grace and goodness that Almighty Jesu hath unto you, and for pity of you, and many more other good men there shall be slain, God hath sent me to you of His special grace, to give you warning that in no wise ye do battle as tomorn, but that ye take a treaty for a month day. And proffer you largely, so as tomorn ye put in a delay. For within a month shall come Sir Lancelot with all his noble knights, and rescue you worshipfully, and slay Sir Mordred, and all that ever will hold with him.'

Then Sir Gawain and all the ladies vanished. And anon the king called upon his knights, squires, and yeomen, and charged them wightly to fetch his noble lords and wise bishops unto him. And when they were come, the king told them his avision: that Sir Gawain had told him and warned him that if he fought on the morn he should be slain.

Then the king commanded Sir Lucan the Butler, and his brother Sir Bedevere, with two bishops with them, and charged them in any wise, and they might, to make a treaty for a month day with Sir Mordred:

'And spare not, proffer him lands and goods as much as ye think reasonable.'

So then they departed, and came to Sir Mordred, where he had a grim host of an hundred thousand men. And there they entreated Sir Mordred long time. And at the last Sir Mordred was agreed for to have Cornwall and Kent, by King Arthur's days; and after that all England, after the days of King Arthur.

Then were they condescended that King Arthur and Sir Mordred should meet betwixt both their hosts, and every each of them should bring fourteen persons; and they came with this word unto King Arthur.

Then said he, 'I am glad that this is done': and so he went into the field.

And when King Arthur should depart, he warned all his host that and they see any sword drawn 'look ye come on fiercely, and slay that traitor, Sir Mordred, for I in no wise trust him.'

In likewise Sir Mordred warned his host that, 'and ye see any sword drawn, look that ye come on fiercely, and so slay all that ever before you standeth; for in no wise I will not trust for this treaty; for I know well my father will be avenged on me.'

And so they met as their pointment was, and so they were agreed and accorded thoroughly; and wine was fetched and they drank together.

Arthur in the thick of a battle

Right soon came an adder out of a little heath bush, and it stung a knight on the foot. And when the knight felt him so stung, he looked down and saw the adder; and then he drew his sword to slay the adder, and thought of none other harm. And when the host on both parties saw that sword drawn, then they blew beams, trumpets, and horns, and shouted grimly. And so both hosts dressed them together.

beam: a type of trumpet

And King Arthur took his horse, and said, 'Alas this unhappy day!' and so rode to his party. And Sir Mordred in likewise.

And never since was there seen a more dolefuller battle in no Christian land; for there was but rushing and riding, foining and striking, and many a grim word was there spoken of either to other, and many a deadly stroke. But ever King Arthur rode through-out the battle of Sir Mordred many times, and did full nobly, as a noble king should do, and at all times he fainted never. And Sir Mordred did his devoir that day, and put himself in great peril.

And thus they fought all the long day, and never stinted till the noble knights were laid to the cold earth. And ever they fought still till it was near night, and by that time was there an hundred

The Death of Arthur

thousand laid dead upon the down. Then was Arthur wood wroth out of measure, when he saw his people so slain from him.

Then the king looked about him, and could see no more of all his host and of all his good knights were left no more alive but two knights; the one was Sir Lucan the Butler, and his brother Sir Bedevere; and they were full sore wounded.

'Jesu mercy,' said the king, 'where are all my noble knights become? Alas that ever I should see this doleful day. For now,' said Arthur, 'I am come to mine end. But would to God that I wist where were that traitor Sir Mordred, that hath caused all this mischief.'

Then King Arthur looked about, and was ware where stood Sir Mordred leaning upon his sword among a great heap of dead men.

'Now give me my spear,' said King Arthur unto Sir Lucan, 'for yonder I have espied the traitor that all this woe hath wrought.'

'Sir, let him be,' said Sir Lucan, 'for he is unhappy; and if ye pass this unhappy day ye shall be right well revenged upon him. God lord, remember ye of your night's dream, and what the spirit of Sir Gawain told you this night, yet God of his great goodness hath preserved you hitherto. Therefore, for God's sake, my lord, leave off by this, for blessed be God ye have won the field; for here we be three alive, and with Sir Mordred is not one alive. And if ye leave off now, this wicked day of destiny is past.'

'Now tide me death, betide me life,' saith the king, 'now I see him yonder alone he shall never escape mine hands. For at a better avail shall I never have him.'

'God speed you well,' said Sir Bevedere.

Then the king gat his spear in both his hands, and ran toward Sir Mordred, crying,

'Traitor, now is thy death day come.'

And when Sir Mordred heard Sir Arthur, he ran until him with his sword drawn in his hand. And there King Arthur smote Sir Mordred under the shield, with a foin of his spear, throughout the body, more than a fathom. And when Sir Mordred felt that he had his death's wound he thrust himself with the might that he had up to the bur of King Arthur's spear. And right so he smote his father King Arthur, with his sword holden in both his hands, on the side of the head, that the sword pierced the helmet and the brain pan; and therewithal Sir Mordred fell stark dead to the earth. And the noble King Arthur fell in a swoon to the earth and there he swooned oftentimes.

And Sir Lucan the Butler and Sir Bedevere ofttimes heave him up. And so weakly they led him betwixt them both, to a little chapel not far from the seaside. And when the king was there

bur: *ring below hand grip*

OPPOSITE
The mortally wounded Arthur lies amid the slain at the end of the final battle

tait le chief voler del bu en mi
la place. Ensi q̃ .j. grãt mortalite del
roi Artu et de mordres son fil la v il
furent tout destruit.

Vant li rois artus vott
cellui cop si dist trop do
lans. ha. dier por quoi
me laissies vos tant abaissier de
proesce trriene. Et por lamor de
cestui cop veu iou a dieu quil co
uient ich morir moi ou mordret
Il trit .j. glaiue gros et fort et lais
se corre ꝗꝗues il puet del cheual
traire vers mordret. Et mor

he thought him reasonably eased. Then heard they people cry in the field.

'Now go thou, Sir Lucan,' said the king, 'and do me to wit what betokens that noise in the field.'

So Sir Lucan departed, for he was grievously wounded in many places. And so as he yede, he saw and hearkened by the moonlight, how that pillers and robbers were comen into the field, to pill and to rob many a full noble knight of brooches, and beads, and of many a good ring, and of many a rich jewel; and who that were not dead all out, there they slew them for their harness and their riches. When Sir Lucan understood this work, he came to the king as soon as he might, and told him all what he had heard and seen.

'Therefore by my rede,' said Sir Lucan, 'it is best that we bring you to some town.'

'I would it were so,' said the king. 'But I may not stand, mine head works so. Ah Sir Lancelot,' said King Arthur, 'this day have I sore missed thee: alas, that ever I was against thee, for now have I my death, whereof Sir Gawain me warned in my dream.'

Then Sir Lucan took up the king the one part, and Sir Bedevere the other part, and in the lifting the king swooned; and Sir Lucan fell in a swoon with the lift, that the part of his guts fell out of his body, and therewith the noble knight's heart brast. And when the king awoke, he beheld Sir Lucan, how he lay foaming at the mouth, and part of his guts lay at his feet.

'Alas,' said the king, 'this is to me a full heavy sight, to see this noble duke so to die for my sake, for he would have holpen me, that had more need of help than I. Alas, he would not complain him, his heart was so set to help me: now Jesu have mercy upon his soul!'

Then Sir Bedevere wept for the death of his brother.

'Leave this mourning and weeping, gentle knight,' said the king, 'for all this will not avail me. For wit thou well and I might live myself, the death of Sir Lucan would grieve me evermore; but my time passeth on fast,' said the king. 'Therefore,' said King Arthur unto Sir Bedevere, 'take thou Excalibur, my good sword, and go with it to yonder water side, and when thou comest there I charge thee throw my sword in that water, and come again and tell me what thou there seest there.'

'My lord,' said Bedevere, 'your commandment shall be done, and lightly bring you word again.'

So Sir Bedevere departed. And by the way he beheld that noble sword, that the pommel and the haft was all of precious stones; and then he said to himself, 'If I throw this rich sword in the water, thereof shall never come good, but harm and loss.' And then Sir Bedevere hid Excalibur under a tree.

And so, as soon as he might, he came again unto the king, and said he had been at the water, and had thrown the sword into the water.

'What saw thou there?' said the king.

'Sir,' he said, 'I saw nothing but waves and winds.'

'That is untruly said of thee,' said the king, 'therefore go thou lightly again, and do my commandment; as thou art to me leve and dear, spare not, but throw it in.'

Then Sir Bedevere returned again, and took the sword in his hand; and then him thought sin and shame to throw away that noble sword, and so eft he hid the sword, and returned again, and told to the king that he had been at the water and done his commandment.

'What saw thou there?' said the king.

'Sir,' he said, 'I saw nothing but the waters wap and waves wan.'   wap: *lap*

'Ah, traitor unto me and untrue,' said King Arthur, 'now hast   wan: *grow dark*
thou betrayed me twice. Who would have weened that thou that hast been to me so leve and dear, and thou art named a noble knight, that thou would betray me for the riches of the sword? But now go again lightly; for thy long tarrying putteth me in great jeopardy of my life; for I have taken cold. And but if thou do now as I bid thee, if ever I may see thee, I shall slay thee mine own hands; for thou wouldst for my rich sword see me dead.'

Then Sir Bedevere departed, and went to the sword, and lightly took it up, and so he went to the water side. And there he bound the girdle about the hilts, and then he threw the sword as far into the water as he might. And there came an arm and an hand above the water and met it, and caught it, and so shook it thrice and brandished, and then vanished away the hand with the sword into the water. So Sir Bedevere came again to the king, and told him what he saw.

'Alas,' said the king, 'help me hence, for I dread me I have tarried over long.'

Then Sir Bedevere took the king upon his back, and so went with him to that water side. And when they were at the water side, even fast by the bank hoved a little barge with many fair ladies in it, and among them all was a queen, and all they had black hoods. And all they wept and shrieked when they saw King Arthur.

'Now put me into that barge,' said the king.

And so he did softly; and there received him three queens with great mourning; and so they set them down, and in one of their laps King Arthur laid his head.

And then that queen said, 'Ah, dear brother, why have ye tarried so long from me? Alas, this wound on your head hath caught over-much cold.'

And so then they rowed from the land, and Sir Bedevere beheld all those ladies go from him. Then Sir Bedevere cried, and said,

'Ah my lord Arthur, what shall become of me, now ye go from me and leave me here alone among mine enemies?'

'Comfort thyself,' said the king, 'and do as well as thou mayest, for in me is no trust for to trust in. For I must into the vale of Avilion to heal me of my grievous wound. And if thou hear never more of me, pray for my soul.'

But ever the queen and ladies wept and shrieked, that it was pity to hear. And as soon as Sir Bedevere had lost the sight of the barge, he wept and wailed, and so took the forest; and so he went all that night. And in the morning he was ware betwixt two holts hoar, of a chapel and an hermitage.

Then was Sir Bedevere glad, and thither he went; and when he came into the chapel, he saw where lay an hermit grovelling on all four, there fast by a tomb was new graven. When the hermit saw Sir Bedevere he knew him well, for he was but little tofore Bishop of Canterbury, that Sir Mordred flemed.

'Sir,' said Sir Bedevere, 'what man is there interred that ye pray so fast for?'

'Fair son,' said the hermit, 'I wot not verily, but by deeming. But this same night, at midnight, here came a number of ladies, and brought hither a dead corpse, and prayed me to bury him; and here they offered an hundred tapers, and they gave me an hundred bezants.'

'Alas,' said Sir Bedevere, 'that was my lord King Arthur, that here lieth buried in this chapel.'

Then Sir Bedevere swooned; and when he awoke he prayed the hermit he might abide with him still, there to live with fasting and prayers.

'For from hence will I never go,' said Sir Bedevere, 'by my will, but all the days of my life here to pray for my lord King Arthur.'

'Ye are welcome to me,' said the hermit, 'for I know you better than ye ween that I do. Ye are the bold Sir Bedevere, and the full noble duke Sir Lucan the Butler was your brother.'

Then Sir Bedevere told the hermit all as ye have heard tofore. So there bode Sir Bedevere with the hermit that was tofore Bishop of Canterbury, and there Sir Bedevere put upon him poor clothes, and served the hermit full lowly in fasting and in prayers.

Thus of King Arthur I find no more written in books that be authorised, nor more of the very certainty of his death heard I never read, but thus was he led away in a ship wherein were three queens; that one was King Arthur's sister, Queen Morgan le Fay; the other was the Queen of Northgales; the third was the Queen of the Waste Lands. Also there was Nimue, the chief lady of the lake, that had wedded Pelleas the good knight; and this lady had done much for King Arthur, for she would never suffer Sir Pelleas to be in no place where he should be in danger of his life; and so he lived to the uttermost of his days with her in great rest. More of the death of King Arthur could I never find, but that these ladies brought him to his grave; and such one was buried there, that the hermit bare witness that sometime was Bishop of Canterbury, but yet the hermit knew not in certain that he was verily the body of King Arthur. For this tale Sir Bedevere, a knight of the Table Round, made it to be written.

Yet some men say in many parts of England that King Arthur is not dead, but had by the will of Our Lord Jesu into another place; and men say that he shall come again, and he shall win the holy cross. Yet I will not say that it shall be so, but rather I will say, here in this world he changed his life. But many men say that there is written upon his tomb this verse: HIC IACET ARTHURUS, REX QUONDAM REXQUE FUTURUS.

Thus leave I here Sir Bedevere with the hermit, that dwelled that time in a chapel beside Glastonbury, and there was his hertmitage. And so they lived in their prayers, and fastings, and great abstinence.

And when Queen Guenever understood that King Arthur was slain, and all the noble knights, Sir Mordred and all the remnant, then the queen stole away, and five ladies with her, and so she went to Almesbury. And there she let make herself a nun, and ware white clothes and black, and great penance she took upon her, as ever did sinful woman in this land. And never creature could make her merry; but ever she lived in fasting, prayers, and almsdeeds, that all manner of people marvelled how virtuously she was changed.

Now leave we Queen Guenever in Almesbury, a nun in white clothes and black, and there she was abbess and ruler as reason would; and now turn we from her, and speak we of Sir Lancelot du Lake.

And when he heard in his country that Sir Mordred was crowned king in England, and made war against King Arthur, his own father, and would let him to land in his own land, also it was told Sir Lancelot how that Sir Mordred had laid siege about the Tower of London, because the queen would not wed him, then was Sir Lancelot wroth out of measure, and said to his kinsmen.

'Alas, that double traitor Sir Mordred, now me repenteth that ever he escaped my hands, for much shame hath he done unto my lord Arthur. For all I feel by the doleful letter that my lord Sir Gawain sent me, on whose soul Jesu have mercy, that my lord Arthur is full hard bestad. Alas,' said Sir Lancelot, 'that ever I should live to hear that most noble king that made me knight thus to be overset with his subject in his own realm. And this doleful letter that my lord, Sir Gawain, hath sent me afore his death, praying me to see his tomb, wit you well his doleful words shall never go from mine heart. For he was a full noble knight as ever was born; and in an unhappy hour was I born that ever I should have that unhap to slay first Sir Gawain, Sir Gaheris the good knight, and mine own friend Sir Gareth, that was a full noble knight. Alas, I may say I am unhappy,' said Sir Lancelot, 'that ever I should do thus unhappily; and yet, alas, might I never have hap to slay that traitor, Sir Mordred.'

'Leave your complaints,' said Sir Bors, 'and first revenge you of the death of Sir Gawain, on whose soul Jesu have mercy. And it will be well done that ye see Sir Gawain's tomb, and secondly that ye revenge my lord King Arthur, and my lady, Queen Guenever.'

'I thank you,' said Sir Lancelot, 'for ever ye will my worship.'

Then they made them ready in all the haste that might be, with ships and galleys, with Sir Lancelot and his host to pass into England. And so he passed over the sea till he came to Dover, and there he landed with seven kings, and the number was hideous to behold.

Then Sir Lancelot spered of men of Dover where was King Arthur become. Then the people told him how that he was slain, and Sir Mordred too, with an hundred thousand that died on a day; and how Sir Mordred gave King Arthur there the first battle at his landing, and there was good Sir Gawain slain; and on the morn Sir Mordred fought with the king upon Barham Down, and there the king put Sir Mordred to the worse.

'Alas,' said Sir Lancelot, 'this is the heaviest tidings that ever came to my heart. Now, fair sirs, 'said Sir Lancelot, 'show me the tomb of Sir Gawain.'

And then certain people of the town brought him into the Castle of Dover, and showed him the tomb. Then Sir Lancelot kneeled down by the tomb and wept, and prayed heartily for his soul. And that night he made a dole, and all they that would come, of the town or of the country, had as much flesh, fish, wine and ale, and every man and woman he dealt to twelve pence, come who would. Thus with his own hand dealt he this money, in a mourning gown; and ever he wept heartily, and prayed them to pray for the soul of Sir Gawain. And on the morn all the priests and clerks that might be gotten in the country and in the town were there, and sang mass of requiem. And there offered first Sir Lancelot, and he offered an hundred pound; and then the seven kings offered forty pound apiece; and also there was a thousand knights and each of them offered a pound; and the offering dured from morn till night. And there Sir Lancelot lay two nights on his tomb in prayers and weeping. Then on the third day Sir Lancelot called the kings, dukes, earls, barons, and knights, and said thus:

'My fair lords, I thank you all of your coming into this country with me, but we came too late, and that shall repent me while I live, but against death may no man rebel. But sithen it is so,' said Sir Lancelot, 'I will myself ride and seek my lady, Queen Guenever, for as I hear say she hath had great pain and much disease; and I heard say that she is fled into the west. Therefore ye all shall abide me here, and but if I come again within these fifteen days, then take your ships and your fellowship, and depart into your country, for I will do as I say to you.'

Then came Sir Bors de Ganis, and said, 'My lord Sir Lancelot, what think ye for to do, now to ride in this realm? Wit ye well ye shall find few friends.'

'Be as be may,' said Sir Lancelot, 'keep you still here, for I will forth on my journey, and no man nor child shall go with me.'

So it was no boot to strive, but he departed and rode westerly, and there he sought a seven or eight days. And at the last he came to a nunnery, and then was Queen Guenever ware of Sir Lancelot as he walked in the cloister. And when she saw him there she swooned thrice, that all the ladies and gentlewomen had work enough to hold the queen up.

So when she might speak, she called her ladies and gentlewomen to her, and said,

'Ye marvel, fair ladies, why I make this fare. Truly,' she said, 'it is for the sight of yonder knight that yonder standeth; wherefore I pray you all call him to me.'

When Sir Lancelot was brought to her, then she said to all the ladies,

'Through this same man and me hath all this war been wrought, and the death of the most noblest knights of the world; for through our love that we have loved together is my most noble lord slain. Therefore, Sir Lancelot, wit thou well I am set in such a plight to get my soul health; and yet I trust through God's grace and through His passion and His wounds wide, that after my death to have a sight of the blessed face of Christ, and at doomsday to sit on His right side, for as sinful as ever I was are saints in heaven. Therefore, Sir Lancelot, I require thee and beseech thee heartily, for all the love that ever was betwixt us, that thou never see me more in the visage; and I command thee, on God's behalf, that thou forsake my company, and to thy kingdom look thou turn again, and keep well thy realm from war and wrack; for as well as I have loved thee heretofore, mine heart will not serve me to see thee, for through thee and me is the flower of kings and knights destroyed. And therefore, Sir Lancelot, go thou to thy realm, and there take thee a wife, and live with her with joy and bliss. And I pray thee heartily, pray for me to Our Lord that I may amend my misliving.'

'Now, my sweet madam,' said Sir Lancelot, 'would ye that I should turn again unto my country, and there to wed a lady? Nay, madam, wit you well that I shall never do, for I shall never be so false to you of that I have promised. But the same destiny that ye have taken you to, I will take me to, for to please Jesu, and ever for you I cast me specially to pray.'

'Ah, Sir Lancelot, if thou wilt do so,' said the queen, 'hold thy promise. But I may never believe you,' said the queen, 'but that thou wilt turn to the world again.'

'Well, madam,' said he, 'ye say as pleaseth you, yet wist you me never false of my promise. And God defend but I should forsake the world as ye have done. For in the quest of the Sangrail I had forsaken the vanities of the world, had not your love been. And if I had done so at that time, with my heart, will, and thought, I had passed all the knights that ever were in the Sangrail except Sir Galahad, my son. And therefore, lady, sithen ye have taken you to perfection, I must needs take me to perfection, of right. For I take record of God, in you I have had mine earthly joy; and if I had founden you now so disposed, I had cast me to have had you into mine own realm. But sithen I find you thus disposed, I ensure you faithfully, I will ever take me to penance, and pray while my life lasteth, if that I may find any hermit, either gray or white, that will receive me. Wherefore, madam, I pray you kiss me and never no more.'

'Nay,' said the queen, 'that shall I never do, but abstain you from such works.'

And they departed. But there was never so hard an hearted man but he would have wept to see the dolour that they made; for there was lamentation as they had been stungen with spears; and many times they swooned, and the ladies bare the queen to her chamber. And Sir Lancelot awoke, and went and took his horse, and rode all that day and all night in a forest, weeping.

And at the last he was ware of an hermitage and a chapel stood betwixt two cliffs. And then he heard a little bell ring to mass, and thither he rode and alit, and tied his horse to the gate, and heard mass. And he that sang mass was the Bishop of Canterbury.

Both the Bishop and Sir Bedevere knew Sir Lancelot, and they spake together after mass. But when Sir Bedevere had told his tale all whole, Sir Lancelot's heart almost brast for sorrow, and Sir Lancelot threw his arms abroad, and said, 'Alas, who may trust this world.'

And then he kneeled down on his knee, and prayed the Bishop to shrive him and assoil him. And then he besought the Bishop that he might be his brother.

Then the Bishop said, 'I will gladly,' and there he put an habit upon Sir Lancelot. And there he served God day and night with prayers and fastings.

Thus the great host abode at Dover. And then Sir Lionel took fifteen lords with him, and rode to London to seek Sir Lancelot. And there Sir Lionel was slain and many of his lords. Then Sir Bors de Ganis made the great host for to go home again; and Sir Bors, Sir Ector de Maris, Sir Blamor, Sir Bleoberis, with more other of Sir Lancelot's kin, took on them to ride all England overthwart and endlong, to seek Sir Lancelot. So Sir Bors by fortune rode so long till he came to the same chapel where Sir Lancelot was; and so Sir Bors heard a little bell knell, that rang to mass; and there he alit and heard mass. And when mass was done, the Bishop, Sir Lancelot, and Sir Bedevere, came to Sir Bors. And when Sir Bors saw Sir Lancelot in that manner clothing, then he prayed the Bishop that he might be in the same suit. And so there was an habit put upon him, and there he lived in prayers and fasting.

And within half a year there was come Sir Galihud, Sir Galihodin, Sir Blamor, Sir Bleoberis, Sir Villars, Sir Clarrus, and Sir Gahalantine. So all these seven noble knights there abode still. And when they saw Sir Lancelot had taken him to such perfection, they had no lust to depart, but took such an habit as he had. Thus they endured a great penance six year. And then Sir Lancelot took the habit of priesthood of the Bishop, and a twelvemonth he sang mass. And there was none of these other knights but they read in books, and holp for to sing mass, and rang bells, and did lowly all manner of service. And so their horses went where they would, for they took no regard of no worldly riches. For when they saw Sir Lancelot endure such penance, in prayers and fastings, they took no force what pain they endured, for to see the noblest knight of the world take such abstinence that he waxed full lean.

And thus upon a night, there came a vision to Sir Lancelot, and charged him, in remission of his sins, to haste him unto Almesbury:

'And by then thou come there, thou shalt find Queen Guenever dead. And therefore take thy fellows with thee, and purvey them of an horse bier, and fetch thou the corpse of her, and bury her by her husband, the noble King Arthur.'

So this avision came to Sir Lancelot thrice in one night. Then Sir Lancelot rose up or day, and told the hermit.

'It were well done,' said the hermit, 'that ye made you ready, and that ye disobey not the avision.'

Then Sir Lancelot took his eight fellows with him, and on foot they yede from Glastonbury to Almesbury, the which is little more than thirty mile. And thither they came within two days, for they were weak and feeble to go. And when Sir Lancelot was come to Almesbury within the nunnery, Queen Guenever died but half an hour afore.

And the ladies told Sir Lancelot that Queen Guenever told them all or she passed, that Sir Lancelot had been priest near a twelvemonth,

"And hither he cometh as fast as he may to fetch my corpse; and beside my lord, King Arthur, he shall bury me." Wherefore the queen said in hearing of them all, "I beseech Almighty God that I may never have power to see Sir Lancelot with my worldly eyen".

'And thus,' said all the ladies, 'was ever her prayer these two days, till she was dead.'

Then Sir Lancelot saw her visage, but he wept not greatly, but sighed. And so he did all the observance of the service himself, both the dirge, and on the morn he sang mass. And there was ordained an horse bier; and so with an hundred torches ever burning about the corpse of the queen, and ever Sir Lancelot with his eight fellows went about the horse bier, singing and reading many an holy orison, and frankincense upon the corpse incensed. Thus Sir Lancelot and his eight fellows went on foot fom Almesbury unto Glastonbury.

And when they were come to the chapel and the hermitage, there she had a dirge, with great devotion. And on the morn the hermit that sometime was Bishop of Canterbury sang the mass of requiem with great devotion. And Sir Lancelot was the first that offered, and then all his eight fellows. And then she was wrapped in cered cloth of Rennes, from the top to the toe, in thirtyfold; and after she was put in a web of lead, and then in a coffin of marble. And when she was put in the earth Sir Lancelot swooned, and lay long still, while the hermit came and awaked him, and said,

'Ye be to blame, for ye displease God with such manner of sorrow making.'

'Truly,' said Sir Lancelot, 'I trust I do not displease God, for He knoweth mine intent. For my sorrow was not, nor is not, for any rejoicing of sin, but my sorrow may never have end. For when I remember of her beauty, and of her noblesse, that was both with her king and with her, so when I saw his corpse and her corpse so lie together, truly mine heart would not serve to sustain my careful body. Also when I remember me how by my default, mine orgule and my pride, that they were both laid full low, that were peerless that ever was living of Christian people, wit you well,' said Sir Lancelot, 'this remembered, of their kindness and mine unkind‚ ness, sank so to mine heart, that I might not sustain myself.'

So the French book maketh mention.

Then Sir Lancelot never after ate but little meat, nor drank, till he was dead. For then he sickened more and more, and dried, and dwined away. For the Bishop nor none of his fellows might not make him to eat, and little he drank, that he was waxen by a cubit shorter than he was, that the people could not know him. For evermore, day and night, he prayed, but sometime he slum‚ bered a broken sleep. Ever he was lying grovelling on the tomb of King Arthur and Queen Guenever. And there was no comfort that the Bishop, nor Sir Bors, nor none of his fellows, could make him, it availed not.

dwined: wasted

So within six weeks after, Sir Lancelot fell sick, and lay in his bed. And then he sent for the Bishop that there was hermit, and all his true fellows. Then Sir Lancelot said with dreary steven,

steven: voice

'Sir Bishop, I pray you give to me all my rites that longeth to a Christian man.'

'It shall not need you,' said the hermit and all his fellows, 'it is but heaviness of your blood, ye shall be well mended by the grace of God tomorn.'

'My fair lords,' said Sir Lancelot, 'wit you well my careful body will into the earth, I have warning more than now I will say; therefore give me my rites.'

So when he was houselled and eneled, and had all that a Christian man ought to have, he prayed the Bishop that his fellows might bear his body to Joyous Gard. Some men say it was Alnwick, and some men say it was Bamburgh.

houselled: shriven
eneled: anointed

'Howbeit,' said Sir Lancelot, 'me repenteth sore, but I made mine avow sometime, that in Joyous Gard I would be buried. And because of breaking of mine avow, I pray you all, lead me thither.'

Then there was weeping and wringing of hands among his fellows. So at a season of the night they all went to their beds, for they all lay in one chamber. And so after midnight, against day, the Bishop that was hermit, as he lay in his bed asleep, he fell upon a great laughter. And therewithal the fellowship awoke, and come to the Bishop, and asked him what he ailed.

The Death of Arthur

'Ah Jesu mercy,' said the Bishop, 'why did ye awake me? I was never in all my life so merry and so well at ease.'

'Wherefore?' said Sir Bors.

'Truly,' said the Bishop, 'here was Sir Lancelot with me with more angels than ever I saw men in one day. And I saw the angels heave up Sir Lancelot unto heaven, and the gates of heaven opened against him.'

dretching: *confusion*
swevens: *dreams*

'It is but dretching of swevens,' said Sir Bors, 'for I doubt not Sir Lancelot aileth nothing but good.'

'It may well be,' said the Bishop; 'go ye to his bed, and then shall ye prove the sooth.'

So when Sir Bors and his fellows came to his bed they found him stark dead, and he lay as he had smiled, and the sweetest savour about him that ever they felt. Then was there weeping and wringing of hands, and the greatest dole they made that ever made men.

And on the morn the Bishop did his mass of requiem; and after, the Bishop and all the nine knights put Sir Lancelot in the same horse bier that Queen Guenever was laid in tofore that she was buried. And so the Bishop and they all together went with the body of Sir Lancelot daily, till they came to Joyous Gard; and ever they had an hundred torches burning about him.

And so within fifteen days they came to Joyous Gard. And there they laid his corpse in the body of the choir, and sang and read many psalters and prayers over him and about him. And ever his visage was laid open and naked, that all folks might behold him. For such was the custom in those days, that all men of worship should so lie with open visage till that they were buried.

And right thus as they were at their service, there came Sir Ector de Maris, that had seven year sought all England, Scotland, and Wales, seeking his brother, Sir Lancelot. And when Sir Ector heard such noise and light in the choir of Joyous Gard, he alit and put his horse from him, and came into the choir, and there he saw men sing, weep, and all they knew Sir Ector, but he knew not them.

Then went Sir Bors unto Sir Ector, and told him how there lay his brother, Sir Lancelot, dead. And then Sir Ector threw his shield, sword, and helm from him. And when he beheld Sir Lancelot's visage, he fell down in a swoon. And when he waked it were hard any tongue to tell the doleful complaints that he made for his brother.

'Ah Lancelot,' he said, 'thou were head of all Christian knights. And now I dare say,' said Sir Ector, 'thou Sir Lancelot, there thou liest, that thou were never matched of earthly knight's hand. And thou were the courteoust knight that ever bare shield. And thou were the truest friend to thy lover that ever bestrad horse.

316

And thou were the truest lover of a sinful man that ever loved woman. And thou were the kindest man that ever struck with sword. And thou were the goodliest person that ever came among press of knights. And thou was the meekest man and the gentlest that ever ate in hall among ladies. And thou were the sternest knight to thy mortal foe that ever put spear in the rest.'

Then there was weeping and dolour out of measure. Thus they kept Sir Lancelot's corpse on loft fifteen days, and then they buried it with great devotion.

And then at leisure they went all with the Bishop of Canterbury to his hermitage, and there they were together more than a month.

Then Sir Constantine, that was Sir Cador's son of Cornwall, was chosen king of England. And he was a full noble knight, and worshipfully he ruled this realm. And then this King Constantine sent for the Bishop of Canterbury, for he heard say where he was. And so he was restored unto his bishopric, and left that hermitage. And Sir Bedevere was there ever still hermit to his life's end.

Then Sir Bors de Ganis, Sir Ector de Maris, Sir Gahalantine, Sir Galihud, Sir Galihodin, Sir Blamor, Sir Bleoberis, Sir Villiars le Valiant, Sir Clarrus of Cleremont, all these knights drew them to their countries. Howbeit King Constantine would have had them with him, but they would not abide in this realm. And there they all lived in their countries as holy men.

And some English books maketh mention that they went never out of England after the death of Sir Lancelot, but that was but favour of makers. For the French book maketh mention, and is authorised, that Sir Bors, Sir Ector, Sir Blamor, and Sir Bleoberis, went into the Holy Land thereas Jesu Christ was quick and dead. And anon as they had stablished their lands. For, the book saith, so Sir Lancelot commanded them for to do, or ever he passed out of this world. And these four knights did many battles upon the miscreants or Turks. And there they died upon a Good Friday for God's sake.

Here is the end of the whole book of King Arthur, and of his noble knights of the Round Table, that when they were whole together there was ever an hundred and forty. And here is the end of 'The Death of Arthur.'

I pray you all, gentlemen and gentlewomen that readeth this book of Arthur and his knights from the beginning to the ending, pray for me while I am alive, that God send me good deliverance. And when I am dead, I pray you all pray for my soul.

For this book was ended the ninth year of the reign of King Edward the Fourth, by Sir Thomas Malory, knight, as Jesu help him for His great might, as he is the servant of Jesu both day and night.

Index

Index